Copyright © 2021 by Ashwin Dav

All rights reserved. No part of this book may be reproduced or
transmitted in any form or by any means, electronic or mechanical,
including photocopying, recording, or by any information storage and
retrieval system, without permission in writing from the author, except
for the inclusion of brief quotations in a review.

This is a work of fiction. Names, characters, businesses, places, events
and incidents are either the products of the author's imagination or
used in a fictitious manner. Any resemblance to actual persons, living
or dead, or actual events is purely coincidental.

Cover design by Tammy Barrett

THE CURRENT DUSK
AWARD 2022
ONLINE PAYMENT
VISA £ 44
A. D. DAVE
RECEIPT 1483-3957

Ashwin Dave was born and raised in Kenya and, following its independence from Britain in December 1963, undertook the first of two 'migrations' that would entail traversing between Kenya, South India and the UK.

On graduating from vet school in Bangalore, South India, the author returned to Nairobi in 1978 after a brief sojourn in London. The homecoming, after fourteen years, ended the first migratory cycle of a personal journey that had started ominously when the family left Kenya in 1964. The author returned to the UK in 1980 after a brief stint with the wildlife department in Nairobi and before an imminent transfer to the Masai Mara game reserve.

The lull in London lasted more than a decade – a phase during which the author gained postgraduate qualifications in toxicological pathology (University of London), aborted a PhD studentship in Biochemistry at the University of Surrey and embarked on a career change – a prelude to the second migratory phase. The four-year self-imposed exile as an expatriate in Bangalore and Nairobi ended with the family's return to London in 1996.

The author's penchant for reading and cricket has served him well; a closet writer with a facility with the cricket bat. The former nurtured by a 'diet' of Perry Mason, Reader's Digest, Beano, Dandy and the like as a child; the latter courtesy of street cricket in 1960s Kenya.

'The Ivory Towers and Other Stories', a compilation of seven short stories, was launched in December 2018.

The debut novel, every bit challenging and scary as showcasing my short stories, is inspired by the magic that Kenya/East Africa represents for us 'wananchi'.

When Elephants Fight

Fight

Ashwin Dave

For mum and my two sons.

'When elephants fight, it's the grass that suffers'

Kikuyu/African Proverb.

ONE

The Buibui Assassin, London.

The chauffeur, adroitly negotiating the fully loaded Mercedes limo through the Knightsbridge crawl, spotted the buibui-clad woman waiting for him on the pavement. Even at that distance, the chauffeur could discern the generous female contours; exclaiming a silent: 'Mama Mia! Bellissimo!' The man's reaction to her feminine charms would have gratified the stranger – the haute couture buibui that she was wearing was meant to elicit wolf whistles. And had he been able to read, understand and act on the intricate embroidered words of Rumi on the buibui – 'Tear off the mask. Your face is glorious' – her veil 'torn off' would have justified the 'bellissimo' exclamation – very beautiful was an understatement.

The young Italian had used the same superlatives a few moments ago as he had sighted the array of luxury cars – Lamborghini, Ferrari, Bugatti, and Maserati - some double parked with apparent impunity. He had to follow suit as he double parked and sidled out of the driver's seat to open the door for his fare.

As she glided into the backseat, gently gathering the silken folds of the buibui, a prerequisite outer garment for females in the Middle East to thwart male attention, he got a whiff of her subtle perfume which aroused tantalising visions of voluptuous belly dancers. In his testosterone-driven world, Turkish delight had a whole different perspective; the 'wrapper' tended to be very sparse and exposing more than it covered – topped with strategically placed tassels.

His reverie was abruptly curtailed by the soft, almost inaudible, clunk of the rear door. As he sheepishly got behind the wheel and engaged the drive mode, he avoided the woman's gaze; his guilt writ large on his youthful face. And as she handed him a card with the name of a Harley Street consultant, she wondered whether it was her attire or her scent that had unnerved him.

He pulled away gently behind the convoy of super luxurious cars, driven by Qataris, Saudis, Emiratis and Kuwaitis, and darted a quick glance in the rear-view mirror. Buibui-clad females were ubiquitous in that part of opulent London, so the driver was unfazed by her veiled look; what enthralled him was the mysterious aura that she exuded. The perfume triggered erotic images of sinuous belly dancers.

The buibui, in keeping with the Arab and Lebanese ethos of the area, had become the badge of wealth and extravagance; OPEC's petro-dollars being the lingua franca. The locals feigned an indifference that belied the lure of rubbing shoulders with the high rollers who, at the throw of a dice at the local casino, could lose a million or two; small change for the uber rich. The abundance of Turkish cafes, shisha bars and Lebanese restaurants, not to forget the belly dancers, was a home away from home – a 'mini Emirates' in the throbbing heart of London. There were many such homes away from home dotted across London and other urban cities; a cosmopolitan melting pot of very many nationalities.

The new nomads of the world – the tax exiles and the non-domiciled jet set – preferred London to the real thing back home. Here they were thousands of miles away from the relentless heat of the desert and the social tensions generated by the 'fish bowl' existence. London afforded them total anonymity; their petrodollars reigned supreme. As did the Bollywood rupee and the Russian rouble; the new rivals in town.

'Harley Street, please,' she said in an accent that was distinct from the normal British-educated Arab clients that he normally ferried around. 'Dr Parker-Jones's clinic.' The chauffeur noted Dr Parker-Jones's clinic, with the W1 City of Westminster postcode, was barely a few minutes' drive away.

The driver, as he took a slightly longer route than warranted, again looked in his rear-view mirror and imagined that, under the veil, she was as exotic as her designer buibui.

Her posture, mannerisms and the pitch of her accented voice were indicative of an upbringing in the laps of opulence; like the green abundance of a wadi or an oasis amidst the arid dunes of the Sahara. The hotblooded Italian was tantalised by his fare – his vivid imagination in overdrive as he struggled to keep his focus on the road ahead.

He tried to conjure up a place of origin, a mental game he often played with his passengers, as he adeptly manoeuvred the sleek limousine, moving at a snail's pace through the London traffic. In this case, with her facial features hidden, he was going entirely by her attire and accent to hazard a guess; Dubai and Beirut came to mind.

And a consultant physician in Harley Street? A twinge of jealousy surfaced at the thought of the frustrating rituals that he had to go through each time to get a GP appointment – the petulant receptionists were a law unto themselves.

The state of affairs reminded him of a line from George Orwell's 'Animal Farm': 'All animals are equal, but some animals are more equal than others.' He glanced at her again and sighed in resignation at his lot; barely managing to keep his envy at bay. Money, not sex, that makes the world go round.

Dr Parker-Jones had acquired a reputation for treating only Hollywood celebrities and latterly, as the Indian film industry exploded on the world stage, Bollywood stars. His patient list was very exclusive and upmarket – he had wondered, at the first consultation, how this elegantly perfumed lady had managed to get past his secretary, Delia, who guarded his elitist reputation with a zeal bordering on fanaticism. He frequently reminded his employee that her wages – and his – were dependent on the very patients that she tried to vet and exclude.

He smiled instinctively – anyone gaining Delia's approval must have been thoroughly vetted. And worth it – just like the sleek adverts of a certain brand. He recalled that on the last visit this patient had paid cash and a premium for booking an out of hours appointment on a Saturday. Back then, he had joked about billing her for all the cancellation charges of the weekend golf at an exclusive championship course in Scotland. Delia had taken him seriously and collected every penny from the woman. The patient had paid without batting an eyelid – not that Delia would have noticed the fluttering eyelids through the veil.

This was her second consult. All he knew was that she flew in regularly for business trips but had been reluctant to provide details of her occupation, her GP or her overseas address. Her attire was indicative of a certain region but then maybe that was what she wanted everyone to believe. The physician was used to celebrities acting the way they did, so ignored his concerns about flying blind – the facial and body language cues blocked by the buibui and the veil. His A-list patients paid well over the odds for his time, so he tolerated their idiosyncrasies.

The flicker of a smile on his distinguished face, which was crowned by a full head of silver hair, was barely noticed by the patient who maintained her poise and silence. He reckoned she was Egyptian. The Sphinx, which he had visited more than once, came to mind. Grudgingly, he returned to the task in hand.

After making quick notes in his spidery scrawl – patient history completed manually because he still refused to use a Dictaphone or any of the gizmos that were the norm these days – he motioned her towards the examination couch.

After completing his examination during which she declined to fully disrobe; the veil very much in place, he paused as if in deep thought. It bemused the physician – some of his recalcitrant patients had no qualms disrobing but still insisted on having the face veiled. In his younger avatar, he would have thrown a tantrum or two but now wiser counsel prevailed – his bedside manner remained impeccable. He could ill afford a drop in his income – a younger high maintenance trophy wife and alimony payments compelled him to be cautious.

His probing fingers palpated her liver and spleen – no signs of enlargement as far as his sensitive touch could fathom. He nodded imperceptibly as he directed her back to her chair – the haematology and gynaecology reports had been perused and filed. He had reviewed both; the blood results had corroborated his initial diagnosis. He had referred her, at the first consultation, to one of the best gynaecologists that he knew – his first wife.

He returned to his chair as she rearranged the buibui and seated herself; her posture ramrod straight, shoulders squared and arms crossed – hostile and apprehensive. He was certain that even without a veil she would be devoid of any facial cues; as inscrutable as the Sphinx.

'I have reviewed all your results and am glad to confirm that clinically I do not anticipate any difficulties treating or managing your conditions. Nothing to worry about.' He paused, more theatrics than to collect his thoughts, and continued. 'However, the presence of uterine fibroids may complicate the clinical outcome, especially, if the bleeding intensifies. It would be advisable to monitor your haemoglobin level, which, at the moment is just above the lower range. Slightly less than the last report. Please have your GP monitor your complete blood count; especially if you plan on becoming a mother. If you wish, we can forward a full report to your GP?

She maintained her stoic silence, so he continued: 'Any questions?'

The patient murmured 'no' with barely a shake of her head.

The rustle of the silken folds of her attire as she collected herself wafted the fragrance of her perfume in his direction. He stood there transfixed; imbibing the sensuous scent.

'Well, see you in six months. Have a safe flight,' he said, almost as a reflex. Subconsciously, still thinking of the Nile and the Valley of the Kings, he had deduced that she was a foreign nubile goddess. No less.

As he ushered her out he made a mental note to ask Delia about the woman's perfume – she would know. His wife's imminent birthday would present the usual annual dilemma of choosing a suitable gift - the exotic perfume would be an easy and a lazy way out.

She left after paying cash to Delia, who was intrigued by the thick wad of currency notes; Sterling mixed up with US Dollars. Delia booked her in for a follow up and handed her the appointment card, marvelling at the slender artistic fingers and the translucent pallor of her exposed wrists. 'Definitely Egyptian,' Delia murmured to herself. Visions of Elizabeth Taylor as Cleopatra flashed through her mind. Delia never quite ascertained what the exotic perfume was. Not that she would have been able to afford such an extravagance.

The nubile goddess left for Heathrow shortly after packing her Louis Vuitton suitcase. The flight was on time and as she looked down from her first-class seat, the grey grim landscape of Heathrow – the terminals and Bath Road dotted with five-star hotels and banqueting halls – receded as the Airbus ascended seamlessly to 30,000 feet.

Despite being a regular visitor to the UK, she never quite got accustomed to Heathrow and its soulless environs and the swift departure always lifted her spirits. She snuggled deeper into her seat as the seat belt sign switched off. A cue for the air hostesses to spring into action.

The flight was mostly empty so she hoped to catch up on her sleep. The past few days had been fraught with anxiety, fretting about her imminent London trip. That sultry day in Lamu, after her exhausting encounter with the over exuberant Brit, had almost ruined her well laid plans.

Her brief and sudden dizzy spell had triggered an anxiety that she could not shake off, even after making allowances for her relentless work schedule and the hot weather. The brief episode was the first time that she had felt unwell. At the time, she had dismissed it as an outcome of her punishing work and fitness schedules. However, the sudden episode of light headedness had convinced her to fly to London.

The physician's soothing words and the near normal reports had convinced her that the transitory dizzy spell in Lamu did not amount to anything untoward; conveniently ignoring the anxiety that had led her back to Harley Street in the first place, rather than consult a local physician. Although Mombasa boasted more than its share of highly specialised UK trained consultants, she had dithered.

She preferred the absolute anonymity that London afforded; even more so than Dubai. In her university days, away from her doting parents, she would always admonish her friends from making any comments of their frequent jaunts to exotic places – 'what happens in Beirut, stays in Beirut' was her usual refrain after a trip. The buibui was her brilliant solution to thwart undue attention; even when visiting London or Paris.

She guarded her identity zealously and could not afford any slip ups; no loose ends and no audit trails left behind. Any mishaps at this stage could be catastrophic – like a house of cards dislodged by a sneeze or a Parkinsonian hand tremor.

She was convinced, as she sipped the red wine served by the pretty airhostess, that the next phase of her grand plan would be a turning point; her crossroads. The moment was hers to seize, especially if she desired to mothball the red fishnet tights and the matching red stilettoes; her work clothes.

'Too much at stake to take any chances.' She looked to the heavens as she repeated the refrain; as if seeking divine assistance. An old hand at meticulous planning, she was hardly a wet-behind-the-ears novice. She was old enough to admit that if things could wrong, they probably would. Her father's words echoed in her mind: 'Man proposes, God disposes.'

Try as she may, she just could not lose herself to the serenity that sleep ensured. Her mind kept going back to her last assignment. The memory of the oversized Brit; his corpulence, the bulk, even now brought her out in a sweat. Things could have gone so horribly wrong. She shivered involuntarily as she downed the last of the Merlot.

Her remit for that day in Lamu had been very specific; the early morning calls had been explicit – execute well and the rewards would be stupendous; virtually a blank cheque. She shunned joint discussions or conference calls; her Chinese walls strategy ensured that London, Dubai and Bombay never got complacent. It suited her – each unaware of the actions or thoughts of the other.

She did not let on, but the money was just the icing on the cake; she relished the challenges; lived for the adrenaline rush – the thrills. It had also become a matter of pride; she had always strived to live up to her sobriquet – 'whispering death'. Death on red stilettos that had never failed to deliver; not yet.

Her contracts were executed with precision and more menace than any bowling excellence that the other 'whispering death' maestro could possibly conjure up on a cold day at Lords cricket ground. She was just as, if not more, clinical in her delivery. Michael Holding's cricketing opponents lived another day to face him; her victims rarely had a chance to survive her fatal onslaught. Her nickname was apt and well earned.

Besides, in this case, there was a lot at stake; all parties concurred. They had come a long way together and had invested far too much to take chances at this late stage of the project.

She sank deeper into her seat and closed her eyes, hoping for at least an hour of deep phase sleep, but it just wasn't to be. Lamu and the near collapse of their plan dominated her thoughts, intrusive and almost obsessive. Even now, harking back to that sultry day in Lamu brought her out in a cold sweat. It had been close. Too close for comfort. Only God's grace had reprieved her. Her Bombay associate frequently quoted the Indian scriptures – 'perform your duty (karma), don't count the fruit'. The harvesting of the fruits was a long way off; the chickens a long way from hatching.

She smiled briefly as the images flashed through her mind; her accidental discovery, the happy accident, had actually paved the way for a volte face, a complete U-turn in her plans. And her fortunes had changed – immeasurably for the better.

Even now, at 30,000 feet, her thoughts went back to the Brit and the only copy of his report, which was now safe in her possession. It was a document that presented an immense opportunity and the feel of the paper and its contents indelibly embedded in her memory.

As the plane passed through pockets of unnerving turbulence, she mentally retraced her journey from Mombasa to Lamu. She travelled back, wide awake, as inexorably the thoughts returned, as did her sense of unease. Deep down there was a nagging thought that something was amiss; a tiny fragment of her memory not quite switched on.

She recalled her solitary journey. She had deliberately changed routes to throw off anyone following her and finally reaching Lamu island via the daily ferry service from Mokowe, the jetty on the coastal mainland.

Despite the fact that she had visited the island many times before, she had painstakingly researched the resort and the villa where the Brit was scheduled to stay. Every entrance and exit and her route committed to memory. She was a perfectionist to the core and her fastidious methods meant that plans B and C were in place, just in case.

Finding the Brit at the luxury resort was the easy bit; getting back to Mombasa without any mishaps was the essence of the task. It had been impressed on her that the Brit was flying off to London soon and had been enticed to Lamu for an all-expenses paid stay at the villa.

She knew instinctively what had been promised to the Brit and her ploy was seduction, a honey trap. His photograph revealed fleshy jowls and a corpulence that indicated a lack of discipline. Gluttony and the ways of the flesh went hand-in-hand.

Under the non-descript buibui – the designer one forsaken for a more utilitarian design – she was dressed in red fishnet stockings and matching red panties and bra that showed off her feminine charms. In that attire she could have tempted even a eunuch. She smiled at that thought – she was proud of her expertise in manipulating men; like putty in her hands. The signature red stilettos completed her professional attire.

She knew that the middle-aged Brit was a bachelor and a self-professed ladies' man. The detailed notes made available to her had one another medical note of interest – he was a diabetic; even better was the note that he was insulin dependent. She reckoned that his age and his Type 1 diabetes made her task manageable – he would not last long with her. She prided herself on her self-taught ways of the flesh; no reason why she could not make a quick getaway – a hit and run operation.

She remembered that initially she had bridled with anger at the thought of performing like a floozy; high class notwithstanding. Until the terms of the deal were presented – virtually a blank cheque plus a share of the profits of the larger joint investment. This assignment would be her magnum opus – its success would mean she could mothball the red work clothes and bring an end to the demanding physical and mental work ethic.

It was easy to locate the beach-side villa – a very secluded and upmarket private retreat for a certain sort of clients. She, sweating under the buibui, knocked gently on the door, hearing the gentle lapping of the waves faintly coming through to the palm-fringed section of the beach. This particular villa was set back from a small cluster of six others – well screened behind the fringe of palm trees and the boughs of fragrant Bougainville.

The beach was all deserted and quiet in the late afternoon sun – siesta time all over the coastal strip, stretching from Mombasa, Malindi to the Lamu Archipelago. Even the birds had retreated to the shady upper perches of the palm trees; the peace breached occasionally by the croaks of frogs lazing in the small water feature that each villa had. The expensive Koi carp, shielded by the aquatic plants, swam languidly in the pond water.

The small water fountain gurgled with the sounds of re-circulating water; the faint drone of the water pump barely audible in the late afternoon silence. Her heart raced under the influence of the adrenaline spurt and her rapid beats drowned all other sounds. She almost spat out the small wad of chewing gum that she habitually chewed to avoid a dry mouth but checked herself just in time to avoid leaving behind a biological specimen. Instead, she added another pellet and masticated furiously to stimulate salivation; the minty taste reinvigorating.

The Brit half asleep after a heavy meal of tilapia fish curry and steaming Basmati rice was groggy with the alcohol imbibed during lunch; several bottles of chilled Tusker beer and glasses of white wine. The promised feast of the flesh, his tryst with the femme fatale, on his last day in Lamu had kept him on tenterhooks all day. His ardour, in spite of the copious amounts of alcohol consumed, was mounting as the hours had drawn closer. Despite the heightened anticipation, he had slipped into a slumber, his snores competing with the croaks of the frogs outside.

The faint and discreet knock roused him. He lumbered, unsteady on his feet, to the door, his fluffy white bath robe barely covering his enormous frame and the rolls of flesh rippling with each step. He saw the buibui-clad woman through the mosquito screen and was momentarily taken aback.

The Brit's disappointment at the shapeless buibui apparition before him was mirrored in his eyes; his heart sank. He had never quite got used to the unique fragrance of the attar, a local perfume, that most local women wore. The distinct home-grown scent conjured up visions of the slave markets that Lamu and Zanzibar were notorious for. He shivered involuntarily – trying to shed the images of cruelty and exploitation that the slave trade was infamous for. He had not bargained for this; his spirits drooped.

As he reluctantly waved her in and closed the door he got a whiff of her exotic perfume and realised it was definitely not cheap attar. Very enticing he thought, much more than the fully clad figure before him – although he did a sharp intake of breath as she flipped the veil over her slim head because she was beautiful beyond his wildest dreams. The gasp of utter surprise was totally involuntary as he stared at the stunning face before him. He was mesmerised by her exotic look, well beyond anything that he had encountered previously. His pulse quickened the blood coursed through as his heart thumped at a frenetic pace. He dribbled.

Her almond-shaped eyes and aquiline nose gave her an almost regal look. The exotic aura of the perfume had dispelled imaginary thoughts of attar and slaves. His mouth gaped, barely controlling the dribble of saliva as he tried desperately to envision what lay beneath the folds of the buibui. Despite the ravages of longstanding Type 1 diabetes, he felt the faint stirrings of passion take hold; he was wide awake and raring to go.

As she came over, she embraced him passionately, deliberately grinding her pelvis provocatively into his groin. She had his total attention as she nibbled his ear lobe and whispered sensuously into his ear: 'Where's the bathroom?' Even in his inebriated state, the caressing drawl of her whisper and the tip of her moist tongue sent tingles of anticipation up and down his lumbar spine; his groin on autopilot.

The seduction so far was in the voice as he had yet to feast his eyes on what lay beneath the buibui. The velvety folds rubbing against his exposed torso – the bath robe had almost dropped to the marble floor – felt crispy cool. The dull drone of the air conditioner hummed in the awkward silence that prevailed; even the frogs had stopped croaking.

All he could do was point her to the far corner, his vocal cords paralysed. He was captivated by her Marilyn Monroe drawl – slow and seductive. The rhythmic rise of her bodice, deliberately exaggerated by her deep breathing, compelled him to lunge at her. She nudged him back into the armchair as she backed off; her feline grace full of promises.

'I'll be back in five minutes,' she purred as she glided off, her hips swivelling in an exaggerated show of tantalising pelvic gyrations. The Brit, poised expectantly in the armchair, followed her sensuous passage towards the bathroom; his arousal mounting with the same rapidity as his tortured breathing.

Her smug smile was saying 'this is going to be a cinch'. It was going to be easier than she had envisaged. His over-the-top reaction would make it very short and clinical. She could take him by surprise; even putty would have been more challenging. He was at her mercy and pliable in her hands.

Within minutes she emerged without the buibui – in red fishnet stockings and red stilettos. The crimson bra and panties; the skimpy apparel with small attached tassels barely concealing her voluptuous contours. As she gyrated towards him, her hands behind her were firmly locked on the Beretta M9 gun in a two-handed grip; the stubby silencer concealing the tip of the barrel.

She followed his eyes as they travelled down the length of her fulsome hourglass figure. 'Perfect,' she whispered to herself – he was distracted; his dopey eyes rivetted on the hypnotic swinging tassels. The swaying hooded cobra playing with the stunned prey.

The last few paces were quick with small strides as she half pushed him back into the armchair and straddled him. The three quick-fire shots thudded into his heart; the sternum breached. He stared at her without focus as he slumped into the chair. Death was too quick for the shock to register in his glassy eyes.

As the Airbus scythed through the skies towards Mombasa, her enduring memory of that afternoon in Lamu was that of his urgency and her battle to control his passionate bravado. His desperate lunges almost toppled her over; a sharp nail doing minor damage.

She recalled that fortunately her ordeal had not lasted long – she had managed to extricate herself from an act that promised him a lot but delivered absolutely nothing; hardly any bodily contact. She had immediately retreated to the sanctuary of the bathroom to regroup. The Brit lay slumped in the armchair.

As she deftly spruced up – wiping off the smudged lipstick and mascara – her finger traced the six-inch scratch on her left forearm; with tinges of blood appearing on the margins. In his passionate and futile attempts to kiss her, his unmanicured nails had done the damage – it had all happened so rapidly that she barely remembered his lunge at her.

She dabbed the blood away and put down the soiled tissue on the toilet cistern. The gentle pressure that she had applied promptly staunched the flow of blood. Greatly relieved that it was a superficial cut, she had wiped clean all surfaces that she had touched; a reflex borne out of years of practice.

The thigh holster snuggling against her left thigh gave her comfort and reassurance. Slipping on the buibui, she slid out of the bathroom, darting a cursory look at the slumped figure in the chair. As an afterthought, she grabbed a tissue and wiped away any debris that may have lodged under his nails – the tissue not soiled with her blood.

She quickly surveyed the room and found the bound report on top of his clothes in the half packed open suitcase. Within minutes she had strapped the report to her torso. She deliberately rifled through his wallet and removed the wad of dollar bills and unclipped his Rolex; both disappeared into the specially stitched pockets of her buibui.

As she was moving towards the bathroom to give it a once over, having flipped back her veil, a flicker of movement in her peripheral visual field alerted her. The movement was close by, just outside.

A waiter from the hotel bar was a few feet away carrying an ice bucket and a wine bottle; just about to enter the mosquito screen covered portico. She could see him bathed in the afternoon sun though she was invisible to him in the dark interior of the room – she had drawn the heavy curtains on the glass frontage of the villa.

She recalled, sinking deeper into her first-class seat as the Airbus glided towards Kenya, that she had frozen for a split second before recovering her poise and dashing towards the rear patio door. She exited and rapidly walked away from the villa. Halfway across she almost stumbled; a momentary blackout. She braced herself against a palm tree until the dizziness abated. As her balance and confidence returned, she resumed her trek back to the pier.

Within minutes she was clear of the clutch of villas and striding briskly towards the ferry; negotiating the narrow, deserted alleys and lanes with an urgency that brought her out in a sweat under the buibui. The town was almost deserted in a post-lunch stupor; the afternoon siesta. Even the ubiquitous donkeys were huddled in twos and threes; somnolent and dopey. The afternoon lull of inactivity pervaded the island; a solitary donkey braying noisily in the distance.

Half an hour later she was on the ferry as she retraced her return journey. The ferry crossing was short and uneventful, as was the rest of her journey to Mombasa. She had deposited the gun with the holster and the Rolex over the side of the ferry as it traversed the short distance to Mokowe jetty. The final evidence of her encounter with the Brit – the dollars and the Rolex – were put in a charity box at a mosque in Mombasa. She had detoured to the mosque to ensure she wasn't being followed.

She had deposited the Brit's report in her safe. A day later while waiting for the call from Dubai, she had flicked through the typed pages – when she caught sight of the words 'oil, hydrocarbons' her interest had been aroused. She read the report twice, very slowly and methodically, making a mental note of the salient findings.

There were maps and images of the Rift Valley and other areas including the coast and the Lamu Archipelago. By the time she had read the report repeatedly, the underlying message was clear – nothing of substance was found; no oil.

The Brit had been thorough and had noted that all past drilling had been unsuccessful. Even if pockets of oil were to be found, the poor quality and quantity would make extraction of the oil commercially unviable.

She had been confused. Why all the fuss about a private survey that had come up negative? There was nothing new in the fact that despite surveys and oil explorations virtually in every decade of British rule in Kenya, oil exploration had not delivered; dry wells abandoned after futile attempts. The existence of a black Eldorado along the coastal strip, stretching from Mombasa to Lamu, was a myth; wishful thinking.

And yet, why had it become expedient to execute the Brit? Unless, the survey had found something that was not reflected in his report. Maybe, he was silenced so that the report could be used at an appropriate time?

As she returned the report to the safe, a germ of an idea had taken hold; a plan had taken shape in her fertile, yet devious, mind. If she kept her wits about her, she may yet profit from the fiasco. Sometimes what does not happen is better.

As the airbus tossed around on hitting further pockets of turbulence, she was jolted back into the present and sat bolt upright, grabbing a tissue to wipe off the small amount of wine that had spilt on the tray. Tissues!

The blood-tinged tissue – she had forgotten about it and left it on the cistern. In the heat of the moment when she saw the waiter she had panicked and fled. She had meant to collect the tissues from the bathroom before she left the villa.

It was too late to do anything about it now. And she reasoned and downplayed her lapse: even if the tissues were found and examined by forensics, her blood could not be traced back to her. She was not on any database; local or international. She had made sure of that – all these years; countless remits and executions.

She thought hard again – she was sure the tissue was not in the pockets of her buibui when she left abruptly and in a panic. She remembered dumping the holster and the gun over the side of the ferry in the warm waters of the Indian Ocean – she had even got rid of the rag with which she had wiped the gun and holster clean.

It was only now, while recapping on the events, that she realised she had left behind a shred of evidence - the blood; a biological sample. She had successfully avoided spitting out the wad of chewing gum on the way in to the villa. Damn. That was a major lapse on her part – leaving behind a biological trail – it had never happened before, in all these years.

She buzzed the air hostess and asked for a glass of mineral water with ice and a slice of lemon. It took her a while to calm her nerves; the evidence left behind looming large in her troubled mind like a dark ominous cloud.

The anxiety stayed with her for the rest of her flight.

The inflight entertainment, showing the concluding stages of the 1990 Marlboro Safari Rally, grabbed her attention initially but she soon switched off when she realised that Kenyan drivers had again missed out. Rally fans all over Kenya had been hoping for a miracle – the last time when Kenyans managed a podium finish was when Shekar Mehta and Mike Doughty won in 1982.

She perked up visibly as she recognised the familiar landmarks of Mombasa as the plane descended for touchdown. That vista of the waters of the Indian ocean crashing onto the Mombasa landmass always quickened her pulse; the sun and the blue skies almost like an elixir.

As she emerged into the arrivals lounge, the reassurance of coming home felt good. Her spirits revived, she was home, in Kenya; safe and secure. The look in her eyes was steely. She relished a challenge and getting her share of the bonanza wasn't going to be easy. Dubai, London and Bombay were in for a fight. She knew exactly how she was going to play this: the words 'hydrocarbons', 'deposits' and 'basin' would be her weapons.

TWO

1960s, Post-Independence, Kenya

The 1964 VW Beetle with its 1600cc four-speed manual
gearbox glistened in the blazing Kenyan sun as it made its way on the
bustling busy single carriageway – also known as the Northern
Corridor – that connected Kenya's cosmopolitan capital city, Nairobi,
to East Africa's premier and busiest port, Mombasa.

The red Beetle had barely covered 104 miles of its 300-mile
arduous journey to arrive at Makindu, when the Dunlops decided to
take a break. For most Kenyans the drive to Mombasa would be remiss
if lunch was not taken at Makindu; subconsciously the vacation started
once the cooler clime and the high-altitude plains of Nairobi were left
behind.

Mr and Mrs Dunlop and many others on that day were
observing the long-practised tradition of visiting the gurudwara, the
Sikh temple, at Makindu. The unwritten rule, which if broken, would
make that trip to Mombasa tedious and unbearably long.

And more importantly, the faithful and the not so faithful, had
an opportunity to have a sumptuous lunch at the temple; another long-
held tradition of the Sikh faith. A religious tradition that had survived
in far flung places; away from the premier shrine at the Golden Temple

in Amritsar, the seat of the Sikh faith.

The gurudwara at Makindu, built in 1926, had over the years blossomed from a tin-roof ramshackle of a hut to a glorious edifice. A legacy of the British East Africa Company which had recruited 32,000 labourers from British-ruled India, to construct the single gauge railway line from Mombasa to Kisumu initially, and, thereon, to Kampala, Uganda. The construction of the temple was undertaken by the migrant workers, although many perished without ever setting foot into the gurudwara. The railway line, often dubbed 'The Lunatic Express', was started in 1896 and was completed in 1901.

The 7000 migrants who stayed behind, after 2500 deaths, formed the nucleus of the Indian diaspora in East Africa; many descendants of those early pioneers subsequently migrated to the UK and further afield to Canada and USA.

Mr and Mrs Dunlop visited the temple briefly to freshen up, genuflect before the shrine and then exited to unpack their picnic hamper; leaving the countless tourists and devotees to pray and then settle down to have their meal in the temple.

The aroma of freshly prepared lentils and chapatis wafting from the temple kitchens was the cue for Catherine Dunlop and many others to unpack their picnic hampers with bottles of Coke, Fanta, Canada Dry and white wine jostling for space along with sandwiches, samosas, chicken curry and chai, Indian tea.

The temple was filled with boisterous school children and their parents, all travelling, like the Dunlop family, for a beach holiday at the resorts and holiday homes dotted along the pristine coastal strip awash with the warm waters of the Indian Ocean. Mombasa, the palm-fringed coastal retreat, was the main haven for the overworked, the stressed and the excited school children. Some ventured farther up the coast to Watamu, Malindi and even Lamu.

An Indian family close by who also were having their lunch smiled shyly at the 'mzungu' family, as they called white people. The aroma of the Indian lunch of lamb samosas, chicken curry and cold chapatis smelt and looked tantalisingly familiar to Mrs Dunlop; similar fare was often served at Rotarian events in her chapter in Nairobi.

A Sikh couple, just like the Dunlops, had decided to give the temple crowds a miss and had unpacked their lunch close by. Mrs Singh, initially shy and hesitant, soon warmed up to Catherine's friendly overtures and launched into a discourse on the Punjabi food that she had prepared for the trip. Before Catherine could stop her, Mrs Singh had unpacked some more food and brought it over.

The generous portion of samosas and chai, served piping hot from their Thermos flask, were received and eaten gleefully. Drew was quite content to sip his white wine and devour the leftover bacon sandwiches while Catherine scoffed the samosas and drank the steaming chai with an appreciative relish.

Mr. Singh, quite taken by the twin lens camera that Drew had on the picnic rug, readily obliged and took a few photographs of the couple – both smiling into the brand new Yashica Mr. Singh took several in quick succession – with the Beetle in the background, and Drew in his white fedora, his head resting on the front bumper, next to the car plates. Most of the shots were of the shapely Catherine, who unwittingly flaunted her charms; almost a Marilyn Monroe type of frolic in the sun. Had she seen the murderous looks that Mrs Singh was darting in her direction, she would have been mortified.

Mr. Singh had already snapped the same sequences of Catherine on his own camera. Mrs. Singh watched with some amount of trepidation, as her husband clicked away; the photogenic charms of Mrs. Dunlop drawing the most attention. The trigger-happy hubby was oblivious to the gamut of emotions cascading across his wife's emotive face; both the lensman and the Anglo-Saxon goddess blissfully unaware of the brewing tempest.

Mrs. Singh, conscious of her ample girth and recognising her husband's wayward amorous glances at the slender-waisted mzungu, had to wrench her man away in a show of ill-disguised ire. She wasn't having his opportunistic flirting sour their holiday even before it had started. There would be several days of torment for her on the beaches of Mombasa where she would have to be vigilant; his roving eyes feasting on the vast swathes of milky white flesh of the mzungu women in their skimpy bikinis. Mr. Singh reluctantly moved, almost bashful, as he was towed away forcibly, like a toddler frogmarched out of a toy store.

Catherine, blithely unaware of the domestic turmoil that she had unwittingly stirred up, lay down next to her husband; arms akimbo to catch as much sun as possible. She did not tan easily so tried to expose as much flesh as would be decent, totally indifferent to the thunderous looks that she was drawing from the other women; the Indian ones watching their husbands like hawks and trying to herd them away to the safety of the gurudwara. By the time the Dunlops left, the Sikh family had already gone into the temple. The Dunlops, after packing away the almost empty wine bottle and other remnants, set forth towards their next planned stop – at the Mackinnon Road mosque which housed a 'dargah' – a shrine.

Catherine, who had never before travelled by road to Mombasa, had decided to visit the tomb that all her Rotarian friends had strongly recommended. As Drew steered the Beetle away from the Sikh temple, she reminded him about her intention to spend a few minutes at the shrine; still hours away on that hot dusty drive towards Mombasa.

An hour's drive out of Makindu, Drew stopped for a comfort break, relieving himself by the roadside. The road was busy and quite a few cars passed by, except the Sikh family's Peugeot. Catherine, certain that they were way ahead, assumed that maybe the Sikh family had stayed back a bit longer at the temple. Drew, somewhat worse for the wear after the lunchtime wine, tossed the Beetle's car keys to Catherine.

'Darling, please take over. I think I will have a shut-eye for a few minutes.' He was soon snoring blissfully next to her, his fedora almost covering his heavily tanned face and shielding it from the glare of the blazing sun. He had rolled up the window to avoid the wind blowing away his hat.

Catherine, still not fully used to smoothly co-ordinating the clutch-accelerator sequences, meshed the gears as she overtook a few slower cars. The tarmac shimmered as the afternoon sun blazed fiercely, sending up waves of hot air eddies. In some sections, one could almost see the heat being reflected from the melting tarmac – like a mirage of convection currents of air, belly dancing upwards. Catherine, conscious of how long they'd spent at the temple, decided to put her foot down to make up for the lost time.

The dargah at the Mackinnon Road mosque had assumed an aura of mystique and reverence – an auspicious spot where even trains and buses slowed down to pay homage. The conflicting reports about the identity of the person buried at the spot – deemed to be a Punjabi foreman who died while working on the Mombasa-Kampala line – added to the mystery and the superstition. The tomb had assumed a reverential significance over the years and stopping at the shrine not only bestowed good luck, but ensured a safe onward journey.

Drew, who had made the road journey many times, had never quite believed in the superstition about the tomb. He convinced Catherine to continue driving past the shrine, despite her protestations and obvious annoyance. She had given in to Drew's argument about reaching Mombasa just before the sun disappeared in a blaze of orange hues; a glorious Mombasa sunset that he wanted her to witness.

It happened just a few miles after passing the dargah. It was never quite established whose fault it was, but the four-car pile-up killed four people: Mrs Dunlop, two employees of the British High Commission in a Mercedes bearing 'CD', diplomatic plates, and a taxi driver in a Peugeot 404.

The mangled mass of the pile-up was photographed by a passing journalist; shattered glass and blood formed a grisly mosaic on the tarmac. The roadside hawkers at the accident scene were the only witnesses apart from the driver following the Beetle.

The police deduced, after taking statements from the witnesses, that in overtaking the Peugeot, Mrs Dunlop had miscalculated the distance and the speed of the oncoming Mercedes. The right chrome bumper of the VW had hit the right fender of the oncoming Mercedes and the drivers had lost control. The tyre tracks of the other two showed the desperate attempts by the drivers to avoid hitting the mangled pile of steel. All four cars had ended up in a pile of twisted metal.

The national papers carried the gruesome photographs of the accident a few days later. The Sikh family, on recognizing the Beetle in the crash photographs, prayed at the shrine for the Dunlop family on the way back to Nairobi. The frivolous images of Mrs Dunlop, posing for the camera, stayed with the Singh family for days and weeks. Mrs Singh, days later back in Nairobi, impulsively agreed to be interviewed and mentioned the bottles of wine in the picnic hamper and the alcohol consumption. Something that would come back to haunt Mrs Singh.

Months later, at the inquest, Mrs. Singh's press interview was dredged up again, much to her chagrin. In the aftermath of the tragedy, Mrs Singh had offered prayers at her local gurudwara – as an act of atonement and contrition. Although she managed to set things right at the inquest by retracting her earlier misguided comments, she would never quite manage to forgive herself for her petty behaviour – her intemperate remarks about the mzungu woman had been driven by jealousy. The full impact of her irresponsible behaviour became apparent when she plucked up the courage to offer her condolences to Mr Dunlop at the inquest. His stiff-upper-lip demeanour just about carried him through as he exonerated his wife by admitting that he had been drinking, not his wife.

That guilt of handing over the wheel to his wife, festered and stayed with him forever.

And overriding that guilt of relinquishing control of the car, were the dark and intrusive thoughts of breaking local tradition – not paying homage to the shrine of the revered soul. He should have acceded to Catherine's repeated requests to stop at the shrine. He had, over the years, gone back countless times and replayed the sequence of events in his tormented mind. And the same questions, repeated in a never-ending loop, remained unanswered – could he have averted the tragedy if he had yielded to Catherine's requests to stop and pay homage to the revered soul? Or, if he had not indulged himself and not had the wine? Or not tossed the keys to Catherine?

THREE

Shenzi, Laikipia, Kenya.

Within the hour, with the sun fast receding and silhouetting the Acacia trees, the five-man group of poachers heard two shots ring out south of their position. The vultures had taken fright at the booming sound of the shots and took to the air; to return later to feast on the elephant carcass, just as the maggots were emerging from the rotting flesh.

Shenzi saw the flight of birds in the distance and was worried that the game wardens may catch up as they made their way towards their parked Toyota Cruiser. Shenzi's ochre-covered face and the bright orange cloth covering his torso and waist could be spotted quite easily at a distance. The other four poachers were well camouflaged in false game wardens' uniforms with the wildlife department logo blazoned across on the front and back. Shenzi regretted donning his signature attire but had not anticipated actual wildlife wardens in the vicinity. The ochre and the bright orange sarong-like covering were authority symbols; just as the cobra uses its puffed-up hood to intimidate.

To complicate matters, the two massive blood-soaked tusks, straddled across the shoulders of his two colleagues, were slowing their progress towards their rendezvous car. Their retreat to Somalia was delayed by the pedestrian pace and the poachers were aware of the sun's transit and the limited time left before sunset.

Shenzi, the leader of the pack, had a quick whispered conversation with the other four poachers and decided to fall back as a look out. The cohort of four poachers went ahead with Shenzi bringing up the rear. He constantly scoured the bush behind him to ensure there was no warden activity behind them.

Shenzi, at 5' 8" and short for a Samburu, was at home in the Acacia-covered bush territory and gradually increased the distance between himself and his team, although he kept them in sight. He was conscious of the AK-47 and the panga carried by his deputy; a temperamental and mercurial character at the best of times. The third and the fourth members had drawn the short straws and were weighed down by the onerous task of carrying the tusks on their aching shoulders; oblivious to anything but their ivory burden.

The fifth poacher, a recent addition to the team, was tagging along and keeping a look out. This was lion territory and all of them were aware of the dangers of an ambush by stalking lions or leopards. The poachers were already envisioning the good times that lay ahead in Mogadishu – once they had cashed in on their bounty.

The shots that had rung out in the distance previously added urgency to Shenzi's pace – they had to be on their way back before the sun dipped and the light faded. It was quite amazing how quickly the sun sets in the African countries flanking the equator and he knew visibility would hamper their progress. The only saving grace was that unfolding darkness would also hamper anyone pursuing them and the big cats.

It was then that he saw the three wildlife wardens.

All they had was a single gun and a walkie-talkie; standard wildlife department issue. Shenzi smiled smugly as he circled behind so that the three game wardens were in the middle; his gang up ahead.

Shenzi made a bird call alerting his deputy who stopped dead in his tracks. The deputy cautioned the others to maintain total silence. They listened intently, quite well camouflaged in the thick bush. The deputy, forewarned by the bird call, knew the game wardens were close, easily picking up the rustle of their movements and the wardens' careless talk.

The deputy, listening intently, picked up two different accents, all speaking English. He readily recognised one of the accents; there were enough of these educated do-gooders – mostly aid workers – in downtown Nairobi and in Somalia. The second accent baffled him although he was sure it was an English one. Though most of the educated lot preferred the safe domain of the 4x4, it was unusual to encounter a foot patrol this far out in the bush. He sniggered – this was his backyard and they were treading into his domain. He had cut his teeth in Somalia on the backstreets of Mogadishu – under the tutelage of Shenzi. The bush was like the wild west; shoot first and ask questions later.

The deputy saw the three wardens as they emerged into a clearing from the cover of the thick bush. He signalled the two tusk-carrying men to go ahead and appear into the open – to take the wardens by total surprise. A bird noisily flapped from its perch and with the wardens distracted by the bird's flight, the two poachers stepped out abruptly, the tusks straddled across their shoulders. The wardens froze, their attention focused on the blood-soaked tusks. In that brief split second, the hot-headed young deputy stepped forwarded and shot the two wardens out in the front. The AK47 shots spooked the antelope and zebra herds who took fright and stampeded away leaving young foals stranded in the melee.

The deputy, emboldened by the felling of the two wardens, walked menacingly towards the stunned third warden and raised the AK47 to finish off the job. There was flicker in his visual field as he saw Shenzi step out sideways from behind the surviving warden.

The third warden, much taller than Shenzi, stared at his two prone colleagues in disbelief and then reluctantly focused on the AK47 and the congealed blood-covered panga. The shell-shocked figure raised his arms in total surrender; staring at the AK47 levelled squarely at him.

The deputy was just about to squeeze the trigger when he heard a terse command, Shenzi's ice-cold voice slicing through the tense air: 'Wacha, hiyu na daktari!' It was then that the deputy saw the red-tubed stethoscope hanging loosely around the neck of the warden; the steel end piece glinting in the sun. Shenzi's timely verbal intervention stopped the deputy in his tracks – a stay of execution delivered just in time. A split second later and the AK47 would have done the deed. The deputy reluctantly lowered the AK47 without a show of dissent. His time would come; for now, he yielded to Shenzi.

The ferocious looking Shenzi stepped forward and ripped off the Rado watch from the raised wrist of the vet and demanded cash. Shenzi rifled the cash from the proffered wallet and pocketed it along with the black dialled Rado, flinging the wallet back, which landed short at the daktari's dust covered Courteney Magnum black leather boots. For a split second, Shenzi was tempted to demand the boots but decided against it.

As the poachers melted into the thick bush, the Brit was galvanized into action and raced towards the two wardens, fearing the worst. The sight of the congealed pools of blood was enough to shatter any hope of rescuing his colleagues from imminent death.

Shenzi and his team retreated and rapidly walked towards their getaway car. They could hear the vet on the walkie-talkie calling for help. They did not have much time; the leader spurred them on; half running as he covered up their spoor just in case a search party from the base camp decided to follow them into the bush.

As they hastened towards their car, Shenzi deliberately fell back, pretending to cover up their spoor. Still very much within range, he withdrew his Smith & Wesson 686 gun from the hidden thigh holster and in one fluid motion shot all four poachers in front of him. The bullets found their marks except the fourth bullet, which was deflected and missed, miraculously, all vital organs.

As he got closer, he shot three of them again; a textbook perfect execution. The fourth team mate had dropped a bit further away and had his face turned towards Shenzi – the eyes seemingly lifeless.

Shenzi took aim to pump another bullet but on seeing the outpouring torrent of blood, inexplicably strode towards the other three. He frisked all three and snatched all their cash, the car keys, the Rado and a dog-eared diary that the third poacher had.

As he quickly counted the haul, Shenzi's parched lips stretched into a wide smile. The British Sterling from the daktari would be worth a small fortune on Mogadishu's thriving black market. He flicked through the grubby-looking diary and frowned in confusion – most of the front pages appeared to be blank. He almost flung it into the bush but instead shoved the diary into the money belt that he had retrieved from the dead poacher.

Shenzi without so much as a backward glance, continued towards the parked car, which carried false 'GK' number plates and was the same make and model as used by the national parks – a ploy that they had frequently used in the past to confuse aerial surveillance teams.

He retrieved the Toyota, hidden among the thick shrubs. Within minutes he double backed to where the four bodies lay – to collect the tusks and the single AK47. The bodies were left behind for the scavengers; the hyenas and the vultures would make short work of the corpses. Before he started his journey towards the Somali border, he wiped clean the 686 and the thigh holster and placed both on the passenger seat; wrapped in an oil rag found in the car. The money belt was strapped to his slender waist; hidden under his clothing.

An hour into the journey, Shenzi pulled off the dirt track into the bush and found a series of termite mounds; some as tall as the smaller Acacia trees. After giving the gun and holster a final clean, he hoisted himself onto the bonnet of the Toyota and dropped the gun and the holster separately into two of the largest mounds – even the local tribesmen kept away from these huge ochre structures which frequently sheltered cobras and scorpions. A cobra bite in the bush meant certain death; instantaneous and excruciatingly painful.

The disposal, well away from the scene of the brutal executions, meant that the final vestiges of his traitorous act would lay buried in the makeshift tombs for eternity. He spotted the circling vultures in the distance – nature's carrion disposal system had begun and once the hyenas got wind of the rotting bodies, all evidence of death would be erased in a few days.

He climbed into the Toyota, nonchalantly humming a popular Swahili melody, as he sped off. 'Malaika, na kupende Maliaka.....' The mouthing of the love song amidst the carnage that had just taken place was incongruous, to say the least – had he been serenading a young buxom maiden then the setting sun and the Acacia trees would have been the perfect backdrop.

The getaway car sped across the dusty dirt track raising plumes of ochre clouds – the border was a long way off and Shenzi had a long, tedious journey ahead of him. He did not mind that – it had been a fruitful expedition; the tusks in the open top behind him and the booty plundered from his victims had made it well worth it. All his to enjoy; no division of the spoils.

As soon as he crossed into Somalia, he sold the Toyota and the A47K at the first market place that he came to – no audit trails or evidence left behind to tie him with the Laikipia incident. Before selling the Toyota, he made the rounds of the various ivory traders that he knew, and sold the tusks after bargaining for almost half a day. He then deliberately put it out there that he was looking for a lift into the interior – towards Mogadishu.

The next day Shenzi doubled back, in the opposite direction, to the border. He had catapulted back and forth all these years without detection or capture; the border between Kenya and Somalia as porous as a sieve.

Back on the Laikipia plains, the Masai children collecting firewood for the evening meal found the four bodies and kept their distance as the hyenas circled the dead group. They heard a faint moan from the fourth who was still twitching a few feet away.

The nimble one among the group ran back to the manyatta to

seek help, while the others kept watch to ensure the hyenas concentrated on the three dead ones. Already the pack was busy tearing away at the bodies and dragging them towards their den and pretty soon the vultures and other carrion would arrive to feast on the spoils.

The fourth poacher, with his life ebbing away drop by drop, was carried back to the manyatta by the posse of Masai morans – warriors. They carried him to the main road, not far from the manyatta. They had managed to stem the bleeding as the rescue party waited for the safari tour cars to return to the game lodges where medical help would be available. The prompt action by the Masai had saved the poacher from certain death.

He was saved by the emergency treatment meted out by a visiting surgeon from Nairobi – running a medical day camp sponsored by the Lions Group. Some of the volunteer doctors were flying back from the airstrip at the camp to Wilson Airport – the patient was swiftly admitted to Kenyatta Hospital under police guard.

Within hours, the wildlife department commandeered the patient and admitted him to Nairobi Hospital where an emergency splenectomy was successfully performed. The press, after being told that the patient was recuperating, was stone walled and in the absence of further details, the media soon lost interest in the survivor. The progress of one of the toughest car rallies in the world, the 1990 Marlboro Rally, merited more coverage than the survival or death of a poacher. The Kenyans and the world had become used to the carnage; be it elephants or citizens.

FOUR

Alec, Nairobi, Kenya.

The Kenya Airways local flight from Nairobi landed at Moi International Airport, Mombasa, as scheduled. Alec made his way through baggage collection and into the arrivals lounge - scanning the multitude of placards; the Sheraton and Hilton signs dominating the waiting crowd in the arrivals area. Somewhere in that throng was his driver for the hotel shuttle service. The Orange Coral Hotel was a short taxi ride away – a family run hotel renowned for its seafood cuisine and its array of water sports, especially scuba diving.

Alec, on the wrong side of forty, had reached the stage in his career as a vet when professional apathy sets in: the 'been there, done it scenario'. He had a thriving small-animal practice in South London and had, early on, gained postgraduate qualifications in small-animal medicine, which then led to lecturing final-year students at the Royal Veterinary College. The prestigious institution in Camden afforded him the opportunity to keep abreast of the latest clinical advances and kept him on his toes imparting clinical skills – best of both worlds; academia and private practice.

A chance meeting with a wildlife veterinarian who was an expert in the capture, transport and release - translocation - of wildlife, especially the endangered pachyderms, elephants and rhinoceros, enticed Alec into wildlife conservation. He joined an elephant conservation charity with a view to spending time in Kenya; allowing him the opportunity to return to Kenya; his birth place. Within months, he had taken sabbatical leave and ended up with the wildlife department's team dealing with elephants, a particular target of the poachers, on the plains of Laikipia.

Alec's fascination with wildlife medicine, in contrast to his small animal practice, gave him the chance to work with the teams at Laikipia and the Nairobi National Park. The dedication of the wildlife vets and the game wardens in protecting Kenya's wildlife heritage resonated with Alec; the plight of African elephants became his new mantra; his newfound passion.

The illegal trade in ivory was endemic to East Africa; stunting economic growth in all three countries - Kenya, Uganda and Tanzania. The high birth rate and the steep population growth encouraged human encroachment into the game reserves – a perfect recipe for human-elephant conflict. The persistent lack of rain in the Laikipia region had intensified the drought cycle. Scarcity of water was a factor that triggered human-elephant conflict. The Laikipia elephants had gained undue notoriety. Rogue elephants had become a nuisance - encroaching on to human habitats in search of water and foliage.

These unruly episodes of aggression were sometimes used as an excuse by the farmers to succumb to poachers' inducements. The balance between wildlife and human habitats was also dependent on tribal sensitivities between the Samburu, the Pokot and the Turkana tribes – all jockeying for the control of the pastoral lands and grazing rights.

Alec's insights into the tribal rivalries and Kenyan politics were primarily based on his father Drew's reminiscences. He was certain that although Kenya had moved on since independence, the old tribal rivalries still existed.

The poachers exploited all these nuances to their benefit – pitting one against the other in elaborate games of mental chess, with real ivory as the currency of discord, decimation and destruction.

His father had had a long and illustrious tenure as a civil servant in colonial Kenya. Born and brought up in Nairobi, Drew Dunlop, had gained a first at Oxford University, reading geology. After graduation he had returned to Kenya – seconded to the Colonial government in the energy sector. Much before Kenya's independence in December 1963, he had joined Kenya Shell as an oil exploration analyst. He had travelled extensively along the Rift Valley and the coastal strip.

Alec's childhood memories of Nairobi and Kenya were as faded as the sepia tinged photographs in the family album. His memories and images of Kenya were second hand – based on Drew's memories. After the accident that killed Drew's wife, Drew had adopted him – the orphan of a British High Commission employee.

Drew had told him much later, after they had moved to the UK, that adopting Alec was his act of atonement and repentance. Especially, when he found out that Alec's dad had died in the same car crash – his father was a clerk with the British High Commission in Nairobi. Alec's biological mother had died a few years after his birth.

Drew had brought Alec back to the UK soon after the tragedy; a disruptive phase in both their lives. His father had returned to Britain to provide Alec with an upbringing that he deserved. He never quite managed to return to Kenya and fulfil his dream of dairy farming on the land in Naivasha which had been in the family for generations.

'Bwana' (Swahili for boss or master) Dunlop, an ebullient soul, had been reduced to an empty shell. He never quite came to terms with the guilt that hounded him for the rest of his life. His conscience, plagued by recriminations and self-doubt, rejected the official verdict that the incident on the road to Mombasa was just a tragic accident; not human carelessness.

The alcoholic stupor that he had sunk into, replayed the same scene in his mind – him falling asleep in the car after handing over the keys of the VW to his wife. And not paying homage at the shrine.

Fortunately, Alec was away at boarding school and missed his father's steady decline into alcoholism and delirium tremens. The pair survived on a generous index-linked pension and a small inheritance, while the farm in Naivasha had to be sold to fund Alec's private school and university education.

Alec, with the resilience of youth had survived the tragedy, seemingly without any emotional scars. He had also survived the rigours of being fairly poor compared to the other well-heeled students. The divide between him and the posh lot aggravated by his accent.

For many, he also became a target of envy and jealousy – he had excelled academically and on the sports field. More importantly, he was a hit with the ladies. The macho brigade never quite understood the fascination that Alec had for women – despite his accent and the financial constraints. Alec was, to all ends and purposes, from the other side of the fence; the wrong side.

By the time he had moved to vet school, he was a strapping six-footer with the debonair looks of a Hollywood star and a fan following to match. His deft touch with the opposite sex had not diminished – his female following was inversely proportional to his male one. Only Ian Ross, also born in Kenya, had stayed a close friend throughout his school and university days. Both of them had started private practice at roughly the same time – Ian had helped with his first business loan for his vet practice and had even stood in as a locum vet at times of professional difficulties.

Alec had just assisted the wildlife capture unit to relocate a few rogue elephants further towards Mount Kenya. The use of the Dan-Inject Dart system to tranquilise and immobilise the elephants with etorphine was standard procedure, as was the use of diprenorphine to promote full recovery and mobility. Most game parks used the dual drug regimen to immobilise large mammals. He found the whole process enthralling, especially the logistics of sedating elephants.

The importance of following set protocols and preventing undue stress to the animals presented clinical challenges, especially as these tasks had to be executed quickly to avoid complications. Even a few extra minutes of prostration or a delay in reversing the tranquilising phase could affect heart and lung function. Fatalities did occur but were thankfully rare.

Just before Alec's return to Nairobi, the game wardens received word that poachers had been spotted on the western plains of Laikipia. There were indications that this was the same network of poachers who had shot down a renowned bull elephant – a shattered tracking collar had been found identifying the tusker as 'Rafiki' (friend).

The Laikipia game wardens had been monitoring Rafiki and knew that its massive tusks, gloriously and extensively romanticised by the press, were the ultimate trophies. In the end, death came at the hands of the poachers who had been tracking the unlucky mammoth. Rafiki's celebrity status was its downfall - just as the wardens had feared.

Fearing the same fate for the herd that they were tracking, the game wardens, some of them armed, set off in the direction of the last reported sightings. The tusks were there for the taking and the conservation taskforce was fearful of further casualties – Laikipia's fast diminishing elephant population was at imminent risk.

The team reached the target area and saw empty cartridge shells strewn close to a cluster of Acacia trees. A blood trail indicated that the elephant herd had not escaped unhurt. No carcasses were found, which was unusual as the poachers had AK47s and could have mowed down any number of elephants. Quite possibly the poachers were retreating or at the end of their 'hit and run' cycle.

Once they crossed the border into war-torn Somalia, the poachers were beyond the arm of international and local law – their immunity and protection guaranteed by the warring factions. The warlords and the militias ruled the land; the law of the jungle prevailed.

It was a couple of hours before sunset when the game wardens came upon a comatose bull elephant who had been shot at point blank range. The gaping wounds where its tusks had been hacked off were still bloody and smothered by swarms of bluebottles. The slashed carotid artery still pulsating with arterial blood – the poacher's panga had made short work of the thick layers of skin, subcutaneous fat and muscle.

A nearby 'manyatta' (a Samburu or Masai enclosure with mud walled huts) had been used as a makeshift slaughterhouse – its expanse of ochre soil stained and damp with pools of coagulated blood. The bluebottles, engaged in a frenzy of egg-laying, would soon multiply and the maggots would be squirming in the rotten flesh within a day. The stench overpowering enough to attract the hyaenas; nature's recycling agents.

One of the armed wardens, shaken by the gruesome sight, shot into the frontal and the temporal lobes of the comatose elephant; euthanasia performed to end the misery of the fallen pachyderm. The shots reverberated in the abandoned manyatta; the sound amplified by the surrounding walls.

The group split up, with Alec following the two seasoned and experienced game wardens. They had only one Heckler & Koch G3 rifle between them; wholly inadequate protection against the firepower of the AK47 armed poachers. Alec's apprehension grew as he viewed the golden orb sinking into the horizon; nightfall not yet imminent but preying on his mind. He fingered the bright red tubing of his stethoscope around his neck to reassure himself that he was a visiting vet out in the wild, not a gun-wielding tourist on a trophy-hunting safari.

Within the hour, with the sun fast receding and silhouetting the Acacia trees, they were ambushed by a group of poachers. Before Alec could react, a short burst of fire felled both the game wardens.

Alec's trauma, on witnessing the brutal execution of the two wardens was hazy and confused. He recalled calling for help after the poachers had fled. He remembered the solemn drive back to the base camp – a gloom had descended on all of them. The next morning, he returned to Nairobi, to be on time for his short break in Mombasa. During the night he vaguely registered a commotion outside his tent.

In the morning, he was told that a poacher had been found

alive by Masai herdsmen. Alec was informed that the injured poacher, under guard, would be on the same flight as him. They had removed a few seats to accommodate the patient. Alec kept his distance and slept all the way to Nairobi; quite shell shocked and emotionally drained.

On landing, he was whisked off to his hotel as he was due to fly to Mombasa later on. He saw an ambulance and a police escort waiting for the injured man. The poacher would be an important witness; if he survived.

Alec's Mombasa stay did little to erase the trauma of the Laikipia incident. His mind kept harking back to that fateful afternoon, especially as he sat on the peaceful beach listening to the soft distinctive sounds of the Indian Ocean. The stark contrast of the brutality of that hot afternoon amidst the Acacia trees and his present serene setting on the beach felt surreal.

After a couple of days of rest and recreation at the Orange Coral Hotel, Alec visited Mombasa's old town and Fort Jesus – both sites had an emotional and nostalgic effect on him, probably because both locations reminded him of his father and his constant ramblings about life in Kenya. He recalled his father's discourses about the historical impact of the Portuguese, the Omani Arabs and lastly the British, who in 1895 declared Kenya's protectorate status under the British Empire.

Visiting Fort Jesus, which was built by the Portuguese in 1593, reminded Alec again about his father's two favourite obsessions – geology and anthropology. Standing on the parapets, looking out to sea, brought back snippets of information. Drew was in the habit of launching into longwinded accounts of Kenya's historical pedigree – the countless journeys that Indian and Arab traders, in their small dhows, would have made to trade spices, ivory, cloves and gold. Alec recalled Drew's particular admiration for the Omani and Indian influences on the coast from Zanzibar, Mombasa, Malindi to Lamu.

It had all started with an expedition by Vasco da Gama – Drew's favourite explorer – in 1497. The Portuguese explorer's discovery of the sea route to India, past the Cape of Good Hope, Mozambique and Mombasa, opened up the Eastern trade routes – for commerce and piracy. Alec wondered whether the poachers used the same traditional sea routes of yesteryears to ferry the illicit ivory from Mombasa to Dubai, Somalia to India and beyond; the traditional crescent sail dhows still operating with almost total immunity.

Alec strayed into old town which was within walking distance of Fort Jesus. As he approached the old town, with its disproportionate number of curio shops, and the harbour, the smell of rotting and drying fish wafted across from the seafront. He could see the small dhows and boats in the distance - shimmering in the sun. The narrow crisscrossing lanes were abuzz with tourists, hawkers and a motley crowd of Indian, Arab and European residents, many of them British and German expats. The buibui-clad Muslim ladies intermingled with sari-wearing Indian housewives out on their daily shopping chores.

Alec paused and watched with fascination as the coffee sellers with their shiny brass kettles and the distinctive patterned ceramic cups meandered through the crowded lanes – it was almost an art, the way they managed to produce a symphony of tinkling sounds just by the rhythmic clicking of the ceramic cups. The scalding black Arabic kahawa (coffee) and the sweet fried dough pastry (mandazi) became the standard fare for tourists and locals alike. Alec sat on the 'baraza', a cement bench that runs along the outside walls of houses, and had the kahawa and the mandazi - the ginger and salty taste of the bitter coffee contrasting with the sweetness of the mandazi. It was a novel experience for him – he had been very young when Drew took him to the UK.

A day later, Alec caught up with his old friend, Musa, who was a wildlife photographer and cameraman. Musa had prospered as a cinematographer and, rumour had it that he had profited handsomely from his Hollywood film contracts – two blockbusters shot entirely on location in Kenya were the making of his international reputation and his fortune. His Hollywood fame attracted more work and led to lucrative contracts – wildlife photoshoots, books and advertising films. Musa had become a minor celebrity. And modestly rich by Kenyan standards, which was a stark contrast to Musa's cash-strapped time in the UK while studying cinematography at the National Film and Television School. Alec had bailed him out on a number of occasions with small loans until his remittances arrived from Mombasa.

The pair had remained friends ever since they had shared digs in London – while Alec was at vet school and Musa on an internship with a film production company in Euston. A deep bond had developed between the two Kenya-born young men.

Alec had caught a taxi from the Orange Coral to Musa's studio near the Mackinnon Market – all excited at Musa's planned day trip to take him sightseeing.

'Alec, meet Ava Patel, she's a family friend.' Musa introduced Ava who, though born in Zanzibar, was brought to Kenya by her young unwed mother. Very soon after arrival, Ava had been adopted by a couple in Mombasa.

Alec was bowled over by the alluring vision of a devastatingly attractive thirty something who exhibited traits of the racial mix that was so prevalent on the Kenyan coast – an Indian, Omani/Arab and Portuguese mixture; a stunning cocktail; a classical and sculptured look. Alec was enthralled by the sheer stunning symmetry of her features; a Nubian queen reincarnated.

'Hi.' Alec was choked for words at first and then continued, 'I hope you are joining us for lunch?'

Ava's smile revealed dazzlingly white teeth and the dimples added to her charm. A smile that could easily have launched a thousand dhows in a bygone Omani era.

'Hope you did not get stuck in the traffic? Where are you staying?' she asked. Musa had informed her about Alec's imminent arrival for their lunch meeting.

'At the Orange Coral, the hotel shuttle uses the priority pre-paid toll lane so we did not have to queue up.' The bridge crossing was a bottleneck and notorious for its exasperating long queues.

'Are you with us for a while?' Ava queried, making small talk while Musa attended to a few routine calls.

'Yes. I head back to London after a stint at the Animal Orphanage and the National Park. There's also an anti-poaching conference that I've been invited to attend. Hopefully, it will give me an overview of the illicit ivory trade.'

Alec was a bit disappointed that Ava wasn't joining them. He would have loved the opportunity to get to know her, especially as he was flying back to Nairobi shortly and may not see her again. He towered over her and smiled broadly to lessen the impact. He was aware that he sometimes intimidated people. He was drawn to her and was subconsciously overcompensating; desperately trying to impress her. Her petite stature overshadowed by her radiance and beauty.

He tried again. 'Are you sure can't join us? It will be a pleasure.'

'Alas, no. I have loads to do, enjoy your lunch. Hopefully, we'll meet before you leave?' Ava remarked casually. Ava had agreed to stand in for Musa at work while he spent time with Alec.

Alec and Musa left shortly thereafter with Ava's words still ringing in his ears. He wondered if Ava was Musa's girlfriend and then dismissed the thought, not before a twinge of envy flashed through.

The lunch at an Indian restaurant gave them ample time to catch up on old times. Whilst the food was delicious, the spicy tang was something that Alec's palate was not accustomed to. He had to down copious amounts of fluids – beer and sweet lassi – to dampen the spicy onslaught. The impromptu stop at the Blue Room for dessert was timely - the dollops of soothing ice cream a Godsend.

They parted at Alec's hotel with Musa promising Alec one final bit of sightseeing before his imminent return to Nairobi. Ava had not featured in their conversation and, although Alec was tempted to ask after her, he desisted. Alec could not get her out of his thoughts and would have jumped at the chance of spending some more time with her.

He was just about to have an early night when Ava called from the lobby asking if he was free for a drink. Alec was so taken by surprise that he floundered for a moment. He quickly brushed his teeth, acutely conscious of the lingering garlic and onion aftertaste, and slapped on some aftershave before hastening down to reception. When he did not spot her in the lobby, he was about to enquire at the night desk when he heard a call from behind him.

As she came closer, Ava flipped the veil of her buibui and burst out laughing.

'Sorry, thought I'd play a prank on you. Give me two minutes, I'll pop into the ladies and take this off.' He had noticed the buibui-clad figure in the lobby but had walked straight past her.

She joined him shortly, the elegant jet-black silky buibui thrown casually over her left arm, arranging and patting her hair with her right hand as she emerged from the ladies. He noticed that she was casually dressed in jeans and a white cotton embroidered top. Despite the lack of makeup, she looked ravishing. The red stilettoes added to her allure but he still towered over her.

'Thought I'd drop in for a nightcap,' Ava whispered in a conspiratorial tone. The lobby was deserted – most of the residents, mainly foreign tourists, were probably lingering over dessert or their cognacs.

Noticing the small embroidered words on the buibui over her arm, he remarked, 'Hardly the run of the mill item – looks very chic. What's the inscription?'

'It's a Rumi poem that reads 'Silence is the language of God, all else is poor translation.' Seeing the quizzical look on Alec's face, she quipped: 'Not just a pretty face, eh? I'll show you my collection of Rumi's work. Very profound. Are you familiar with his poems?'

'Nope,' Alec said. He was glad that she had taken the initiative to come over. He had no idea who Rumi was. He'd have to visit the library and bone up, especially if he wanted to make a good impression on this demi-goddess.

'Very cerebral,' he mused. Poetry wasn't his forte – Wilbur Smith and Robert Ludlum were more his thing. He had been a

voracious reader until he went to vet school. And a film buff. He
recalled that Ian had shared his penchant for Hollywood films and both
were members of the British Film Institute. Going for a movie in
Leicester Square, followed by a curry and a pub crawl was their Friday
night routine – often their dates joined them. Musa would do so as well
but would avoid the pub crawl.

'Let's get that drink, I'm parched,' Ava said, as she led the
way. Alec followed, admiring her denim-covered slim legs in the
stilettoes and her hour glass figure. 'Umm, good things come in small
packages,' he almost said aloud. The red stilettos clicked on the tiled
floor.

'Let's go to the poolside bar,' Alec suggested.

'No, let's walk down to the beach, there's a night spot that
serves exquisite cocktails and, among the cosmopolitan crowd we
won't stick out like sore thumbs.'

'One sore old thumb, you mean? You hardly qualify with your
youth and looks.' Alec was away again, plying her with compliments,
which she seemed to take in her stride; signs that she was used to male
attention and more than adept at fending for herself. Alec smiled,
obviously she'd had plenty of practice. He'd have to sharpen up. After
his acrimonious breakup, he had kept his distance from women; until
tonight. He was completely out of practice.

The bar was packed with a very mixed crowd of Europeans
and locals, predominantly younger couples. There were a few buibui
and sari wearers among the majority of Western women; smart casual
attire interspersed with designer evening gowns. Most congregated
around the dance floor, festooned with pulsating strobe lights. A live
band with a female lead singer was already warming up for the late-

night session.

After a few drinks, Ava led him to the dance floor – despite Alec's protestations about having more than two left feet. He was more worried about standing out in the crowd – they made an odd couple with Ava nestled against him, barely reaching up to his shoulders.

Ava's youthful appearance accentuated his age; he felt like a relic especially on the dance floor. However, they had polished off a bottle of red wine, so, the wine fuelled bravado and the tangible frisson of excitement, generated by the chemistry between them, blunted his inhibitions.

After a while, realising Alec's discomfort, Ava switched to a slow dance as she cuddled up to him. Despite their height disparities and much to Alec's relief, they were hardly noticed in the cosmopolitan ambience of the dancing couples. He could have danced all night.

No one gave them a second look; Mombasa with its bonhomie culture afforded them that freedom; the melting pot that it truly was. Something that Nairobi could never match.

There were a few older couples dancing at their own pace which reassured Alec. It had been a while since his last foray onto a dance floor; especially with someone as stunning as Ava.

They lost all track of time and were content to move languidly, almost pedestrian, until Alec recognised the melody- 'Malaika' (angel), an international love song that had catapulted Miriam Makeba, a South African exile, into the charts.

'That's Makeba, isn't it?' Alec asked. The Swahili melody captured the pathos of unrequited love. The lyrics were lost on Alec but he danced, as best as he could, to the soulful tune. It gave him the opportunity to draw Ava closer. She didn't seem to mind as she responded, synchronising her movements to his tempo.

'Well before my time,' exclaimed Ava cheekily. 'Yes, well spotted, it is Makeba. Right up your alley, my old friend.' She continued the ribbing, with an exaggerated emphasis on the word 'old'. Alec ignored the barb about his age and refused to rise to the bait. He was certain he wasn't more than four or five years older but let her have her fun at his expense.

'Makeba is famous all through East Africa and her songs, especially 'Malaika', opened doors for other talented Africans. For us Kenyans, she holds a special place, especially after her duet with Harry Belafonte at the independence-day celebrations on 12th Dec 1963. The crowd went berserk with the rendition of 'Malika' – in the presence of Jomo Kenyatta, the first Prime Minister of an independent Kenya,' Ava elaborated as she looked up into his eyes.

'Actually, my dad attended those boisterous celebrations at Uhuru Park. He met Mzee Kenyatta soon after, at an oil conference in Nairobi. There's a group photograph with my father, standing next to the Prime Minister – it's a treasured item in the family album.' Alec fell silent as he recalled that and other photographs in the family album.

Briefly, in the fleeting hours of their nocturnal tryst, 'Malaika' became their song. Alec was flattered by the attention Ava showered on him. He was overwhelmed by the attention – maybe the wine had gone to his head. It could be a toxic mix – wine, women and song. He barely remembered the other songs belted out by the band. Boney M, he knew for sure; especially 'Rasputin' and 'Brown Girl in the Ring'.

When the 7am wake-up call came through from reception,

Alec reluctantly got up – his head felt sore and he then realised that the other side of the double bed was vacant. The short note on the rumpled pillow caught his eye.

'I had a wonderful time. You did well, mzee (old man), despite the red wine! Got to get back to my flat and then to work. Hopefully, we'll catch up before you leave for Nairobi. Kwaheri (goodbye) for now.'

The note was signed as 'kidege' (little bird). Alec noticed, with a wry smile, that she had appropriated the 'little bird' epithet from the lyrics of the 'Malaika' song. He recalled Ava translating the lyrics while they were dancing. He had heard Makeba in a live concert many years ago; the melody always reminded him of Kenya. Now it would remind him of Ava as well.

He was smiling as he jumped into the shower still reflecting on the night's events, not least her tongue-in-cheek references to their age difference. She had also told him that she was from Zanzibar. Musa and his family had taken her under their wing.

Alec, softly whistling the melody, felt the nostalgia sweep over him – he hadn't realised how profoundly he missed his birth country; his visit had struck a deep chord within.

His melancholy had disappeared by the time the tour got under way and Musa took him to their last landmark – Moi Avenue, the dual carriageway adorned by two pairs of massive elephant tusks, straddling the busy carriageway.

The Mombasa tusks probably defined Kenya on the tourist trail just as the Big Ben highlighted London and Britain – iconic structures. The replica tusks had been erected in 1956 to commemorate Princess Margaret's visit to Mombasa. Initially made of canvas and sisal, the tusks were later replaced by aluminium ones to save on refurbishing costs.

Musa took a few shots of Alec, dwarfed by the giant replica tusks in the background. Alec had seen smaller versions of replica tusks at Musa's studio; props used in the film trade. The local craftsmen were extremely talented and skilful – from a distance, but for the size, the props looked like real ivory.

Alec spent his last night in Mombasa at the Orange Coral with Musa and Ava his dinner guests. It had been a pleasant evening as they dined at the poolside restaurant with the roar of the waves as they cascaded onto the pristine sandy beach and the palm fringes silhouetted against the milky white moonlight.

'Well, I guess all good things come to an end.' Alec toasted his two guests with the last of his wine. Looking at Ava, his tone had a wistful ring to it. Ava was quieter than usual as the evening and the dinner drew to an end.

'Remind me, when do you return to London?' Musa asked.

'I am shadowing Dr Pinto at the National Park for a while and then we are attending a conference. I fly back in roughly a month's time. If either of you are in Nairobi, do please call me – I'm at the Hilton.' Alec said the last bit looking fondly at Ava; Musa had missed the glow on Ava's face as she shyly averted her eyes from Alec's ardent gaze.

Alec knew that Musa was always jetting off to photo shoots, so the invitation was implicitly for Ava; more in hope than anything else. The last couple of days had flown by and he was quite taken by this vivacious Aphrodite.

Musa went off to collect his Range Rover and as he drove up

to the front of the hotel, Ava slipped Alec a note and dashed off with a cheery wave.

The note had her address and telephone number with a post script – 'come to the flat for our last nightcap. PPS: I live on my own, 'mzee' Alec.'

Alec was still clutching the note as he descended from the cab at an address in the old town – he could hear the faint sounds of late-night revellers on the harbour front. He had managed to buy an excellent bottle of Merlot from the wine bar at the hotel and as he rang the bell, Alec thought about the 'Malaika' melody and hoped it would invoke the same magical feelings as the previous night; 'mzee' notwithstanding, the 'kidege' was in for a repeat performance.

Alec returned to Nairobi to join Dr Pinto at the animal orphanage. His brief interlude in Mombasa, especially the time spent with Ava, had reinvigorated him. On the flight back, he just could not get her out of his mind and regretted that his tight schedule did not give him any chance of meeting her again.

The Nairobi Animal Orphanage, inaugurated in 1964, was initially used to house and treat orphaned wildlife before releasing the animals in to the wild. Over the years it had evolved into a shelter for treating and rehabilitating abandoned and injured wildlife. The orphanage, sited near the entrance to the Nairobi National Park, had a fully-fledged veterinary clinic attached to it. It was at the clinic that Alec hoped to shadow the attending veterinarian, Dr Pinto, before returning to the UK.

Before the end of his stay in Kenya, Alec accompanied Dr Pinto to a pan African conference convened by the wildlife department. The central theme was the illicit ivory trade and the impact that poaching was having on elephant populations. Alec was astounded when one of the guest speakers, presenting a paper on the illicit ivory trade, revealed the stark statistics of the systematic and organised killing of elephants. The disturbing statistic, that drew a collective gasp from the eminent gathering, was that Africa had only 350,000 to 400,000 elephants left; down from an unconfirmed census report of 1.3 million.

A hush descended in the conference hall as the dire statistics brought home the gravity of the situation and the realisation that the world would soon lose all its African elephants; an abject indictment of human greed. The conference passed several resolutions to curb the wanton decimation of African elephants – financial incentives for the tribes to foster and protect wildlife, latest arms for the game wardens, public education and awareness and fund raisers.

Alec wondered if Kenya had the resources to save its wildlife – the West certainly needed to take an active role, otherwise the pachyderms and many other species would just vanish off the face of the earth.

The elephant in the room had, indeed, been the lack of global legislation to ban ivory sales – without this important measure, everything else was just cosmetic tinkering.

A quote by a delegate stayed with Alec as the conference concluded:

'When two elephants fight, it is the grass that suffers' – in the geo-politics of the regions, the elephants were the grass caught between governmental apathy and the aggression of the poachers and the cartels.

Before the delegates departed, an open invitation was extended to all to attend a unique and special fund-raising event – the burning of confiscated ivory by a private lobby of business sponsors. The money raised by the business community would be pumped back into wildlife conservation. The idea was to encourage the business community and the sponsors to play a full role in raising funds.

This was a small hoard of ivory retrieved from the poachers in the Laikipia region. The corporate sponsors had lobbied the government to allow a specially set up charity to manage the event. It was envisioned that the business sponsors would bear all the costs of the event thereby maximising the funds raised for future conservation projects. This would be a pilot project – the first time for the corporate sector to undertake such an event without any government involvement.

A few days later, the seized ivory was set ablaze on a specially cleared plot in the Nairobi National Park. The ivory was arranged in a conical pattern with wooden logs piled around to form two towers. The confiscated ivory gleamed through the gaps in the concentric layers of wood.

Amidst tight security, the guest of honour, an international business tycoon, lit the aviation fuel doused timber logs. As this was a corporate event, potential donors were given priority invitations – an official representation kept to a bare minimum. The press, both local and global, was conspicuous by its low attendance – the sponsors had made their own arrangements to film the entire event and merchandise the film to maximise its advertising revenue.

Two days before the event, the Bollywood studio contracted to film the ivory burning was forced to abandon the project after a fire destroyed all its production facilities. The organisers, unable to make alternate arrangements with another Bollywood studio at such short notice, turned to Musa – the homegrown talent. Musa, aware that the Bollywood fraternity was attending, accepted without hesitation. He had to rope in Ava to help manage the shoot on the day.

Alec accompanied by Dr Pinto and other colleagues, took full part and stayed back to enjoy the almost festive mood. Earlier in the day, Alec was pleasantly surprised to get a call from Musa – apparently, he had been recruited, at short notice, to film the entire day's proceeding, with a view to producing a short documentary film – which would be used to promote public awareness about poaching, ivory smuggling and to raise funds.

The Bollywood fraternity, Bombay and Dubai based, participated as well – a film production opportunity to use Kenya's exotic locations and take advantage of the tax incentives offered by the authorities. It was hoped that the economic benefits of increased tourism to Kenya's game parks and holiday destinations would more than offset any tax concessions.

As ivory takes an inordinately long time to burn completely, the committee of corporate leaders had outsourced the entire process – an off-shore company registered in Panama had won the contract following a well-advertised international tendering exercise.

The pyres were left burning for hours whilst the charity event and the partying continued. Chilled Kenyan beer and 'nyama choma' (meat, barbecued) sustained the festivities late into the night.

The partying fizzled out once the dignitaries and their entourages were whisked away in a gleaming convoy of Mercedes Benz and BMW limousines; the private security escorts orchestrating the journey home.

The ashes from the burning piles of embers were destined for use as souvenirs to raise money for the charity – clumps of ash sealed in replica tusks or in glass to be used as paperweights. It was envisaged that the funds raised from merchandise would be ploughed back into various conservation projects. The business sponsors were confident that the event would raise considerable sums, going by the attendance and the pledges of support.

As the private security personnel guarding the site were busy escorting the dignitaries out, some of the game wardens stood in as interim sentries. Alec asked Dr Pinto to get a small sample of the ashes and debris as a souvenir of the event. A sterile 30ml container, filled with the ashes, was duly handed over to Alec.

As Dr Pinto handed over the vial, he caught sight of someone he knew in the sponsors' tent.

'Excuse me, Alec. I recognise someone whom I haven't met in ages,'

Pinto remarked as he walked towards the foreign sponsors' enclosure. 'On second thoughts, why don't you come over, I'll introduce you to the sponsors?'

Alec had barely managed to enter the sponsors' enclosure, when Dr Pinto was dragged away by Musa to pose with some of the dignitaries; leaving Alec stranded on his own. After spending a few minutes on his own, he decided to backtrack to the barbecue tent. As he was leaving, he noticed a small plastic pillbox under one of the tables – it contained two capsules and a white tablet.

Alec, having spotted Musa with the film team, waved at his friend, who looked flustered and preoccupied; dashing around to capture the best angles for the shoot. Musa panned the camera and followed Dr Pinto for a while until he reached the group of the sponsors; all engaged in an animated discussion about the impact of poaching activity on the Kenyan economy.

Having captured the majority of guests, including a bevy of buibui-clad women, the filming units were confident that they had enough footage of the actual ivory burning event. Musa had been instructed to ensure there was sufficient footage of all visitors; especially the foreign guests from Bombay, Dubai and even far-flung London.

One of the Indian sponsors had flown in a group of Bollywood starlets to add a bit of glamour and glitz to the occasion. Musa had his hands full and would have to edit out enough extra footage to have a sleek marketable short film – to be used along with other merchandise to raise much needed funds.

In all the commotion, Alec barely had a few minutes to spend time with Musa and Ava. It was his last chance to interact with her before he flew back.

As Alec prepared to return to his hotel, he remembered the small pillbox and handed it to Dr Pinto. 'Here, found this in the sponsors' tent. Maybe you can trace the patient – there's no label. The capsules seem to be a cod liver oil supplement but the tablet is difficult to identify. Might be important medication.'

'Thanks. I am escorting the sponsors back to their hotel so will try to locate the owner of the pillbox,' Dr Pinto clarified as he pocketed the box.

As Alec had made a generous donation, he was on the mailing list. Just before he flew to London, he received the commemorative souvenirs – miniature ivory towers encased in a glass cube doubling as paperweights. These mementoes had been specially designed and prepared by Musa's studio in Mombasa.

A month later, Alec caught a connecting Emirates flight from Dubai into Heathrow. With several flights landing at almost the same time, it took a while to collect his baggage and proceed towards the 'nothing to declare' green channel. Heathrow was buzzing with returning residents and tourists predominantly from the Caribbean, Nigeria, Ghana, Pakistan and India.

It was well past midnight and Alec, tired and exhausted, was not looking forward to the backlog of work waiting for him. The anti-climax, after spending time under the Kenyan blue skies, hit him like a sledgehammer. He headed for the green channel as he raced towards the exit, anxious to get to bed for a few hours of sleep before reporting back to the vet school in Camden.

The customs officer scanning the throng of passengers entering the green channel spotted the towering figure and the anxiety flagged by Alec's body language. Alec sighed in exasperation as he was pulled up and asked to haul the suitcase onto the counter and to unlock it. He should have known better – in his rush to get home to bed, he had inadvertently flagged his anxiety.

He was wont to lecture his final-year students to look for a change in behaviour as part of their clinical exam of the patient. And, here he was 'red flagging' himself to the officer. He smiled and made eye contact with the young officer; knowing full well that it was too little, too late.

The officer was almost at the end of his search when his probing fingers felt the bulge in a pair of pyjamas. When the officer held aloft the 30ml specimen bottle filled with greyish white debris, his arching eyebrows seemed to say it all. Alec had forgotten all about the souvenir paperweights, the replica ivory towers and the 30ml sterile container – all loosely wrapped in clothing to avoid breakage.

'A memento of my visit to Kenya.' Alec responded to the arched eyebrow. 'Laikipia to be precise. It's a souvenir of the symbolic burning of confiscated ivory.' The word ivory made the officer do a double take and he glanced at Alec's expensive suitcase and his three-piece crumpled Armani suit. The fact that Alec's arrival had coincided with flights from flights from India, Pakistan and West Africa did not help. Alec's tired and curt responses were misread by the overzealous officer as evasive and obstructive.

'Sir, if I may, what is your occupation?' Before Alec could respond, the officer, waving the C902A declaration form continued, 'I assume you have read this through?' The officer was alluding to the Customs declaration form. The arched eyebrow was defying gravity by now and the attendant expression of disbelief and dismissal on the younger man's face did not go unnoticed – Alec's ire almost exploded.

Alec's brusque words were regretted as soon as they slipped out, 'Veterinary Surgeon and, I am well aware of the regulations, including the more stringent protocols of the Convention on International Trade in Endangered Species, better than you could ever fathom. The ashes represent ivory that was burnt at a very high temperature, so there is absolutely no chance of any contagion. The sample is virtually sterile. Please take my qualified word for it.' Alec's temper got the better of him as he reached into the breast pocket of his crumpled suit and flashed his Royal Veterinary College staff ID at the, by now, surly officer but he regretted it immediately as his abrupt reply clearly struck a raw nerve and the officer's brow creased with overt irritation.

The officer excused himself and sought his supervisor. Just as Alec's patience was running thin, a crestfallen officer returned and advised Alec that all the material would be held back for further forensic tests. The officer, unwilling to look Alec in the eye, quickly concluded the paperwork and handed over a copy of the confiscation note. Alec, relieved at the abrupt reprieve from further delays, repacked his suitcase and proceeded towards the arrivals lounge. The officer watched Alec's progress through customs with palpable dismay – he had hoped to exact his revenge for the vet's arrogant behaviour.

Alec had forgotten all about the customs investigation until he received a fairly detailed report from a CITES-approved forensic lab. He skimmed through the technical report and the concluding words 'no evidence of any ivory' stuck in his mind. He stuffed the report in his briefcase with a mental note to read it later on. It wasn't until the weekend that he managed to re- read it.

The findings were summarised as: 'Spectrophotometric and DNA tests performed on the samples – ashes and debris - had detected bone/cartilage of animal origin. The report confirmed that the DNA present was derived from cattle bones. The test was negative for elephant ivory.'

As the findings sunk in, he went back to the photographs from his trip, especially the high-quality professional ones taken by Musa in Mombasa. His intuitive thought was that he was missing something glaringly obvious, although he could not put a finger on it. He read the report again and reviewed the photographs.

The Moi Avenue shots of the giant replica tusks. Something about the tusks... Musa had said something about the tusks that escaped him. The more he tried, the more it receded into the recesses of his mind. He decided to sleep over it, confident that the elusive piece of the jigsaw would pop into his head.

And it did – popped into his head as he stepped into the shower in the morning.

Musa had explained that the replica tusks on the dual carriageway in Mombasa had been redesigned with fabricated aluminium ones – to save on maintenance costs.

Replicas! That was it; the tusks burnt on the day in Nairobi were replicas, not real ivory. The conspirators had burnt plastic or resin props and cattle bones to create an illusion; a charade. The real ivory that was meant to be burnt had been swapped with fake ivory. Alec's brow furrowed. The real ivory shipped out and then sold? To perpetrate a scam? And who knew the truth?

His mind went back to the day – the way the towers had been created. The bulk of the so-called ivory that was burnt on the day was cattle bones, piled up in the middle to make up the mass; the outer layers of the towers were plastic and resin fake tusks. The logs of wood encircling the conical mass in the middle added to the imagery – it looked as though ivory was going up in smoke.

'Quite a clever ruse, the 'smoke and mirrors effect,' Alec muttered to himself.

Alec surmised that the real ivory had been switched at some stage and the conspirators had stage-managed the entire show. It was quite apparent and obvious that this was an elaborate and well-planned conspiracy. With the amount of time elapsed, the authorities would be hard pressed to, firstly collect enough evidence, and secondly, whether that evidence would stand up to scrutiny in a court.

The only saving grace was that the day's proceedings were well documented and recorded – Musa's film may just throw some light on the matter. The corporate sector who had organised the event would become the focus of the inquiry, especially the international tendering process.

As for the cache of the real ivory, it would be unreasonable to expect it to be sitting in a warehouse somewhere on the coast; the chances were that the loot was already on its way to the lucrative markets of the Far East.

It had not escaped Alec that if the souvenirs had not been confiscated at Heathrow, the theft and the scam would have gone unnoticed.

Almost on an impulse and without giving it much thought, Alec picked up the phone and called Nairobi. When the technician in the lab at the orphanage told him that Dr Pinto was on his rounds, he left brief details about the ivory test with a request for Dr Pinto to return his call ASAP.

The assistant, working late to catch up on the backlog of blood smears, instinctively knew that he could ingratiate himself; his masters would be pleased. The curio shop owner listened to the hushed tones of the technician - Alec's words were repeated verbatim. The tinkling of ceramic coffee cups could be heard in the background.

Within minutes, cascading calls were made, local and international, the last one was routed to the portly trader in the spice bazaar. The coded message in Urdu and Hindi was scribbled by stubby, nicotine-stained fingers on a scrap of nutmeg-stained paper. The coded terse message, with a whiff of nutmeg – a two-layer authentication process – would be deposited at a designated drop off point in Meena

Bazaar, Bur Dubai; not far from Dubai Creek.

The trader was content with the cash payment that he received every time a successful drop was made; not for him to delve too deeply into what did not concern him. He had survived this cloak and dagger work since he became a 'conduit' a decade ago. He knew that any slip-ups would get him into deep trouble – the creek would become his watery grave. The generous pay helped feed many mouths back in India.

Meanwhile, the curio-shop owner, on receiving the tipoff call, dashed off to a warehouse near Kilindini harbour. Unknown to him, he was followed by an unmarked police car. A taxi, with a buibui-clad figure in the back, joined the two-car entourage in front – the Indian driver, his curiosity piqued, kept glancing in the rear-view mirror at the veiled female passenger. He noticed that her buibui looked expensive and was a designer brand that had become popular in recent months, especially with the younger generation. The figure-hugging contours and the elaborate embroidery on the veil and the upper torso were in stark contrast to the floppy shapeless factory range ones.

His eyes were drawn to the rhythmic rise and fall of the bodice with each breath and the fragrance of her Chanel perfume filled the enclosed environs of the cab – the Parisian scent was a welcome change from the normal Persian 'attar' that most buibui-clad women wore.

The driver was admonished swiftly in accented Swahili to keep his eyes on the road and to follow the target car. The young driver, mindful of the strict guidance issued by his employer with regards to single female passengers, looked away guiltily, concentrated on the two cars ahead and steadfastly kept his gaze on the road.

The officers and the female taxi passenger watched from their respective parked cars as the curio shop owner knocked discreetly on the roller shutters of a warehouse. An Arab emerged from a side door and the two had an animated discussion. The curio shop owner seemed agitated, going by his gesticulations and demeanour. He left abruptly, visibly annoyed, as the Arab shrugging his shoulders in a gesture of indifference returned to his air-conditioned office on the mezzanine floor. He saw his irate colleague drive off but failed to notice the unmarked car and the taxi. He swiftly returned to the warehouse; his staff having left well before the arrival of the curio shop owner. The unmarked car followed the curio shop owner back towards old town.

The buibui-clad figure noticed the Arab move away from the window, paid off the driver and walked swiftly towards the warehouse. As she knocked on the warehouse door, she flipped back the veil, exposing a heavily made-up face.

When the Arab answered the door, still grumbling and swearing under his breath, he was taken aback – he was half expecting the curio shop owner and another furious argument.

The buibui-clad figure shot him twice through the heart. As the Arab slumped backwards onto the cement floor, she stepped closer and shot him again. After failing to feel a pulse and the dilated pupils confirming death, she veiled herself and exited into the stifling heat, pulling the door shut behind her.

The gun disappeared in the folds of her buibui as she swiftly walked to the next block where she flagged down a passing taxi; the cool interiors of the taxi came as a respite from the blazing temperature outside. She ended the journey half way through into town and paid the driver. She joined the throng of worshippers into the mosque. After a short stay, she left the mosque and walked a fair distance before catching a taxi home; alighting half a mile away from her flat.

The police found the Arab in a pool of blood – the three gunshot wounds to the chest easily demarcated by their entry through the white shirt; both had pierced the heart causing instantaneous death. The point of entry of the third shot at the temple was partly covered by the Arab's henna-dyed hair and clotted blood.

The lab assistant in Nairobi watched the breaking news broadcast about the police investigation in Mombasa with trepidation – he never returned to his job at the orphanage. He made his way to Dubai as instructed; he had no idea that the Arab had been executed as the police had kept the news off the air for operational reasons.

His body was fished out of the Dubai Creek, several weeks later by the Sea Rescue department of Dubai Police. The police had received several calls from passengers of the 'abras' (water taxis) that plied the creek. The corpse lay in the mortuary as an unclaimed 'John Doe', as no identification was found on him. The technician had been shot thrice through the heart.

The arrest of the curio shop owner and the subsequent raids across Mombasa and along the coast, unearthed fake export invoices and several consignments of cattle bones. Ivory was found mixed up with the bones or secreted into false compartments. The warehouse where the Arab had been executed became a focal point of the investigation - consignments of bones addressed to clients in Dubai, Abu Dhabi, Bombay and Yemen were found, crated and ready for despatch.

The officer attached to the police station at Kilindini harbour called up the officer in charge in Nairobi and relayed a synopsis of the confessions of the curio shop owner and other employees at the various warehouses.

The evidence retrieved suggested that tons of ivory had been smuggled out. Tusks, sometimes broken down into smaller pieces mixed up with full-length tusks were exported with false documents. The exports mixed up with genuine cattle-bone consignments meant for rendering into animal feeds and for the manufacture of gelatine. The monetary value of the smuggled ivory ran into millions of dollars, signifying a massacre of elephants on an industrial scale.

Alec's BA flight landed in Nairobi on time and he was escorted through the VIP lounge and to his hotel – the Hilton in downtown Nairobi. Alec had been briefed by the Foreign and Commonwealth Office – FCO – in London and was not surprised to see two CID plain clothes officers accompanying him everywhere. It all seemed very droll and melodramatic to him but he felt reassured, nonetheless, by their presence. He was excited to be back; even more so if he could somehow contrive a way to meet Ava.

With organised crime gangs involved and the huge amounts of profits at stake, the FCO had alerted the British High Commission about Alec's imminent arrival – to ensure his safety. Certainly, both the UK and Kenya governments were not taking any chances. The FCO had also forwarded the Customs & Excise report about the fake ivory to both parties.

While Alec was aware that the case was tied up with the illicit ivory trade, it was much later when he was ushered into the offices of the man in charge that he realised the significance of the Kenyan covert operations.

As he walked down the corridor and into a well-furnished

vestibule, a figure moved towards him. The three-piece handmade suit sat well on his well-muscled frame. Sam Samana, seconded from Kenya CID to the anti-poaching unit of the wildlife service, gripped Alec's hand in a bone-crushing handshake. Alec wondered if his metacarpals had just been rearranged as he tried hard not to wince.

'Karibuni, daktari! Welcome, doctor,' Sam boomed as he looked at the vet dressed in a Harris Tweed jacket. Alec looked on puzzled as Sam continued, 'Good to see you again.'

'Do I know you? Have we met before?'

Sam smiled and repeated the terse command: 'Waacha, hiyu na daktari!'

Alec gaped at Sam, recognition dawning finally. 'The voice that saved my life? I was sure the AK47-wielding hothead was on the verge of shooting me.' Alec looked in awe and confusion at the officer in front of him. 'Didn't recognise you in your three-piece suit.'

'The braided locks and the ochre clothing – that wasn't me. That was the gang leader. I was behind him. I shouted out those words, that warning, which he repeated. You were lucky, Alec, that you weren't gunned down. You were that close,' Sam said making a gesture with his thumb and index finger.

Alec looked on in stunned silence as Sam elaborated. 'The gang leader whom we know as Shenzi, the barbarian, fled with the tusks after gunning down all four of us. I was lucky to survive – Masai herdsmen found me in the nick of time. I was barely alive when the wardens flew me down to Nairobi.'

'Oh, that was you? I saw a stretcher on the plane. You are part of the...?' Alec left his sentence incomplete.

'I managed to infiltrate the poaching gang about a year ago, although the investigation has been going on for years. We stumbled upon your team by pure chance. We were heading towards our getaway Toyota when we saw you guys. Shenzi is a psychopath – we have been tracking him for a while now. He kills for pleasure; he would have killed you without batting an eyelid. I think your British accent and your stethoscope saved you. He knows better than to mess with international aid workers and medics – that would have rallied the authorities into action.' Sam paused and continued: 'I'm sure my cover has not been blown. Don't think so. I reckon he just wanted the booty all to himself and did not want any witnesses. He murdered two of my wardens that day. I won't forget that, nor will I let him. They died on my watch – both were married and with young children.'

Alec had only an inkling about what was going on but was glad that Sam was in charge. He seemed in total command although the constant warfare between the poachers and the wildlife agencies presented difficulties for those caught up in the middle; the locals and the elephants invariably lost out. Sam was Sandhurst trained and had been put in charge of the commission investigating the illegal ivory trade. The gravity of the economic toll on the East African countries was so huge that Sam was given carte blanche to protect the tourist industry. His remit, approved by all three nations, extended internationally – the slaughter had to be stopped; any which way.

While the investigation was progressing well, the Kenyan authorities had not yet had any breakthroughs and the culprits were still at large. The curio shop owner had been identified as a link almost a year ago. Kenya CID had been tailing him in the hope that the chain of command would be exposed.

The investigation was confident that in due course the culprits would be brought to justice. With the raids on the warehouses and the arrest of the curio shop owner, it remained to be seen if the evidence collected stood up to legal challenges. The crime warlords reigned supreme - the fear of reprisals ensured that innocent people caught up in their web, never spoke up; their silence was guaranteed.

It came as a relief for Alec to be told that Musa was not a suspect. Alec recalled that Musa had taken him to the same curio shop that afternoon in Mombasa. The police had been tailing the various suspects for some time. Musa, with his ostentatious life style, was initially a suspect but had been cleared after a thorough scrutiny of his background and finances.

Alec was disappointed when his attempts to connect with Ava failed. He almost thought that Ava was ignoring him until he mentioned it to Musa who told him Ava had gone away to Zanzibar to attend a family wedding.

Alec could not for the life of him recollect if Ava had mentioned that her family originated from Pemba Island; one of the larger islands of the Zanzibar Archipelago. Their magical moments together barely extended to such mundane matters. Ava, according to Musa, had fallen out with her family and had cut all ties so her explanation of attending a family wedding in Zanzibar was out of character and Musa was concerned that she had not contacted him so far.

A few days later, Sam escorted Alec through the VIP lounge at Jomo Kenyatta International Airport and on to the tarmac where his BA flight was being refuelled for the flight to London. Alec's departure was tinged with regret – that he could not meet Ava.

'Kwaheri, daktari. Goodbye, doctor.'

He knew that Shenzi was quite high up in the ring and the cartel was behind the sustained slaughter of elephants in Kenya. It may well be that the same set of poachers was involved in the illicit ivory trade in Tanzania as well. Sam's team had, over the years, come to recognise the wanton mutilation of elephants as the work of Shenzi. The panga wielded with gratuitous violence – tails docked, eyes gouged out or even trunks sliced into pieces.

Shenzi for now was immune to any action, especially if he was deep in hiding in Somalia. Sam's cover was pretty much intact; Shenzi did not know he had survived and the wildlife dept had kept it under wraps about a 'poacher' surviving and being in custody. Except for a few at the top, the wardens and others had been told that the captured poacher had died before any information could be extracted. The press had been kept at bay to safeguard the operation.

Just as Sam's car was emerging from the airport's perimeter and onto Uhuru Highway – the route back into town – a buibui-clad figure flipped her veil back into place and retreated towards the airport car park; her red stilettos and the buibui barely drawing any attention.

She had watched from the periphery as Sam and the 'daktari' had used the fast-track checking system reserved for VIPs. It was early days but she knew that the involvement of the Brit in the accidental exposure of the fake ivory fiasco could draw the attention of Her Majesty's Government – Kenya enjoyed the reputation of being a frontrunner in the fight against poaching and the illegal ivory trade.

After the instructions to eliminate the Arab in the warehouse, the first of the two cogs, she had expected more assignments to follow – watching the news of the police raids had sent a shiver down her spine. She had walked away just in time before the police raided the warehouse – her next target was the curio shop owner but the police raided the shop first. It had been a blessing in disguise that she did not walk into an unintended trap. The lab technician was an easy target – lured to the vast expanses of the desert. He had been promised a payoff and wasn't expecting the buibui assassin. She knew that the curio shop owner, still in custody, was a minor cog in the wheel - would not have any relevant information to pass onto the Kenyan authorities.

Alec was astounded by the stories picked up from the Kenyan press about his escapades in Laikipia and his unwitting role in unearthing the scam. The business community and the sponsors were under the spotlight – although even they were taken in by the sheer audacity of the scam.

The tycoons and business leaders all volunteered to co-operate with the authorities and carried out a blitz to protect their various trade bodies – damage limitation had become paramount. His colleagues at the Royal College and the veterinary fraternity were delighted that a UK vet had made an impact on the world stage in an important area of wildlife conservation, albeit unintentionally. Alec had become an accidental celebrity.

It had been years since a vet had hogged the headlines – not since the popularity of the Yorkshire Dales vet, James Herriot. His runway bestseller 'All Creatures Great and Small' had caught the imagination of readers all over the world. Alec tried in vain to deflect attention and could only hope that the commotion would soon abate; he was not, by any stretch of imagination, in Herriot's exalted league.

He also knew that the flipside of all this misplaced attention could be detrimental; he certainly did not want to be under the microscope. The poachers and many others might be plotting some kind of a comeback against the Kenyan authorities. And probably everyone associated with the investigation. The sooner he got back to his mundane but safe world, the better.

FIVE

Ava, Mombasa, Kenya.

Mombasa police, on a tip-off, raided a flat in the old town, not far from the harbour. The flat was vacant and had been picked clean; the occupant had fled days or weeks earlier and nothing was found. The forensics team combed the flat for clues and finally marked it down as an unspecified burglary – fingerprints lifted off did not come up as a match on the police database. The case of 'breaking and entry' was left open, pending further enquiries.

Musa contacted the police when Ava failed to return to Mombasa. When the police realised that the address of the missing person matched that of the flat that they had examined recently, a senior officer decided to contact Sam. His suspicion was that the flat may be at the centre of the recent reports of ivory smuggling and when Sam took charge of the matter, the officer sighed with relief. He was glad to be off the hook – he'd rather let Sam deal with the intense media scrutiny.

A few days later, a press release from the investigative team indicated that Musa had been interrogated at length and had been absolved from any involvement. As per his declarations, Ava had gone to Zanzibar to attend a family wedding. When repeated efforts to contact her had failed, Musa had no choice but to report her disappearance to the police.

The flat, according to the police, had been examined thoroughly and did not reveal anything. It was the police's contention that a 'cleansing operation' had been performed – nothing was found; not even traces of hair. The forensic search had failed to shed any light on Ava's mysterious disappearance.

Out of courtesy, Sam contacted Alec and mentioned Ava's failure to contact Musa. He was careful and guarded in his exchange with Alec – the press speculation about her involvement in the ivory scandal was deliberately avoided. Sam was glad that Alec was in London and far away from the rumours flying about.

A few weeks later, Alec received a package at the surgery, delivered by FedEx: it contained a pre-recorded cassette - Makeba's hit songs and a hand-written note.

Hey Mzee,

I am passing through London – shame we can't meet. I often look back to the brief time that we spent together in Mombasa. 'Malaika' our song for that one night, brings back very fond memories. One of these days God willing we shall meet again.

Kwaheri and Au Revoir,

'Ndege' (Your little bird).

Alec had forwarded the cassette to Sam, more out of courtesy than any conviction that it may shed some light on the case. He followed up with a call to Sam.

'Habari, did you get the cassette?' Alec greeted Sam, using one of the few Swahili words that he had picked up while in Kenya.

'Hey, Alec. Yes, I did, it's with our forensics people, although I doubt it will throw up anything new. Since our last conversation, I am now deeply concerned – she has disappeared without a trace. We know for sure that she certainly did go to Zanzibar,' Sam said guardedly.

'Concerned because she is missing and you think she's involved?' Alec surmised.

'The pattern of behaviour is a giveaway, if you think about it. We are dealing with a professional outfit – no trails or clues have been left behind. The flat was stripped bare – it is quite obvious that either she or someone she knew did a thorough job of 'cleansing' the place. No family albums or photos left behind. I wouldn't even know what she looks like but for the photograph of you two taken on the night at the beach restaurant.'

'Really? I don't recollect posing for any photographs that night. And Ava wasn't with us when Musa took me around.' Alec's tone was of surprise and puzzlement.

'We got lucky, a beach photographer, a freelancer, took photographs of the diners that night. One of the tourists must have paid the freelancer – you two were caught in the frame. Kenya CID was tailing you on my instructions and we got the details of the photographer from the restaurant manager.'

'You had me followed? Why?' Alec's truculent response brought a smile to Sam's face.

'Pole, pole, go easy, my friend. Don't lose your shirt. It wasn't you – quite a few Mombasa residents were under surveillance – if you recollect this is an old operation. Musa was also under surveillance at that early stage as were many others. So, while you were in Mombasa, we decided to keep tabs on Ava as well. It was for your safety.'

'You think she is implicated? Working for the cartel? And I thought it was my charisma that drew her to me.' Alec paused knowing that his intimacy with Ava, albeit very briefly, would be viewed as a holiday fling. And yet he had not been able to get Ava out of his thoughts. 'I find it hard to believe that she is implicated in any way.'

'I do as well. Let's hope there is a plausible explanation for her absence. Nothing sinister.'

'Sinister? You mean a honey trap? Whoever is behind this is using Ava?'

Alec asked, incredulous and anxious at the way things were unfolding. 'I don't get it – her role?' Alec pondered loudly after a brief silence; still battling with his emotions.

'Her trail goes cold in Zanzibar. All we know is that she comes from a very prosperous family – her ancestors were Khoja Kutchi sailors from Gujarat in India, some of them settled permanently in Zanzibar. The Indians were known for their expertise in designing and making dhows and the Khoja community has been sailing the Monsoon winds for centuries. Her great-grandfather was a prosperous businessman with several properties and clove plantations. Ava fell out with her father's family. Her westernised lifestyle and her values were seen as transgressions that led to her being ostracised. She was a pariah and they hadn't seen her for years,' Sam said.

'We barely discussed her background – vaguely recall Ava mentioning that she was born in Stone Town, Zanzibar. I don't even know what she did for a living. Musa just said to me that she was helping out at his studio and that she was almost like family. Surely, you have asked Musa?' Alec was still floundering to make sense of Ava's disappearance.

'All Musa knows is that she was attending a family wedding in Zanzibar. He alerted us when she did not return as scheduled. The flat, we are still investigating. If she owns it then that would be a surprise; even renting in that part of old town can be expensive. Though it looks as though she had money – her Western lifestyle does not come cheap in cosmopolitan Mombasa. The expat community and the tourists have driven prices higher; most local residents can't afford that kind of a lifestyle.'

'You reckon she had other sources of finance? Meaning she is complicit?'

'We will have to wait until we have more information. I am not saying that she is involved, but neither am I ruling anything out. Too early to draw any conclusions. For your sake, I hope she turns up and clears herself.' Sam paused. 'For now, things have stalled – we have no leads to follow except try and find Ava.'

'What happens to your investigation now?' Alec asked.

'The poaching activity has died down. This cessation of activity more or less confirms my suspicions that the poachers are keeping a low profile here in Kenya. We will liaise with our partners – let's see if the poaching operations shift to Tanzania or Uganda. Our joint operations have a common goal – to protect our wildlife and to safeguard our economies which are heavily dependent on tourism. My broad remit is to prevent the plunder of our natural resources. At the moment, the thrust of our investigation is focused on the business sponsors and the consortium that underwrote the ivory-burning event. We are certain that the scam revolves round the tendering process and on the international company that organised the ivory burning. As far as we can be certain, we can rule out any local involvement – this has all the hallmarks of an international operation – a cartel.'

'Ava came over to my hotel for a nightcap – in a buibui, which she changed out of to emerge in Western clothes and red stilettoes. She said that it was just a prank.'

'The buibui is quite popular on the coast, usually donned to conform to religious or cultural norms. She probably put it on to blend in and not draw attention to herself,' Sam expounded.

As Alec put the receiver down, it occurred to him that Sam had not elaborated on Ava's occupation or background. He reread her note again and briefly recalled their time together in Mombasa. Her disappearance made no sense to him. Her absence had left a huge void in his life – any hopes of a reunion were receding fast. The future looked bleak; full of despair.

A few months later, the Kenyan press carried a few lines about an unidentified body of a buibui clad female found in the creek across from Mombasa town. The only reason the UK press carried the news was because a British family on holiday in Mombasa were the first to sight the floating body and report it to the police.

Some days later, Sam called Alec with the sad news.

'It was her, my friend, I am sorry – the woman found floating in the Tudor Creek not too far from the old harbour. We had DNA samples from your night out at the beach restaurant – lipstick and saliva left behind on the wine glass. The restaurant manager had bagged the glass for us. It was a bit of a break – her saliva on the wine glass considering that her flat did not yield any DNA samples.'

'That's bit much isn't it? Not even a strand of hair in the shower or a clipped nail in the flat?' Alec interrupted.

'Exactly – the absence of any trail proves my suspicion that a professional outfit was sent in to 'sanitise' the flat,' Sam replied.

Alec was saddened at the way it had ended – no conclusive proof of her involvement; only circumstantial evidence.

'Alec, are you there?' Sam was aware of Alec's emotional conflict.

'Yes, sorry. I am still convinced that she would have cleared herself had she survived this ordeal.'

'There is more I am afraid – she was executed, probably on the mainland and the body then dumped at sea. The post-mortem report also mentions a recent tattoo across the back of her right shoulder which exhibited signs of contact dermatitis;

probably an allergic reaction to the dye used. The tattoo read: 'Mzee's Malaika''. I know you had mentioned the live band and you guys dancing to the Miriam Makeba song. The tattoo was a declaration, a cryptic message for you?' Sam enquired.

'When I sent you the cassette, I did not enclose her note. Now that you mention it – maybe there was a message in there about her intentions. Let me forward the note,' Alec whispered barely getting the words out.

'Pole, pole, my friend, go easy. My profound sympathy and condolences.' Sam commiserated noting the hint of melancholy and despair in Alec's voice as he ended the call.

Alec found her note and re-read it:

'...... One of these days, God willing, we shall meet again....' Not to be he muttered to himself. As an afterthought, Alec Xeroxed the note and despatched the original to Sam.

SIX

Roxana, Bangalore, South India.

The Air India flight from Bombay to Tehran, normally filled to capacity, had plenty of empty seats. Roxana had half reclined on the vacant seat next to her when the male mellifluous tones woke her from her indeterminate sleep pattern – the last few days had taken its toll on her.

'Roxana! Hi, what are you doing here?' Roy asked. The flight purser in charge of cabin crew on the Air India flight to Iran leaned across the aisle and whispered. His winsome smile softened his sharp chiselled features.

Roxana was genuinely pleased at the coincidence of Roy being on the same flight. It comforted her that Roy, who had been instrumental in engineering her first campus romance, was there for her if she needed a shoulder to cry on. Roy's best friend and Roxana had dated for almost a year; the usual campus romance that had fizzled out – the senior tiring of the sophomore female. The two couples had double dated for a while until Roy and his girlfriend had quit the course to join Air India.

Roy had never quite ascertained the reason for Roxana's abrupt breakup. 'Such a shame,' he thought, looking at her stunning elegance

- even under the subdued lighting of the cabin he discerned the classical features that would have won any beauty contest anywhere in the world. Roy had always carried a torch for the beautiful Iranian foreign student and had managed to hide his feelings for her. He had never quite forgiven his friend for treating Roxana with such callousness.

Roy had envied his friend at the time – the pair had been inseparable and were deemed to be the star couple on the campus. Roxana and her beau were 'made for each other'. Roy was reminded of the blurb from an advertising campaign, 'Made For Each Other', run by a famous brand of Indian cigarettes. The marketing blitz had triggered the intense ribbing that the beleaguered lovers had endured on the campus - mostly good natured.

That was the start of the malicious gossip about their covert meetings on the infamous terrace. The terrace, mostly deserted during the day, transformed itself into an impromptu 'lovers' lane' as the shadows lengthened. The terrace sightings became a barometer of most campus romances.

'Roy! I didn't see you when I boarded the plane, otherwise I would have sought you out,' Roxana gasped ending Roy's reverie.

Roxana, despite her sombre mood, smiled sheepishly. Her romancing of the most handsome final year student on the campus was well known; a matter of record. As was their cantankerous break up. Roy had been there for her during that phase; a willing shoulder to cry on.

She whispered tentatively: 'May I impose? I need a favour?'

'Sure, what are you after – get you a complimentary drink? A glass of Shiraz?' He had always wondered whether her wine preferences had anything to do with her family's origins from the southern Iranian city of Shiraz.

'No, thanks. Would you have any news about the situation in Tehran?' she queried keeping her voice low, almost choking with emotion. They were a tad over two hours away from touchdown.

'Oh, I am sorry - of course, the rioting in Tehran?' Roy chided himself for missing the signs – the red rimmed eyes and the subdued responses; in stark contrast to her normal vivacious manner. 'Let me have a word with the flight engineer and I'll come back to you. Although I don't think the situation on the ground is any worse off otherwise we would not have had clearance to take off. The final briefing before take-off was that the riots had abated and order had been restored on the streets.'

The Indian press had meticulously covered the uprising and the Shah's troubles. He smiled nervously and went back to the galley; promising to come back as soon as he had an update.

A Few Days Earlier in Bangalore:

Roxana Shirazi, the only female student in the group of fifty Iranians, remembered the 16th of January 1979 as the crucial and cruel day when her world collapsed around her; midway through the final year of a Bachelor's degree course in Organic Chemistry.

She would indelibly remember the awful day for years to come just as many people recalled the exact moment when JFK's assassination was broadcast to the world. Her father had always maintained that Kennedy's premature death in Dallas, that fateful day on 22nd November 1963, had incalculably damaged the world; probably a more drastic event for Iran. For her father and for many all over the world, the American President's demise was a watershed – always used as a yardstick for all future upheavals.

In 1970s Iran, the Pahlavi regime's modernisation plan, driven by its vast oil reserves, earmarked education for its youth as a top priority. Iran needed trained professionals to wean itself away from its overreliance on expatriates.

The Shah's dreams of success and fortune for the Persian kingdom were ambitious – to recapture Iran's geopolitical dominance and regain its historical position. He had surrounded himself with able and educated Iranians whom he had enticed back from England, Europe and the USA. And Abbas Shirazi was one of the first to return to Tehran – to carry the torch for the Shah's vision of an Iran reminiscent of the glories of Cyrus the Great, the first Persian Emperor.

Dr Shirazi, Roxana's debonair and dashing father, a Rhodes scholar and a geologist, initially joined the oil ministry as a petrochemical engineer. Over the years, as his stature grew, he was hand-picked by the Shah and inducted into national politics. His remit was to modernise and upgrade the education system and was formally appointed to take charge of overseas scholarships and educational programmes.

The scheme incentivised hundreds of Iranians students to venture abroad for qualifications in science, medicine, engineering and agriculture. In keeping with the Shah's 'White Revolution' which was rolled out in the 60s to reform and modernise Iran, Dr Shirazi introduced equal opportunity educational programmes for Iranian women. His daughter was one of the earliest applicants to win a place on the degree course in South India. Iranian students flocked to Indian universities in droves – the cost to the Shah was miniscule compared to exorbitantly expensive programmes in the west.

The Shah's policy of empowering women had its detractors and set him up against the clerics. Dr Shirazi, with a PhD in petroleum engineering, was tainted with the same brush as countless other politicians. The Shah's rivals were waiting for an opportunity to negate the push towards modernity and the Shah's progressive reforms became synonymous with American decadence.

Roxana's father was caught in the crossfire – he became a target by association and affiliation with the ruling regime. His Oxford education and Anglophile ways became impediments. The vultures were circling, waiting for an opportune time to swoop down.

Roxana had a premonition of bad tidings when the khaki-clad postman shouted 'telegram' as she was leaving the hostel to make her way to the campus. As she tentatively took the distinct brown envelope marked 'Telegram – Indian Postal Service' – she shivered involuntarily; an intense foreboding flooded over her. The postman hesitated briefly expecting a tip – the pretty Iranian was known to be a generous tipper.

The look of anxiety on Roxana's face, as she fumbled nervously to tear open the envelope, was missed by the middle-aged married postman - he just could not resist focusing on the sensuous curve of her pink lips, the clear blue eyes capped by perfectly shaped eyebrows and the sheer radiance of her beauty.

'Only 'apsaras', celestial females, were meant to be this beautiful,' the postman murmured. She barely looked at the postman as the message sunk in. The man turned and walked away; disappointed at not being rewarded.

Roxana tried to focus on the message; the words, a terse single line, blurred by the unsolicited tears welling up in her azure blue eyes.

She had just heard on the morning Voice of America broadcast about the enforced departure of the beleaguered Reza Mohammed, the Shah – ostensibly for medical treatment. In essence, the Shah had abdicated the Peacock throne and the Pahlavi regime for the face-saving sanctuary offered by the Egyptian President, Anwar Sadat. It was the beginning of the end for the Shah dynasty as far as Iran was concerned. It was the beginning of the end for Dr Shirazi too.

With an effort, she forced herself back and read the telegram again: 'Come home immediately'. Three abject words that heightened her anxiety – her demons let loose. Her father was exposed and vulnerable, at the mercy of his political enemies.

She prayed for her parents' safety; knowing that the religious fervour gripping Iran would consume one and all – the innocent and the not so innocent.

Her father, an erudite man who tended to live in his ivory tower, had always shunned political roles and was a reluctant politician. He was jettisoned into that role because the Shah wanted people with a vision. He had signed up only to ensure that his knowledge and training could be put to good use – the common good. He believed that Iran's oil wealth was for all its citizens, not for the elite to fritter it away. In that respect, Dr Shirazi shared the Shah's vision about Iran's aspirations to capture past glories. In keeping with those dreamy aspirations, Dr Shirazi travelled far and wide as the Shah's unofficial ambassador.

Roxana half ran to the local post office to place an overseas call to her father and when the repeated attempts by the operator failed to connect, she feared the worst. On her way back, she stopped at a temple and prayed for her family's safety; she just felt the need to be in God's house; any God's.

The Shirazi family's pedigree went all the way back to the Byzantium Empire – Constantinople's Orthodox Greek Christian roots. And then Iranian Zoroastrian connections. Dr Shirazi and his recent ancestors belonged to a very tiny minority – Persian, Zoroastrian.

Roxana sat down, cross-legged, on the cold granite floor of the roadside temple, along with other devotees, and closed her eyes to concentrate. She listened intently to the strangely comforting unintelligible stream of words intoned by the priest; the eerie sing-song tempo of the mantras was soothing and very calming. She remained at the temple until a semblance of control was restored; only leaving after most devotees had left.

The next few days were spent in a state of troubled hysteria – the constant worry and the lack of any news from back home had her on edge. Her attempts to book a flight had failed and she was put on a waiting list. Many Iranians like her were all trying to get back home, worried that they would be trapped in alien lands – far from home.

It was during this phase of suspended reality, a state of troubled limbo, that she decided to visit a local yogi's ashram - within a few hours' bus ride from her campus. A couple of her friends at college who regularly visited the ashram at times of personal stress, had advised her to spend a few hours there to regain her composure.

The huge open-air assembly point under an amber canopy was where she was directed to and despite the noisy recital of Sanskrit mantras over the PA system, a serene atmosphere prevailed. The place was only half full and she selected a seat at the back and sat down. She copied the stance of the other devotees – crossed legged on a small mat with the back straight and arms straightened and resting on each folded knee.

She closed her eyes and focused on the soft shehnai -a north Indian oboe- and the mantras. The sounds of the shehnai, considered to be auspicious, had an immediate calming effect. Roxana, regulating her breathing with the incantations of the 'Om' sound, continued for almost an hour - until the numbness and pain of her crossed-legged position became unbearable.

She got up cautiously and lingered a few minutes for her peripheral circulation to restore feeling in her leg muscles. She moved gingerly, her muscles still aching, towards the exit, hoping to catch the next bus back to the campus.

As she waited at the bus stop, she closed her eyes to continue the meditative calm, until she felt unease – as if she was under scrutiny. She thought she was alone at the bus stop and opened her eyes to reassess her surroundings.

It was then that she noticed the vendor with his cart full of green coconuts all arranged in a huge mound, and the tall stranger watching her intently as he leaned against a huge banyan tree. He did not avert his gaze as he sipped the refreshing fluid. She looked straight back, almost challenging him to blink first.

'May I offer you this sweet nectar?' the stranger shouted from across the road. 'It's very refreshing and the perfect pick-me-up.'

He continued in an accent, the nuances of which she failed to place. Certainly not Indian she thought to herself. Even at that distance she was spellbound, lost in his hypnotic unblinking stare.

As she walked towards him, she could feel his intense examination, to her great annoyance. The stranger smiled as he saw the blush suffuse her face and neck. He then offered her a freshly prepared coconut as his fervent gaze continued downwards to the neckline of her simple cotton top. She crossed over in a trance, almost hypnotised. Her hand instinctively moved to shield her cleavage, trying in vain to button up. All the while, his eyes never wavered, his sipping uninterrupted.

He was dressed in homespun Indian trousers and an open-collared shirt, the first two or three buttons undone to show hair covered pectorals. She deliberately, tit for tat, let her blue eyes travel down the length of his shirt, which wasn't tucked in. He blinked first, acknowledging her fiery defiance.

She looked up into his eyes – he kept on smiling, smug at having almost read her mind and her arousal. She sipped the cool refreshing water and deliberately avoided looking into his eyes – she knew if she did, then she would lose control. Her recent enforced calm, induced by the mantras, was diminishing by the minute.

And, lose it she did, as she felt his warm palm on the small of her back gently steering her away. The next thing she remembered was entering his small flat above a clutch of shops at the end of the road. The mantras could still be heard in the distance as they climbed the chipped red oxide painted cement staircase up to his lair; his domain.

They made small talk, she babbled on about Tehran and the riots to mask her confused capitulation; the simple coir mattress on the red oxide floor loomed in the background. His rejoinder that he was spending some time in the South learning about herbal medicines and yoga barely registered with her.

His steely blue eyes and fair complexion almost flagging his origins; Middle Eastern or Persian like her. He did not elaborate despite her hesitant queries. A compatriot, she fervently hoped; kinship established. She felt safe, at home with someone from that part of the world. She dropped a few Farsi lines but he failed to take the bait, his intent clear as he led her on.

The next few hours and even the night that she spent with him were lost in the haze of total surrender and pent-up passion – she remembered the ferocious lovemaking that continued unabated once they returned from a simple dinner at a roadside café. She did recall briefly smoking something at his place, probably hashish as it seemed to enhance her responses. This was so unlike her, the impulsive indulgence with a stranger. Her first one-night stand and she had sleep walked into it.

The next morning, she caught the first bus back to the campus, the guilt overwhelming her. They had barely exchanged words as she quickly dressed and left; he did not try to stop her.

As she sat in the bus speeding towards Bangalore, she realised that they had not even exchanged any information – she did not even recall asking his name. She convinced herself that her emotional upheaval of the last few days had sought release in a few hours of abandonment. She wished she could have dealt with it in a different manner. Not bolt away like she had.

SEVEN

Roxana, Tehran, Iran.

On the short Indian Airlines flight to Bombay and the subsequent connecting Air India flight into Tehran, she was bereft with worry – no tears left to shed. She read and re-read the terse 'come home immediately' message as if re-reading it would make it any less intimidating or ominous. When her final attempt, while waiting for her flight at Bombay airport, to contact her parents also failed, thwarted by an engaged tone, she felt numb; there was no turning back now. She'd soon know their fate and, indeed, hers.

The news coverage in the Indian press about the rioting and the purge that had taken place to erase the Shah's memory, enhanced her panic – her father's prominent position and proximity to the ruling political elite meant that he was a marked man. The tsunami raging through the country would be used as a cover, a pretext, to settle old scores; the daggers of jealousy would be wielded with impunity. She feared for her parents especially as her father had lost the Shah's protection.

Anything to do with the exiled Shah was taboo and her father tainted by his association with him. The purge taking place was just the beginning of an explosive phase that she knew would change everything for her and for her beloved Iran.

It was much later, when she returned to Tehran, that she discovered that her father had been erroneously labelled as a 'shahdoost' (friend or admirer of the Shah) – that epithet in itself was literally a death sentence. Such was the paranoia being whipped up to destroy the memory of the Shah that all vestiges of the Pahlavi throne were being removed or erased.

Little did she realise, on returning to the family home in Tehran, which had been ransacked and stripped bare by the looters, that she would never ever see her parents again. Nor would she have closure of any sort – they had disappeared into thin air.

The chilling accounts about her parents' disappearance in the dead of night confirmed her suspicions about police connivance. The police, despite repeated emergency calls by the neighbours and friends, never attended. No one knew what had happened and the police were indifferent to her pleas of opening an investigation into the missing couple.

Roxana's visits to the police station did not yield anything that mattered; initially the officer in charge commiserated but soon got weary of her continued presence. The usual excuses of the lack of manpower and resources were repeated; as were the catalogue of pending and unresolved 'missing person' reports. Despite the litany of excuses, she persisted, like a dog with a bone, and camped for hours at the police station, pestering the officer for news, any scrap of information about her parents.

Her daily vigils at the police station only ended after her father's friends feared for her wellbeing and convinced her to stop. The standoff at the police station was being noticed and the repercussions of her dogged resistance was in danger of spiralling out of control; the local clerics were beginning to take an interest. Eventually, her visits tapered off and she holed up at home, a reclusive and lonely figure.

Roxana, rejecting calls from well-wishers to move out, decided to stay put at the derelict structure that once had boasted of music-filled dinner parties and cultural gatherings with her father playing the perfect Persian host. The recital of Rumi's poems, her father's favourite pastime, had rubbed off on her – she turned to Rumi and music; her solace in her hour of need.

She should have heeded the words of caution from her father's friends – her enemies came stealthily in the night and tortured her with unspeakable acts of intimidation and retribution; her father's perceived sins visited upon her. They wanted her out of Tehran – the threats became more persistent and more graphic.

But for the timely intervention of some powerful allies, Roxana would have disappeared as well; a mere statistic on a 'missing persons list'. To remain in Tehran was not an option, especially for a lone woman without the patronage or protection of a man.

Eventually, shell-shocked and emotionally fragile, Roxana slipped away under cover of darkness and the anonymity afforded by the hijab, which had been declared compulsory for women. She did not wish to endanger the lives of her father's friends and others who had provided guidance and refuge to her. The Tehran that they all loved was a thing of the past; her exile from the city of her birth was a foregone conclusion.

Burning with a zeal to somehow hit back, take revenge, she reached out to several militia groups after SAVAK – the Shah's security organisation that was thought to have had links with the CIA and the Mossad – had been disbanded. It was an opportune time to align herself with a militia or splinter group that might aid her in locating her parents and quench her thirst for vengeance.

She was trained in hand-to-hand combat and became quite proficient in the use of guns and other weapons. Little did she know that she was being used by each unit's commander for their own agenda; sexual or otherwise. Roxana was so traumatised by the events after the revolution that she latched onto any person in authority who might empathise with her. Her mental condition was extremely fragile and it was years later that she realised that the trauma of that phase was embedded deep within her subconscious, like a virus hijacking the host cells for its own purposes.

After almost six months of being passed from one unit to another, she realised the futility of her position. One night, the commander who had monopolised her, tried to bully her into submission – in the heat of the moment she castrated him and fled. Her first kill. She had tasted blood and had crossed that threshold of brutal retribution – the finality of taking a life.

She fled to Turkey – to Rumi's birthplace to subdue her conscience and atone for her sins. In her disturbed emotional state, she fell back on her passion for poetry. Her deep love of Persian poets, especially Rumi, triggered an old long forgotten hobby – she immersed herself in Rumi's work.

On an impulse, she set forth to visit Konya where Rumi was buried – her homage to her father who was also a fan of Rumi and Sufi music. They had dreamed of visiting Konya together – it was to be her graduation present.

Now that he was gone and graduation deferred for now, she felt compelled to bring that dream to fruition. Her journey to Rumi's shrine would be her salvation.

She trekked from Tehran to Iran's north-west border with Turkey and thereon to Konya – where Rumi was buried in 1273 AD. The order of the 'Whirling Dervishes' was formed after his death and became a pilgrimage ritual for many followers, especially the Sama Ceremony. Roxana headed for that emotional sanctuary – the mausoleum dedicated to Rumi's memory. Her father, who knew most of Rumi's poems verbatim, would be pleased with her. The thought that her father was with her on this, comforted her and brought a measure of closure.

Roxana lived on a trust set up by her father in London – although she knew that the trust had assets that she could live off for a while, she was scared of running out of money. She lived frugally as she travelled through Iran and Turkey – echoing Rumi's simplistic life style.

Konya with its deep spiritual ambience became a haven for her, the ultimate solace. She was driven towards a way of life that she had long ignored. She immersed herself in the mystical music and its profound interpretation; a respite from her troubles. After months, her emotional pendulum vacillating from one extreme to the other, she had some inner peace; a normal sleep pattern restored and a semblance of sanity.

The emotional scars of unstable relationships had left her with a deep mistrust of men; her psyche damaged to shun male attention. She deliberately dressed as an ascetic to hide her considerable womanly charms; her shapely figure frequently hidden under shapeless clothes to avoid drawing undue male attention.

It was during this profound all-consuming spiritual phase - a re-awakening - reading Rumi and listening to Sufi music that precipitated a turning point. An incident, after the annual performance of the Whirling Dervishes and the Sama Ceremony – which marks the death anniversary of Rumi – almost ended her new-found serene existence in Konya.

Whilst returning late at night from the ceremony, she was waylaid by a group of men all high on hashish – she was bundled into a car and taken to a deserted and derelict building site. She had almost resigned herself to a repeat of what had happened in Tehran, when the fortuitous intervention of an ascetic, who heard her screams, saved her from unfathomable atrocities.

The self-assurance of the man and his intrepid behaviour seemed to mesmerise her captors – they fell silent under his fierce hypnotic gaze. Roxana held her breath as the culprits paused in their indecision; rudderless.

The ascetic then did a strange thing – he took out his reed flute and rendered some kind of a mystical musical composition. The culprits were aghast at the sheer audacity of the man. They listened in rapt attention.

Roxana recognised strands of Rumi in the surreal composition. She too was frozen, as enthralled as the goons. The sounds emanating from his magical flute fixated one and all – total silence reigned as they absorbed the music. His rendition of Rumi transfixed her and the thugs.

Roxana looked in marvel as the ascetic, still playing the flute, forced the thugs to retreat, a step at a time, apprehensive of forces that lurked in the dark recesses of their own minds. In their drug-filled stupor, the fluting ascetic assumed the ephemeral force that the Sufi poets thrust upon their followers – the rhythmic sounds casting a spell. They fled like rats scurrying into the darkness. Roxana heard the car speed off, danger ebbing away, with her eyes fixed on the man. As the ascetic walked away still playing the flute, Roxana followed the Pied Piper out of the dilapidated building.

For the next few months, she just followed him around. A feeling that she had met him before haunted her.

He was a shaman, a faith healer, on a spiritual journey through Turkey, especially Konya, to observe and imbibe the traditional healing practices; the use of music to heal the soul. His Zanzibari origins, the land where generations of Indians and Arabs had co-existed for centuries, led him to India – to add Ayurvedic and Tantric practices to his repertoire of treatments.

By the time he met Roxana, he had almost mastered the traditional healing methods of the Byzantium – all related to chanting, Rumi and Sufi music. His stay in Konya and other parts of Turkey had opened up new avenues that he had hitherto ignored – rituals dealing with the occult and reminiscent of similar skills practised by the traditional healers on the Kenyan and Zanzibari coastal regions and, indeed, by many in India.

She later learnt that he was of mainly Omani pedigree – a Zanzibari Arab. His ancestors had travelled all the way from Oman and settled along the coastal strips collectively called the Swahili coast. The Sultanate of Oman, established in Zanzibar, held sway over the coast from Mozambique to Mombasa to Somalia and beyond.

The young Roxana was instantly drawn to this unorthodox

man with the brooding dark eyes, tall and with aquiline features that strangely brought Rasputin to her mind. Despite his annoyance and insistence to leave him in peace, she ignored him and followed him around like a groupie tagging a rock star.

His total defiance of her dazzling blue eyes and her voluptuous feminine charms intrigued her. She was irked by his indifference, his matter-of-fact dismissal. It hurt her pride. His rejection of her considerable feminine charms goaded her to try even harder, seeing it as a challenge to break his resolve. He had, despite pampering and cosseting her since rescuing her, not laid a finger on her.

One moonlit night she deliberately, after having been to her favourite hammam – Turkish bath – entered his chamber. Her perfumed body, still warm from the bath, slithered tentatively into his bed; Eve on the prowl, the serpent unleashed.

As she re-played imaginary erotic scenes in her head, she showered the full force of her substantial physical attributes on her man, whispering seductively several of Rumi's love poems in his ear. Her recitation of a particular favourite poem, which ended with the evocative words: '…the warmth of your cheek against mine' egged her on.

As she brandished her passionate caresses in an elaborate ritual of titillation, she could feel his resistance melt away underneath her. Roxana paused for a moment to look into his eyes, which were partially hooded but she knew he was very much conscious of her body. She smiled wickedly as she went to work on him. It was going to be a long rapturous night.

It was while they were in the throes of intense passion that the memories and images of her one-night stand flashed through her mind.

Back then he was a neophyte – a willing student of Tantric rituals - but here an accomplished tutor. She asked, still in a stupor: 'We met at that bus stop outside the ashram in Bangalore. Did you spike my drink – the coconut? I often thought about that night I spent with you.'

'Nope,' he said laconically. 'I spent most of my time in South India doped up on hashish and herbal stimulants. The years I spent there are a total blur. I don't recall you or any other woman during that phase in India.'

She turned over without responding, annoyed. Most men rarely forgot her or could resist her ample charms and here was this rare specimen who did not recall anything. She knew he was lying. His intervention that night was proof enough for her that he had recognised her.

After that torrid night, she noticed a change in him – almost as if he was resigned to her presence. They spent the next year or so travelling together. For Roxana it was a calming phase – a transition from the heightened anxiety state after her flight from Tehran to her present blissful phase in Turkey. Deep down she knew that this status quo was an illusion. At some stage she would have to return to Bangalore to complete her neglected education.

The break came out of the blue - when the ascetic realised that the cosy existence in her company was hampering his training and spiritual growth. The imaginary notch on the belt – the conquest – once achieved had lost the thrill. Her presence was becoming irksome; almost suffocating.

The parting of ways was just as abrupt as their first encounter. Roxana was distraught initially – she had got used to his comforting presence. Turkey had been a mirage; an interlude. She could not meander through life aimlessly. As her paramour had frequently reminded her : 'shit happens, life continues.'

The ascetic's departure was actually yet another turning point in her life and her return to Bangalore almost predestined. With her father's estate frozen by the Iranian regime and her trust fund diminishing in value, Roxana had to regroup and reassess her plans. Fortunately, her father's foresight had anticipated a run on her finances – her trustees had instructions to liquidate enough of the trust fund's assets to finance her postgraduate studies if need be.

When she returned to Bangalore, it came as a shock that she would have to repeat her final year. She did graduate and, in the absence of any scope to return to Tehran in the short term, promptly enrolled for postgraduate qualifications.

The next pivotal phase of her life began when she met Sanjay Ray, a foreign student from Kenya who had recently transferred to Bangalore University to complete his English literature degree.

Sanjay, short and of pedestrian looks, would have gained his university degree in the UK but for his below par A-level grades – thanks to the time spent in Soho's nightclubs and in a new bed every night. The dusty corridors of the elitist Harrow School and its library were as alien to him as the unexplored coral reefs of his native Kenya.

He was recalled to Nairobi in disgrace and packed off to Mombasa to learn the ropes in one of his father's subsidiaries –beach resorts along the coastal strip, stretching from Mombasa to Lamu. When that failed to rein in Sanjay's debauchery and heavy drinking, he was summoned back to Nairobi in disgrace; the Ray clan in a quandary about the prodigal's future. Sanjay's predilection for the three Ss – sun, sea and sex – had Manu Ray, Sanjay's widowed father and head of the

Ray clan, constantly rescuing his son from one catastrophe to another.

The father, fondly referred to as 'Senior' as he was the eldest among the brothers, had even tried to cure Sanjay's wayward ways by resorting, in desperation, to faith healers and shamans. Not that it made any difference to Sanjay's testosterone-powered affairs. The only saving grace was that Sanjay concentrated on foreigners; any local entanglements would have been perilous. Nonetheless, the family feared that the heir to the Ray fortune was open to blackmail and manipulation.

Sanjay's father was at pains to defend him to the extended family and his business associates by asserting that his son was not stupid, just lazy. He did all he could to protect his son from the gossip and innuendo that his affairs generated, but he had no choice once the extended family lost its patience and suggested packing him off to the harsh reality of India. Might make a man of him, they said in unison. Senior relented.

It did not make an iota of a difference. Sanjay continued in India where he had left off in the UK and in Kenya. He flourished in Bombay – not on the campus though. The night life in the company of hangers-on who saw him as a meal ticket, deteriorated into a familiar, practised routine. Sanjay was back to his old ways – heavy drinking, sex and drugs. His obvious wealth drew parasites, both male and female 'leeches'.

His financial pedigree was part of the problem – thanks to being heir to a vast fortune accumulated over generations of hard graft by his entrepreneurial ancestors in East Africa, especially in Kenya. An only son, his pampered life in Kenya had resulted in a privileged and sheltered upbringing – he was ill-prepared for the opportunistic vultures who preyed on the ultra-rich. Being filthy rich and a foreign student in Bombay was a double whammy; he enticed sycophants and pimps like rotting flesh attracts flies and maggots. Devoid of any family or local support in an alien harsh land, he was a sitting duck.

Sanjay was caught with his pants down with a faculty member who sensing an opportunity to extort money, tried to blackmail him. It had been a honey trap and it soon escalated beyond Sanjay's control. The local thugs muscled in; the scent of easy money attracting the human sharks, just as the chemical signature of spilt blood draws in the real sharks.

The college's English faculty found out about the sordid affair and Sanjay was threatened with immediate expulsion – the threat withdrawn promptly when the college became aware of the salacious gossip doing the rounds. The college, in order to avert a PR disaster, swiftly issued a 'no objection certificate' and facilitated Sanjay's transfer to another university. The thugs, fearing that their prey was about to abscond, redoubled their efforts to extract money.

Eventually, Ray Senior had to fly to Bombay and intervene – he paid off a young upcoming local gang leader to silence all the other petty opportunists. Fortunately, the local mafia boss's timely mediation prevented Sanjay's indiscretions from mushrooming into a free-for-all. Ray Senior's tactful damage limitation exercise paved the way for Sanjay's safe passage to Bangalore – to continue his degree programme.

Fearing that history may repeat itself in Bangalore, Ray Senior tried, once again, to convince his son to return to Nairobi. Sanjay, knowing that a move back would entail an arranged marriage, refused unreservedly. The thought of living under the gaze of the joint family in an arranged marriage with the prospect of fathering 2.3 children nauseated him. The bribe of a hefty 'marriage allowance' and a mansion in any city plus the portfolio in Cyprus was also rejected.

Until kismet intervened; saved by the bell - or so he thought.

For Sanjay it was love at first sight – the vision of Roxana, ravishing and exquisite, emerging from the swimming pool of a five-star hotel, was kismet; his destiny. Roxana's blue eyes and her glowing complexion captivated him. She was his Aphrodite emerging from the sapphire waters of Cyprus, where the Ray clan had seven holiday resorts – the largest one not far from Aphrodite Rock, the birthplace of Aphrodite, the Greek goddess.

Sanjay, familiar with the legend of Aphrodite and her cult following in Paphos, had just met his goddess who had her own cult following of admirers, on and off campus. He had grown up watching Bollywood movies where the actresses were enticingly fair-skinned and their co-stars even more so. To him, Roxana was no less than any Bollywood superstar, with the starry looks and the chutzpah.

It was a done deal as far as he was concerned. For the first time in his vacuous mind, his bed of promiscuity assumed the magnitude of a bridal chamber – he had found the perfect bride: the perfect trophy that he could take back to Kenya.

The family's previous attempts at arranging Sanjay's marriage had failed as a suitable girl would need to have the same social and financial pedigree: third or fourth generation Kenyan Gujarati. The early migrants, mostly Gujaratis, who built the Kenya-Uganda railway, would have looked in awe at their descendants who had amassed such vast fortunes – and even bigger chips on their shoulders.

Sanjay, unlike the others in the clan, was anything but

attractive. His chances of an arranged marriage were thwarted by the absence of even a single redeeming physical attribute. The vast Ray fortune, not even a potential future Forbes listing, was enough to tempt anyone into matrimony.

For Sanjay, Roxana was the perfect opportunity to avoid the poisoned chalice that the arranged marriage system represented. She was the one for him, period. He ignored the fact that his ultra conservative family would have major concerns about their heir marrying a foreigner; a Persian at that. Not in their wildest dreams would they have imagined a Zoroastrian bride instead of a Hindu daughter-in-law. He knew that resistance to his marriage would be immense, even if Ray Senior sanctioned it.

His initial overtures towards Roxana had been futile – she had nothing but disdain for his puppy dog trailing of her all over the campus. It never occurred to him that his advances would be rebuffed; his previous conquests had been all too easy – women who were seduced by his immense wealth.

For weeks Sanjay's dogged persistence was met with total and abject indifference. The puny and spoilt brat was inconsolable – he drank away his sorrows in the popular pubs dotting the Bangalore landscape. Roxana's defence against his charm offensive was resolute and steadfast.

Sanjay persisted, she resisted. He knew he was the ugly duckling but with enough gold to buy his way into any debutante's bed; here though he had marriage in his sights. No more fly-by-night affairs or one-night stands. For once, he was the predator, albeit with bona fide intentions.

Roxana's disdain was genuine until she read about his family's considerable business interests and assets. The news of the Ray clan's dispute with the Cyprus authorities regarding the development of an exclusive five-star golf resort in Paphos made the headlines for all the wrong reasons – its proximity to the Tomb of Kings, a UNESCO World Heritage site, was the bone of contention. In the end, the environmentalists won and the project was shelved. The fiasco, reported all over the world, opened Roxana's eyes. It looked as though the ugly duckling had some merit.

Roxana's interest was piqued enough for her to request her trustees in London to look into the Kenyan family's financial history. Her trustees, initially bemused, swiftly responded – the UK and European assets were worth millions; considerably more if the Kenyan and other global assets were included. On a separate issue they reminded her of her perilous finances especially as the Iranians had frozen Dr Shirazi's assets. More importantly, she was reminded that her trust would soon run out of money. The trustees advised her to negotiate with the Iranian regime. If she failed to gain access to the assets then she would be virtually insolvent.

Roxana, mindful of her precarious finances, had no option but to execute a volte-face, a U turn that landed Sanjay squarely in the frame. Short of finding that plum job that would support the huge legal costs of squaring up to the Iranian regime, Sanjay appeared to be her only hope. She found him repugnant and gauche but if kissing the frog was the princely key to his coffers then so be it - desperate times need desperate measures.

Her smile was sardonic as she muttered to herself: 'Just my luck that I had to draw the short straw.' The short straw here was the joint family and the clan hierarchy that she'd be up against back in

Kenya. Marrying the 'beast' would be easy; using her womanly wiles to gain an upper hand with the clan would be the challenge. Marrying the frog and having his tadpoles frightened her but facing up to the patriarch – going by the business write ups and profiles – was even more daunting.

She sighed mightily as she fashioned her strategy – the man seemed to be besotted so the difficult task would be to camouflage her gold-digging designs. She used the Tantric techniques learnt in the bed of the ascetic – Sanjay did not stand a chance; his hedonistic cravings propelled him to her bed on several occasions. Roxana employed all her sexual wiles to bait him, without quite going the distance. He was left gasping; titillation was all he got.

He was so beguiled by her that he readily accepted her alleged reservations about a pre-marital relationship, erroneously assuming that she was saving herself for the bridal night.

Roxana was taken aback when Sanjay gave in and accepted her plea of no sex until the wedding night. She was puzzled at first – he seemed almost relieved. This was at odds with their tumultuous courtship where he was so eager to get her into bed. Maybe, he was bowing to pressure from the family to get married and settle down. She had paid genuine heed to his ramblings about family bonds and Indian cultural ties – to get an insight into what she was buying into.

She demurred each time he raised the issue of marriage – until he proposed on bended knee. She pretended to be surprised and then accepted his marriage proposal, feigning jubilation. Her genuine concern was that Sanjay seemed so diffident and unsure of himself when he was alone with her, at odds with his alleged Lothario reputation.

They were married in the registrar's office in Bangalore on the same day as the Indian cricket team triumphantly arrived in Bombay after winning the 1983 World Cup. The newlyweds flew to Kenya on completing their respective degrees – Sanjay returning with a trophy wife on his arm and a swagger that belied his inner turmoil. He was apprehensive – his father was a force to be reckoned with, who might just carry out the oft repeated threats of disinheriting him.

Sanjay was relying on his wife's considerable charms to woo one and all. Roxana was secretly relieved that Sanjay had not consummated their marriage. His impassioned excuse was that he wanted to sire his children on Kenyan soil, just as the past four generations of the Ray clan had done. Roxana was relieved at the stay of execution. Not that she had any intention of having his tadpoles. She had still not figured out a modus operandi for deferring the consummation of their union.

The Ray clan welcomed the new bride, tentative but overawed by her radiant beauty and her blue eyes. Most of them, resisting the urge to repeat the beauty and the beast comparison, secretly envied Sanjay's good fortune at bagging such a trophy; a princess no less.

Even Senior, experienced in the ways of the world, wondered how his son had managed to bag such a catch. The patriarch's thoughts were tinged with apprehension. Roxana seemed very cultured and he hoped that, whatever her intentions, she would treat Sanjay fairly; let him down gently. When it happened, not if it happened.

He admitted, much later on, that Roxana was no Bollywood B-star airhead but a Rumi reciting Tantric priestess, who turned out to be a formidable adversary. His fervent prayer had been that Sanjay would survive the ordeal of a breakup.

Within days of Roxana's entry into their palatial home on the outskirts of Nairobi, Roxana confronted the patriarch.

'You knew, didn't you?' Roxana challenged.

'Knew what?' Senior tried to hide his shock and looked away, her intent quite confrontational. He was puzzled. He had hoped that she knew and hence her acceptance of the alliance.

'When exactly did you figure out that your son is gay?' Roxana blurted, close to screaming at him. She continued before he could respond. 'He failed to consummate our marriage in Bangalore. His excuse was that he wanted to start a family on Kenyan soil. It has been a while since we got back – he keeps shying away. But you knew. Sanjay made out as if he had had an affair with the wife of a faculty member. He was having an affair with the husband! Obviously, the wife caught them. Right?' The fury in her voice was controlled; barely.

'Yes, I am afraid, several times in London, Bombay and even in Mombasa. When he informed us that you had accepted his proposal of marriage, we were elated. We thought that, miraculously, the shaman's treatment in Mombasa had somehow changed him.' The patriarch looked away, refusing to look her in the eye. He was honest, liberal minded and a man of the world but Sanjay had placed him in a dilemma. Ray Senior feared for Sanjay – the ultraconservative Gujarati community and even some in his own family would not be as tolerant and lenient as he would have wished for. Keeping silent was the only option.

'This is going to cost you,' Roxana retorted.

'Please, don't do anything in haste. I am prepared to help out as long as this remains between us. No one need to knows. Do you understand?'

As she walked away, her back to him, her smile said it all. She was relieved that she would not have to share the conjugal bed. The histrionics were for the patriarch's benefit. A few sleepless nights for the patriarch and a heightened state of anxiety would all work in her favour. She was in no hurry; let him sweat. The longer the intervening wait, the better the outcome for her.

By the weekend, and after subjecting Senior to the silent treatment, she laid down her demands; a win-win scenario for her.

The patriarch thought long and hard and accepted without any resistance. It was the expedient thing to do – it bought him time, and more importantly it bought her silence. Any untoward disclosures at this juncture would damage Sanjay and the extended family.

The old man agreed partly to her demands – a slice of his cash fortune and the chain of hotels and resorts in Mombasa and Lamu. Plus, the small cargo and freight company with its clutch of bonded warehouses, dotted across Mombasa, Dubai and Bombay. He refused to part with the warehouses on Bath Road, near Heathrow and the seven resorts in Cyprus. He would reconsider the London warehouses only if she moved to London with Sanjay.

He was not surprised that she knew about his assets; all listed companies and all above board. In his time, he had seen too many families destroyed by greed; their dynastic achievements squandered by questionable practices. He had always played by the rules and was not about to change course to accommodate Roxana or anyone else for that matter.

The Heathrow units were the crème de la crème of his freight operations. The

patriarch was hoping that if Sanjay moved to London, then the family would retain some control and, crucially Sanjay would be protected by his UK domicile status. Tax was the least of his worries; Sanjay's legal status in Kenya was at risk. He knew that she knew.

The Ray clan would be under the cosh, permanently. Her gloating smile was an answer in itself; she knew Kenyan law. She had no intention of divorcing Sanjay; not in a million years. And moving to London would play into Senior's game plan. Her continued presence in Kenya was her best bet; her trump card.

'No chance,' she told Senior. 'I am staying put, for now. If and when I decide to move, it will be on my terms, not yours. You can keep your warehouses and your Cyprus resorts – for now.'

She was adamant. He argued and pleaded, to no avail. He needed to get Sanjay out of the country and the sooner the better. Reluctantly he agreed, on the condition that the couple moved to Mombasa and maintained the appearance of a blissful marriage. And she would be discreet, not flaunt her lovers.

'If you expose Sanjay or damage him in anyway, then I promise you, we will not stand by idly.'

She smiled sweetly back at him, knowing that these were empty threats. Sanjay's murky past was her trump card – as long as she stayed married to him and remained in Kenya.

The deeds of the properties and leases were transferred to Roxana Ray – she had insisted on taking the Ray surname in order to bank on the family's business reputation. Roxana Ray was more bankable than Roxana Shiraz.

And, arguably Roxana Shiraz, had disappeared; no one knew her whereabouts – neither friends nor foe. Even her last lover, her Rasputin, would find it difficult to trace her. Her strategy of maintaining a low profile had worked since fleeing from her Iranian tormentors. There was no reason not to exercise the same caution.

Within a short span of seven years, Roxana had established her hold on the business and then on, it was a matter of consolidation and expanding – even the patriarch was impressed. Even though he knew that each passing year and each success, diminished the chances of her quitting Kenya.

Despite his pleas to her, Roxana took on a legion of lovers, although he was relieved to note that discretion became her middle name. Even her business activities, the conferences and the business meetings, were conducted from behind the scenes. After the trauma of Iran, it had become second nature for her to stay away from the public gaze.

Sanjay sank deeper into drugs and alcohol; Roxana had a big hand in driving him to that. Soon news filtered out to the Ray clan that if something was not done to get Sanjay away from Roxana and from Mombasa, there would be calamitous consequences.

On the pretext of a family celebration, Sanjay was lured away from her clutches. It was then that the scale of Sanjay's addiction to drugs and alcohol dawned on the family. The patriarch had heard about his promiscuity and a new threat appeared on the horizon – his weight loss and gaunt look prompted concerns about HIV/AIDS.

Sanjay was flown to London and straight into a rehab centre. Within months, the diagnoses of alcoholism, HIV infection and clinical depression were multiple death sentences. Sanjay flitted in and out of rehab, the specialist liver unit at Hammersmith Hospital and gay bars. He died in a hospice six months later.

The family flew Sanjay by private jet one last time to Nairobi;

cremating him on Kenyan soil. The Ray clan's four generations of the Kenyan cycle of birth and death remained uninterrupted. The patriarch sent several messages to Roxana, requesting her presence at Sanjay's funeral. When she failed to respond he rang her offices in Mombasa. He was told that she was away on business.

Senior had anticipated this eventuality; the business had been restructured after the last blackmail attempts in Bombay. Sanjay's share of the conglomerate had been placed in a trust; ringfenced to protect Sanjay and the clan.

The Ray clan was premature in thinking that Roxana's hold on the family's assets had waned after Sanjay's death. Senior was wise enough to know that it was too early to write her off. Roxana's Zoroastrian ancestors had survived persecution for centuries and Sanjay's demise was hardly a setback for Roxana. It would be a grave folly not to expect a legal challenge and a claim on Sanjay's estate. Senior cautioned his extended family with the words - 'hope for the best; prepare for the worst'.

EIGHT

Abbu, Mombasa, Kenya.

The dark dank front room of the house on Vasco da Gama Street was sectioned off from the rest of the ground floor dwelling. A faint aroma of fried fish wafted in despite the potent incense that bellowed out plumes of scent from the small brazier that was in the middle of the front room. The haze created by the spirals of fragrant smoke added to the mystique of the occasion, like the hypnotist and a swinging pendulum.

Several candles were burning on the window sill and on the ramshackle table next to the brazier – the yellow flames shimmering languidly in the room. The blazing sun outside – well past its zenith – on that Friday afternoon bathed the throngs of tourists and local residents as they bustled past the small dwellings with ornately carved wooden doors, testimony to an Omani legacy.

The consultation room was deliberately kept dark with thick black curtains on the barred windows and across the old-fashioned carved wooden double door at the front; the threshold raised a foot or two by a cement stair. There were hard cement ledges, as broad as a bench, on either side of the front door – many houses in the old quarter had this 'baraza' feature, more often than not occupied by mangy old dogs than old men.

The sitting outside, sometimes with wooden balustrades, was an anachronism left over from the past when men would smoke the hookah and slurp noisily as they drank the hot salty and ginger spiced kahawa. The dark, bitter coffee drinking and the exchange of idle gossip, out in the blazing Mombasa sun, were rituals that preceded a game of cards, carrom or draughts.

As the shaman prepared for his next patient, the buibui-clad lady in the kitchen, separated from the 'surgery' by a full-length curtain, sautéed finely diced onions on a Primus stove that spewed kerosene fumes – the pungent smell of onions and the fuel hung heavy in the air. The soft music playing in the background – an Indian flute rather than Arabic verses – did little to change the sombre mood in the surgery.

The young man and an Arab ayah had been ushered in – the faith healer had watched them walk the short distance from the junction at the main road where an elegant Mercedes had driven up and parked; the narrow interior lanes left very little leeway for most cars to pass through safely. Doves and crows using the low-hanging telephone lines as perches, routinely deposited their urea excretions on pedestrians below, their cooing and cawing adding to the cacophony of sounds. The salty air wafting in from the old harbour added to the humidity.

The shaman's penetrating gaze could just about discern a well-dressed mzungu (white man) in the back seat; the driver resting against the bonnet, calmly watching the passing humanity. Another car parked behind had burly bodyguards in attendance.

The patient, apprehensive at the strange looking décor – the candles and the incense – was in pain as he lowered himself onto the cushioned hard wooden chair. The healer could not but notice the wince of pain flash across the face of the fair-skinned effeminate young man; a grimace of considerable discomfort.

Abbu, with his decades of experience as a traditional healer, arrived at his 'spot diagnosis' as soon as he connected the symptom – what he thought was anal pain – with the patient's looks, the presence of the mzungu in the sleek car and the ayah as a chaperone.

The shaman's examination of the patient, after he had undressed, was all but abandoned as he caught sight of the small patch of blood on the white Y-front. Abbu smiled indulgently as he weighed the chances of a rich mzungu driving down to the old town to consult him rather than a GP were all but negligible – unless he had something to hide. He rubbed his hands gleefully as he prepared his concoction of Vaseline and other secret ingredients for the patient; an ointment that smelt as bad as it looked.

He went back to his window and had another look – the sleek Mercedes and the mzungu were still very much there. He was a bit surprised that the man had driven up in broad daylight rather than send his minions. The shaman, in his haste to cash in on the situation, dismissed it as the mzungu's arrogance – some of these foreigners, with their fancy cars and fancier mansions, still looked down on the local residents of old town as backward.

The bias against the old culture and faith healers had its roots in the dark reputation for voodoo and black magic practices; amulets and tokens sold for every misfortune known to mankind - from unrequited love, infidelity, betrayal to passing exams. Mombasa's potpourri of racial mix of Arab, Indian, Portuguese, Bantu and other races contributed to the practices and ethos of the town.

The old town had over decades of steady decline lost its inhabitants, leaving behind curio shop owners, warehouses, older poorer residents, faith healers and an assortment of retailers. Remnants of a bygone era. The preponderance of buibui-clad healers was notable as pregnant patients, unable to afford the services of medics, relied on the female shamans to look after mothers and their babies; midwifery, obstetrics, neonatal care and paediatrics all rolled into one. There were many who preyed on the minds of the vulnerable with black magic and voodoo practices.

Abbu, as he dispensed his concoction and discharged the patient, advised the ayah about keeping the area clean and to apply the ointment regularly. He reassured the patient and the chaperone that the anal tear would heal as long as untoward straining whilst opening the bowels was avoided; any straining would aggravate the bleeding.

He also recommended a small amount of Castor oil orally as a laxative and cautioned against an enema - the rubber tubing if inserted vigorously could damage the delicate network of blood vessels of the rectal and anal regions.

The ayah almost corrected the shaman but checked herself – constipation remedies on the back streets of Mombasa were hardly relevant to the wealthy mzungus; they had access to well-trained doctors not charlatans advocating weekly rituals of Sunday morning enemas. It wasn't her place to comment. She paid up without a quibble despite knowing that the shaman's fees were well over the top. The mzungu's instructions were explicit - to avoid any confrontation or argument about the charges, no matter how exorbitant.

Both hurried away down the narrow bustling lane towards the

main road and the waiting car; the driver still resting against the bonnet and the man sitting in the back reading a newspaper. The other two men looked bored as they continued to chain smoke.

Even at that distance, the shaman could see the self-importance of the man in the car – the chauffeur and the presence of the body guards gave it all away. He watched as the young man got in and the car moved away; the ayah walked off towards Salim Road. He knew that she'd be back soon.

Sure enough a few days later, the same chaperone came in with another young patient; he attended with care and precision to his new patient. As they left, he popped his head through the curtain and spoke to the henna-haired woman. As per his terse commands in Arabic – she quickly donned her buibui and followed the ayah and the patient to the end of the narrow-cobbled street where the Mercedes was parked.

The shaman's housekeeper ran the last few paces to arrive within striking distance of the waiting car – she memorised the car registration and turned back. Within minutes she was back in the kitchen preparing the fried fish and rice for her man. He made a note of the car registration in a small black diary that he kept strapped to his money belt under his vest.

A pattern soon developed with the same ayah turning up with different young adults once or twice a month. Neither the chaperone nor the healer engaged in any conversation – each knew their role. He would attend to the patient without bothering with a physical exam, prepare the ointment and collect his fees, which increased with each visit. The ayah duly complied and escorted her ward back to the car.

After almost six months of the constant flow of patients from the mzungu, the healer managed to extract information about the owner of the white Mercedes. A patient who worked at the local police station near Naaz cinema owed him a few hundred shillings for dispensing love potions and amulets. The besotted clerk, reliant on the shaman's expertise to win over his fair lady, readily supplied the details.

The car belonged to a wealthy white politician who had stood as an independent candidate for local elections. He had failed to get elected despite spending vast sums on vigorous campaigns. The man, a bachelor, had made his fortune in property. The shaman found out, later on, that the man's wealth was spread all over the world, especially in the UK.

Over the years, the healer kept track of the man's political rise with great interest. The shaman watched and waited for an opportune time to move. Both progressed in their respective political arena; both were fiercely passionate about Mombasa's cultural and historical roots, going back centuries to the Omani domination. The healer had begun to admire the man from afar – at council meetings, at voluntary community organisations and various charities.

There was one particular charity that caught his eye – the mzungu was patron of a charity that organised scholarships and financial support for destitute young adults, for study locally or abroad.

And the healer had been watching this slow ascent to the top of the political spectrum. He was patient too, as he waited year in and year out, happy to bide his time. He was convinced that when the time came, he would be able to call upon the faithful to do his bidding; the mzungu politician would have to yield to his political demands or face personal ruin.

Abbu was certain that the mzungu's political dominance would be an asset and can be used to fulfil his own agenda. The politician had one other star quality – he was white which meant that he held an unfair advantage over the blacks and the Asians.

Abbu's inside knowledge of the mzungu's sexual preferences and his sordid record would be his Achille's heel – even a whiff of a scandal would end his political aspirations, and certainly put him behind bars. The shaman, the self-professed kingmaker, smiled, one pawn safely on the chessboard, poised to do his bidding. One more pawn was needed – without the Asians on board, it would be difficult to carry his agenda through. Like the mzungus, the Asians had the firepower to sway political opinion – their cash-rich businesses could be tapped for the shaman's agenda.

The arrival of a woman, a budding tycoon, whetted his interest even further. The tycoon with an Indian surname had walked away with all the business accolades – woman of the year, Chair of the Chambers of Commerce and many other such achievements; all within the last seven years. That was some achievement – to be running one of the largest conglomerates of holiday resorts and cargo/freight and bonded warehouses. Although he had not met the reclusive figure, she seemed to have the right pedigree – the wealth and the family name – Ray. If he could draw her in, then the others would follow suit.

The Patel and the Shah clans were omnipotent; they dominated the retail, wholesale and manufacturing sectors. They controlled the trades. And the flow of money.

And Abbu had the means to manipulate these cash rich families – their fear of political uncertainty. He had every intention to use the expulsion of the Asians from Uganda by Idi Amin as a seminal moment. The legacy of Amin's actions was the single most potent political weapon at his disposal – Kenya's Asians lived in fear of the same fate befalling them.

Abbu was wily enough to recognise that all the pieces were in place, all he had to do was to pull the drawstrings just like the diamond merchant drawing the purse strings of the velvet pouch, trapping the diamonds in the pouch.

It was time that he did things his way. In Africa, for too long the two elephants, the whites and the Asians, had fought each other for supremacy. The whites for political supremacy, the Asians for financial gains. The natives had become the 'grass'; always the losers in the battle of the elephants. The tussle between the two elite classes would play out to his advantage. It was his mission, his dream, to change this order. It did not bother him that nothing would change for the downtrodden masses, except that he would oust the other two; the power would be his to wield.

His birth in Zanzibar and the subsequent traumatic journey to Mombasa had left scars – the Zanzibar Revolution on 12th Jan 1964 had ended the political and financial power wielded by the Arabs and the Indians.

Abbu's family had fled to Mombasa and had lived in total obscurity, refuge provided by elderly relatives. He had grown up with his maternal grandparents firstly in Mombasa and then in Lamu. His father's small boutique in Zanzibar had been ransacked by the rioting mobs who were intent on ejecting the Arabs and the Indians. The majority Swahili masses had long rued the domination of the economy and the purse strings by an elite minority. Abbu's family, despite their part Bantu ancestry, got caught up in the middle – neither fully of Arab nor of Swahili descent.

Abbu had given up schooling, despite the bursaries available from the Aga Khan. He had instead joined his maternal grandmother who had long practised as a faith healer. His initial years were spent in running errands for his grandmother and later on being trained as a shaman to take over the family-run faith-healing enterprise. He had inherited one ramshackle practice on the demise of his grandmother. That old town surgery soon mushroomed into a chain – across the coast embracing Mombasa, Malindi, Watamu and Lamu.

His eventual ambition was to establish several such practices all over Kenya – once he had honed his skills. His travels through India and Turkey to acquire the traditional methods of healing practised in both those countries became his apprenticeship. His flair and passion for Sufi music was kindled by his expertise with the flute. And being inspired by Rumi – the 13th century Persian poet.

NINE

Alec, Dubai, UAE.

The British Airways flight climbed steeply after take-off –
Alec Dunlop looked down at the rain-soaked Heathrow landscape and
the linear flow of cars on Bath Road; all diminishing in size as the
plane soared upwards. For once he felt no remorse or sadness at
quitting London.

The last year or so, since Ava's death, had been difficult; an
emotional rollercoaster. Alec had tried desperately to regain his focus
and get his career back on an even keel. He needed to realign; gain a
new perspective in life.

While he had managed to escape to the USA, after handing
over his practice to Ian Ross , his associate, the emptiness that he had
felt after her sudden demise was very much there – palpable and
gnawing.

Having completed a short course in Zoological Medicine, he
was charged up to return to Kenya – his brief introductory stint in
Laikipia and at the Nairobi National Park had whetted his appetite for
wildlife medicine and conservation. The thought of returning to the
blue skies and Acacia studded landscapes of Kenya was appealing. It
would be the perfect antidote to his mundane existence in London.

Sam's persuasive and repeated calls to return had been encouraging – he had promised that a one-year tenure at the vet school at Kabete could be arranged. The clinical role at Kabete and the opportunity to contribute to wildlife conservation would be the perfect opportunity; a stepping stone to other assignments. Sam reminded Alec about Nairobi being the regional hub for very many international organisations, including the UN and many research institutions where Alec could easily slot in. Sam cited ILRAD (International Laboratory for Research on Animal Diseases) as something that may interest Alec.

Alec debated long and hard. Eventually, he reasoned that he needed full closure on Ava's death before he ventured back to Kenya. He had escaped to the US to distance himself from Kenya; his guilt of having contributed to her death was irrational and corrosive. The thought that, had he not discovered the ivory scam, she would still be alive, hounded him.

The tipping point was Dubai – when he came across an advertised vacancy in the Veterinary Record. The advert looked ever so tempting on a cold winter's day in his South London surgery.

''MRCVS urgently required in Dubai for a new state of the art camel hospital and racing stables...........''

It was the bit about the racing camels that intrigued him – he had heard about the astronomical sums paid for the right breeding stock and the huge prizes that owners vied for. A stint as a clinician at the hospital and stables was as exotic as it could get. The thought of endless expanses of sand and the solitude that the desert provided was too tempting to forego – he was hooked.

Several flights to Dubai for personal interviews followed. He was still unsure but when he received a confirmed offer from the Chairman and the Board of Directors, he was swayed into accepting the position. Alec was suitably impressed that the private hospital and stables enjoyed widespread patronage – the Emiratis loved their racing camels, just as the Aga Khan loved his horses.

The proximity to Kenya – a mere five hour flight away – was at the back of his mind when he committed himself. He felt guilty about changing his mind but was sure that Sam would understand; for now, Kenya was on the back burner.

He called Sam to explain his decision. 'Sorry Sam, I had to go for the Dubai offer. It's too early for me to consider coming over there. Maybe after this contract. You know my predicament.'

'Yes, I do understand. Ava's spirit is still looming over you – one can run but one can't hide, so have your closure. My offer is still open, so let me know if your circumstances change. And don't get lost in the desert like your hero, T E Lawrence. 'Alec of Arabia' somehow does not have the same ring as 'Lawrence of Arabia.' He continued: 'I am convinced that the Emiratis would be compelled to send out a search party – not so much for a Brit but for their prize-winning camel.'

Alec laughed out loud. 'You bet!'. Alec had read T E Lawrence's autobiography, 'The Seven Pillars of Wisdom', and had as a result, become an ardent fan of Peter O'Toole – he had never missed the re-runs of David Lean's film 'Lawrence of Arabia' on the telly.

The camel hospital was a state-of-the-art new clinical facility built on the outskirts of Dubai; one of the seven emirates that constitutes the UAE. There were six other veterinary hospitals spread across the other kingdoms. All the seven hospitals and the attendant clinical laboratories were manned by foreign vets and technicians – mainly from the UK, India and Pakistan.

By the time Alec joined as Director of Clinical Services, the UAE conglomerate consisted of several subsidiaries embracing racing and stud stables, dairy, veterinary hospitals and laboratories and farms growing the specialist fodder for the camels. Including a new venture, in collaboration with a Swiss chocolatier to make chocolates from camel milk. Alec had been given a box of these exclusive chocolates on his first visit and had become addicted to them.

The holding entity was a privately held company with the majority shares controlled by seven Emirati families – effectively they ran the show; foreigners owned barely 20 per cent of the shares. The Emirati shareholders had ambitions to list on the London Stock Exchange in the near future. Alec had been promised share options if that listing occurred during his tenure at the hospital. This was in addition to his generous salary package.

The Emirates flight to Dubai was full and as they disembarked after a six-hour flight from Heathrow, the scorching heat rendered his shirt unbearably damp, despite the airconditioned terminal. The sleet and the wintery chill of London felt almost endearing in comparison to the intense searing heat.

Alec wondered how the Bedouin and other tribes survived in these extreme conditions – a marvel of human endurance. Even more of a wonder were the camels who had evolved over centuries into a lean, mean machine.

The camel's evolutionary adaptations, apart from its ability to withstand high temperatures, conserve water and 'turbo charge' fat and glucose metabolism, also included slit like nostrils, two rows of eyelashes and a third eyelid to keep out sand. With its oval shaped red blood cells, the camel's amazing ability to withstand extreme variations in temperature and hydration, made it, without a doubt, the beast of burden of the desert. For Alec, as he recapped on the finer details of the camel's arsenal of tricks, the racing breeds presented a new frontier. The thought excited him, especially the steep learning curve ahead of him – camel medicine was a new frontier for him; just as Laikipia's elephants had been.

As he made his way through immigration, he was struck by the long queues of Asians waiting to be cleared by officious immigration officers. The queueing migrants looked forlorn. The officers had absolute powers to send them back if their visa documents were not in order.

Alec, even at a distance, could feel the depth of the migrants' fear and despair. It was a scene or emotion, that would confront him time and time again over the months of his stay in the Middle East. In due course, like most expats, he would become accustomed to it and develop a thick skin. The culture of disparity between the Western expats and the impoverished migrant workforce, mostly from the Subcontinent, was striking and that made Alec uneasy. He would be confronted with this inequality time and time again; reigniting his memories of school life and the bullying that he had endured.

Little did he realise that as CEO of one of the largest conglomerates of veterinary hospitals and laboratories in the UAE, he would soon get used to the double standards. The vast oil wealth of the Middle East enticed people from all over the world; his lucrative contract and share options would soon lull his conscience into accepting the abnormal.

The smooth journey from the airport to the vast hospital complex, just outside Dubai, which was going to be his base, was seamless and effortless in the luxuriant interiors of the company car. The airconditioned convoy of Mercedes and Rolls Royce cruising rapidly through the vast desert expanses – totally uninhabited except for a few stray camels trekking through with their solitary riders – would soon lose its charm and become as pedestrian as catching the tube in urban London.

'This is heaven,' Alec mused, comparing the empty carriageways to the congested roads of London. The sand dunes stretching into infinity – sand as far as the eye could see – were a better visual than the grey concrete blocks of inner-city London.

The newly built residential quarters for the clinicians and lab staff were dripping with five-star luxury – a vast collection of small villas built around a central domed structure that housed the dining facilities and a fully equipped gym. It was rumoured that the state-of-the-art kitchen attached to the dining hall would have been the envy of any Michelin star chef in London or Paris.

In this instance, an Indian chef had been lured away from a prestigious group of hotels in Delhi to cater to the mostly Indian and Pakistani staff. Alec's introduction to real Indian cuisine had begun; an exciting culinary voyage that would supplant his favourite London fare of onion bhaji and chicken korma with Haryali kebabs and Hyderabadi biryani.

The camel hospital with the adjoining small racing and exercise track could be seen in the far distance – the setting sun silhouetting the several glass and steel structures and their fluorescent lights twinkling in the distance. Out in the still darkness of the vast dunes, the steel fluorescent domes looked surreal, straight out of a sci-fi movie set. The sheer opulence of the vast hi-tech complex was breath taking; a mirage of suspended reality.

Alec soon hit the deck running after a brief induction by Dr Reddy, an Indian vet, whom he had met on earlier visits. The clinical teams all took turns to familiarise him and accompanied him to the other hospitals. He was the only MRCVS vet; all the others had qualifications vetted and licensed by the Gulf authorities.

It was much later that he realised that, as a member of the Royal College of Veterinary Surgeons, his salary and perks package, paid tax-free in sterling, was obscenely exaggerated, compared to what the Asian vets were paid. He fretted that this financial chasm between him and the other vets would cause professional friction.

He was right to be concerned except that the inequality in the pay scales among the Asian vets was a bigger catalyst for the internecine feuding between the various factions – those brought up in the cities, those who had access to English medium schools and those who belonged to a certain section of society.

The factions were more apt to fight among themselves than envy an MRCVS licensed Brit's super-duper package. The board were paying Alec the going rate for Western expats whereas the others were easy to manipulate – the supply far in excess of demand meant that the board had the upper hand.

What he did not know was that the board had deliberately appointed an outsider, although unwittingly, they had overplayed their hand. The choice of a Brit as a CEO was based on merit. However, the directors in opting for a Brit, had ignored the legacy of British rule –

not only in the subcontinent but also in the Middle East. The 'them and us' division, in addition to the factional rivalries and the over inflated egos, made Alec's job that much harder – the lines in the sand already drawn before his arrival.

Alec's excitement at being involved with the racing stables and the close-knit racing fraternity blinded him to the darker forces at work. In a very regulated and monitored environment, the triad of the owners, the race authorities and the vets took centre stage for policing and compliance. In a three-pronged entity, the triad had to work in total harmony.

With the vast sums involved, the racing camel signified just as much economic value in the Middle East as the racing horses to the UK, sometimes more so, as owning a prized camel was a matter of pride. Most owners treated their camels as pets and as family members and family honour taking precedence over everything else.

The specialist camel hospital was an embodiment of that sentiment – camels were part and parcel of the tightly knit family centric community. 'Izzat' became a central part of life in the racing circles. And winning was a matter of 'izzat'; the honour far outweighing any financial rewards.

Alec's background in small-animal medicine had not prepared him for this kind of high stakes political play – it became an issue; a steep learning curve. Clinical challenges he could surmount but the machinations of people with vested interests was as alien as the concept of 'izzat'. He was a political novice, as he was soon to find out. Success has its own side effects.

Alec's and the company's first taste of victory came within months of participation in the first racing season. At an event in

Sharjah, the stable's young camel won the race on its maiden outing. While the prize money was paltry compared to the enormous capital invested in the young champion, even the first small prize was noteworthy. It became a matter of pride for the company's investors and for Alec's team.

It was at the celebrations in the owners' enclosure where Alec proudly introduced his clinical team to share the limelight and kudos for the win. It was here that the first subtle move was made by an emissary of a distinguished business rival; all the trappings of power and wealth on display – the silken robes, the gold dagger in the cummerbund, a fawning retinue of staff and bodyguards, convoy of classic cars, the works.

The emissary, escorted Alec to the tycoon, Chatzi Kostas, who it was rumoured was one of the richest camel owners in Dubai and extremely well connected. He came from a long line of shipping magnates. His small armada of dhows regularly sailed the trade routes to India and beyond, laden with cloves, cashew, gold and allegedly, ivory. Camel racing was a passion; an indulgent hobby.

'Good afternoon Dr Dunlop. Great pleasure at finally meeting you.' A cryptic remark delivered in an accent reminiscent of a Western education; London School of Economics or Harvard. Alec was momentarily taken aback. He was intrigued by the distinct emphasis on the word 'finally'. To the best of his knowledge, he had never met the gentleman.

The Greek Cypriot, in full regalia, including a ceremonial gold-plated 'khanjar' dagger jutting out from his cummerbund, presented him a card and said: 'We have been following your progress with immense interest. If you ever decide to broaden your horizons, then please call us. We have a much bigger setup – hospitals and stables here in the Emirates and several private wildlife ranches in Kenya. In fact, my Cypriot and Byzantium ancestors were famous for ivory trading. It wouldn't surprise me if some of them ended up in either German or British East Africa, Tanzania and Kenya, respectively. We were impressed with your Laikipia adventure.'

Alec was bemused by the royal 'we' usage and the gauche attempt at offering him a job. It occurred to him that the man was trying a tad too hard to impress him and he wondered where this was heading. The deliberate reference to Kenya mystified him. He could not recall meeting the man – the only possibility would have been the ivory-burning event in Nairobi where international sponsors had played a major part in the fundraising.

Before Alec could enquire, Chatzi turned and walked away. Alec smiled ruefully – he had been dismissed. They must know of his brief encounter with the poachers and his attendance at the ivory event. He made a mental note to probe Sam on this – Sam's investigation into Kenya's illicit ivory trade had floundered in the desert – the trail going cold after the discovery of Ava's body in the creek. Maybe, their adversaries, the cartel, were based here?

He turned to his deputy who was more conversant with the camel-racing fraternity; the whirlwind introductions and the meetings were already confusing him.

'Dr Reddy, would you have any idea who that man is?' Alec asked still staring at the retreating figure with a wake of burly body guards. The Indian vet followed the direction of Alec's nuanced nod and screwed up his eyes behind the heavy lenses of his spectacles.

'A recent arrival from Cyprus, I am informed. Rumour has it

that he is a man in a hurry on an acquisition spree to take over camel hospitals and racing stables. He is a predator with a war chest to match – comes from a long line of Greek shipping magnates. He has a chip on his shoulder and wants to win his own spurs so as not to be dependent on his rich family,' Dr Reddy replied with inflections of awe in his voice. His admiration for the Cypriot probably stemmed from the family's immense wealth and his aggressive business methods.

Dr Reddy had a head for financial management and their roles reflected that – Alec concentrated on clinical practice while Dr Reddy spent more time with the Board than out in the clinics. That arrangement suited Alec and, it seemed to Alec that Dr Reddy preferred the rough and tumble of the boardroom slightly more than the clinical role. That explained the Indian's admiration of the Cypriot. Alec wondered if Kostas had tried headhunting his deputy.

Although clinically Dr Reddy was more than a match for Alec, the business acumen surprised him. His belief was that clinicians rarely switched sides, certainly not before retirement. Alec recalled details from his deputy's CV - the broad experience of working in a camel hospital in Rajasthan, followed by years spent at the faculty of Veterinary Medicine at the vet school in Bangalore and eventually gaining a PhD from the same faculty.

Alec peered closely at the gold-embossed card given to him by the Cypriot. 'Very intriguing,' he murmured as they walked towards the celebrations going on in the airconditioned enclosure.

Dr Reddy, looking at the ornately embossed card, said offhandedly: 'Ignore the bluster. He's a bully. It would have been better if he had stayed back in Cyprus and played with his father's ships than to try and play with camels here.' Alec stared at the Indian; maybe he had misread his deputy. He was a dark horse and certainly no fan of the Cypriot nor his wealth.

For the first time Alec felt uneasy in the corporate world, just as he had felt in Kenya when confronted by the armed poachers and Shenzi. He was out of his depth and comfort zone, the business world and its political nuances worried him.

A few weeks later, Fedex delivered a parcel – a luxury line of Swiss chocs made from camel milk by a rival and a hand-written invitation to attend a party for selected vets.

Two days later, a follow-up call turned ominous when he politely refused the invitation. By now Kostas' secretary had turned belligerent and quite obnoxious – even suggesting that a refusal to join the group would be regretted. The implied threat was quite obvious.

'Thank you for the offer. I am flattered. However, my work here is not done so please convey my regrets to Mr Kostas.' With that Alec, before the secretary could remonstrate, politely indicated that he had a case pending and tried to put the phone down. He heard a rustle and the oleaginous tone of the businessman come through before Alec could disconnect.

'Dr Dunlop, I understand that you are new to Dubai and probably not fully conversant with the way we do things here. Please hear me out.' Kostas continued before Alec could interject: 'We are the largest, by market share, company in the sector and have grown rapidly. That kind of exponential growth means that we are on the right track and need to innovate and expand. Please consider the offer and sleep on the matter. I am prepared to renegotiate – for the right candidate and I am quite confident that you would fit in very well – we could double the salary and include share options after a year's service.

And….'

Alec, interjected before his formidable rival could say another word. 'My apologies for interrupting, but please, I must insist – I have to go. Thank you, but no thank you.'

Alec, recalling his previous run in with Kostas, fumed with exasperation as he slammed the phoned down. The man's arrogance, barely hidden by the veneer of cultivated respectability, did not bother Alec as much as it brought back painful memories of his school days. He could well imagine Kostas throwing his weight around and expecting instant obedience.

The conference call initiated by the Cypriot, after a long tirade against the Englishman, degenerated into a monologue about 'ways of skinning cats, flogging dead horses' and threats about 'running Alec out of town'. The participants in Bombay, London, Nairobi and Stone Town all commiserated without offering any solutions.

The Cypriot's offices in downtown Dubai, once the tallest skyscraper, had been dwarfed after several newer ones had popped up. He had never liked being second best so it was time to take the gloves off.

A day later a transcript of the call landed in Sam's office – hand delivered. Sam's eyes lit up – finally he could see his way forward. He knew it was time for Alec to meet Kay and more importantly for Kay to be paraded in public with Alec. He smiled, mischief in the air. He was looking forward to Alec's reaction. And, Dubai's. It was time the cat was put amongst the pigeons; predator and bait at the same time.

Within six months of Alec's arrival, the parent company had doubled in size with the merger or takeover of several small camel breeders and medium-sized camel hospitals. So much so that Alec was spending quite a bit of time streamlining these operations across all seven kingdoms. Their clinical teams expanded as well with more vets joining the company. Although Alec had sat on the interview panel, most of the candidates chosen were selected by the board's directors rather the clinicians.

The recruitment of new vets and technicians, yet again, was dominated by corporate profits rather than ethics. The board's emphasis on employing the Asians instead of Western expats delivered the same clinical expertise at a fraction of the costs.

Alec was beginning to worry that all these management issues were hampering clinical outcomes and performance because of the flagging morale. Friction about the workload and pay scales festered under the surface.

With the immense workload, sometimes Alec did not get back to the headquarters for days or weeks. He started delegating, depending more and more on his cohort of Asian vets. Alec's increasing absences and his reliance on Dr Reddy added fuel to the fire, intensifying the jockeying for position between the convent educated fluent English speakers and those who did not share these attributes. Dr Reddy's rapid elevation to a position of power, despite his modest origins, antagonised some of his colleagues.

The convent educated vets erroneously assumed that the directors would overrule Alec's choice so they were caught off guard when the board accepted and endorsed Dr Reddy's promotion to the deputy's role. Their rancour was directed more towards Dr Reddy, an easier target for their bitterness than Alec or the board.

Alec had sown the seeds of his own downfall and a maelstrom

was brewing out of control.

TEN

Sam, Dubai.

It was during this phase of galloping expansion and huge investor interest that Alec had a call from Sam.

'Habari, daktari. How are you?' Sam's booming voice came through as Alec prepared for a clinical-case conference at the hospital. A recent outbreak of mastitis in the milking camels had become problematic – milk production had dropped in the affected herds.

'Hi. Haven't heard from you in ages. I thought you were upset at my decision to decline the Kabete position.'

'I was initially but on reflection your decision makes sense. It may be too early to come back; you need time for closure. My only concern is that you might be vulnerable there. We have a fair insight into the transit routes used by the ivory traders,' Sam expounded.

'Alas, too many demons for me over there in Kenya. I suppose the possibility of the cartel being based here can't be discounted.'

'True. Anyway, the offer is still on the table. I am hearing great things about you and your state-of-the-art camel hospital. In a sense that's why I am calling. I have free time in Dubai after I finish my work there. Perhaps we can meet up?' Sam said and gave Alec the dates and the hotel that he was staying in.

'That's great. You are not too far from our offices in town. Look forward to seeing you soon,' Alec responded.

'I am bringing along a friend I want you to meet. Her name's Kay. She's attending a parasitology conference. Sorry, Alec, got to go,' Sam said and signed off before Alec could get a word in edgeways.

The Kenya Airways flight landed at Dubai airport on time. Sam and Kay were staying in different hotels as Kay's four-day sojourn had been arranged by the conveners of the parasitology conference.

Kay Patel's hotel, the Sheraton Grand, became a focal point for the trio – a short distance from the World Trade Centre. They met in the evening in the foyer – a table had been booked at the restaurant. Alec had been intrigued by Sam's reticence about the mystery woman.

Alec had arrived early, as he normally did, and was having a cup of gahwa, the Arabic coffee, when Sam walked in without his guest. The two greeted each other with gusto, the camaraderie between them quite apparent.

'Where's this mystery woman that you wanted me to meet?' Alec asked casually. He was used to Sam's pranks and was outwardly feigning a calm that he did not actually feel. It was too good to be true that it was all a co-incidence, Alec reflected with mounting anticipation.

Alec, after Sam disappeared towards the gents, was left scouring all the diners as they arrived and settled in. His eye was drawn to a couple of incoming guests but quickly dismissed them – both women found their friends in the busy throng of diners and walked past him.

As Alec twiddled his thumbs and waited impatiently for Sam

to end the bizarre game that he was playing, he looked around him at the other diners – a mixed crowd of ex-pats and locals. His gaze was drawn to a middle eastern lone diner who he thought was watching him. The man, in a linen suit a couple of sizes too small for his frame, quickly averted his gaze and got busy with rearranging the silver on his table. He had neatly lined up all the cutlery to his right. Just as Alec finished counting the seven pieces of silver, he was brought back by the exquisite perfume that wafted across him.

'Dr Dunlop, I presume? I am Kay Patel,' Kay said extending her hand, using the Dr prefix so commonly used by vets in Kenya. Sam had briefly mentioned that Alec had a small animal practice in South London and had recently taken up a clinical position with a specialist camel hospital.

Alec lurched and splattered the gahwa all over his white shirt and his Levi jeans, because Kay Patel was the spitting image of Ava. He stared in stunned disbelief at Kay, barely conscious of the coffee dripping down his shirt. The reflex tidy up exercise, a brief distraction to regain his poise, failed miserably as he silently mouthed : 'For the love of God! Sam had better have an explanation for this!' He managed to clean up most of the spilt coffee except for a small barely noticeable patch.

Alec, still smarting at Sam's callousness, hurriedly rose to shake the proffered hand. For a split second, he was transported back to Mombasa and to the flashing visuals of Ava as they sat listening to Makeba's song. Alec with a monumental effort at regaining control, smiled sheepishly at Kay; desperately ignoring the striking resemblance to Ava. Thankfully Kay was distracted by Sam's abrupt entry and missed the gamut of emotions being played out on his face.

Sam, annoying Alec even more by ignoring the frosty daggers-drawn look on his face, made the formal introductions.

Alec soon recovered and warmed to the graceful scientist, her exceptional dusky looks drawing appreciative glances from the other men; much to the annoyance of their female partners. For a split second, there was a hush on the surrounding tables, broken by the deliberate efforts of the female companions to deflect attention away from the beauty and her two male companions.

Alec was smitten – he could not take his eyes off Kay who almost melted under his intense scrutiny. The flushed look enhanced her almost translucent complexion which made her look Persian. Alec gulped and looked away to regain his composure. His annoyance with Sam diminishing by the minute.

'You did not warn me that Kay is the spitting image of Ava,' Alec said in an accusatory tone. Before a sheepish Sam could respond, Alec looking directly at Kay, explained: 'You have a striking resemblance to Ava, a common friend of ours – almost as if you are her identical twin. Ava died in a drowning accident,' Alec added, after the briefest of pauses.

'I am sorry to hear that.' Kay demurred softly looking at Alec and then at Sam. Alec felt guilty for having raised the spectre of Ava. It wasn't Kay's fault that she looked like his dead...what had she been? Girlfriend? Lover? Either way, Alec felt bad for making Kay feel awkward.

Sam, suitably contrite, passed the menu to Kay and Alec as he summoned a waiter. The dinner passed in a flash, as is common when the food, the décor and the company all gel. Alec had instinctively taken to Kay, the initial awkwardness forgotten as the dinner progressed. Before dessert arrived, Kay excused herself to go to the ladies.

'Dammit, why didn't you warn me?' Alec rasped, barely controlling his temper. He took a few deep breaths before trusting himself to ask: 'What the hell were you trying to prove? We'll lock horns later as she might pop back. Anyway, where did you meet her?

Alec's gamut of emotions – awe, confusion, attraction and instant rapport – to Kay's out-of-the- blue presence, were reactions that Sam had hoped for and anticipated; albeit with some amount of guilt. His pleasure at his friend's expense, although tinged with contrition, was all in a good cause – he was pleased that the two were hitting it off.

'She used to work for us and then took a sabbatical to finish her PhD in Parasitology. Kay re-joined the wildlife department recently – got back from London a few weeks ago. I met her at a departmental conference and, just like you, her striking resemblance to Ava threw me as well.'

'Just a thought, but is it safe – the cartel may think she is Ava, just as I did?' Alec enquired.

'I am hoping that they do – maybe flush them out,' Sam said. 'I am hoping that we can convince Kay to assist us. With the investigation stalled, we might need to use entrapment tactics; bait the cartel.'

As they left the restaurant, Alec's gaze was again drawn to the table nearby - the lone diner had left. Alec noticed that the pattern of seven pieces of forks, knives and spoons lay undisturbed on the right.

Before the two friends parted in the lobby – Kay had already retired to her room – Sam briefly explained that he had plenty of loose ends to tie-up; the Laikipia investigation had ground to a halt for now, despite following leads to London, Bombay and Dubai. Sam's enquiries abroad had resulted in more questions than any definitive answers; the trail had gone cold.

Although he had initially thought that the 'epicentre' was in Dubai, his gut feeling was that maybe, just maybe, that's what the cartel wanted the authorities to believe. The cartel's arrogance was in assuming that the Kenyan team was ill equipped – financially and intellectually – to handle a complex multinational case and that the Kenyan team would soon give up.

More than ever, it firmed up Sam's resolve to persist. He had taken a personal oath that, irrespective of the end result, he would pursue Shenzi and deliver justice – his retribution for the brutal death of the two wardens.

'I need you, my friend, to go along with me on this,' Sam entreated. Alec nodded his assent, not quite sure what he was getting into.

Once the conference was over, Alec assumed the role of a tour guide as this was Kay's maiden visit to the Emirates. Although Alec would have preferred Kay to witness, first-hand, the parasitological impact of tick, mite and fly infestations on the camel herds, they never quite had the time. She just about managed to see Dubai city's highlights – dune safari, visit to a wadi, sailing the creek in a dhow and a belly dance extravaganza in the desert.

ELEVEN

Musa, Dubai

Just as Alec and Kay were returning to the hotel after their day in the desert, they bumped into a private tour guide and his clients.

Alec casually glanced at an opulently dressed Indian male and his female partner. They were discussing the dune safari – in an alien language, interspersed with English words.

Just behind them was a stocky man who looked distinctly familiar, Alec thought, as the man was studiously scrolling through stapled pages; totally oblivious to his surroundings. He was struggling, eyes screwed up in the dim light.

'Musa!' Alec blurted out as the man came into focus in the fading light; the glow from the parking lights of the limo providing the only illumination. Alec had to shout to drown out the blaring Arabic melody from the massive speakers mounted around the marquee.

The man almost jumped out of his skin and looked past Alec – his sight fixated on Kay as if he had seen a ghost before he focused on the tall figure.

'Alec! What on earth are you doing here?' Musa asked, still half looking at Kay, almost in a daze and not believing his eyes – his brain flummoxed.

Alec introduced Musa to Kay as Musa briefly mentioned that he had just completed a short shoot for his client, a Bollywood producer. Musa introduced the portly Bollywood producer and his young leading lady. Alec was officious but courteous without paying much attention to the producer, his wide-eyed gaze drawn to the man's female companion.

Despite the dim light, her sculpted features were enhanced by the interplay of light and shadows, very much like the haunting retro look of an Ingrid Bergman movie. The lady was exquisitely attired in a pair of tight- fitting designer jeans and a low-cut blouse; Bollywood's answer to the Brigette Bardot look. It felt like an eternity before Alec could drag his eyes away and he wondered if the actress could have got away with that brazen show of flesh in downtown Dubai.

The woman looked radiant and elegant; every inch the Miss India pageant winner that she was. The Bollywood star in the making had, after winning several other local pageants, been signed up by an elite modelling agency. The producer, on the judges panel of the Miss India contest, had signed her up well before the rumours of their secret wedding started doing the rounds.

On a previous assignment in Bombay, Musa had been introduced to the producer who had professed an interest in his bespoke safaris; a full package that included filming their entire honeymoon in Kenya, with a stopover in Dubai. The producer, aware that the Kenyans were keen to give tax incentives for filming in the country, had approached Musa for advice.

Musa's aspirations to gain entry into Bollywood gained momentum when the producer, in turn, agreed to assist in raising the finance for Musa's directorial debut – as long as his wife was offered the lead role. The quid pro quo arrangement suited both parties and a memorandum of understanding was duly signed.

Alec smiled at the young woman as he turned to Musa who was still staring at Kay, his mouth agape. Alec excused himself as he pulled Musa away.

'I know what you are thinking,' Alec said looking at Kay who was making small talk with the gorgeous starlet. 'I was fooled as well.'

'She's the spitting image of Ava,' Musa barely managed to articulate the words, still gawking at Kay. For a brief moment, both old friends, looking at Kay, were transported to their dinner with Ava at the Orange Coral in Mombasa.

After a brief stilted conversation with Alec, Musa excused himself, explaining that they were flying to Nairobi in a day or two for the bespoke safari which included Laikipia, Mount Kenya and Masai Mara.

Musa whispered his admiration of Alec's date and winked in a conspiratorial gesture. He promised to keep in touch with Alec as he backtracked his way towards the limo and his clients.

All the way back to Jumeira Beach Hotel, where he was staying with the Indian couple, Musa had a surreal feeling about the out-of-the-blue meeting with Alec and Kay. With all that had happened between Ava and Alec, he wondered how Alec was coping with an Ava-lookalike entering the fray. He certainly would not want to be in Alec's shoes.

It was a pensive Musa who flew back to Nairobi the next day with the Bollywood couple. An exhausting shoot of the Dubai-Kenya trip had been suddenly thrown into disarray by the accidental meeting with Alec and Kay. He could not eject Kay out of his mind nor could he banish Ava from his thoughts; a state of mind not too dissimilar to Alec's.

TWELVE

Alec, Dubai

Alec was preoccupied along similar lines - the encounter with Musa in the desert had brought back vividly the trauma of Ava's disappearance and the subsequent abrupt news of her demise. The upsurge of memories and the dark intrusive connotations sent an involuntary shiver down his spine. His pain was still palpable – made more acute by the sudden appearance of Kay in his life. His recent interaction with her was still fresh in his mind and he wondered, not for the first time, if there was a purpose to all that had transpired recently.

'What is it that they say? We meet people for a reason, even if it is very transitory,' Alec murmured to himself. Now that Kay had appeared in his life, he was apprehensive about the future.

Shortly after Kay returned to Nairobi, Alec ploughed back into his work with a vengeance – the time spent with Kay was a welcome break from his hectic schedules but he was aware of the pressures that Dr Reddy and his team were under. His deputy had managed to hold the fort in his absence with tact – despite the tensions that existed between the warring factions.

Alec met Sam for a drink the next day before Sam's flight to

Bombay. He wondered about the globetrotting Sam – both of them had come a long way from that hot dusty evening in Laikipia; their lives intertwined since that confrontation in Laikipia.

Sam did not elaborate but his imminent trip to Bombay was more a matter of following through with the links thrown up by the Mombasa raids. The false cargo invoices found in the Mombasa warehouses were the only tangible links to Bombay. Sam was not very optimistic and was convinced that it would probably be a dead end or he would be stonewalled.

He asked by way of distracting himself, 'You seem edgy and overwrought – are you happy working in this restrictive environment?'

Sam had noticed Alec's frustration. The bureaucratic processes and the onus of being answerable to the shareholders were issues that weighed heavily on him. The novelty, and the sense of adventure were wearing thin; his romanticised version of Dubai finally encountering the real one.

He was a fish out of water in the uber-rich backwaters of a trading outpost where, unlike his open and unrestricted lifestyle in the UK, the closed nature of society came with shackles. While he had adapted to his new clinical duties, the onus of dealing with cultural and political aspects of his CEO role became challenging especially as the managerial functions were impacting on his clinical role.

Something had to give. He was glad that Dr Reddy seemed to be on top of things, especially with the political sabre rattling between the board and the clinical teams.

'I may have erred in coming here. With the 20/20 vision of hindsight, I should have accepted your Kabete offer – the professional discipline of academia and the ethos of a teaching hospital – the vet school at Kabete – are more my style.' Alec responded rather wistfully, a contemplative look in his eyes. He had been guilty of chasing dollars in the desert.

He felt weary and jaded, although the sudden appearance of Kay and her youthful exuberance had perked him up. Suddenly, Kenya and Kay seemed far more appealing.

'I wasn't aware, when I accepted the job, that I was walking into a geo-political mess,' Alec continued, his face showing the strain of his juggling act between his clinical and non-clinical roles; the two warring groups adding to his burden.

'What exactly are you referring to?' Sam was perplexed at the change in Alec's tone.

'I have had my eyes peeled since I arrived. The double standards - in how I am treated as a British expat compared to the Asians. And then add the constant bickering about professional hierarchy and pay scales and we have a recipe for disaster. I am no Henry Kissinger, just an 'imposter' Lawrence of Arabia.' Alec sighed and looked at Sam with a wry smile, not sure if Sam understood his dilemma.

Sam, noting the deepening worry lines on his friend's visage, patted Alec on the shoulder. 'The offer is still open, so let me know if you get fed up with the heat and the sand. If you ever are in a bind here, give me a call. We have a lot of goodwill here. Strictly off the record, I can pull levers here as well if needed.'

Alec acknowledged his thanks. 'I will bear that in mind.' Little did he know that he'd have to call upon Sam soon, very soon.

After Sam's departure, Alec threw himself into his work. Just as he was getting to grips with it all, Dr Reddy walked in with a grave look on his face. A look that Alec had seen many a time before – especially when India was losing on the cricket field.

Dr Reddy had always boasted about his cricketing track record – that he had captained his university cricket team for several consecutive years; an unbeaten feat. Strangely, Alec noted that Dr Reddy rarely mentioned his alma mater back in Bangalore – except when it came to cricket. And yet, as a cricket enthusiast, Dr Reddy's reluctance to play in the local tournaments seemed at odds with his passion for the game. His usual excuse was that he had enough on his plate - the camel hospital and the racing calendar taking up most of his time.

'Why the glum look – don't tell me that we have another outbreak of mastitis on our hands? Or even worse, India got thrashed?' Alec loved to rib his deputy although making fun of the Indian's allegiance to his national team was dangerous, especially if India was on the receiving end.

'Yes, unfortunately. It looks as though we have a resistant strain – just got the culture results; Staph aureus positive. All under control though – we've isolated the milking ones and started intra-mammary antibiotics. But that's not why I'm here,' Reddy continued after a dramatic pause, anticipating Alec's full attention. 'It's Dr Joshi – the trap that we had laid has worked.' Dr Reddy paused again to see if Alec was listening.

'You know the drill – isolate, treat and manage. Hopefully, milk production won't be too impacted. Now, what about Dr Joshi?' Alec frowned at the thought of the huge sums lost in stock pilferage. The spate of recent drug stock thefts had been flagged by the in-house stock control procedures.

Just before Alec's brief break whilst Sam and Kay were in town, they had discussed the issue – the sporadic theft of expensive meds from the clinic's pharmacy. The thefts soon became entrenched and endemic. Both of them realised that the matter needed to be nipped in the bud before the stock deficits became unmanageable and needed to be declared to the board. The culprit, having got away with the initial smaller thefts, was getting bolder - with bigger and more frequent pilferages.

Alec's sombre tone and total attention placated the agitated vet; cricket and the outbreak of summer mastitis pushed out of the frame in the face of a grave ongoing crisis.

The hospitals and the stables only used branded products – the consignments were delivered directly by the manufacturers, not via local wholesalers. Most of the pharma stock was flown in from Europe under special deals struck by the board at a hefty discount. In return, the board ensured full access to the manufacturers for advertising and other promotional campaigns. The huge popularity of the racing events and camel auctions created marketing opportunities for all concerned. With the presence of large expatriate communities, even pet foods and small animal medications became winners.

It was a mutually beneficial arrangement. The downside was that these branded products commanded a premium price on the black market, so unscrupulous employees were tempted into stealing, despite the risk of arrest, instant dismissal, deportation, prison or even a public flogging.

Although Alec had initially resisted Dr Reddy's proposal of installing secret cameras, he had to yield to using entrapment as the only resort.

'We've got him on tape – the evidence is here.' Reddy pointed to the tape that he had placed on Alec's desk. They moved to the board room so that Alec could be appraised of the evidence. Alec watched in grim silence, his anger mounting, as the tape rolled.

'Just dismiss him – make sure he signs a statement to that effect.' Alec said as his brow furrowed with rage. Despite Dr Reddy's advice that the police be informed, Alec decided to avoid going down that route. The scandal of a long drawn-out affair and the punitive measures of licence and visa cancellation, public flogging and imprisonment deterred him.

Although he did not verbalise his thoughts, he had some sympathy for the poorly paid Asian staff, a serious situation created by the double standards that existed.

Alec did not want to be embroiled in a cause celebre case – he knew that with the tension existing between the factions, the fallout would be very divisive and disruptive. The fact that the trap had been set by Dr Reddy would be used to conjure up a conspiracy scenario.

Once Dr Reddy had agreed with him, Alec advised the board that it was best to just walk away. Dr Joshi was asked to resign once a non-disclosure agreement had been signed meaning that both parties were bound, mutually, not to disclose confidential information.

Two months later, Alec bumped into Kostas at a Dubai racing event. Alec was greeted like a long-lost brother. Alec again politely refused the job offer and joined Dr Reddy at the lunch that had been arranged.

As they were leaving the event after the prize-giving ceremony, Kostas made it a point to come over and bid his farewell.

'Dr Dunlop, I forgot to introduce you to our new deputy chief of clinics and operations, Dr Joshi.' Kostas gestured towards the beaming vet as he came over and shook hands with Alec and pointedly ignored Dr Reddy. The snub was apparent only to the two Asian vets – the others, including Alec, missed the underlying current of hostility between the two professionals.

Dr Reddy was unusually subdued as the Toyota Cruiser made its way back towards their hospital campus.

'Penny for your thoughts?' Alec asked as the massive four-wheel drive vehicle cut across the sand dunes – they were briefly stopping at one of their outstations because one of the camels had been limping at an earlier exercise session. They had decided to have a quick look and have a short comfort break. Alec quite liked the strong coffee that the desert café served; strong and bitter with an aftertaste of cardamom and cinnamon.

'We should have reported him to the police,' Dr Reddy blurted out, not looking at Alec and instead gazing out at some of the camels being put through their paces. 'I fear he may retaliate in some way, now that he has inveigled himself into our rival's establishment. Things here move in strange, oblique ways. Connections are everything – higher the link up the hierarchy, greater the power wielded.' Dr Reddy's voice reflected the gravity of their predicament. The Indian wasn't convinced that the matter had ended and expected more ripples to follow.

'Well, we have a signed confession from him so I am sure he would not want to incriminate himself to his new employer. Kostas is not stupid. he would not want to harbour a corrupt vet – that would harm the professional reputation of his stables and his organisation,' Alec countered, although his voice failed to carry any conviction. He earnestly hoped that he had made the right decision in not reporting the matter to the police.

'I hope that you are right and this has been buried,' the Indian said wistfully. Dr Reddy fervently hoped that Alec, whom he admired for his clinical acumen and for his outspoken 'no nonsense, straight from the shoulder' methods, did not become a pawn in the emotionally charged board room politics. If they went after Alec then his position would become even more precarious. Dr Reddy was aware that the board would sooner pick on him than the Brit; he was eminently dispensable.

Kostas had his fingers in many pies and more importantly, it would be suicidal to ignore the man's ego and his ambition to dominate the corporate landscape – to be the best camel racing and hospital group. The stakes were very high and, in the corporate world that Kostas inhabited, winning was everything. Any which way.

The altercation had just started. It was a powder keg waiting to explode and Alec was, unwittingly, the fuse that had started it all.

With the start of the new racing calendar in November, Alec and his team, were too thinly spread on the ground. Between controlling the mastitis outbreak, managing the camels –both racing and milk herds – and complying with the stringent protocols of good governance, it was a busy time for everyone, especially for the newly recruited interns and stable hands.

On reflection, Alec acknowledged that this was probably the time when the error occurred, which led to the racing authority opening an investigation into suspected doping. At the outset, when his team received a notification about an audit of their clinical protocols, it was viewed as a random audit rather than a specific complaint.

Shergari, one of their upcoming racing stars, won the Gold Cup with the top prize of $200,000, on debut in the first event of the racing calendar.

Alec and his team were feted at the post-race celebrations. Alec had just made it back after attending to a difficult calving in Sharjah – one of their clinical hubs. The euphoria of the win was short lived when an initial notice was followed up by a phone call putting the stables on notice for further action.

Next morning when the inspectors arrived at the stables to quarantine the winner, Alec rushed into an emergency board meeting – the directors had been informed that the two urine samples collected before and after the race had tested positive for ketoprofen. Consequently, the remittance of the $200,000 prize money had been suspended, pending a full official enquiry.

The presence of ketoprofen metabolites in Shergari's urine was central to the allegations of impropriety – an illegal attempt to influence the race results. The authority's allegation was that ketoprofen, a painkiller, had been used fraudulently as a performance enhancing drug.

Whilst, the administration of ketoprofen in cases of injury or lameness was accepted therapy, its use was banned in racing camels within four days of any competitive event.

Alec and his team refuted the charge categorically – both Alec and Dr Reddy had full confidence in the team's compliance protocols. Alec was incandescent with rage.

Addressing the board and the investigating team, Alec declared: 'I recall I was in Sharjah when I took the call from Dr Reddy – this was...'

The chief investigating officer, a prominent solicitor, who had been head-hunted to chair the forensic team, interjected quite abruptly: 'When was this – date and time of the call?'

Alec, annoyed at the apparent hostility and abrupt manner, continued: 'I was just about to. This was Friday 27th of November – three days before the race. However, my clinical team has admitted that ketoprofen and dexamethasone were prescribed for Kismet, who had presented with acute lameness during an exercise routine – the treated camel did not participate in the race. I am sure there is some confusion – Shergari wasn't prescribed anything in adherence to the race protocols. Could the positive result be an aberration, an error? What about the mandatory second-sample testing and spectrometric confirmation?' Alec was battling to control his anger; the accusatory and biased tone of the audit team had put his back up.

The audit team stood frozen and looked to the solicitor for guidance. For some of the younger Emiratis this was their first face-to-face close encounter with a Brit. They were so accustomed to the Asian vets that most of them found it difficult to understand Alec's rapid delivery and diction. Alec's apparent over-the-top reaction was partly due to the use of Arabic; he had found this unnerving even at board meetings, despite the presence of competent translators. The solicitor, knowing that the Brit would be on the back foot, capitalised on Alec's discomfort. He continued to pepper his arguments with Arabic phrases.

Dr Reddy, reading the annoyance on Alec's face, shuffled his feet and avoided eye contact with Alec, worried that the Brit was in danger of alienating the panel.

'Absolutely. Yes. That's why we are here – the second urine

sample was also positive,' the solicitor retorted quite smugly. 'We have looked at the clinical notes of all the camels – Kismet, the alleged lame camel, has no treatment protocol listed. There is an entry, endorsed by Dr Kingsley, for the administration of the two aforementioned drugs...' The solicitor paused briefly to look around and then completed the sentence, '...to Shergari. Not, I repeat, not to Kismet, the lame one.'

As the import of the solicitor's words sunk in, Alec looked at Dr Reddy and wondered, for the first time, if Dr Kingsley had blundered in mixing up the case notes.

'Friday the 27th? On a holiday? Would you say only a skeletal team would be present on the site? The probing continued, abrasive and relentless.

'We have clinical rotas to ensure both clinical and support staff are on duty,' Alec rebutted. He was, after more than a year in the UAE, still not used to Friday as the day off rather than the weekend.

After a heated debate that lasted for almost an hour and with recriminations levelled at the clinical team, Alec and Dr Reddy belatedly realised that Dr Kingsley, the new intern, had injected the wrong camel. Instead of treating Kismet, the limping camel, he had treated Shergari. Alec reluctantly acknowledged that an error had occurred; a serious lapse considering the race result. Both Dr Reddy and Alec were puzzled at the apparent mix up – camels participating in any competitions were not only isolated but stabled away from the other non-participating camels.

The smug cat-got-the cream look on the solicitor's face told its own tale. Alec realised that there had been deficits in protocol – Dr Kingsley, an intern under the tutelage of Dr Reddy, had not followed procedures. A serious lapse under any circumstances but all the more damning in this case because of racing protocols. Alec offered his unreserved apology to the forensic team which was followed by a written one.

Dr Joshi and Kostas both celebrated when the local news carried a brief indictment of lax practices at Alec's hospital. Swift action by the race authorities was taken – Shergari was stripped off the trophy and the prize money and a full investigation initiated, pending further legal action.

After a protracted hearing behind closed doors, it was finally concluded that a performance-enhancing drug had been administered to a race participant. Whilst the enquiry could not prove, beyond a reasonable doubt, that there was malicious intent by Alec's staff to manipulate the outcome of the race, Alec's clinical team was guilty of not following clinical protocols and a total failure to supervise an intern. The allegation by the authority's solicitor that Kismet was deliberately kept in the same stable as Shergari, as a decoy in the event that an alibi was needed later on, was struck down as pure conjecture. The authority's action was deferred till an appeal could be lodged by Alec's team.

In due course, the authority dropped all charges of premeditated malicious intent and upheld the minor charge of negligence – protocols not followed and Dr Reddy's lack of supervision of an intern.

Eventually, the authorities suspended Dr Reddy's licence indefinitely and a hefty fine was imposed; effectively it meant that the Indian vet could not sustain himself in the UAE. Dr Kingsley, surprisingly let off with a caution, resigned and left without any explanation.

On a matter of principle, Alec fought for his deputy and sought to have the suspension revoked. He argued that as the CEO, he should have been held responsible, not Dr Reddy. The action against Dr Reddy was unfair especially as Dr Kingsley had ignored all clinical protocols. Alec even offered his resignation if the authority spared Dr Reddy. The pleas fell on deaf ears.

Alec came away from the hearing feeling that justice had not been served and had a sneaking suspicion that even the directors of the group, his employers, had their own agenda and were using the Asian vets as scapegoats.

On the way back to the campus, Alec voiced his concerns to his deputy.

'I'm sorry Dr Reddy for not being able to save your job. If anything, I did fight for you and the team by offering my resignation. I had hoped that by taking responsibility for the actions that led to this mess, you could be spared. Anyway, just so you know, I have already resigned in protest – I have decided to return to my practice in London. What about you?' Alec enquired looking at his deputy who seemed quite at peace despite the adverse consequences that he faced.

'Thank you for your support. However, you should not have given in. I have a sneaky feeling that there is an agenda, an ulterior motive, to all this. Even possible collusion between Kostas and Dr Joshi and, maybe, Dr Kingsley. We shall soon know. I am heading back to India. I can go back to private practice if I can't get a faculty position.'

Alec looked at his deputy's inscrutable expression and marvelled at his calm composure and remarked: 'I must say you are taking this quite well. Considering that you and your wife will have to uproot and go back.'

'I have dealt with much worse turns in my life. This will pass as well,' Dr Reddy replied in a matter of fact tone.

That was their last conversation about the case.

While Dr Reddy was in the process of winding down and returning to India, unknown to both, there were discussions behind closed doors about Dr Reddy's imminent arrest and possible expulsion from the UAE as a 'persona non grata.' The charges could also lead to a public flogging.

In order to make the case cast- iron, Kostas's minions were hell bent on politicising the case and bringing forward a criminal case against Dr Reddy. Although the case was still being dealt by the licensing board, there were proposals to involve the immigration authorities.

To further complicate matters, an additional criminal charge was levied at the last moment – the use and sale of expired medicines.

The charge was brought against the commercial wholesaling section of the hospital; a case of fraud. The two-pronged strategy of implicating clinical and commercial negligence meant that the group's operations would be severely compromised. The direct impact would then be on the company's share price – a plunge in its market value.

The board and Alec were the last to know of the impending leak to the media – once the matter was in the public domain the impact on the company's share price would be immediate and devastating. It would not take long for a predator to acquire enough company stock to make a hostile move. The writing was on the wall – Kostas would swoop and take over the company.

Alec also realised that his status as a British expat had afforded him protection. It would be easier to implicate Dr Reddy, the weak link in the chain, who would then be at the mercy of the new directors of the merged companies.

More importantly, Alec would not be able to save the Indian vet from prison and/or a public flogging for fraud. Alec and his team were stunned by the rapidity with which the case had progressed – a clinical accident was one thing but fraudulent trading would be hard to defend.

Within a month, Kostas's hospital group swooped and took over Alec's clinic and all other facilities. The steep decline in the company's share price, after the heavily publicised scandal, made it a sitting duck. It was easy for Kostas to buy up the depressed shares and acquire a majority holding in the group.

Days later, when Alec heard that Dr Joshi had become the chief vet at the merged and combined corporate entity, he reappraised the chain of events and recalled Dr Reddy's words regarding a conspiracy and collusion.

Finally, it all made sense – the head-hunting approaches, Dr Joshi's defection to Kostas's team and the gloating and acrimonious statements made by Kostas's team following the ketoprofen enquiry.

The muddied waters became crystal clear when Dr Joshi, the chief group vet, recruited Dr Kingsley to the Kostas group. Very soon, some of the vets from Alec's team resigned and joined Kostas and Dr Joshi. The cleansing operation against those perceived to be loyal to Alec was absolute and complete.

Just before Kostas's group gained control of Alec's hospital, Sam had a call from Dubai and his blood turned cold. The caller was specific and to the point.

Sam caught the next flight to Dubai – forewarning his connections that he needed their help. He managed to catch Alec just as he was leaving for a board meeting where the merger with the Kostas group was going to be debated and voted in.

Alec listened intently to Sam – it took just a few minutes for Sam to draw a picture of dire consequences for Alec's continued stay in Dubai and more importantly, for Dr Reddy. Alec made quick notes as Sam guided him through what he needed to do – his contacts in Dubai had given Sam the broad outline of actions to be taken within the next 48 hours. After that everything would be in the public domain – then the law would take its own course; a public flogging a strong possibility.

Both went to Dr Reddy's staff quarters.

'Morning Dr Reddy. May we come in?' Dr Reddy had not been forewarned as Alec did not want the Indian to panic and give the game away. The Indian vet's surprise was genuine.

'Of course, please come in.' He was looking at Sam wondering what Alec was up to so early in the day. He knew about the board meeting.

When Alec introduced Sam and explained the purpose of their visit, Dr Reddy sank back into his armchair, confused and pleased that Alec was true to his word about assisting him in any which way he could. The discussion was briefly halted as Mrs Reddy came in with cups of South Indian coffee.

As soon as she left after exchanging pleasantries, Alec continued: 'You were right back then – we should have reported Dr Joshi to the police. We probably would not be in this mess today if we had. Obviously, someone must have planted the outdated stock or deliberately not taken it off the shelf. Anyway, Sam here has inside info that there are moves to use the false charges of fraud against the company to create problems – specifically for you.'

Dr Reddy listened in rapt attention, knowing fully well the implications – imprisonment, public flogging and the tortuous way things would progress while he would be thrown to the dogs. His immediate concern was about his wife and his family back home; all dependent on him.

Alec continued, quite contrite for having heaped all the troubles on his Indian deputy: 'Here, keep this statement for your record. I have issued a payment – your wages to-date and a pro-rata bonus remittance. This will save you the bother of chasing Kostas for your accrued payments,' Alec said as he handed the statement to Dr Reddy.

After Sam's call, Alec had instructed the accounts department to finalise Dr Reddy's accrued salary to avoid any interference once Kostas gained full control of the company.

'Sam has inside information of impending action against you. He has suggested that you and your wife catch the first available flight out of here. Go before we lose control.'

Sam who had hardly said anything, extended his hand to Dr Reddy. 'Good luck and Godspeed. I have it from the highest authority that no one will question you about your travel plans – you have 48 hours to fly out. Contact him, he's expecting your call,' Sam said as he handed over a business card.

Dr Reddy was moved to tears. 'Thank you for your help – both of you. I will not forget this favour.' As they left, Mrs. Reddy gave Alec a small statuette of Ganesh, the Indian deity.

'We believe in him as the Protector. Carry it with you – small enough to slip into your wallet as a good luck charm.'

Alec and Sam shook hands with the couple and left; Alec was sure that he would not see his deputy again. As an after-thought, just as they were leaving, Alec said: 'We've never had dinner together at my place, why don't you and Mrs Reddy join us tonight? Sam is staying the night so we can have a proper farewell dinner.'

Dr Reddy hesitated briefly, looking at his wife for guidance, but she politely declined. She said to her husband: 'Why don't you, it will take your mind off the events of the last few days?'

Dr Reddy readily agreed to come over later on. As Sam and Alec returned to the villa, Alec stopped over and had a word with the chef at the canteen – to arrange for food to be delivered to the villa at 8pm.

The three of them had a pleasant evening discussing politics, ivory and the poaching problems that Africa faced, especially Kenya. All through, the telly was broadcasting a cricket match being played at Lords – a charity match to raise funds for wildlife conservation. None of them were paying much attention to the televised match.

When the phone rang, Alec excused himself to take the call from Kay in his study. He was away for a good 15 mins and when he returned, he caught a few stray words about the match – it seemed to him that Sam was debating a cricketing rule and the umpire's decision. Both of them ceased talking about the match at Alec's entry.

Alec remembered later that the meal had been pleasant and after almost two hours Dr Reddy decided to return to his wife – guilty that she had been toiling away at their villa. They parted with Alec promising to keep in touch and even inviting Dr Reddy and his wife to

Kenya for a Masai Mara safari.

Within days, the details of the alleged fraud were leaked to the media. The pieces fell into place like clockwork; the Kostas Group bought controlling shares at next to nothing and swooped; taking full control.

Alec left for Nairobi well before the domino pieces fell into place – the havoc that was caused by the false allegations and the repercussions. He knew that Kostas and his cronies could not have harmed him in any way and he was thankful to Sam for his timely intervention in saving his deputy from untold misery. It was a relief and reassuring that his deputy had made a timely exit from Dubai; the best outcome under the circumstances.

Just before Alec left Dubai, the grubby-fingered spice trader received another message – after a long break. He nonchalantly dropped the small hand-written message at its designated drop point.

The recipient of the message in Bombay placed a call to Dubai.

'He'll soon be on a flight to Nairobi – to your backyard,' Kostas said smugly to the caller from Bombay. 'As per our deal, I have gained control of the merged group and you have your man.'

Kostas had no hesitation in co-operating with the caller. He had no interest in whatever that was cooking in Bombay and in Kenya. He had full control of the merged groups and was well on the way to establishing a monopoly of the camel hospitals.

THIRTEEN

Dharavi, Bombay, India.

The constant interference on the line and the noise in the small ramshackle office in an unassuming corner of the densely populated Dharavi area, made the telephone conversation barely audible.

The two – caller and recipient – were at different ends of the spectrum of order and chaos; Dharavi, the slum in Bombay, probably financed the careers of many who had made it to Dubai. In fact, the recipient, sitting in his slumlord office in Dharavi, controlled substantial swathes of businesses in downtown Dubai; including the swanky office building the caller was lounging in.

The caller in his air-conditioned office in Dubai having visited Bombay and especially Dharavi, Asia's largest slum, on many occasions, waited patiently for the clicks interspersed with buzzing sounds and crackling to subside. He had to distance the phone from his ear to avoid the noise then promptly brought the handset back into play as he heard the distinct voice, full of authority with an abrasive intonation.

'Hello', said the Dubai caller. 'We have set the ball rolling. He's heading back to Nairobi and the camels are heading our way.' The scandal splashed across most newspapers was the reason for the call.

'Shabash. Well done. You know the drill. Have you started working on it?' asked the Dharavi caller, raising his voice to overcome the disturbance down the line. The cacophony of blaring horns, hawkers selling their wares and the sounds of the heavy machinery did not help.

The front of the warehouse was a hive of activity as a consignment of animal bones, skins and other animal waste from slaughterhouses was being off loaded. The lorries, laden with several consignments, were parked further away to avoid blocking the narrow lanes. The throngs of coolies sweltered in the heat as body odour and the stench from the open sewers assaulted the senses. Their frenzied unloading of the consignment assumed a brief urgency as the monsoon deluge trickled to a drizzle.

In a corner, farther into the dark interior, children and adults squatted on the uneven mud floor sawing the buffalo, goat and sheep bones into smaller pieces. The assembly line of workers further along loaded the pieces into wheelbarrows and a team of adult women, some with their faces veiled by the ends of their ragged saris, emptied the bones into large vats boiling and bubbling over huge coal fires. The congealed mass, after repeated processes of boiling and filtration, would be eventually rendered into gelatine. The entire gelatine end product was meant only for export - not for local use - to Kenya exclusively. The Kenyan importer, based in Nairobi, used the gelatine in the manufacture of capsule shells. Nothing was wasted – even the remnants of bone were rendered into bone meal for animal feeds.

'Well, not yet. We have a problem with both operatives in Mombasa. Both have become liabilities. That needs to be resolved.'

'How so? We need the buibui woman for further assignments.

Placate her for now; the other one is very dispensable – his debts have become unmanageable and with the Bollywood strike here, his movie won't be released. Once, he's out of the way, we'll deal with the buibui insurgent. First though, send in the sanitisers – retrieve the Laikipia film.' The impatience in the Dharavi voice was obvious and menacing.

'Easier said than done,' said the lugubrious voice in Dubai. The minute the words slipped out, he regretted them; boss man did not like to be challenged. He waited a split second too long to temper his words with conciliatory noises.

Before he could cajole and waffle, the man retorted: 'Saala, mujay sikhata hai. Don't teach me, you idiot. Just do it and if you can't, then let me know – it will take me a single phone call to activate the 'supari', contract killing.'

Before the matter could descend into a monologue of expletives in colloquial Hindi, which the caller struggled to understand at the best of times, Dubai disconnected. For all he knew, the Dharavi mongrel may well have put a contract on his life. The mongrel had become unstable since his foray into Kenya had reaped untold riches; everyone had benefitted but some more than others. The minion, sitting in Dubai, wondered, not for the first time, if the spoils were going to materialise at all. He hadn't seen any so far, the Dharavi beast's excuse was that the proceeds had been re-invested.

FOURTEEN

Sam and Alec, Nairobi.

Sam, as he waited for Alec's flight to land, mulled over the recent events. The warning call from Dubai about Alec's troubles had been unnerving. Sam had always felt that his friend would be stifled by the lack of freedom and control in Dubai – the Emirati directors could be a fickle lot; fickle and dangerous.

He had used his contacts to sound out the vet school in Kabete; the wildlife fraternity had a good rapport with the academicians. He had used his considerable charm and persuasive tactics to land Alec a visiting lecturer's position. The immigration approval and the temporary veterinary licence were the easy bits. The warning from Dubai hastened the process and Alec accepted the one-year tenure with heartfelt gratitude.

Alec's enforced departure from Dubai meant that someone was orchestrating his friend's return to Kenya. It occurred to Sam that he needn't have gone to all that bother with setting up Kay as bait. Only time would tell if Alec relocating to Kenya was going to be conducive to the investigation. Sam smiled. He was learning Alec's lingo; translocation to a safe haven was just about right.

Whoever it was must know that Alec was under his protection and must feel confident that they wielded more control in Kenya than in the Emirates. Maybe the cartel did not want to take chances, too close to its home territory? Sam had assumed that cartel was operating out of Dubai but this new development brought Kenya back into the equation.

He sighed – the jigsaw was still muddled – and muttered 'pole, pole' under his breath as he saw Alec chatting animatedly with the pretty air hostess escorting him towards the VIP lounge. He would have to watch over Alec like a hawk. The cartel may well try the same tactics as they had done in the UAE.

Sam wondered, not for the first time, if his secondment from Kenya CID to the anti-poaching unit of the wildlife service had been compromised after the Laikipia events. The cartel was always a step ahead.

A lot was riding on how things shaped up from hereon. 'Pole, pole' was indeed a mantra that all of them had to adhere to. They were nowhere near nailing the culprits.

Alec's return to Nairobi was partly driven by his new-found fascination for Kay. His first instinct, after the debacle in Dubai, had been to return to his small animal practice. But the allure of Kay's world dragged him back to Nairobi; her pull more compelling than any logical analysis of his professional situation. He was comforted by the thought that Ian, his vet school classmate, had promised to step in if his vet surgery ran into difficulties. That gave Alec a lot of professional leeway to accept assignments away from the UK.

Sam, back in Nairobi on the trail of the poachers and the cartel, was glad to have Alec in his corner. They had got on splendidly and there was mutual respect. He was hoping to entrap the cartel into showing its hand. He wasn't quite certain why the cartel wanted Alec back in Kenya – unless it was some kind of payback for exposing the scam of burning the fake ivory. Even that did not gel – Alec could have been dealt with quite readily in Dubai. Unless the cartel was taunting him. Either way, Sam was optimistic that it would only be a matter of time before his luck changed. Although the cartel held all the aces at the moment, Sam was banking on the cartel slipping up and/or a lucky break. In retrospect, the idea of using Alec as bait was irresponsible.

Sam had received quite a bit of intel from his field officers, especially from Dubai, about the cartel's annoyance at the perceived British interference. They equated Alec's and Kenya's involvement as British moves to thwart the thriving illegal ivory trade.

This over-the-top response from the cartel indicated to him that the cartel was rattled. His playing cupid by taking Kay to Dubai had alerted the cartel. Maybe the cartel had mistaken Kay for Ava; just as Alec had initially. He had worked hard to ensure that Alec, on quitting Dubai, did not return to London. Alec's presence in Kenya could well be the stimulus that triggered an exaggerated response from the cartel; the break that Sam was waiting for.

A few days later, after having settled in his visiting lecturer role at the Kabete campus, Alec called Kay to continue from where they had left off in Dubai, hoping that the vibes were still very much there.

Alec was pleasantly surprised when Kay readily agreed to fly down to Mombasa and spend a weekend with him at the Orange Coral Hotel. Much against his better judgement, he had decided to revisit all the haunts that he and Ava had shared, albeit so briefly.

Two days later he received the air tickets and the hotel holiday package with several brochures of various tourist attractions. Flicking through the colourful brochure of the Orange Coral Hotel, especially its beach and the poolside bar, triggered a memory. Alec shivered involuntarily and all the demons of the past came flooding back.

On an impulse, his better judgement prevailing, he picked up the phone and rescheduled their trip.

Their weekend break on a privately owned luxury beach hotel on Manda Island in the Lamu Archipelago was almost over. Kay was booked in an adjoining room. There were moments when he felt that there was that look in her eyes which Ava had when she teased him or when she flirted outrageously with him. For a brief moment, he almost yielded to the tantalising thought of knocking on her door and inviting her for a nightcap, just as Ava had done.

The fear of rejection held him back; the coward in him winning – although he convinced himself that he was following the dictum 'he who retreats, lives to fight another day.' Wiser counsel prevailed and he retired for the night. He slept like a log and for once, after the recent experiences, without his demons taking centre stage.

Alec and Kay flew back to Nairobi – both lost in their thoughts. The silence between them on the flight back was a sign of deepening friendship – rather akin to the comfortable silences that happily married couples endured without any awkwardness or guilt.

As they disembarked and emerged into the arrivals lounge, Kay dashed off towards the pick-up point where she knew her dad, who was in town for a brief visit, would be waiting in the car, after shyly giving Alec a peck on the cheek. She turned back and waved before disappearing from view.

Alec went back to Kabete, none the wiser about Kay's feelings towards him. It was much later that he realised that Kay had dashed off without introducing him to her dad. He found that quite disturbing – negating all the euphoria of their Lamu break.

Alec spoke to Sam later from his office at Kabete. He could not stop raving about Kay. He wondered if he was reading too much into Kay's reluctance to introduce him to her father at the airport.

'Pole, pole my friend. Maybe, she's not ready yet to acknowledge her feelings for you. Her cultural background – Indian traditions and customs – may warrant a measured approach. Don't rush her – she'll take you to her parents when the time is right. Don't fret, give her the space.'

Sam cringed as he put the phone down. His conscience was hollering – loud and clear. He regretted not revealing the truth to Alec right at the outset – too late now. It would now be a question of damage limitation – and hoping that the repercussions would not threaten the investigation and their friendship.

Not now, soon, he convinced himself. His day of confrontation with Alec was looming. He had been blindsided by his concern for

Alec; playing cupid, in retrospect, had been a huge mistake.

FIFTEEN

Zubin, Mombasa.

Mark Woolf, the son of a British dairy tycoon from Naivasha, had fathered many children – his promiscuity knowing no bounds. After failing at most trades – the luxury of having a rich father – his astute investments in property, the oil sector and Footsie stocks on the London Stock Exchange blossomed.

When he died in Mombasa in the arms of his mistress and consort, Yasmin Adamjee, the conflicts between his legitimate and illegitimate heirs were like volcanic eruptions; the tectonic plates of his immense wealth crumbling under the onslaught of legal battles.

His property estate encompassing Mombasa, the coastal territories and the Lamu and Zanzibar Archipelagos was just a miniscule fraction of his East African and global assets; the global holdings were the mainstay of his wealth. Mark loved to regale his friends, especially when propped up at the Norfolk Hotel bar, with stories of his pioneering ancestor moving from Devon to Kenya in 1908 to hunt lions for the Kenya-Uganda Railway.

Mark was the epitome of the colonial old-boy network that had thrived in East Africa after most of the colonies had won independence

– Mark and many like him were diehard romantics who had refused to quit Kenya, come what may. Most, though not all, had dual allegiances – their British and Kenyan roots intertwined and going back generations.

That innate pride in the land of their birth – Kenya and other parts of East Africa that had seen Omani, Portuguese, German and British political control – had engendered a breed of successful and dominant men who had thrived and prospered. A similar wave of transformation had taken place with the Indian diaspora. Some of them had transplanted themselves in East Africa centuries ago, initially as shopkeepers and artisan craftsmen.

Yasmin had planned well in advance while she still had emotional control over Mark. His convoluted relationships with several women – wives and mistresses – were nothing short of a legal powder keg and the fight for the spoils of his considerable estate was destined to be epic. Yasmin's reading of the situation was instinctive – the concubine well ahead of the curve.

Over decades of their passionate relationship, she had planned and engineered her pregnancy, knowing that he would not be able to deny anything to a male heir.

With the birth of Zubeid Mark Adamjee, their only son, she had skilfully wrested control of all his Mombasa, Lamu and Zanzibar holdings in one fell swoop; transferred legally to her under joint ownership with Zubeid. She had the foresight to predict, decades in advance, that his extended family would look down their toffee noses at Mombasa and the coast as the 'backwaters' of the colony; malaria-infested and not worth the bother. She knew that any claim on his Nairobi or London holdings would be futile.

She had called it right – the courtroom brawls concentrated entirely on Nairobi and the 'white highlands' – the centre of European settlement in Kenya – and beyond into the UK. The assets signed off by Mark to his brown concubine and her pup were considered financially insignificant and not worth contesting.

They were content for Yasmin to inherit that part of Mark's estate – not for a moment did anyone imagine that the same Europeans and their descendants would flock to the backwaters in droves, as would other foreigners, all seeking their Shangri-La, earthly paradise, by the sea be it Mombasa or Zanzibar.

In a sense, their disdain and arrogance suited Yasmin – she was content and happy in her world on the coast with her son beside her as far away as possible from the mzungus. In contrast to their education and sophistication, she revelled in her humble upbringing and passed on the same sense of humility to her son, constantly borrowing from the Sermon on the Mount: 'Blessed are the meek, for they will inherit the earth.'.

Zubeid had also inherited several offshore shell companies and the passion for oil from his father. Mark, in moments of early recognition of Zubeid's prodigious intelligence, paid for his boarding school and university education in London. Mark's ultimate gift was dark blue and hard covered, and it opened up the world for Zubeid. A British passport; a paternity test confirming his bona fides.

Just before Zubeid entered university, he changed his name to

Zubin by deed poll in keeping with his Persian ancestry. Zubin, meaning a short spear in Persian, was deliberately chosen, tongue-in-cheek, as 'Shorty' had been his nickname at school.

After reading Economics at the London School of Economics, Zubin with the looks of a modern-day Adonis had only one gripe – that he had inherited his mother's short stature. He had excelled at cricket – gaining a cricket blue – his prowess on the field gained him more female admirers than his scholarly achievements in the classroom.

Fortunately, by the time he had moved to university and beyond, the derogative school moniker had been laid to rest. His university mates were more apt to call him 'Mercury' for his physique and passing resemblance to the legendary singer who was born in Zanzibar.

Most of his university mates knew where Zanzibar was because of the Freddie Mercury connection; very few would have been able to locate Zubin's birth place – Lamu Island, founded in the 12th Century and 150 miles from Mombasa, off the coast of Kenya.

Zubin's substantial inheritance provided the springboard to his burgeoning property empire which grew exponentially – as most of his portfolio was based in London and the suburbs. The jewels of the crown for him were several residential blocks of flats in Kensington, Hammersmith and Chelsea and commercial units in Hatton Garden.

With prudent tax planning, skills learnt so well under the tutelage of his father and with the help of a battery of accountants, his wealth was sheltered in offshore tax havens in the British Virgin

Islands, Jersey and Isle of Man. The use of shell companies registered all over the world added the final touch of finesse – the movement of assets between these companies to avoid tax liabilities. Most of these tax savings and a considerable portion of his income were donated to charities nominated by Yasmin.

By the time he returned to Kenya in his early thirties, he was a rich man by any standards – the only reason he did not appear on the Forbes magazine list was because he chose not to showcase his wealth. He had learnt well under Yasmin's tutelage – shunning hubris became a way of life.

He moved to Mombasa to look after Yasmin who was suffering from psittacosis – a lung disease acquired from the Grey African parrot that she had inherited from her family. The parrot was her only company in later years, especially when Zubin was in London. Her lung function gradually declined over the years; she was dying a slow death and entirely dependent on oxygen therapy.

She and Mark had lived for a while in Nyali – in a ramshackle bungalow that became their hideout from the prying press. Zubin refurbished it for her without spoiling the colonial façade and the old-world charm that she so revered because it reminded her of Mark. He moved in with her before she died from pulmonary failure. The bungalow was named Yasmin House in her memory.

He never moved out from Yasmin House despite having several other properties in Mombasa. As he was fond of saying to his friends who all wondered why he was still content to stay put in 'that old relic': 'I don't have a wife so I am blessed and I don't need a new kitchen nor a walk-in wardrobe.'

His avowed bachelorhood gave his very many detractors and rivals a chance to question his sexuality. Although he was irked by the senseless gossip, he rarely commented on the matter.

As actions speak louder than words, he had the perfect riposte each time –Zubin would promptly throw lavish parties to offset the gossip. He would fly in a bevy of Bollywood actresses to his yacht and ensure that the papers and magazines were flooded with photoshoots of his liaisons; recorded by Musa, a distant cousin from Yasmin's side of the family.

He was quite well known in Bollywood and was constantly being linked with actresses, single and married. Zubin was a prime catch and many a newcomer would deliberately start the gossip of an affair or even a secret marriage to enhance their prospects of landing juicy acting roles.

It was while he was in Mombasa that he came across his father's papers – Mark had studied geology at Oxford. It took Zubin almost six months to index and file all the papers that were left behind in old suitcases and brown boxes.

One particular report, going back to the 1950s and 1960s intrigued him. The papers rekindled his interest in oil and local politics. The copy of the report mentioned exploration by international oil companies. Although there were reports of oil exploration in the Lamu region dating back to 1954 and in other areas back to 1930, most of these forays came up dry; including the first oil well drilled in 1960 in

Lamu.

Any interest in finding oil in Kenya fell away when these initial attempts came to nothing. Among the papers were copies of old reports – photos, geological, gravity, aeromagnetic and seismic surveys carried out in and around the Mombasa coast and Lamu – thick files of paper, sepia tinted and dust laden. The surveys had not resulted in any fresh exploration.

Zubin came across a similar report in Mark's files in London which was dated in the early 70s. It talked of exploration in the Lamu Basin, the presence of cretaceous rocks, seismic data revealing salt diapiric structures along the coastal regions of Kenya. Again, most drilling had been unsuccessful and the dry wells abandoned. Buried among all this were handwritten notes in old note books or newspaper clippings with annotations in the margins. He recognised his father's spidery scrawl.

The only personal photograph he found among the oil files was a sepia-tinted dog-eared black and white photo on a beach of his father and another individual. He flicked the photo to see if there was a notation on the back – something that his father was in the habit of doing with family photographs – notations of dates, names and places in his writing.

This one did not have a date on it – just the initials MW and DD and LAMU. He wondered who DD was but had found a small note, an appendix, to one of the oil surveys which had been initialled as DD. It briefly mentioned the presence of cretaceous rocks in the Lamu region and his initials DD again on an oil report about an offshore survey in Lamu. It looked as though all of these surveys were conducted privately at Mark's behest on his tracts of land. There was a map of Zanzibar – hand sketched but without any notes.

When Yasmin died, Zubin buried her in Lamu rather than Mombasa – he built a tomb around her burial place as a mark of respect and something to come back to Lamu at least once a year, on her death anniversary. Yasmin had retained the old house in Lamu where both had been born and Lamu became a second home –away from Yasmin House in Nyali.

He raised a lot of funds locally in aid of a charity that looked after patients with chronic debilitating illnesses – in memory of Yasmin and called it 'The Y Foundation'. Gradually over the years he became quite well known in the voluntary sector and at the local political grassroots. Although he did not stand for local-council elections himself, many local candidates sought his help to raise campaign funds.

Over the years he unwittingly, on the back of the 'Y Foundation', got involved with a lot of religious and cultural organisations; so much so that he would be invited to annual celebrations – be they Hindu, Christian or Muslim festivals.

At the Diwali celebrations of a local Hindu cultural group, he was the chief guest at their annual prize-giving ceremony. Following the festivities, he was having a post-dinner coffee with some of the trustees and was introduced to their chair– a retired GP well into his eighties.

Dr Arya a fourth generation Kenyan, whose ancestors had

steadfastly refused to register as British citizens, was a fount of old school memories, having studied locally at the Aga Khan School and later on at Makerere Medical College in Kampala. On graduation, he set up a GP practice in the Nazi Moja area in central Mombasa. A chance remark by the octogenarian brought up the topic of oil and exploration.

'There's plenty of oil in them waters,' the frail GP said laconically, gesturing towards the ocean where a Likoni ferry was going through the creek.

'Really?' asked Zubin, more a rhetorical query to indulge an elderly wizened old man than a factual one.

'There's scepticism in your voice young man.' The older man said in an accusatory tone. 'I've lived in these parts for decades – don't let the hair fool you,' the old timer quipped pointing to his fringe of jet-black hair – he was bald as a coot except for a horse shoe-shaped band of dyed hair stretching from ear to ear. That was the only band of hair that the GP got his barber to dye jet black on his fortnightly hairdressing visits.

The white goatee that the GP sported was left untouched; pristine white. It did give the old man a distinguished look, faintly smelling of cigars and Old Spice aftershave. His talk of the good old days and his ramblings reminded Zubin of his mother – Yasmin's wisdom and knowledge of the coast was second to none. Zubin listened intently, more out of respect than interest.

'I'll have you know,' the GP continued, 'that all the majors – including Shell - surveyed the Lamu Basin for oil – this was in the

1950s when Kenya was still a colony. There were press reports at the that time that all the wells had come up dry and all exploration subsequently ceased. I am convinced that there must be reports in Whitehall, buried among reams of colonial papers, that point to some evidence of oil. Otherwise, why would oil companies waste resources drilling? There have been other attempts, in almost every decade since the 1950s. Zilch.' He formed the zero sign with his index finger and his thumb.

Before Zubin could be drawn into the what seemed to be the retired GP's favourite topic, the medic continued. 'There is anecdotal evidence about oil,' he said, again gesturing towards the ocean. 'I recall a gentleman, whom I knew only by his initials, writing to a local newspaper proposing that the movement of the tectonic plates that formed the Rift Valley may well have exposed oil-bearing seams. He firmly believed that the Rift Valley must have oil deposits and by extension the coastal strip as well.'

'Surely, that's just conjecture,' Zubin said softly in order not to offend the old timer who seemed convinced of vast oil reserves under his feet. A point that the old man emphasised by stamping his feet every time oil was mentioned; almost expecting oil to gush out.

'Well, there's oil in Egypt and in the Sudan, isn't there?' Dr Arya asked arching his white bushy eyebrows which had not been touched by a pair of scissors or trimmers in decades. The wayward eyebrows and the goatee gave the Indian GP an absent-minded professorial look.

'Yes, of course, there is oil in North Africa but that hardly means anything,' Zubin remarked to avoid another monologue, aching to get away, without appearing rude.

'Well, my friend, the letter writer DD seemed convinced – purely because the Rift Valley system extends from Egypt to Kenya and all the way down to Mozambique.'

Zubin wondered whether the DD mentioned in his father's papers was the same DD who had written to the press? Although Zubin remained impassive he pondered on the possibility that the old coot's ramblings may well have some merit.

'This DD – any idea who he was?' Zubin asked.

'Only met him at parties, while he was holidaying here – I recall that he was a geologist in the Ministry in Nairobi. He was adamant about Kenya's oil reserves. He even carried out his own informal surveys around the Rift Valley. Not sure if he pursued it any further with the authorities here in Kenya or in England. I was saddened to read that he went back to England after his wife died in a car crash.' The GP fell silent for a while, engrossed in his thoughts. He recalled the press reports about the accident. 'Douglas or Dunlop I think.'

They had a further discussion about local politics and how the colonial government had always short-changed Mombasa and the coast in the allocation of federal funds. As often happens, others joined in and personal opinions came to the fore; the main being that economic development was concentrated mainly in and around Nairobi Province. The Coast Province, which included Mombasa, was treated like a pariah – despite contributing vast sums to Kenya's GDP.

Although Yasmin had never believed that there was any deliberate bias against the coast, the sentiment persisted amongst the local population. Zubin only found out about his mother's political affiliations after her death – her ardent support for unity candidates who did not play the race card.

The incessant discussions about Mombasa's pariah status were old hat as far as Zubin was concerned. He valued his mother's position – that Mombasa and the coast needed to present a united forum for the prosperity of all its citizens.

Zubin, after Yasmin's death and in her memory, set about using the Y Foundation to spread that message of unity. While he did not actively campaign for any political office, he chose to back local candidates who espoused the same ideology. The Y Foundation, adopting an inclusive approach, achieved some measure of success in stimulating economic growth in the Coast Province.

Over the next few years, Zubin frequently recalled the old GP and their conversation about oil. He had researched the archives at the central library in Nairobi and even in London. The same information kept popping up – drilling programmes that had failed to find oil. He firmly believed that there was no oil on the coast.

The news of a British geologist, shot dead in Lamu made the headlines. The mysterious death stayed in the national papers longer than anticipated; even some UK newspapers ran the story for a while.

It was after the Lamu killing, that he received a call from

Dubai. It barely lasted a minute but he was informed that he should contact Dubai once he received some information in a few days.

Two days later he received a log of his visits to old town and a grainy photograph, probably taken at a fair distance, using a telephoto lens.

It showed a driver resting against a Mercedes with the car registration visible. He recognised himself in the back seat. The non-descript brown envelope did not have a sender's address. A handwritten note saying 'we are watching you' was enclosed.

Zubin dismissed it as a prank and promptly forgot all about it.

A year later, an old issue about Mombasa's governance came to the fore during frenetic campaigning for municipal elections in Mombasa. The old fissures based on religion, something that had been simmering for years, resulted in factions splitting from major political camps. Although, the Christians, Hindus and Muslims had, over centuries and decades, integrated quite well and shared common interests – either by marriage or commercial ties – election fever led to tensions building up. Sporadic attacks on local businesses, tourist resorts and the affluent sections of Mombasa led to questions being asked about the motive behind these organised incidents. Civic awareness finally caught up with reality – the electorate realised that it was an orchestrated campaign of hate to disrupt the economy of Mombasa – and to foment divisions.

At one of the meetings where the Y Foundation was invited to make campaign donations for the forthcoming local elections, Zubin was approached anonymously – the waiter told him that a message had been left at reception. The receptionist was very much in the dark as well – all she knew was that a courier had asked for him by name and had handed an envelope to the doorman. Frustrated at not finding anything from the receptionist, Zubin pocketed the envelope without opening it.

Later on, on the way home, he looked at it closely and opened the envelope gingerly. In the dim light he just about managed to see what it was – three photographs: one of his driver leaning against his parked car, and young men entering or leaving the old town house, which he later found out was a shaman's surgery.

At first, in the dim lit interior, he did not see the paper – his fingers brushed against it. Aware of the driver and the fact that they were close to home, he inserted everything back to be looked at later in the privacy of his home.

Zubin's face had turned a bright hue of crimson when he looked at the photographs again after kicking off his shoes and collapsing in his armchair, the nightcap on his mahogany desk forgotten as he read the typed note; the salutation was 'Shorty'.

The precise and terse words were meant to intimidate and to create anxiety and fear – of the unknown; a tacit message of blackmail. An initial remittance of $100,000 was requested via a bank transfer – details of a bank that he'd never heard of were listed. 'Pretty polite for a blackmailer,' Zubin muttered under his breath. No one had called him Shorty in decades.

'Only someone from his past would recall and quote his 'Shorty' tag', Zubin reminded himself and his mind was drawn back to the monstrous time he had spent at a private boarding school in England; a victim of school bullies. He had been a miserable lonely kid from Mombasa whose accent was at odds with the majority of the white children.

There was an implicit threat if the first remittance was not forthcoming within days – a deadline was indicated. He was struck by the language – 'first' remittance, meaning there was more to come. That did not surprise Zubin. It was classic and standard methodology used by those who used extortion; all par for the course. A blackmailer never gives up and, therein, lay Zubin's dilemma. He knew there would be more demands for more money and more threats. He spent sleepless nights debating as the deadline crept closer. Serious consequences were threatened if he defaulted.

The following morning, he took a gamble and decided to try doing it his way, otherwise he would need to call on his friend for assistance. While he was reluctant to drag old connections into this quagmire, an outsider's insight may present new solutions. Or they could all be sucked in; quicksand territory.

He requested his solicitors in London to try and trace the links to the bank details. His solicitors were unable to unearth anything that he already had not surmised – a series of offshore accounts under different shell companies and lodged in tax havens across the globe. A maze of information that he knew was designed to stonewall any snooping.

Zubin instinctively knew that forensic audits of what he knew were hawala transactions would prove futile. It was time to seek help because the vortex of deceit and machinations may be a front for something even bigger and nastier.

He placed a call to Nairobi and waited impatiently as a series of verification clicks ended, as the voice, muffled by the sounds of azan in the background, came through quite clearly.

'Sema sasa, rafiki. Habari.' Zubin quickly launched into his narrative not responding to the salutation; a code in itself that assured both parties about the authenticity of the call.

Zubin, as he terminated the call, wondered whether his friend was in Dubai or Bombay; the call to prayers, the azan, was another code that constituted a two-layer verification process. The only thing that constantly changed would be the prayer; next time it could be a hymn or a mantra.

His friend advised that he make the remittance well before the deadline. It would give them time to figure out a strategy and ascertain how seriously Zubin was compromised.

Within a week further demands were made. Zubin transferred four separate remittances of $100,000 into the designated account; a total of $500,000 collected within a short span of time. After the final payment he received a thank you note. 'Someone has a sense of humour,' Zubin noted.

There were no more demands for money but over a period of weeks and months he received instructions to issue pro-forma invoices for export cargoes – for cattle bones to Dubai or to Tanzania, Zanzibar and Uganda.

Zubin realized that a pattern of exports – by sea and road – was emerging. He knew that the slaughter houses of the whole of East Africa would not generate those amounts of cattle bones – the beef consumption would not match the export values of cattle bones; the strategy was obviously one of mis-declaring the true nature of the consignments. He shivered involuntarily – just hoped that it wasn't arms or something as sinister as launching a coup. He had been sucked in very cleverly – a financial audit trail was established and now it would be difficult to extricate himself. He wondered whether it had been wise to have dragged his friend into the mess. He was complicit by succumbing to the threats.

The next contact surprised him even more – he was couriered a copy of a report – a geologist's survey report. The typed report revealed details of oil exploration in and around the Rift Valley and in the Lamu Archipelago. The geologist had drawn his conclusions from his own private survey and from previous such attempts.

While Zubin barely understood the technical jargon used to describe the findings, the concluding statement of the private survey was that there were huge oil deposits on the coast, especially in the Lamu Archipelago. He was being asked to join an investors' club referred to as the 'Mag Seven'. The oil exploration shell company had a substantial cash holding to fund its activities – part of the $500,000 payment already made had been invested for each investor. There was no indication of the total share capital so Zubin assumed that the 'seven' investors were part of the Mag Seven club.

Zubin was immediately reminded of the 'them waters have oil' remark by the old GP and the DD initials on some of the papers that he had found. Unless the document had been altered or edited in any way, he knew that this report wasn't part of the DD papers. This was something entirely different and undersigned by an anonymous British geologist and seemingly a private survey conducted by a group with deep pockets on behalf of a private client or clients.

He recalled the press reports about the discovery of a body in Lamu – the man had been fatally shot. The coincidence of Lamu cropping up on a secret oil report and an unsolved killing in Lamu intrigued him. He wondered whether the several incidents, the Mag Seven demands, the false cargo invoices and the killing of the Brit, were part of something bigger?

As he continued reading his anxiety mounted at the mention of an historical event:

*11th Nov 1964 - Unilateral Declaration of Independence (UDI) by Ian Smith's government to form a sovereign state. There were bullet points about Harold Wilson's retaliatory actions and the bush wars waged by Robert Mugabe's forces. This was Zimbabwe's birth following the attempts by Smith to break away from Britain.

As Zubin finished reading the report, not the first time, the hairs on the back of his nape bristled.

Although the veracity of the private oil report had not been established, the Lamu killing and the reference to the UDI seemed to imply an imminent crisis; the discovery of oil and the UDI being part of a web of inter-connected events.

Zubin found his mother's worry beads and rolled them through his nimble fingers – the added dimension of sexual blackmail guaranteed his sleepless night. As the night progressed, as did his insomnia, the UDI would be perceived as a grave matter by the laws of the land. His brow furrowed in deep thought with fear rearing its ugly head. Even his vast wealth would not protect him from criminal or political repercussions. In an ironic way his opulence had made him a target.

Out of the blue he thought of Yasmin, his mother. With her long and close association with local politics, her insight and vision had been valuable in the past. A good listener and very empathetic, he missed her dearly; the umbilicus intact even after her death.

Within months, Zubin was indoctrinated into the club. There was nothing on paper; all the contacts were via reports and sometimes anonymous untraceable calls. He was also made aware that he was the last to be recruited – there were six others. He realised that 'Mag Seven' was short for 'the magnificent seven; also referred to as 'M7'. The tongue-in-cheek reference to Kurosawa's 'The Seven Samurai' and 'The Magnificent Seven' led him to believe in a Hollywood or Bollywood connection. He recalled snippets of information about the Kenyan authorities declaring substantial concessions for movies shot in Kenya.

Although he had frequently heard the refrain 'Mombasa for Mombasa born residents', he was certain that the perpetrators were playing on peoples' fear and confusion. There was more to all this than met the eye. He also admitted that the touted discovery of oil and the forecasts of huge deposits and profits to be shared were carrots – oil as bait.

When Zubin received word that he had to present himself at a private airstrip near Mombasa for a short trip to Lamu, he baulked at the thought and sought his friend's opinion. Despite his misgivings, he yielded to his friend's advice to play along.

As his chauffeur dropped him at the private airstrip, he noticed the Cessna 172 Skyhawk parked close to one of the hangars. 'Mag Seven' was distinctly emblazoned in red across the white fuselage.

He saw two other passengers waiting anxiously in the hangar which was manned by a single employee. He introduced himself to the other two men whose foreign passports were on the counter; Zubin's British passport laid atop the other two. He wondered where the other four were – probably flying in from other locations.

The single engine plane took off with the three passengers; the pilot effortlessly taking to the blue Mombasa skies. They landed at Manda Airport in Lamu after a short two-hour flight – it had been ages since Zubin had flown in a single engine plane; the bumpy ride adding to the anxiety of flying into the unknown.

On landing, they were ushered on to a boat – a short trip took them away from Lamu Island and towards a much smaller island. Zubin got the feeling that they were being dispatched as far away from Lamu Island as possible. The island looked desolate as their small boat moored at the jetty. As they disembarked, he saw an armed dozen or so guards patrolling the perimeter of a small hotel. As they entered the lobby, he saw the missing four passengers.

He never quite ascertained the nationalities of the other six but guessed they were all prominent East Africans. There was a distinguished looking older Indian gentleman who, going by his command of Swahili, seemed local or maybe a British expat.

Strangely, there were two buibui-clad women already seated at different ends of the auditorium; he assumed they were staff. They sat quietly throughout the presentation.

It was quite a slick customised documentary – the history of oil drilling in Kenya. All the visual clips were totally non-descript and it was virtually impossible to identify the locations. The texts and subtitles mentioned the prospects of offshore discoveries; there was no mention of dry wells or previous failures. The message was very upbeat echoing the 'there's oil in them waters' proclamation. The presentation, professionally put together, promised barrels and barrels of oil.

There was no mention of any governmental or political agency and the entire operation had the stamp of private enterprise. The texts mentioned that a shell company had been formed and investors invited to participate in the float.

The presentation ended with a switch over to a live-TV broadcast or so it looked. A very brief news clip showing armed garrisons patrolling the narrow lanes of a coastal town, ostensibly Lamu, with gunfire echoing in the background. The group were shocked to realise that some kind of a coup seemed to be unfolding, with the background fuzzy with smoke spiralling upwards from a building. It looked as though the police station was set ablaze.

A verbal commentary had been provided with the visuals – the seven passengers watched in awe while Zubin wondered what he had walked into. Some of the others looked at the others and had the same thought – 'I never signed up to a revolution'. Some kind of a unilateral declaration of independence had just been graphically shown.

The disbelief on the faces of the seven investors was blatantly obvious, while the buibui-clad women still remained aloof and silent; not a whimper from them. Zubin turned and looked at both of them, but they were both staring straight ahead at the unfolding drama.

The ending credits that rolled out had a statement declaring that the Lamu Archipelago had declared itself as a self-governing sovereign state – divorced from the mainland. There was a collage of print news declaring that troops had seized the ferry and mined the waters between Lamu and Mokowe on the mainland. Manda Airport had also been taken over. The lockdown of the archipelago was total; a successful bloodless coup.

As the presentation ended and the lights came on – the seven 'samurai' were stunned as were the personnel of the hotel who had all congregated at the back. The pin-drop silence was all pervasive – as if the world had stopped to exist, broken only by the raucous braying of donkeys by the waterfront.

The manager rushed to the colour TV in the corner and switched it on – no broadcasts except for an AV message on a loop – that Lamu had declared independence, all communication links had been severed with the mainland and a total blackout of the archipelago was in place.

For more than an hour, the seven and the other personnel sat in almost stunned silence. The manager did a quick tour of the island – no sign of the garrison nor of any boats or the speedboats – Zubin could have sworn that he had seen a couple of dhows moored further away. The beach looked deserted and all inhabitants had been evacuated. There was no way of getting off the island. They were stranded without any links to the outside world. The silence, even for the solitude that the islands provided, felt unnatural and eerie. The phone lines were dead, they were cut off from the world. Both the buibui-clad women had disappeared.

Thousands of miles away, pre-programmed transactions were being carried out; funds siphoned off from the seven victims across several banks and countries. There was no coup, only a financial raid on the cash reserves of the victims – a scam as audacious as daylight robbery.

The remittances, siphoned off the offshore accounts by a well-planned hacking exercise, transferred into the recipient's account in a bank in Panama. These funds were in addition to the $3.5 million sitting in the account – the initial £500,000 demanded from each investor. The funds then transferred to other offshore accounts and then onward via hawala transfers.

It would be apparent to all concerned that the perpetrators had hacked into the seven investors' accounts and had siphoned off all available funds. In a twist that the victims would comprehend much later, the hackers had programmed withdrawals even from linked or affiliated accounts. It would take days and weeks before the victims discovered the true scale of the scam. Millions were ransacked from their offshore accounts.

The perpetrators had done their homework well – the millions pilfered collectively from the several accounts amounted to a sizeable fortune but individually for the seven investors, who were all billionaires, the theft barely mattered. The scammers knew that the thefts would not be reported as the cash deposits, accrued over decades, were of dubious origin. Not only untaxed but also transferred out via hawala dealers; the illegal cash transfer system that bypassed all recognised banking and foreign exchange regulations.

The perpetrators were aware that the 'mag seven' members would not report the thefts to the authorities to avoid incriminating themselves. It was in their interest to maintain the status quo of silence; anything else would have meant imprisonment, penalties and years of litigation.

It was a whole 24 hours before the seven managed to attract a passing speed boat. The captain looked at them in disbelief when they mentioned their isolation and the news clip of a coup in the archipelago.

'What coup?' the captain asked, still thinking that the party of seven was pulling his leg. 'I've just ferried a honeymoon couple from Lamu town to one of the resorts. Barely an hour ago. Everything is normal.'

Zubin smiled ruefully – they had been had. A massive hoax; a coup that never was. Lamu, where they disembarked, was normal. The seven caught the ferry to the mainland. Before parting company at Mokowe, they all agreed to keep tight lipped about the day's experience. Any admission to the authorities would be even more damaging and the criminal proceedings would destroy companies and families.

Zubin proposed that they exchange contact details and form an alliance in case further attempts were made to extort money. Only the distinguished Indian agreed and exchanged contact details with Zubin. All the others slipped away, barely able to make eye contact.

Zubin had been forewarned by his friend – he had escaped unscathed as he had put caveats on all of his bank accounts – each transaction to be verified verbally and in writing by his accountants before any withdrawal.

The $500,000 that he had already paid had been refunded into his account as promised. He had been assured that he would not be out of pocket for any future transactions.

While he had the last laugh, thanks to his friend, the fact that his accounts were shielded and blocked meant that the perpetrators may be forewarned. In the end, it was decided that it was a risk worth taking – Zubin had been assured of full protection by his friend. He had been used as bait.

Unknown to Zubin, the distinguished Indian victim had been sucked into the Mag Seven by similar blackmail and extorsion tactics. The victim had been wily enough to isolate his accounts with caveats in place that prevented carte blanche withdrawals. His outlay also was restricted to $500,000.

Zubin was hoping that the blackmailers would not come back for more. In his mind, he knew that further attempts would be made to extort money – the perpetrators knew of his assets and wealth in Kenya and in Europe. He was hoping that the interim period would give him breathing space to confront the person he knew was responsible, failing which he would have to revert to his friend again. Zubin had been assured of repeatedly about this high-level intervention.

Much later after Zubin was back in Mombasa, he received a call – he was advised to keep a low profile – best to take that long overdue holiday to London. The Sanskrit mantra playing in the background told him all he needed to know. His friend was tipping him off. Zubin knew that by blocking his accounts, he had not only 'flagged' himself but also endangered himself.

Zubin rang his flat in the Mayfair – the girlfriend who was in residence got all excited at the news. Zubin was arriving at Heathrow – and she had instructions to send the chauffer to receive him.

Before Zubin put the phone down, he said to her: 'Congratulations, Miss World contestant. Goodluck, do Kenya proud. Next stop Hollywood or maybe Bollywood?'

'If that happens, you'll be the first to know. Have a safe flight and see you soon. And, don't get up to any mischief on the flight!' Simone giggled as she recalled their last flight together. Their drunken antics in the first class toilet had almost got them into trouble.

He was pleased for Simone – he had attended her two

crowning glories last year. Miss Mombasa, Miss Kenya and now Miss World contestant. He tried to figure out what had gone into her coastal cocktail of genes – Indian, Portuguese and Omani? Whatever it was, the end result was truly enchanting. Hakuna matata!

The Indian victim, much older and exhausted, was on his way back to Nairobi. The sting had left him breathless – the anxiety and the dust – had triggered his asthma. The Ventolin inhaler that he always carried had helped ease his breathing but the tightness across his chest persisted. The blackmail and extortion tactics used on him to recruit him into the 'Mag Seven' were linked to the skeletons in the closet that he thought had long being buried. The mention of his son right at the outset was the clue – he had a fair idea who was behind the 'Mag Seven' scam.

SIXTEEN

Musa, Eastleigh, Nairobi.

Musa's debut Bollywood movie, as a cinematographer and director, had run into trouble – with still two more weeks to completion. The producers fretted about the budget overrun and his detractors celebrated. In the dog-eat-dog world of tinsel town, debut entrants, especially foreign ones, evoked strong feelings of antipathy. Musa had a lot to learn about the workings of Bollywood; the patronage of a godfather was vital for survival. Or bloodline. Talent without one or the other often withered.

He had borrowed heavily to bring his maiden directorial venture to fruition. Like everything else in India and in Bollywood, life flows at its own pace and he had lost control. The shoot schedules had been delayed and cancelled on several occasions for no apparent reason. Musa, accustomed to the strict disciplines of punctuality and professionalism, was on unfamiliar territory; here the tail wagged the mongrel dog.

On the verge of a nervous breakdown, foisted upon him by the financiers, the stars and his rivals, he had to seek his benefactor's benevolence, yet again, to keep his head above water. His mentor and benefactor, whom he had escorted on his bespoke safari, had become an investor as well. Musa considered himself as a protégé but his detractors used decidedly unflattering terms – mostly colloquial expletives.

In his enthusiasm to get the project off the ground, Musa had thrown caution to the wind in signing deals without due diligence. As an outsider, he was easy fodder for the loan sharks. Faced with the prospect of abandoning the film when he overshot the budget, he took on more debt – the sharks kept lending on extortionate terms. He ignored even his mentor and continued shooting.

He would have sailed through but for the bolt that struck overnight when the All India Federation of Cine Artistes balloted their members and decided to strike for better wages and working conditions. Overnight Bollywood came to an abrupt standstill. There was no filming in any of the studios and all other affiliated activities ceased.

The strike lasted two months by which time Musa's last tranche of finance had dried up – and this was just the interest that he needed to pay every day, week or month to service the loans.

Most of his bona-fide lenders empathised with Musa and deferred or suspended his interest charges hoping that the movie would be completed quickly once the strike ended. The hard-core ones, with dubious motives, just moved in and occupied his offices. The crunch came – the sucker punch – when inexplicably henchmen of a major financier moved in and confiscated his incomplete film, holding him to ransom. The completed spools of celluloid would not be released until a full payment was made.

Musa had nowhere to turn to – he had exhausted all sources of financial help. A man at the end of his tether, confused and desperate, he made the cardinal mistake of bolting to Mombasa, high on nicotine, alcohol and anti-depressants.

The word of his flight spread, and as time elapsed, the gossip got more and more ugly. Rumours of his suicide, mental breakdown, admission to rehab and other nasty outcomes became rampant. When the alleged invocation of a 'supari' contract killing became an open secret, even his well-wishers abandoned him, fearful of incurring collateral damage.

His mentor's silence was even more damning; he had not come out in support of the bankrupt Kenyan. The rumour doing the rounds was that the mentor had finally pulled the plug and withdrawn all support.

Months earlier, the precipitating moment that sealed Musa's fate was inadvertent and an accident – on the bespoke safari during a stop-over in Laikipia. He was so busy filming the producer and his wife, that he failed to notice Shenzi and his companion. Musa, unaware that he was in the wrong place, at the wrong time continued filming.

Months later when Musa fled Bollywood to return to Kenya, the contract was put into place – knowing fully well that Musa's financial mess would be blamed for the punitive action.

The buibui-clad figure, with the Chanel perfume, made her way to the scribbled address. Days later the woman would be remembered for the exotic perfume – a strong fragrance. Shoppers and bystanders remembered the fashionable Prada Milano insignia on the large bag. The flight from Mombasa and the taxi ride to Eastleigh on the outskirts of Nairobi had been uneventful.

The buibui afforded total anonymity. Eastleigh, the predominantly Asian gentrified area of the post-colonial era had been colonised by the arrival of Somali inhabitants and the buibui had replaced the sari.

As the buibui-clad woman walked past small stalls selling goods from Dubai and Somali delicacies, the ramshackle ground-floor flat down a narrow alley came into view – sandwiched between stalls selling camel milk and miraa, the intoxicant.

The buibui figure double checked the scribbled address. The tracking of the courier parcel and its delivery confirmed that the target was holed up at the address. The parcel of Malindi halwa, a decoy, was deliberately sent to confirm the man's presence in the seedy environs of Eastleigh.

Musa still groggy from late-night drinking and anti-depressants, opened the door without any hesitation – the fragrant perfume wafting through the flimsy door put him off guard.

The soft thud of the silenced handgun was heard before the bullet pierced his heart and he slumped to the ground. The assassin stepped in and closed the door and shot him again and again; the signature three-shot routine.

The assassin checked that the victim was dead and before turning around to exit, noticed the courier package on the dining table. Remnants of a previous meal and unwashed dishes littered the Formica-topped table. Several empty bottles of Stoney Tangawizi ginger beer lay strewn on the cement floor. Scraps of mandazi and the famous Malindi 'halwa' (a sweet gelatinous dessert) attracted flies to what probably was the last supper. The flies buzzed back as the assassin left the flat.

A few days later Sam received a call from the team – Musa's body had been discovered and a summary of the police pathologist's findings briefly relayed.

The modus operandi seemed similar in all three deaths – the Arab in the Mombasa warehouse, the British geologist and now Musa. The sightings of the buibui-clad female – most witnesses recalled the strong perfume – and the point-blank shootings formed a definite pattern. Sam had been informed that the ballistics reports did not match – meaning that the same gun was not used for all three killings. And Sam noted that Musa's killing was the first one away from the coast – the execution taking place in Nairobi rather than Mombasa or Lamu.

A pensive Sam rang Alec at Kabete and informed him that Musa's body had been discovered in Eastleigh.

'Alec, my sincere condolences. You guys go back a long way,' Sam commiserated.

'Indeed. We used to share digs in London and had kept in touch ever since. I thought he was in Bombay shooting his debut movie?' Alex asked.

'He was. Apparently, he got into financial trouble after the strike halted everything overnight. He fled, rather than sweat it out. This was an execution – the presence of the buibui figure in Eastleigh points to a contract,' Sam said

'Looks as though the cartel got to him first. Musa's only connection to the ivory scam was that he filmed the event.'

'And he knew you and Kay,' Sam added.

At a hastily arranged funeral, Musa was buried at Mbaraki Cemetery in Mombasa. The funeral was very well attended. The local boy who had earned his spurs as a wildlife photographer and cameraman, had put Mombasa on the Hollywood map.

Both Sam and Alec flew together to attend the funeral. Present among the funeral cortege was the Bollywood producer – Alec instantly recognised him as the portly man with the young starlet in the desert where they had bumped into Musa. He had others with him, probably associates or people from the film fraternity.

On the flight back to Nairobi, Alec reminisced about Musa and the times that they had spent together in London. Sam listened quietly as Alec unburdened his grief.

'Quite a change from the self-effacing young Musa I knew in London to the accomplished photographer and cinematographer of today,' Alec mused.

'How did he end up in Bollywood – a graveyard for dreams and newcomers? Sam asked.

'We were both movie buffs and addicted to regular visits to the cinemas in Leicester Square. Musa took it a step further by pursuing cinematography and chasing his dream of making movies. The producer and his wife took one of his bespoke safaris with the intention of scouting for locations for his next production to be shot in Kenya. Musa told me that the man was impressed with Musa's Hollywood track record. That's how they ended up working together. The rest is history.'

'Yes, I am told that Musa had to sell his 'soul to the devil' to extricate himself from the financial mess that engulfed him.'

'Meaning that he had fallen foul of the law?' Alec queried.

'Not exactly but the amount and sources of his funds – the rapidity with which he managed to finance his project beggared belief. Maybe his circumstances compelled him to borrow at unsustainable rates – quite often the loans become unmanageable.'

Just as the flight was landing, Alec remembered something that

Musa had mentioned after the bespoke Kenya safari had ended.

'The producer was keen to invest in Kenya. Not just a studio – a film production facility – but pharma manufacturing. I gathered that Musa was acting as an intermediary – to access tax incentives, licences and visas for businesses that created jobs for Kenyans. Musa had indicated that there were other investors involved in the project.'

Sam promised to explore if any applications had been lodged with the Pharmacy Board and the immigration department.

Sam and Alec were at the historic Norfolk Hotel in Nairobi – built in 1904, its development and history mirroring the changes that Kenya had undergone after independence. They were in the restaurant that overlooked the University of Nairobi campus. The restaurant, an important watering hole for foreigners and locals alike, was buzzing with frenetic activity.

Alec was overawed by the aura of the place, from the imposing Tudor architecture to its famous clientele; his movie-buff 'antenna' excited by the thought of being in the hallowed, iconic hotel that had seen Richard Burton, Michael Caine, Robert Redford and Meryl Streep pass through its mighty portals. Michael Landon, the star of the Western TV serial 'Bonanza', struck a particular chord – Alec had seen the repeats while growing up in London.

'To absent friends!' Alec toasted Sam as they discussed the investigation.

'Musa was right. There are several applications with the Ministry. The one that caught my eye – guess?' Sam quizzed.

'By the Bollywood producer or others?'

'Not sure – it's an Indian outfit based in Bombay going by the company name, A. D. Enterprises. The manufacturing application details processes dealing with bones, gelatine and pharmaceutical capsules. The jargon got too much for me,' Sam remarked.

'Gelatine is derived mainly from animal bones and skins and has several uses in the pharma industry; mostly in the production of capsule shells – which can be filled with medicines, vitamins etc. The capsule shell or casing is similar to the sausage casing into which meat is filled,' Alec explained. 'But how does that tie up with the producer or Bombay though?'

'The Mombasa team found false cargo invoices – bones exported to an outfit in Bombay. Some of the consignments had bones mixed up with illegal ivory; the main conduit to ship out the illegal ivory. At the moment, Bombay is the only connection,' Sam elaborated.

Alec pondered on the conundrum. 'Couldn't you haul in this Bollywood guy for questioning?'

'Not really. Unless we can join the dots somehow. We need to connect the Mombasa false invoices and cargo destined for Bombay, the Bollywood producer and the application for manufacturing. That's purely circumstantial even if manage to tie up all three variables. There's a big Indian expat business lobby in Kenya – very well connected. Tricky. We don't want to ruffle anyone's feathers and we certainly don't want to tip anyone off,' Sam reasoned. 'I'll have to ask my contacts in Bombay and Dubai to help.'

SEVENTEEN

Sam, Nairobi

A forensic report of Musa's murder in Eastleigh was passed onto to Sam. The case remained on file and there were no clues as to the motive for the killing. Sam made notes and brief annotations on the margins of the report:

Fedex parcel trace – dead end. Client had paid cash; false Mombasa address.

Nothing stolen as victim's personal effects (watch, ring etc) and cash were found in the room.

The press, pestering the police for a statement, had to be content with a terse message that investigations were in progress. What had been withheld was that a silver crucifix had been found on the bed and political leaflets proclaiming Mombasa's right to federal funds and an equitable share of the revenues generated by tourism. Affirmative action for jobs and affordable housing were the other essential demands.

Sam underlined the words 'silver crucifix' with a red Biro. He looked for it in the file exhibits and found it along with the leaflets. He stared at the two items for a while and then sighed.

The Christian connection – the crucifix – was a new

perspective. Or it could be a ploy to distract the police? Sam mulled on these matters as he closed the file.

EIGHTEEN

Alec and Kay, Nairobi

Alec and Kay had been going out for a while and all their friends and colleagues knew that it was only a matter of time before they 'outed' themselves as an item. Their Mombasa trip had nudged things along quite nicely and the ice had been truly broken.

Alec had initially tried to fight the huge attraction and affinity that he had for Kay but had gradually succumbed to the inevitable – total capitulation. Sam's 'pole, pole' advice and, indeed, Kenya's oft-repeated words had merit – go with the flow made more sense than to fight or resist.

He reflected joyously about the time that he had sent her a spanking new Slazenger tennis ball – gift wrapped in the biggest box that he could find with an enclosed note – 'the ball is firmly in your court'. She admired his sense of humour and had responded in a similar vein.

She presented him foil wrapped dry ice cubes with a note – 'consider the ice broken'. They had met up at their favourite watering hole – the Thorn Tree Café housed in the small open-air atrium of the New Stanley Hotel in central Nairobi.

Over the years, the acacia tree in the middle of the open-air bistro style café, had become a legendary makeshift post box for travellers. A huge board on the tree became a mailbox, where tourists left messages on small cards, pinned down by shiny drawing pins and tacks. The café was a hugely popular rendezvous point with in transit travellers, well-heeled as well as backpackers.

Although he had not realised it back then, that Thorn Tree café meeting had assumed the same emotional connect as the 'Malaika' song. That evening as Alec waited for Kay to arrive at the Mayuri Lounge in the Westlands area, abutting the dual carriageway, he wondered why she had opted for a vegetarian restaurant. His new-found passion for spicy meat cooked in the tandoor meant that he opted for Indian non-vegetarian cuisine every time; any attempts to wean him away from the spicy chicken wings or shish kebabs met with staunch resistance.

As he arrived at the Mayuri – Sanskrit for peacock - the ambience and the aroma of cumin and coriander fragrances that were no longer alien, calmed his nerves. The waiter attired in a traditional costume, led him to his table.

For all he knew, he could be in a royal court somewhere in Jaipur – quite a few of his clients in south London hailed from India and had always urged him to visit Rajasthan, the desert state famed for its royal palaces and forts.

There was a live band tucked away in the background playing the sitar – soft classical sounds that Alec was vaguely familiar with; the piped music so common in the Indian restaurants in the UK.

Although the Mayuri Lounge was a class above the Dubai restaurants that he and Dr Reddy had frequented, he felt uneasy and his discomfort showed. The task ahead looked decidedly difficult without his favourite Indian fare and Tusker beer. His dismay was written large on his face as all he saw on the tables around him seemed downright alien. There was not a tandoori chicken wing in sight.

His spirits sagged. He wasn't sure if he could go through with what he had meticulously planned. His unease mounted as he glanced through the menu – there was hardly anything that he recognised and his fears were magnified when he noticed the absence of alcohol on the menu. Oh, ye Gods, have mercy!

The little Dutch courage that he had summoned for this special evening was draining away rapidly. Alec was beginning to sweat – something that hadn't happened even when he had faced death on the plains of Laikipia.

He dragged himself back to the soft tinkling notes of the sitar with great difficulty. His hand instinctively went to the inside pocket of his Armani suit – reassured by the bulge and the rustle as he fidgeted. He almost took it out to bolster his flagging spirits, when he saw her approaching the table, smiling radiantly.

She was a sight for his sore eyes, the ornately embroidered silk top tucked into the slender waist band of her designer jeans and her jet-black hair tied back in a pony tail, showcased the elegant curve of her slender neck. The dimpled smile adding to the allure of her face.

Her stilettos, crimson red, made muffled soft noises on the hard timber floor. The bare aisles between the tables shimmered in the light, with each table sited on a circular patch of Persian carpet; the 'islands' representing a male peacock's colourful and dazzling plumage.

The restaurant was oddly named Mayuri instead of Mayur. By the time the error was spotted it was too late to undo the damage. The iridescent blue and green décor that had been applied with great finesse and at a huge expense was characteristic of the male instead of the female peacock. The feathers of the female peacock, in stark contrast to the male's dazzling colours, tend to be either brown, grey or cream.

Alec was enthralled by the soft swish of her pony tail – keeping rhythm with her dainty paces towards him. 'Child-bearing hips', he muttered to himself. He was glad that he had donned his lucky Armani suit.

He was aware that most heads had turned, especially the male ones, at her drop-dead gorgeous look. A hush had descended on the floor and that made him even more nervous.

'Hi, you look stunning,' he ventured trying to enthuse confidence in his voice, which was off key by several decibels. His throat was parched and he was hankering for that cold beer.

'Thank you,' she crooned, as she settled down in the chair opposite him. She beamed at Alec and he preened under her gaze, hoping that she noticed that he had forsaken his usual blazer and denim jeans for an elegant suit.

'Fancy opting for a veggie place?' he teased. 'I would not have minded some red-blooded masala lamb chops and, definitely something stronger than passion juice or sweet lassi.'

'You asked me to choose, so here we are,' she said expansively spreading her slender arms. 'Besides, I wanted you to sample some vegetarian delicacies. Wait until you have their chilled desserts,' she added pointing to the dessert menu on the linen-covered table. He recalled the sweet fare that Musa had offered in Mombasa – Alec found most of the Indian desserts a tad too sweet - cloying for his English palate.

'Mayuri was the premier vegetarian restaurant in town back in the 60s. It used to be located in the middle of town, not far from the fire station,' Kay offered by way of a historical reference. 'This present site is more in keeping with trendy Nairobi although if you were to ask my dad, he'd say that he preferred the simple minimalist look of the old place.'

She noticed that Alec was decidedly fidgety and very quiet, panic writ large on his handsome face. And the lucky suit.

'What's up doc? Decking out for a mere dinner date? Didn't you once tell me that you always wear this particular three-piece Armani suit for good luck? Don't tell me you are going to get down on your arthritic knees'? she said facetiously – until she saw the blood drain from his face. 'Oh my God…Alec?'

'Trust you to say the right things at the wrong time,' he parried, recovering his composure, as he laid the envelope on the table. She looked at it as if he had thrust one of his small exotic patients, an iguana, on to the table.

She threw a quizzical glance at him; her eyebrow arched like a perfect parabola. She felt her heart thump against her ribs and fervently hoped that the envelope had what she thought it had – an affirmation of his intent. She feigned indifference, despite the ripples of excitement building up to a climax – her left hand reaching tantalisingly across the table to take the envelope.

'Go on open it. It won't bite.' He was now smiling at the role reversal – she was perturbed, her eyes wide open, pupils dilated in a state of heightened anticipation.

She did open it with exaggerated caution. As she dexterously slid the note out, she recognised his spidery illegible scrawl, scripted with a fountain pen, not a Biro.

'Alec! What the flip – I can't decipher this. What is it – read it for me, if you can – bet even you can't read your own writing?' she challenged him. She chided him as she had on many an occasion on his handwriting. She had proposed that medics deliberately scrawled to create an air of mystery and an aura of control. Her writing was precise and neat which gave her the moral right to preach to him; not that Alec paid any heed to her impromptu sermons.

'Stop playing for time – you did read it. I saw the flicker of a smile around the edges,' he countered. 'Turn over the note – I had anticipated that you'd try to bluff your way out.'

It was short – a few typed words: 'Will you do me the honour of becoming Mrs Dunlop?'

Alec

'You are such a coward, Dunlop – you didn't have the wherewithal to go down on your gammy knee and propose like an ordinary mortal,' she prevaricated, buying time and baiting him. 'This must be a first – a written proposal? Oh, I get it – no wine served here, ergo, no Dutch courage to tide you over. 'Here', she pushed the glass of passion juice towards him, 'have a sip, it might inject a wee bit more conviction into your efforts.'

'Coward? Really? What's more binding than a written proposal? Come tomorrow I could very well lose my nerve and revoke my proposal. Surely you do not want to take that chance?'

Alec looked at her expectantly as she got up and excused herself. 'Need the ladies, be back shortly.' She hurried away with her brown Louis Vuitton handbag clutched in her left hand, her ponytail swishing like a pendulum.

'Typical. Running away from the battlefield. And you have the gall to question my courage, Dutch or otherwise,' he shot back at her retreating figure. All he got was a hip wiggle and the 'V' sign, which he missed because the tantalising swivel of her hips was engaging his total rapt attention. He wasn't alone – the other men were watching the same sensuous undulations as she glided away.

Alec waved the hovering waiter away without taking his eyes off the retreating figure – hoping that she would look back and give him a clue to her answer. The waiter backed off as Kay disappeared.

She glided back shortly and, as she slipped gracefully into her chair, opened her handbag with great fanfare to retrieve an envelope.

For a moment Alec was taken aback when he saw the sealed envelope, the Sellotape glistening in the bright lights of the restaurant.

'Touche!' He slit it open using the silver knife embossed with 'Mayuri Lounge' across the handle. He was seasoned enough to still his hands; no tremor as the knife did its work.

The compliment slip, with 'The Mayuri Lounge – Supremely The Best' embossed across the top of the letter-head, was blank. He turned it over expecting an answer – blank as well. He looked at her puzzled.

Kay, gripping the crimson lipstick firmly in her right hand, scribbled neatly in bold capitals: 'YES!' She looked straight back at him, very deadpan and queried: 'Shall we give the meal a miss and go straight for dessert – at my place or would you rather have the passion juice here? I'll spare you the blushes by not insisting that you put that ring on my finger in front of this motley crowd – that bulge in your pocket is a ring, I presume?' Her soft brown eyes crinkled and her shy smile reflected the easy repartee that they shared, parrying words like two poets locked in a duel. He had certainly found his match; she drew blood more often than not. His excuse was that her dusky looks befuddled his mind, sometimes rendering him speechless.

'Here, this is now your property for safekeeping. Let's go back to your place and I'll happily put it on your finger and serve dessert in a fitting passionate manner.' Alec smiled as he handed over the ring, glad to be rid of the bulky box.

They headed for the exit after he had apologised profusely to the manager and the waiter, earnestly hoping that the generous tip would compensate for the inconvenience caused.

They walked hand in hand towards Alec's modest-looking VW Beetle, parked a few yards away in an Acacia-tree-lined street with the well-lit front of the restaurant behind them. The car, bathed in the shadow cast by a tree, came into view as they ambled towards it, barely paying attention to their surroundings.

Neither of them saw or heard the two figures emerge from behind a larger tree that they had just passed. Before the engrossed couple could react to the footfalls behind them, a gun was prodded into Alec's back and they were both cautioned not to make a sound – nicotine-stained chubby fingers were clasped around Kay's mouth as a precaution.

'Kukaa kimya!' the burly figure whispered in her ear, just loud enough for Alec to catch the caution to keep silent. Kay recoiled at his smoker's bad breath and the stench of nicotine emanating from his fingers. The thug thrust his groin suggestively into her and Kay blanched at the implied sexual threat.

The subtle fragrance of her perfume almost lulled him into relaxing his grip on her mouth as his thoughts strayed, his right elbow feeling the soft contour of her breast. Kay's sharp bite into the flesh of his thumb brought him back to the job in hand. He pushed her towards the car as they were bundled unceremoniously into the cramped back seat of the VW after Alec was forced to hand over the keys.

Briefly the threat of death and Laikipia flashed through his mind. He was hoping that this was just another carjacking that Nairobi was so notorious for; an opportunistic incident. They had been caught in the wrong place at the wrong time – the euphoria of their pleasant tryst had dulled the normal caution that they would have exercised. The tree-lined side lane, bathed in shadows, was a perfect setting for a 'snatch and grab'. The restaurant's night watchmen were oblivious to the drama unfolding on their doorstep with the deep shadows reducing visibility.

Within minutes, the VW was abandoned on a slip road – off Wayaki Way. They were bundled into an old Merc and were spirited away on to the dual carriageway towards Lavington. Once they had sped away from the abandoned VW, the driver pulled over and Alec and Kay were blindfolded and their mouths taped up. The car pulled out and sped away.

Thousands of miles away, Kostas picked up the phone and heard a series of clicks – an overseas call. The female speaker repeated a coded message: 'We have both the packages. They will be delivered as per the manifest.' The tycoon in his villa in Dubai switched the bedside lamp off and snuggled closer to his Russian wife; his fourth one and the youngest.

Before the crack of dawn, they lifted off from – what Alec assumed – was a private airfield. Their blindfolds had been left in place during the bumpy flight with the mouth tapes removed so that they could drink water. Alec reasoned that it was a small plane going by the turbulent flight and the bumpy landing. They were then bundled into a car and driven a short distance through dense outgrowth – Alec and Kay could hear the branches brushing and scraping against the side panels of the car.

Alec started feeling queasy especially as the kidnappers had not yet removed the blindfolds. Suddenly, the car stopped and they were forced out – Alec scraped his elbows as he stumbled and fell against a small thorny shrub. He could hear Kay's sharp intake of breath as she too landed heavily.

They heard the car speed away and the inhaled plume of dust set up a bout of coughing. They heard a distant call: 'Kwaheri bwana Alec. Kwaheri Ava!

'Ava?' Did they just call you Ava?' Alec asked assuming Kay was close by.

They lay there for a while, still bound and still blindfolded, without a clue as to where they were until a series of whoops sent a chill down their spines.

'What was that?' Kay asked. The tremor in her voice was unmistakable.

'Hyaena!' We seem to be in the bush somewhere.' Alec grunted as he sat up and pushed his back against a shrub. He felt the thorn pricks.

Then they heard the snap of a branch.

'Is anyone out there?' Alec blurted out. 'Help! We were kidnapped.'

No response, just total silence until the next thing they heard was a soft thud and a scream from Alec as a bullet hit him in the upper arm; the fleshy part of his biceps. Kay screamed too – worried that Alec was badly injured.

'Alec? Are you okay'?

'I've been hit – I can feel blood running down my left arm.' His arms tied behind his back were beginning to ache and his circulation compromised by the tight ties.

There was a second pop followed by a thud further away.

'Kay!' Alec screamed as he heard another shot. He had no way of knowing how close Kay was. And then there was silence. He could faintly hear Kay breathing but no more shots which was puzzling until he heard cow bells and the voices.

The Masai morans hurriedly herding their cattle home before the sun disappeared over the horizon had just emerged from the bush onto the dirt road that ran past an abandoned manyatta. The trio of morans stopped short as they saw the couple struggling to get to their feet - barely visible through the spirals of dust kicked up by the cattle.

Shenzi, who was lining up another shot, saw the Masai corralling the herd and withdrew into the thick undergrowth. Even with a rifle he would not dare confront the Masai – the Laikipia plains were their backyard and he wouldn't stand a chance in hell tangling with the ferocious fighters. More importantly, there could be more returning herds and morans nearby.

Shenzi backtracked and ran towards the parked Toyota cruiser, hidden in the thick bush. He swore under his breath. The inopportune appearance of the Masai had disrupted his plans. Both targets had survived and it was going to be difficult to explain the aborted mission.

Shenzi drove past the spot where he had first encountered Alec and the two wardens. But for his verbal outburst that afternoon, Alec would have died at the hands of his deputy.

Sam's frantic attempts to locate both Alec and Kay were instigated when Alec had failed to turn up at his Naivasha farm – it was the conclusion of the 42nd Safari Rally and they had arranged to be at the finish line at the Kenyatta Conference Centre in downtown Nairobi.

The car rally, one of the toughest on the world circuit, was first started in 1953 to mark the coronation of Queen Elizabeth. For Alec being present at the finish of the 1994 season had a special significance – he had treated the pets of an ex-rally winner at the Kabete hospital.

Sam grew concerned when all his calls went unanswered. This was unusual – Alec would have called and cancelled. Something was amiss. He drove down to his office to trigger an official search. He had alerted the police and his team.

Two long days later, he had an anonymous call. The call was identified as originating in Dubai. Just a short curt message.

'Bwana Sam, call off your search. We have both your friends – Alec and Ava.' The line went dead before Sam could react.

His heart skipped a beat. The caller had said 'Alec and Ava'. Not 'Alec and Kay'.

Sam called Mombasa and then Dubai, his heart racing as he thought about the consequences of what he had just heard. The mention of Ava raised the hairs on the back of his neck – this was the first time Ava had been brought into the frame by anyone other than Alec. That too, an overseas caller.

Sam twirled the glass paper weight in his hand as he mulled over the matter – his office desk exhibited the usual organised mess with papers and files resting precariously one on top of another.

He smiled ruefully as he looked at the paper weight in his hand

– it was the Ivory Towers memento of the ivory burning. 'Fake ivory, you mean,' he repeated to himself as he recalled the events that had pitted him and Alec against the poachers.

He picked up the paper weight and shook it – the small ash residue trapped in the triangular paper weight floated like snowflakes.

'Strange how small coincidences sometimes lead to cataclysms,' he reminded himself. He looked at the paperweight and sat bolt upright in his Chesterfield chair. 'Maybe this was a coincidence as well – picking up the fake ivory paperweight? Could the cartel have arranged the kidnap? Maybe they were dealing with something much bigger than just poaching and illicit ivory?'

Sam muttered loudly to himself, his brow furrowed in deep thought. He was about to call his contact in the police department, when the phone rang.

'Sam, Alec here. Bet you were sweating,' Alec said.

'Alec, where the hell have you been?' Sam blurted. 'I just had a call claiming that you lovebirds were in their custody.'

'We were, but luckily the timely appearance of the Masai saved us. Guess where I am?' He continued before Sam could answer, 'In Laikipia – same place where we ran into the poachers. Near the abandoned manyatta. We were kidnapped as we emerged from the Mayuri Lounge, flown here and then dumped. Lambs for slaughter, for sure – had it not been for the Masai, the hyaenas would have feasted on us.'

'Are you or Kay hurt?' Sam asked.

'No, except for a flesh wound to my upper arm. You need to send the cavalry – don't fancy spending the night here. This place gives me the creeps. Second time I came very close to being bumped off.'

Alec was about to ask Sam about the kidnappers mistaking Kay for Ava but decided to defer till they were safely back in Nairobi. He just remembered that Kay had remained silent as well.

'Sam, one more puzzle – whoever it was, the kidnappers I mean - how did they know that we had stopped at that exact spot to euthanise the comatose elephant? Near the manyatta? Could this be the same gang?'

'Only the leader of the poachers is missing, everyone else is accounted for. He's known as Shenzi, the barbarian. We had lost him. He's probably in Mogadishu, the tusks must have fetched him a tidy sum,' Sam paused, then he continued. 'You guys sit tight – let me liaise with the wardens in Nanyuki. They may have a patrol nearby in Laikipia.'

They were lucky – a game warden in the vicinity picked up Sam's SOS call. Still charged up after their escapade, Kay sat next to Alec, as the Toyota Cruiser hurtled towards Nairobi. She felt his eyes on her but avoided his gaze, not sure what to say. Silence reigned as they sped towards the capital.

'Cat got your tongue, Kay?' Alec asked. 'Or should I be calling you Ava? When were you planning on telling me? Not even at the restaurant when I proposed? Surely, that was your cue to come clean?'

'I am so sorry Alec but I had to yield to Sam's explicit instructions. I had no choice. I tried to convince Sam to take you into confidence much earlier but he was worried about the investigation. After getting the intel about imminent trouble in Zanzibar, where I was attending a conference, he pulled me out. Joyce, who was the same build as I, replaced me, dressed in a buibui. Our misfortune was that

Joyce was mistaken for me and executed. Sam decided, on the spur of the moment, to play along and mislead the cartel by planting the news that Ava's body had been recovered from the creek. A press statement released by the police and instigated by Sam, deliberately added the false news of a tattoo. Sam then arranged for me to go to London – to drop out of circulation.'

Alec listened; dismissive, distant and silent. His jaw clenched tightly and with his arms folded across his chest, Ava sensed a steely reserve shutting her out. Like roller shutters coming down with a thud.

'I am sorry Alec to put you through all this. We had no choice – if we had taken you into our confidence then the cartel would have known too. It was all done to safeguard the operation and lives. At that time, playing you was the best course of action,' Ava said, relieved that she was rid of Kay, Sam's creation, and the attendant skulduggery.

Alec remained silent, intent on watching the Acacia trees and the landscape zoom by as they sped towards Nairobi. Ava tried to muffle her sobs, not wanting him to feel sorry for her – she felt bad enough. But then Alec turned to her, and said, deadpan: 'Does this mean that I will have to propose to you again?'

Ava, ignoring his feeble attempt at levity, wiped away the tears, relieved that he seemed to have forgiven her. She fervently prayed that the investigation would not cost them dear. The death of Joyce and all the others had already taken a heavy toll. Any further collateral damage to their relationship would bury all hopes of a future together. They finished the rest of the journey in silence.

The chill between them lasted barely a week. Ava, miserable at the way they had parted took fright at the prolonged radio silence. She took matters into her own hands and booked the best suite at the New

Stanley for the weekend. All the acrimony and the anxiety of the last few days melted away when he walked into the suite to encounter Ava dressed to kill – in just a lacy face veil and red stilettos.

The dimmed lights, the wine and Makeba's recorded rendition of 'Malaika' were as superfluous as the words of reconciliation that Ava did not get a chance to deliver. In the heat of the moment, even the spicy tandoori chicken wings and the lamb chops that Ava had laid out lost their zest. The fizz was entirely in the dessert; once the veil and the stilettos had been shed.

NINETEEN

Zubin, Mombasa.

Zubin returned to Mombasa, after the Lamu incident, none the wiser about the Mag Seven club or the persons behind the scam. Although initially everyone had agreed to keep in touch to present a unified front if further demands were made, once they were on safe ground, the mood changed. Except for the senior Indian gentleman, all the others declined to exchange contact details. Zubin tried to reason but eventually gave in to the majority. They parted as strangers.

As Zubin relaxed in his beach house, with a cool sea breeze gently parting the net curtains, he recalled the advert that he had first responded to while on a short visit to London – an MI6 routine recruitment drive. He had briefly returned to the UK to meet up with his accountants to finalise the annual tax returns.

Military Intelligence Section 6 (MI6), the overseas branch of MI5, had long followed anecdotal evidence of the illicit ivory trade in East Africa funding the nefarious activities of rogue organisations. Zubin had been headhunted, partly because of the family's wealth but mainly for the established ancestry on both sides. The reservations about his sexuality were easily dismissed by the precept that 'hell hath no fury like a woman scorned'. Zubin's past was littered with several

such furious women – many scorned and yet determined not to pursue
paternity tests. He became MI6's 'man in Africa'; the prefix 'good'
was added by the female operatives of the secret service.

Historically, Zanzibar had always been the hub of the slave
trade. Ivory, cloves and Omani influences were interwoven into the
fabric of the islands. Zanzibari dhows laden with gold, spices and
ivory, plied the historical sea routes to Dubai, Oman, India and far
beyond. Mombasa and Lamu, both outposts of the Sultanate of Oman,
were vital cogs.

Zubin, on a routine visit to Century House, the HQ of MI6 in
Lambeth, had been alerted to a shadowy organisation based in
Mombasa that was fielding candidates in the local elections. Zubin's
active role in local politics because of the Y Foundation meant that his
MI6 remit to monitor 'rogue individuals and organisations' would not
arouse suspicion. The Y Foundation took the lead on many campaigns
to develop the coastal strip – better housing, education, jobs and an
impartial allocation of federal funds. The Y Foundation gave
legitimacy to Zubin's snooping; he was truly in the eye of the storm.

The political rivalry between the various religious groups had
its roots in the 19th century political formation of the Zanj Empire by
the Omani Sultanate – Mombasa, Lamu and Zanzibar were part of the
Swahili Coast. The beliefs that once united these lands were distorted
to divide communities. Zubin's task to observe and monitor became
even more onerous once vested interests took root.

These feelings of dissatisfaction and frustration, built over
decades of federal inactivity, led to the political rumblings and
eventually demands for full autonomy for Mombasa and the coast.

Zubin recalled Yasmin mentioning that the call for autonomy became an aspiration at each cycle of local and national elections. More often than not, the matter was swept under the carpet under the guise of losing foreign investments and hampering national development.

It was via the Y Foundation that Zubin managed to tap into the political machinations that were prevalent at the grassroots. His exposure to a shadowy organisation preaching the 'Mombasa for the Mombasa born' mantra led to Abbu, his grassroot networks and his faith healing. The man had cleverly distanced himself from standing for office – he campaigned only for his chosen candidates.

Abbu was off the radar – his reputation, built over decades, as a faith healer and shaman placed him at a huge advantage. He wielded a huge amount of power and had the ability to swing voters; his mass following was almost legendary. The authorities had under estimated the man's charisma, just as Zubin had – in the beginning. Gradually as the layers were peeled off, Zubin realised that the man used his legitimate reputation of a faith healer as a front for illegitimate political wheeler-dealer practices via blackmail, black magic and voodoo rituals. He was the kingmaker.

It was at this stage, knowing the pivotal role that Abbu played in local politics and the anecdotal reports of his absolute power that Zubin entered the fray. A deliberate ploy to get close to him.

Abbu's penchant for advertising his services – the touting of his expertise as an accomplished shaman – gave Zubin the perfect opportunity. The shaman's range of treatments for the troubled mind – unrequited love, love potions, exorcism – and bodily ailments were regularly advertised. The gossip mills also mentioned other alternate remedies for sexual disorders – only divulged at special one-to-one consultations.

Zubin had also heard the sinister allegations about blackmail – the rumour was that any patient, especially a young adult, who presented with anal bleeding would be targeted. The practice of frequent enemas for chronic constipation – so prevalent in certain communities – would be ignored as a legitimate reason for the bleeding. The young adults would be cajoled to reveal the identities of male relatives or friends and then blackmailed, especially if the victims turned out to be celebrities or politicians.

It was Zubin's idea to offer himself as bait – his prominence in local politics would endear him to the shaman as a target for political mileage.

The sting was set up – deliberately using young adults who looked vulnerable or effeminate. The actors chosen from the amateur dramatic clubs from Mombasa and beyond. The Y Foundation ran several charities for homeless adults – this was public knowledge so Zubin was confident that Abbu would assume the worst. Zubin became the bait – he projected himself as a predator.

And it wasn't long before the shaman took the bait. Zubin deliberately positioned himself next to his car – in broad daylight – as the ayah chaperoned the young 'victims' to the shaman's surgery in the old town. He knew the shaman had taken the bait when he noticed Abbu's buibui-clad housekeeper follow the ayah and the patient back towards the waiting car. The simple ruse of using credible actors and chicken blood had worked – only the first patient had been genuine; a case of chronic constipation.

It was several months before the shaman started making demands – on each occasion the fees were paid, no matter how outlandish. Gradually, the shaman got bolder and bolder until he traced the man accompanying these patients to be the rich and famous bachelor – Zubin. The Y Foundation became the shaman's main focus – as a source of funds but also for political gamesmanship.

When Abbu 'blackmailed' Zubin into joining the 'Mag Seven' club and the ransom demands were made, Zubin sought the advice of a 'friend' – Sam, who was the contact set up by MI6. Zubin in collaboration with Sam had finally gained a foothold. Sam had hoodwinked his way into the poaching rings using the same methods.

In the early stages neither Sam nor Zubin had any idea of the ramifications of their 'lucky break'.

TWENTY

Alec and Sam, Naivasha, Kenya

Alec had arranged with Sam to spend the weekend at the farm, both aware that their brainstorming sessions in the past had unravelled many things; clarity restored during or after their 'think tank' sessions. Alec had indicated that he needed to explore the circumstances of Dr Pinto's death.

Their favourite spot, under the huge Acacia tree, afforded them stunning panoramic views of the lower lying areas of Naivasha. The sun was gradually sinking over the horizon as they finished the first of many ice-cold Tuskers that Sam's valet-cum-chef-cum man-Friday, Henry Karuiki, had served. The lamb samosas with the green chilli-coriander chutney that Henry had served went down well with the cold beer.

'Kissinger, that was perfect. Asante sana.' Alec thanked Henry as he replenished their beers.

'Karibu sana, bwana Alec!' Kissinger shyly responded to Alec's comments. The warm smile lighting up his face and revealing toothless gums.

By now Alec had also got used to addressing Henry as 'Kissinger'. The story went that Sam had inherited the chef when he bought the farm from the Vaz family. The Goan couple had trained Henry Karuiki to cook and had nicknamed him 'Kissinger' - the passing resemblance to Henry Kissinger, the American diplomat, became more striking as Karuiki grew older. Over the years, the moniker 'Kissinger' had stuck.

Karuiki wasn't too displeased with the nickname, especially after Sam had explained the important role the American diplomat had played in American and world politics. This had prompted the chef to make one of his rare forays to the McMillan Library in town to read up on the American. It did not take long for the chef to sport the same black thick-framed glasses; an affectation that enhanced the 'Kissinger' effect.

Sam had ribbed the chef endlessly for using glasses as a theatrical prop and had, in the presence of Alec, reminded Henry that had it not been for the repeal of the 'McMillan Memorial Library Act of 1938', which barred entry to all except Europeans, Henry would not have been able to enter the library and bone up on the US diplomat.

This disclosure of Kenya's colonial past dented the chef's exuberance and he abandoned the spectacles – until Alec remarked that the glasses gave him a certain gravitas. The bifocals made a swift and permanent return to the low perch on the chef's hooked nose.

'What's on your mind about Dr Pinto?' Sam asked as he started on his second Tusker of the evening. The last sightings of the missing Goan vet had been in the Masai Mara where he had been tracking an injured lion.

'We know that Dr Pinto's remains were found in the national park by the wardens some months back,' Alec responded still maintaining that air of mystery and slipping into their Sherlock

Holmes-Dr Watson role playing. They parried constantly about who assumed the superior mantle of Holmes, the quintessential English detective.

On this occasion, Sam yielded to his friend: 'Go on maestro, enlighten me,' Sam replied with an air of resignation. Alec was unstoppable once he got into 'that mode'.

'At the time, we all thought Dr Pinto had strayed too far on his own. There had been reports of this pride, led by a young injured male, of aggressive behaviour. This was just after Dr Pinto's transfer. We were forewarned about flying to Masai Mara at short notice,' Alec explained; prolonging the air of mystery.

'Ok, bwana Holmes. Can we get to the point?' Sam said, not without a trace of irritation at Alec's grandstanding.

'Hold your horses. It will take longer if you keep butting in. I don't think I have mentioned this but just after Dr Pinto had handed me the 'ashes' souvenir, he had recognised someone in the sponsor's enclosure. Much later I saw him chatting to this dignitary who had an entourage of his aides milling around him. I did not get a look, as his back was towards me. Anyway, when Dr Pinto re-joined us, he said something about knowing the dignitary from 'USA' or words to that effect – unfortunately, as you may recall, there was a display of fireworks and I lost his words in the noise.'

'Meaning his death is connected to what happened on the day?' Sam queried, wondering if his friend was onto something; even if the connection was nebulous; vague and wafer thin.

'Dr Pinto had mentioned that his alma mater was in Bangalore – his vet school was part of the University of Agricultural Sciences – UAS – campus in Bangalore.'

'So?' Sam was now more than intrigued by Alec's train of thoughts. He still had no idea where this was leading. Probably, 'a fishing expedition' - Sam borrowing the words from the Perry Mason TV legal drama series.

'Don't you get it? The abbreviated form of his alma mater is UAS. What if he meant UAS and not USA? He had recognised someone from the vet school in Bangalore?'

Alec stopped abruptly trying to regain his thought trail. After a minute or two he looked at a very puzzled Sam.

'What if Pinto's death in the Masai Mara was not an accident? Maybe he was killed because he identified someone, a culprit? It would be easy to dump the body in the Masai Mara, knowing that the lions or other scavengers would make short work of the corpse.'

'He was silenced, you mean? I recall that the sparse remains recovered were so badly decomposed that the post mortem was inconclusive. Or so we were led to believe.'

Alec subsided into a long silence – just drank his beer as he tried to mine his mind for memory bytes of details that lay buried. Sam looked on without a word – for fear of interrupting his friend's train of thought.

Alec could not shake off the feeling that something that was said to him in Dubai after the camel-racing fiasco was at the centre of his thoughts about the ivory scam.

Dr Reddy had been his forte and had been by his side all along during the acrimonious trial and investigation. He even recalled that Dr Reddy took all the blame for the mix up with the two camels.

Towards the end of the case, he recalled that he had agreed to resign and accept the blame if it saved Dr Reddy's job. The last bit of conversation at Dubai Airport where Dr Reddy said farewell before Alec had boarded his flight to Nairobi.

Alec sat up and looked at Sam. 'The last time anyone mentioned 'UAS' was Dr Reddy!' Alec blurted out. 'Dr Reddy had indicated that he would have no option but to return to UAS and maybe get a faculty position at the vet school in Bangalore.'

'Dr Pinto went over to greet Dr Reddy – both from Bangalore?' Sam asked.

'Just a gut feeling at the moment.'

They just sat there – two friends lost in the intricacies of the case. The Laikipia encounter seemed a long time ago – so much had unfolded since then.

'Do you have any high-level connections with UAE immigration?' Alec questioned his friend who jerked out of his own reverie.

'Yes, I assume you want access to Dr Reddy's immigration file to ascertain if he's still in Dubai?' Sam countered.

'Simple. If he is still in Dubai, despite the gravity of charges levelled against him, then the hostile takeover was just a ruse to serve a higher agenda? All pre-planned as Dr Reddy probably felt that he had been recognised at the ivory burning. Everything that has happened since then has been a cover-up to stop you, the commission, from finding out the truth.'

'Huh', Sam said still not convinced. 'I thought you were very taken with Dr Reddy – now he's your prime suspect?'

'Well, we have no option but to keep digging. Maybe, it would be easier to contact the vet school in Bangalore and see whether Dr Reddy has re-joined the faculty.'

Two weeks later Sam phoned Alec at Kabete. Alec was engrossed in a post-mortem being carried out on a pet Alsatian which had died of liver failure. Kenya, especially Nairobi and other urban cities were going through a spate of canine deaths; all showing signs of liver disease. The 'hob nailed' appearance of the liver and signs of jaundice pointed to cirrhosis of the liver; very much akin to alcohol abuse and liver disease in humans. Alec and the pathologist were both aware of recent press reports about fungal contamination of dog food; the link between aflatoxin and liver disease.

'Your hunch was right – there is no record of any vet licence or visa being cancelled. Meaning he is very much in Dubai. Probably running the camel hospital – that's his cover if he is indeed part of the ivory cartel,' Sam elaborated.

It was during this phase that Sam flew to Bangalore to try and pin down the connection of Dr Reddy or others to the Bangalore campus and the ivory burning event in Nairobi.

Both Sam and Alec had jointly looked at Musa's film – with all the smoke and crowds criss-crossing through Musa's film, even using expert techniques to zoom in, the dignitary remained a blur, obscured partly by Dr Pinto who was clearly visible as he walked past Musa. In one shot, Alec and Dr Pinto were clearly visible – Alec examining the souvenir of the ashes that Dr Pinto had just handed over.

The faculty of veterinary medicine at the veterinary hospital on the campus was a short distance away from the grey-stoned edifice of the vet school. The front of the hospital had a couple of tennis courts that looked the worse for wear, overgrown with weeds. The front of the vet school was in a better condition – a huge water fountain spewing jets of water and rolling lawns down to the main entrance on an extremely busy road; a major artery of transport connection to the outer ring of the city.

The faculty was very accommodating. Dr Jacobs, the erudite head and professor of medicine, more than willing to talk to Sam. After taking Sam on a brief tour of the hospital – his pride and joy – they returned to the head's office. Sam had used the excuse of assessing the needs of the several Kenyan students pursuing the various courses offered by the vet school. Sam did not want to tip anyone off or create waves.

Dr Reddy had been a merit student through his undergraduate years, to his Master's in Small Animal Medicine and followed by his PhD. The academic progression – starting as an instructor to associate professor and finally to professor and head of department – was the routine slow and steady climb up the academic hierarchy.

Dr Jacobs was initially reticent about Dr Reddy's background – but grew very effusive in his outpourings as the conservation progressed. Sam got the feeling that the current head was in awe of the previous one. There was genuine warmth and admiration in the head's voice.

As the discussion came to an end, Sam asked by way of a closing question: 'Would you have Dr Reddy's address – maybe I could meet him?'

'I'm afraid, Dr Reddy died a few years ago,' the professor said.

'Really? Where? In Dubai?' Sam asked. It was his turn to be puzzled. He had met the man just a few months ago.

'Here in Bangalore. He retired a few years ago. I didn't know he had gone to Dubai. He dabbled in private practice and even managed his local cricket team.' The professor explained that cricket had been a lifelong passion. Dr Reddy had been such an accomplished cricketer that the vet had almost taken up cricket as a career.

Alec was astounded when Sam called from Bangalore and conveyed his findings – that Dr Reddy, BVSc, MVSc, PhD, professor and head of the department of vet medicine, had died a few years ago.

The Dr Reddy that Alec knew in Dubai was also from the same vet school and had the same qualifications declared on his CV. He agreed with Sam – something did not stack up.

On the flight back to Nairobi, Sam had more time to ponder over his Bangalore trip. As Sam settled down to a long night's flight, he made a mental note to call Dubai once he got back to Nairobi. He needed access to the Dubai man's CV. The licensing authorities in UAE would have one on file. It was standard procedure before issuing a visa to work in the UAE.

Shortly before he fell asleep after requesting a nightcap from the airhostess, he tuned in to the BBC on the inflight entertainment screen. The cricket coverage about India winning against Pakistan reminded him of Dr Reddy. At the farewell dinner, Alec had left the room to take a call from Kay leaving him alone with Dr Reddy. They had tuned in to watch a cricket match being played at Lord's Cricket Ground in St John's Wood, London.

The nightcap almost spilt in his lap as he lurched forward – Dr Jacobs had mentioned Dr Reddy's abiding passion for cricket. Sam was wide awake – the nightcap's effect totally nullified.

Dr Reddy had enquired about a simple umpire's call as they had watched the match – a no-ball signal – which any school boy cricketer would have known about. Dr Reddy's ignorance of a simple umpire's signal did not square with the Bangalore vet who had almost taken up cricket professionally.

Why would Dr Reddy lie about his cricketing background? The call to Dubai to cross check Dr Reddy's details became even more imperative.

Two days later, as he put the phone down after his call to Dubai, Sam rang Alec at Kabete.

'Guess what? The Dubai visa application has our Dr Reddy's address as somewhere in Bombay – an area called Dharavi. Are you sitting down? The two are different identities – one, a distinguished academician who was into cricket and died sometime back in Bangalore and our Dubai vet who has never played cricket. The Dubai file has the qualifications and the academic record of the Dr Reddy from Bangalore. Our Dr Reddy has veterinary qualifications from the University of Rajasthan and has worked for a number of years in a camel hospital there – so he's got the clinical expertise to work in Dubai. He 'borrowed' the PhD qualifications of the real Dr Reddy at the vet school in Bangalore to land the Dubai job. My contacts in Bombay have just confirmed that Dr J A Reddy has Bachelor's and Master's qualifications but no PhD. Both vets have the same initials – 'J A.'

Alex listened in silence as the import of Sam's words sank in. Dr Reddy, his colleague in Dubai was an impostor.

'The same – J A Reddy – same first names but the middle names were different, although both started with the initial A. Long names, I dare not even try to pronounce,' Sam went on.

'This means that the imposter Dr Reddy is still in Dubai. The expulsion was a sham, a ruse? Hang on a second,' Alec blurted. 'Kay and I met Musa and his clients, an Indian couple in Dubai. I'm sure

Musa said he was a businessman and a Bollywood producer. The portly producer had given me a business card – I recall it had a Dharavi address. He boasted about his humble origins in Dharavi – he still retains the business premises and the site for sentimental reasons. And, Dr Reddy and this producer were both present at the Nairobi event, both hail from Dharavi. Too much of a coincidence, don't you think?'

'Agreed. That places a lot of people in the same frame at the ivory event – Musa, the Bollywood producer, Dr Reddy, the impostor, and you. Quite a few who were present that day in Nairobi are dead. Ergo, that event was central to everything else that has unfolded since,' Sam said.

'And I was present and was just kidnapped and almost bumped off,' Alec mumbled. 'And Ava almost died with me. If the impostor Dr Reddy is still in Dubai as our sources have confirmed, then he must have been complicit in the conspiracy to eject me? In cahoots with Kostas? Somehow I can't imagine him being part of all this,' Alex said.

Sam heard the same scepticism in his friend's voice as the time when Musa had been interrogated after Ava's disappearance.

A few days later, they managed to track down Dr Reddy in Bombay. He confessed that he had used the real Dr Reddy's qualifications to land the job in Dubai. Without a PhD, he could not have beaten off the intense competition for the UAE positions. The attractive salary package was his chance to clear all his debts and secure the family's financial future.

Dr Reddy had flown out of Dubai as advised by Sam. He remained beholden to Sam and Alec for their help – otherwise he would still be in UAE trapped by Kostas's scam or even in prison. Dr Reddy was suitably contrite for his actions, and assured Alec and Sam of his support, if needed, to bring Kostas to heel.

Another dead end, Alec thought. He was glad though that Dr Reddy was not involved; not part of the ivory scam or part of the cartel.

TWENTY-ONE

Abbu, Mombasa.

Abbu understood the psychological impact of using omens and amulets and used them to his advantage. His travels through India, where he had followed the tantric practices, also gave him an insight into other rituals – black magic or similar rites invariably associated with religious folklore. The shaman was well versed in some of these practices and had added these and many more to his bag of tricks.

The residents of Mombasa and the coast were bombarded with a concerted campaign of psychological intimidation – the supremacy of evil and how it would affect one and all if traditional and time-honoured practices were not followed. Only amulets and exorcism would protect against the demons unleashed by planetary mis-alignments.

Green chillies and lemons are used in India to ward off evil. Mombasa traders and householders had these 'amulets' strung up in doorways. Chicken heads and feathers on car screens or left in doorways were omens of evil and bad luck to follow. In one instance an albino child was kidnapped and turned up washed ashore near the creek. There were several such campaigns carried out all over Mombasa especially in electoral wards in and around old town. With no one claiming responsibility, gossip and innuendo added to the fear factor.

Sam and his team had even visited Mombasa to reassure the populace that the police were still in charge and well on top of the events. The acts of intimidation were pervasive – the reassurances by the local politicians and the authorities only created further confusion.

Abbu and his shaman persona had succeeded in creating fear amongst the local population. Right from the outset, Abbu had skilfully kept the two separate – Abbu the faith healer and Abbu the shaman. The shaman role conjured up to control the mind, whereas the faith healer attended to the sick body.

The most sinister aspect of the campaign was the 'Mombasa for the Mombasa born' agenda that the anonymous group or groups hoped to impose. Despite the repeated attempts at spreading dissent and chaos, most voters knew that this false propaganda was just old wine in a new bottle. In certain sections, the false campaign actually united people against the movement. However, there remained an undercurrent of unease in the less well informed or more gullible populace. The electorate was well aware that any disruption to the inbound tourists would affect their livelihoods. Tourism and associated hospitality sectors were major employers on the coast.

Abbu had his finger on the pulse of Mombasa and thought he had an opportunity to seize political control. His influence over a vast network at the grass roots afforded very many advantages and his work as a shaman and a faith healer helped – he had a presence on the ground that made him a central figure all along the coast; a kingmaker.

This was his chance to hijack the campaign for his own benefit – not by opposing any particular ideology but by projecting himself as some kind of a messiah who was going to liberate the populace.

All done in a very subtle and covert manner – donating sums of money for renovating the crumbling mosques and the madrasa schools in the provinces. He used coercion, blackmail and other subterfuges to recruit powerful people – those with the political clout to do his bidding.

One of his early targets was the Y Foundation – he had a strong hold on Zubin via the multitude of photographs in his possession – the compromising images of young adults, if released to the press, would destroy Zubin's reputation, whom he thought of as a political rival. Similar tactics were used against anyone who dared to speak up –blackmail and extortion used to silence rivals.

TWENTY-TWO

Sam and Alec, Naivasha.

Alec and Sam were at their wits' end – prime suspects either killed or inaccessible. The investigation was floundering. And the upsurge in ivory poaching filled Sam with dread — they had been on the wrong track all along. Dr Reddy was no longer a suspect. The cartel was intact and very much active.

As Kissinger went back into the kitchen, Sam said: 'We are back to square one.'

The men fell silent for a while as they inhaled the aroma emanating from the starters that had just arrived. The vista of sizzling food on their plates enticed them to forsake all conversation as they assailed the chunks of lamb, chicken and fried mogo with unbridled relish.

They paused for a while until Sam quipped: 'I guess Musa could have been a great help or even Dr Pinto – if they had been alive. Both were present at the ivory-burning event that day. Maybe your team could look at Musa's film again? Might trigger a memory?'

A few days later Sam called just as Alec was leaving the small animal clinics at Kabete.

'I've had another closer look at Musa's film. I saw Dr Pinto talking to the group huddled in the sponsors' enclosure but most were facing the other way. Even had my guys blow up the frames – nothing. Only Dr Pinto is clearly visible. The obvious inference is that many of the attendees are linked one way or another which makes the film crucial evidence. However, without Dr Pinto's or Musa's personal input, the picture remains incomplete.'

'There's something that I forgot to pursue – your comment about Dr Pinto and the sponsors reminded me. That day at the ivory event in Nairobi, I found a pillbox which I had handed over to Dr Pinto. Not sure what happened to the two capsules and a tablet that were in the pillbox. Probably took it back to the Orphanage.'

The pillbox was still sitting in the lab with a label in Dr Pinto's writing – 'Alec – meds found in the sponsors' enclosure'.

The report from the Government Chemist, the Kenya Medical Research Institute (KEMRI) at the Ministry of Health confirmed the two capsules as cod liver oil and the white tablet as citalopram, an anti-depressant.

TWENTY-THREE

The Indian, Stone Town, Zanzibar and Leicester, UK.

The Indian's office was in a side street parallel to Kenyatta Road; a stone's throw from where Freddie Mercury was born and lived until the age of eight. The narrow lanes were flanked by terraced houses which had barazas - cement ledges built into the walls - running along the length of the external walls.

The baraza served as seats or as narrow footways on which one could walk during the heavy rains and floods. The ornately carved Zanzibari doors were a common feature on the coast. The front doors frequently identified the owners – Muslim carvings denoted Arab origin; Indian, if it had carved lotuses.

The lotus, a symbol of wealth in India was prominent on the door of the Indian's house; a visual clue to the origins of the occupant. The entire building was once residential; now used as an office.

From his first-floor window, seated in his Chesterfield leather chair, behind his mahogany table, he could see a sea of crowded narrow by-lanes and terraced houses - all with tin rooves. Most of the Stone Town properties had that faded and dilapidated look as if one had stepped back into the 1800s.

Although the external façade was non-descript and in keeping with the surrounding white-washed peeling walls, the massive handcrafted carved door gave the building a look of medieval distinction.

Once one entered the large court yard on the ground floor and ascended the small creaking timber staircase to the first floor, the faded and tired worn look disappeared. The interiors boasted a modern décor with a mix of soft pastel paints and handcrafted Persian screens. The hum of the air con was another modern incursion in a house full of old-world charm. These Indo-Arabic architectural edifices, flanking narrow crisscrossing lanes, were commonplace across the Swahili coast from Zanzibar to Lamu.

The Indian loved the retro feel of the place – he preferred the unostentatious look which belied the vast wealth that he had accumulated over the years as an ivory and spice trader. His clove plantations were the envy of many. Cloves and ivory were the making of him but he had since diversified into property and other trades.

His main administrative base was in Dar-es-Salam where he had a plethora of MBA qualified managers and employees running his vast legitimate empire of travel agencies, resorts and hotels, freight and cargo and bonded-warehouses in the harbours of Mombasa, Zanzibar and Dar-es-Salam.

There were similar hubs in Nairobi, Dubai, London and Bombay. No one knew about his various bolt holes; calls to his Dar-es-Salam office were rerouted to Stone Town. Even his staff based in the offices across the globe weren't aware of his whereabouts.

The Indian had delved into the history of the African continent in meticulous detail and the more he read, the greater was his ire and discontent. He realised that between the Germans, the British, the

Belgians, the Portuguese and the Italians, his part of the world had been conquered and controlled by the European colonials for centuries.

The only exception to the rule was the sovereign control of Zanzibar – and, at different stages, parts of Kenya and Lamu – by the Omanis. It heartened him to read that his hero and mentor, Tippu Tip, a Zanzibari, had travelled as far as the Belgian Congo and eventually ended up being the Governor of Zanzibar.

As the Indian sat in his mansion on the outskirts of Leicester in England, he relived the Zanzibar Revolution – the riots against the Indians and the Arabs had torn apart his family. They had fled to Mombasa and had eventually landed in Bombay – on an abstract belief that India would provide a safe haven. It hardly did – after a life full of criminal intent and activities, he was forced to move out to Dubai and then to London.

He had no skills that could prepare him for a career, but his sharp brain and mental agility provided the escape route from menial jobs – his ability with numbers landed him a job running illegal lotteries and gambling dens for a local thug. It took him thirty years to graduate from a penniless nobody to a drug dealing and money laundering kingpin. He became the hawala king - the illegal and parallel money system that controlled cash transfers across currencies and countries.

The Indian smiled. He was a banker who moved money across borders; just like the big banks. His parallel banking system was more important than the legitimate one especially in countries where the lines of demarcation were blurred. It was later, after he moved to the West, that he realised that the lines were blurred much more in the developed world; his perception that only the colonies were corrupt had been based on a false narrative. After all, the colonies had learnt well from the colonial masters – excelled at the game and eventually surpassed the masters.

Sitting in that mansion in Leicester reminded him of the two vows that he had made to himself that day at the British High Commission in Nairobi – when the family's visa application to settle in the UK was rejected by the officious immigration officer.

That, one day the very same system will felicitate him for the wealth that he had created – he was fortunate that the barriers to his upward mobility had been loosened by the tremendous success of the Asian diaspora displaced from East Africa. His adopted city, Leicester, became the epicentre of revival for the 'refugees' from Uganda, followed by many others from Kenya, Tanzania and Zanzibar.

The second promise was that he would establish a homeland for all those who wished to return to their roots. The Ugandan Asians had managed to achieve some success in returning to their homeland, though his return to Zanzibar - at the head of the timeshare brigade was work in progress.

It was with pride that he looked back at the pinnacle of his achievements – as head of the cartel that had its tentacles all over East Africa, Dubai, Bombay and beyond.

All the proceeds of all the scams perpetrated by his minions – Abbu profiteering via political shenanigans, Bollywood movies, ivory trading, Roxana's and Kostas' endeavours were funnelled by way of his global hawala networks – he knew that but they did not. The minions were deluded into thinking that the cartel was their 'baby'.

After the deaths of Abbu, Shenzi, Roxana and many others, he knew that he was on the cusp of his final onslaught – to create a homeland in the Zanzibar Archipelago. His chain of timeshare resorts was the first step in the fulfilment of that dream. The timeshare properties were exclusively sold to the Asian diaspora – all those displaced by the upheavals in East Africa. Most of these 'refugees' had prospered in the UK, Canada, Australia and the USA.

There were two main criteria for the timeshare membership – that each wananchi – citizen - had to be born in East Africa and have an individual asset value of at least £1 million and a disposal income of £100,000 annually. The high-net-worth individuals were offered prime slots and moved up the hierarchy in direct proportion to their financial viability. Those who were second, third and fourth generation East Africans were accorded the 'some are more equal than others' Orwellian status.

Although the timeshare properties were spread across East Africa, the Archipelago of Zanzibar was his personal preference, not just because it was his birthplace but because his mentor, Tippu Tip, had governed Zanzibar. The island archipelago had another unique and attractive feature that he hoped to exploit – its political discord with the mainland.

That day in Stone Town when he recognised Ava Patel and her consort, Alec, led to his panicked withdrawal – their presence was too close for comfort and he had jumped to the rash conclusion that he had been outed. The police raid that he feared imminent never materialised.

He had erred on the side of caution by retreating to Dar-es-Salam initially and later to Leicester. His 'Chinese Wall' strategy afforded him some protection from detection, as did the maze of shell companies spread across the world. The convoluted business model, designed and refined by him over the years, was deliberately embedded in each country as a standalone entity. Only he knew how the different entities were connected and only he controlled the flow of cash.

Ray Senior was one of his mini failures – neither Roxana nor Abbu had been able to coerce him to join his grand plan. He had a strong suspicion that Ray Senior had been tipped off by Zubin aka Shorty, the MI6 minion in East Africa.

He yawned and sighed as he prepared to go to bed – he opened a new package of the Seven Seas cod liver capsules that he always had before retiring. He looked at the two capsules – the shiny gelatine shells that encapsulated the oil – and wondered whether it had gelatine manufactured by his minions in Bombay and Nairobi.

He smiled, not for the first time at his reflection in the crystal water of his indoor swimming pool – not bad for a penniless stateless Zanzibari thrown out of the British High Commission offices in Nairobi. The mansion was owned by an offshore company – a part of the maze of global companies that his accountants had established over the years. All his properties were similarly owned – virtually impossible to trace back to him.

His grand plan was similarly a slow process to create the right conditions - back home in East Africa – for the multitude of Asians, the diaspora, dispersed all over the West. He was on the cusp of attaining the dream of a homeland – a back to the roots – an African retreat. As they say 'you can take an African out of Africa but you can't take Africa out of an African'. He was very close to the finale; all the chessboard pieces were in place.

The next morning as he completed his seven-lap routine swim in the heated indoor pool, he was on schedule to have his breakfast at 7am. The Indian's ivory trading encompassed East Africa and beyond and most of his illicit ivory was sourced from Tanzania where the slaughter of elephants and the harvesting of ivory were carried out on a monumental scale.

The poached ivory was shipped out to Zanzibar in small dhows and then transported to the hub – Mombasa and onwards to the main markets in Dubai and beyond. East African ivory was prized, as compared to Asian tusks, because the soft composition of the ivory made it easy to carve into ornaments and artefacts.

The head of the cell picked up the call and exchanged the usual Muslim salutation of 'peace unto you'.

'Have you had any further progress about our discussion? Has Sam arrived yet?' The Indian asked referring to Sam's arrival in Dubai to track down and interrogate Dr Reddy.

'Yes, all done. Our contact within the UAE immigration had tipped us off about Dr Reddy's immigration status. He was interviewed at length about his background.'

The Indian did not let on but knew straight away that his ploy of forcing Alec, the vet, back to Nairobi had not worked. The duo, by the seat of their pants, had managed to outwit him. More importantly, they must have worked out or would soon do so – that he had engineered the takeover of the camel hospital and the stables. His plan to take over the conglomerate and list the company in London was in imminent danger of exposure.

He quickly disconnected the call and thought deeply about the Kenyan team, Sam and Alec - their combined presence was a peril that he needed to nullify.

The Indian acknowledged that the he had failed to capitalise on the crisis that he had initiated at the camel hospital. He wondered how

Tippu Tip, his mentor, would have played the Dubai hand? It pained him that Shenzi had failed to eliminate the threat posed by Alec – somewhere along the line he had wasted an opportunity. He had not followed the wisdom of Churchill – 'never let a good crisis go to waste'.

A voracious reader, he had discovered Hyman Minsky, the American economist, and many others in his youth. His investments in global property were usually impulsive, however, with property and land purchases in East Africa, he had a well-thought-out strategy in place to buy low and hold into perpetuity.

In Mombasa and on the coast, he would wait patiently for political upheavals that triggered the sudden and substantial loss of asset values – signals to buy. The Indian, with precision and some amount of luck, bought swathes of land over several years or even decades – at rock-bottom prices. He did not act alone but orchestrated the participation of other cartel members – each member was led to believe that the scheme was their 'baby'.

In some cases, he would cut them loose after landing profits – as he had done with Kostas after his swoop on the camel hospital. With Abbu, the shaman, he was determined to take it to the wire and step in at the last moment – he had spotted the commercial potential of Abbu's hoax agenda about taking over the coastal region.

With Roxana, the lines were very clear – all she wanted was the money; her head was not messed up with political or social ideologies. He liked her and his use of her as a buibui assassin for the cartel was a stroke of genius. In order to maintain control, the introduction of Shenzi as her understudy assassin was even cleverer – kept her in check.

The Asians, nervous at the best of times, did not need reminders of their precarious position in East Africa. The several coups in the region, Amin's expulsion of the Asians and the war that led to Amin's overthrow all created a climate of fear and confusion.

The Indian, at the helm of the cartel and the vast numbers of enlisted members – 'back to the roots' campaign disguised as timeshare clients – had the world at his feet. The vast resources of the cartel augmented by the assets of the ultra-rich timeshare members, made him invincible. Or so he thought.

All this and more added to the uncertainty that he had created by the false reports of a separatist movement all along the coastal strip – the 'Mombasa for the Mombasa born' was a scam. His minions and political proteges had, for decades, played on the fears of the people that their hard-earned money was being misused for economic development elsewhere. The entire campaign was a sham, led ably by Abbu.

And here he was, many years later, on the cusp of banking obscene amounts of money – yet again. And he had the firepower, his band of 'dogs of war' mercenaries, to unleash as he saw fit. His dream of creating a 'land of the Zanj' was well within reach – he considered himself an African; Indian genes nurtured by the African continent. He would create the perfect harmony between black and brown – his Zanzibar of the future.

The plan had almost floundered when the contract killing of the British geologist and the retrieval of his oil report were used by the buibui assassin to further her own agenda of greed. Having read the report, which categorically stated that there were no oil deposits, the assassin correctly figured out that the negative report had 'other higher value' purpose – open to manipulation. He had to give in to her extortion and yield to her demands in order not to disrupt the next phase of his grand plan.

Once the report was safely in his possession, his most trusted co-conspirator went to work and forged the report – to show huge deposits of oil in the Lamu Archipelago. This fake report was deliberately leaked and judiciously circulated with a heading 'for your eyes only'. Those four words ensured that the report gained maximum exposure within his target group of scapegoats.

This was the fillip that would drive property prices upwards – the first stage of his grand plan to create a bubble. The next step was to drip feed the positive news to his legions of followers, and their followers and so forth; it became the best-kept secret. And like all best-kept secrets, the false news became the currency of his opportunity. The more it spread, the more he profited.

The value of his property estate started creeping up, especially the swathes he held on the coast – Mombasa and Lamu. The rumours of an oil find fed well into the psyche of the country, especially as the discovery of oil further afield in other African countries had raised expectations of the public. Property prices sky rocketed and drew in investors in droves.

After the bubble reached a peak, his team of estate managers and estate agents sold discreetly; sale agreements subject to privacy of transactions. The instructions were to liquidate the portfolio gradually so as not to threaten the price bubble – the supply cleverly controlled to maintain a shortage. The Indian was a master at work – the supply and demand curve under his control. He had honed his art to perfection – the psychology of human greed at the heart of his strategy.

His accountants worked quietly in the background; sale proceeds filtered and salted out of the country; via his global hawala networks. The shell companies formed in the UK and other exchanges were manipulated and many share price bubbles also emerged. Huge loans, using the listed shell companies, were raised and disappeared into other shell companies and offshore platforms. His majority shareholding sold as soon as the value had spiked or reached a pre-determined 'sell signal'.

The Indian sighed; a job well done. Now he had to take care of the finale of his misinformation tactics – the years of groundwork to create an illusion – the pseudo separatist movement. He had no interest in the establishment of a purported separate state carved out of Mombasa county. Like the oil scam, the idea of creating a separate Mombasa state was also a hoax. His loyalty and aspirations lay elsewhere; his grand plan for Zanzibar.

TWENTY-FOUR

Alec and Ava, Nairobi.

Ava and Alec were back at the Mayuri Lounge at her insistence. She had ignored Alec's moans about vegetarian food and how he was looking forward to his weekly restaurant binges on tandoori cooked meat.

'Why have you dragged me here – you know I can barely stomach the veg fare?' Alec asked.

'You have already forgotten – on the way back from Laikipia, you had promised to propose again.'

'Where's the ring'? Alec asked looking at her ring finger.

That's when she blanched – the blood draining from her face and the smile wiped off. The thugs had bundled them into Alec's Beetle, switched to another car and then dumped them in Laikipia.

Ava frowned, trying to retrace the sequence of events in her mind. She could not recall what she had done with the ring. The kidnappers had rummaged through her handbag and thrown it back at her in disgust when the search did not throw up anything of value. The thugs took the few shillings in change that she always carried for the parking meters on Kenyatta Avenue or to tip the street children who guarded parked cars.

Ava opened the bag and tipped everything on the table. No ring, some change, a credit card and Alec's written proposal of marriage – with the lipstick 'yes' scribbled across it.

Alec looked at her, deadpan and asked, almost in a whisper: 'You've lost it, haven't you?'

'It'll come back to me. I had it in my bag when we left this place that night we got kidnapped,' she said without much conviction. 'I must have hidden it in the Beetle, before the goons switched cars.'

'Never mind. Shall we defer the repeat proposal; no point going down on my knee if there's no ring,' Alec asked, enjoying the temporary reprieve.

She just nodded, her mind on the New Stanley suite and how they had managed to resolve some of the issues. The memory of how she had worked on Alec that night raised a smile.

'We could not talk that night but I'm curious. When did you first suspect that Kay did not exist?' Ava asked tremulously. Sam and she had debated long and hard about coming clean.

'It took me a while but my gut feeling was that things did not stack up. There was no great hoo-ha about your disappearance and alleged death – only a police statement about finding a body with a tattoo. No inquest and the press were strangely silent. Considering that Mombasa is a popular tourist destination, the discovery of a body in the creek hardly mattered. Not even to the hoteliers and the resorts who would lose European tourists. Musa's silence, almost apathy, was a huge giveaway, especially as he had mentioned that his family had taken you under their wing. Did Musa know?' Alec continued after a pause. 'One more thing. You are right-handed and Kay, left-handed. Back in the restaurant, you fell for my trap – I asked you to sign your name on the note. You did, with your right hand; Kay would have used her left hand.'

'I am ambidextrous but my right hand is dominant – which takes over when I lower my guard. It was Sam's idea for Kay to be left-handed – he said that you might recall Ava as being right-handed.' Ava explained.

'What happened in Zanzibar was terrible, a disaster with Joyce ending up dead but I think both you and Sam took an enormous risk.'

'We had no choice, events overtook us. In retrospect, Sam could have taken a different course but that's hindsight for you. Had you known that I was alive, your reactions and behaviour would have given the game away, especially in Dubai where you were being watched. My cover was about to be blown in Zanzibar despite the use of a buibui. Zanzibar was the hub for ivory trading in the old days and I thought I could snoop around for Sam while I was there on a short work assignment. The intel report and everything that followed went against us. Sam arranged for a private funeral for Joyce – with her family's consent. The body fished out of the creek in Mombasa was a 'Jane Doe', an unclaimed body, from the public mortuary. Once, I returned to Nairobi, Sam and the wildlife department arranged for postgrad training in Parasitology at Imperial College, London. Effectively decommissioned and 'exiled'. Musa had to be taken into confidence – right at the outset. He was Sam's eyes and ears on the ground in Mombasa. Until he got the Bollywood bug and moved into the glitter world of celluloid.'

'You were born in Zanzibar. How did you land up in Mombasa?' Alec asked.

'My mother, who was single, was ostracised by her family

when she became pregnant. She was packed off to Mombasa soon after the birth of twin daughters. Musa's father hailed from Zanzibar so she was given refuge. Unfortunately, mum died along with my twin sister, three months after arrival in Mombasa and I was put up for adoption. My adoptive parents, both GPs, took over and I grew up in Mombasa until I graduated from the University of Nairobi and joined the wildlife dept as a newly qualified parasitologist. Sam, when he realised that I knew Musa, recruited me to his team. I was working at Tsavo National Park when you accidentally got involved. And was drafted in to keep an eye on things – our meeting at Musa's studio during your Mombasa visit was not an accident.' Ava paused and added: 'Although, everything that followed wasn't – I was blown away by your charm.'

'And, the cartel bought it – that you were dead?' Alec asked.

'We think so, but the important thing was that you accepted it. Sam knew that they were keeping tabs on you,' she continued. 'I resurfaced as Kay and was deliberately brought to Dubai to meet you – to parade me and to bait the cartel. Sam had checked out that my mum's and twin sister's deaths had been duly recorded so if anyone snooped around, it would all tie up. That's how he came up with the name Kay – my twin sister's name on the death certificate. The rest you know – Dr Reddy, the racing scandal and your ouster. Your ejection afforded Sam the perfect opening to bring you back to Kenya. Both of us were bait for the cartel – but this time we were in control; on home territory and in Sam's backyard.'

Alec held up a finger to pause Ava. 'The buibui killer in Mombasa, the Arab in the warehouse, was that you?' The anxiety on his face was evident as he waited, barely daring to breathe, for an answer.

Ava smiled for the first time. 'No, that was the buibui assassin; employed by the cartel. We figured out later that there was more than one assassin involved.'

'What about the Brit, the geologist?' Alec raised an eyebrow as he continued with his interrogation. 'And Musa?'

'Not us. Unlike your James Bond, we are not licensed to kill. We think the geologist was killed by an assassin engaged by the cartel – the blood-tinged tissues may be a vital clue. Sam is convinced that the geologist's killing is connected to his visit – he might have been carrying out surveys. He was seen in Mombasa, along the coast and on various islands in the Lamu Archipelago. Sam reckons his report, which wasn't found in his villa, may have vital information.'

'And Musa's death?'

'Not sure. We all know that his foray into Bollywood bankrupted him. Musa's debts, after the failed Bollywood venture, and his film of the ivory-burning event probably made him a target. We know there was a big contingent of sponsors from Dubai, Bombay and the UK. Could be any one of those present,' Ava speculated.

'A very possible scenario. Musa did mention that his Bollywood dream was sponsored by many private investors in Bombay; especially by his mentor – the Bollywood producer who was one of the first to go on Musa's bespoke safaris. With the movie incomplete and the huge debts, many were baying for his blood.'

'Enough of a motive to order an execution,' Ava stopped and then looked at Alec, wondering if he would forgive her – for all the skeletons. 'I am sorry, Alec. I have carried the guilt for so long that it's a relief. There's one more thing that we need to discuss,' she said tentatively.

It was then that Ava confessed that she had debated long and hard about revealing their wedding plans to her parents. The euphoria of Alec's marriage proposal rapidly diminishing in the face of unfinished business – the final hurdle of informing her parents about Alec was still pending. Alec had yet to meet her parents.

'That explains your behaviour at the airport when your dad picked you up. You did not want your dad to meet me? You haven't told them about our relationship, have you?'

Alec knew what was coming – he had been through this scenario many times. All his life in London; job interviews; girlfriends, the whole caboodle. But then, London was a melting pot of races and cultures and Nairobi very insular, very closed off. He recognised Ava's dilemma – he had gone through the same scenario with his last serious relationship.

'Oh, they know that we were in a relationship. That day on the way back, dad had joked about meeting his future son-in-law. I managed to fob him off. They know that you are a British vet on a work permit here. I don't think I have even mentioned your name because I was scared that they might read about your exploits in the papers.'

'Don't tell me! They have no idea that I am Kikuyu by birth?' Alec gasped, in total disbelief. 'Gosh. They know I am British and...' Alec's voice trailed off. He let Ava confirm the truth.

'They have assumed, erroneously, that you are white. I am sorry, Alec. I was scared, am scared, that they may not accept you.'

Her brown eyes brimmed up with tears. She kicked herself for being so indecisive; reason and logic replaced by emotion and sentiment. Ava wasn't looking forward to the epic encounter with her parents. She'd almost prefer to take on the cartel any day.

For once, Alec maintained a stoic silence worried that his instinctive use of humour in a crisis could be misunderstood.

'We have a monumental battle on our hands,' Alec declared, almost reading her thoughts.

In the end, Ava's courage failed her. Much against his better judgement, Alec had to give in to Ava's stubborn stand of getting married without informing her parents. She decided to have the wedding in Stone Town, Zanzibar – ostensibly because it was her birth town but Alec surmised that the distance probably was the deciding factor. Ava's secret wedding, away from Kenya, meant that her parents were unlikely to stumble upon the truth.

TWENTY-FIVE

Abbu, Mombasa.

The call from Dubai woke the buibui-clad figure – the assassin had waited for the call and had dozed off. The echoing of the azan could be heard in the background.

'Ignore my previous instructions. Go down to Nyali – I have already couriered the file. Execute ASAP, without fail. And I want your confirmation - the male and the female targets. If the female is not present when you arrive, bide your time. Wait till she arrives. I want both killed. There is no one else in the house.' The long-distance caller disconnected before any questions could be asked.

The file included the address details and a photograph of the man, but not of the woman. The Nyali villa looked secluded and well away from the bridge and the main causeway.

The same call and details were repeated to the second assassin, who was donning the buibui. The red stilettoes would be the last to be put on. The caller emphasised that the killing of the man had to be executed at a set time. The caller clarified that the servants were out and the male victim would be the sole occupant.

The buibui assassin was perplexed for a moment – this was the first time that a photograph of the victim was not attached. The only clue of the hit was an address and a brief hand drawn sketch of the floor plan of the villa. The assassin was pleased that the place looked secluded and had a beach side rear entrance; more than one escape route was always an advantage.

Abbu was waiting at his large but unostentatious villa in the Nyali area – Dubai had called and set up an urgent meeting with one of the other directors. The short notice of the meeting was explained – the director was on a short vacation and was in the vicinity for barely a day. It was imperative that the meeting took place.

Abbu was puzzled about the urgency of the meeting. He knew his domain – the Swahili coast stretching from Tanzania, Zanzibar, Mombasa and the coastal strip up to and including the Lamu Archipelago. This was definitely his patch and any incursions on his territory were an intrusion and violated the unwritten rules of the cartel. The presence of a director willing to conduct business while on holiday seemed odd.

'The Mombasa for the Mombasa born' agenda, the false narrative that he had formulated over the years, was his baby and his game plan – to play the way he pleased. Falsely portraying the Coast Province and Mombasa residents as economic scapegoats bought him votes and clout; not for him to worry about the political ramifications.

The recent press reports and police bulletins about the capture of Shenzi were fake – he knew that because Shenzi was his minion and had called him to refute the news of his alleged capture. He knew that the police were on a 'fishing expedition' – using psychological warfare to ferret out possible weak links in the cartel.

The Lamu coup was his baby; to be used as he saw fit. To his amazement and shock, he had been ordered to abort the entire project.

This had never happened before and his protestations were roundly overruled. All the captives, the Mag Seven members, were held on the island for a day and released.

In his younger days he would have rallied against such incursions but desisted from rocking the boat. Substantial funds had already been collected from the seven victims and, he later found out, that bank accounts were hacked into and more cash stolen. None of the victims reported the thefts.

The huge amount that he had generated for the cartel – the Lamu hoax and the repeated buy-sell cycles after the deliberate leak of the false oil report – was probably the reason for the short notice meeting – to congratulate him for the work done. The timing was right – he had just delivered the deeds of several blocks of land – it was long overdue, the recognition for his stupendous achievements. He felt the tension ease.

Abbu broke his reverie and looked at the time – his visitor was due at any moment. The champagne that he always had on ice would be an ideal way to celebrate – his hour of glory; he meant to relish it. He was alone at home – having dismissed his houseboy and cook for the weekend. It would be the perfect celebration, without any disturbance or interference.

He sighed as he looked at the time – the guest was late. He was about to call Dubai when the chimes jingled, reverberating through the vast corridors and front rooms of the villa. As he quick stepped to the front door and flung it open, his welcome smile froze – there was no one there. He looked around, slightly flustered, as he ventured to the front gate and back before shutting the door and retreating towards the front room.

The buibui figure, having rung the bell, double backed to the beach side and entered the villa through the rear porch door – the floor plan committed to memory aiding her. She had been told that the rear door would be open.

She moved into the front room and decided that she did not have enough time to stick to her modus operandi – entice the victim by disrobing and using her semi-nude presence to stun and confuse. She did not have even a moment as she heard the front door slam shut.

She just had enough time to remove the gun from the thigh holster and prepare her stance. She made sure that the folds of her buibui did not hamper her movements as she waited in anticipation, her arms behind her, gripping the gun for reassurance. Her palms were clammy against the gun frame and the grip. It was a sultry Mombasa afternoon and the air inside the villa stifling and uncomfortable, especially as the aircon was switched off.

Abbu re-entered the front room, cursing under his breath; the pesky kids from next door probably messing about. They frequently came round to look for their beach ball or their wayward Dachshund. The dog spent more time in his garden than in the neighbour's.

He stopped mid-step when he saw the buibui-covered apparition standing in the middle of the room. It then dawned on him. The hair on his nape bristled at his mounting anxiety and he shivered despite the heat.

The buibui assassin here, on his patch, in his house? They had remained anonymous to each other all these years – the cartel's execution contracts conducted over the phone or via drop-off points. Abbu wondered if the call earlier about a meeting had been a well laid trap; he was disoriented enough to remain silent.

She would not have recognised him had she not followed and tracked his political campaigns; pulling the strings in the background. She always made it a point to attend his rallies whenever she could – the buibui used each time to provide total anonymity. She knew that her target had no clue about her and did not know who she was or the purpose of her visit. Not yet.

She could see the beads of sweat on his brow – the years had not been kind to him; the hashish and debauchery had taken their toll. The weather-beaten visage sagging at the jowls and the receding hairline gave him an aged, haggard look. He was a shadow of the man that she had first met in Bangalore and then in Konya.

Only the radiance in his hypnotic eyes was undimmed; the Rasputin gaze very much potent. And the flute – her eyes briefly strayed to the reed instrument on the coffee table, evoking vivid images of their time together in Turkey.

She was puzzled for a moment – he just stood there, in total stunned silence until she realised that she had not taken the buibui off. She still kept the gun gripped behind as she flipped the veil over her head with her left hand.

There was a split-second lapse – a hesitation – before he recognised her.

'Roxana?' What are you doing here? I am expecting company. It's a business meeting.' His voice trailed off as the first seeds of doubt sprouted in his mind. Maybe Roxana was the guest that he had been urged to expect.

She smiled at his confusion. Her plan of keeping the two roles separate – that of the cartel's head and the buibui assassin – had worked. She had her own Chinese walls in operation. No one knew that the successful tycoon, Roxana, was also the buibui assassin – not the authorities and not even the others in the cartel. Her anonymity had kept her off the radar and out of trouble.

This was the first time she had not used her feminine charms to stun the victim, the target. It felt unnatural, being fully clothed before an execution. It felt weird as she brought the two-handed gripped gun forward, pointing it dead straight at her target.

Her gambit had been successful, Abbu's stunned expression was proof enough. The cartel's identity was shrouded in secrecy – all she knew was that the different cells were autonomous and associates put in charge of their respective domains. She was not only an associate or principal, as she preferred to call herself, but also the appointed assassin. She had long suspected that Shenzi was her understudy as an assassin.

Abbu, his brain furiously assessing the situation, had the single most important moment of clarity – the gun pointing at him was full of menace and he was unarmed. Even the khanjar was out of reach. The memories of their brief passionate tryst in Turkey and of her womanly charms were displaced from his mind by the cold hard thought of mortality.

'You are the boss; the company that I was expecting?' he asked in an incredulous whisper. Abbu was sweating, he had not engaged her – which meant that there was a third party over and above everyone. It had become obvious to him, in these moments of clarity, that he was not alone in assuming primacy, even Roxana seemed to be under the same delusion.

The look in Roxana's eyes, the assassin's eyes, told him all he needed to know. The king checkmated by the queen; once his queen many years ago. Turkey seemed eons away, almost in a parallel world. He had got it so very wrong, deceived into thinking that he was running the operation. Each leader of a cell or domain led to believe the primacy of their cell and leading role. Abbu wondered if Roxana would figure out that all these years they had been hoodwinked. Someone somewhere had planned this and was probably laughing all the way to the bank. The only difference between him and Roxana was that he knew the game was up; belatedly. She did not – not yet.

'Just like the Lamu coup and the cartel's plan, my plan, to create an independent Zanzibar governed by the cartel– all hoaxes? Surely that can't be it? The seizure of Zanzibar was going to be retribution, vengeance, for the treatment meted out to us, Arabs. We Arabs had suffered the most – we lost everything, including our future when we were compelled to leave – death or exile.' Abbu stopped to take a deep breath. He was rambling, buying time for a way out. He willed her to look at him. Her eyes were not on him

Roxana remained silent, deliberately avoiding his gaze. She knew too well the danger of drowning in those soulful eyes. And, if he started on the flute then she was done for good; her resolve would break. She spoke more to keep her doubts at bay.

'You reckon the Swahili majority would let you and others take back the fertile lands? Put back power in the hands of the old guard –the elite – and undo the gains of the revolution, the shackles broken on that day in Jan 1964? I am a product of the carnage that took place after the Shah went into exile – my parents were butchered and I was left almost penniless and bereft. That's when I found solace in your arms in Konya. And what did you do? You walked away, abandoned me. That was my eureka moment and I decided never to trust a man again. Your ambitious dream of dominating the land that you were ejected from is futile – never to be fulfilled. Your fanciful dream of your Shangri-La will remain unconsummated. You don't even know if that is the final plan.' Her mind went back to Lamu and the oil report that she had retrieved

'Roxana, please look at me. We can make this work. The grand plan is yet to unfold. Once we have our hands on the timeshare portfolio – we can walk away. Between the two of us we'll have a fortune. We could go back to Konya – and recapture the magical moments of our time in Turkey.'

She was looking at him, finally. He could sense her slight hesitation. He picked up the flute and threw the final dice to save his life. He played the same melody that he had many years ago, when the thugs were about to ravage her. The Rumi recitals floated back from another land, another timeframe. He was fluting for his life. She listened, motionless, her resolve beginning to crumble. They could have a go again; settle in Konya.

And then a car backfired in the distance, the loud clap of thunderous sound jolted her and distracted her - she looked away. He noticed the fine tremor of her hands and the slight pause as she raised the gun and lowered it briefly for a millisecond. He stopped playing and refocussed on her eyes; the blue irises accentuated by her pale complexion. Even after all these years, her beauty took his breath away. He wished, not for the first time, that he had not walked away and abandoned her in Turkey.

The pin-drop silence that followed the backfire broke the spell. The split-second hesitation and the flicker of a movement behind her Rasputin, saved her life. She dived sideways just as the buibui-clad figure behind Abbu fired twice in rapid succession. Abbu toppled forward as one of the bullets dissected his renal artery; blood spurting and pooling in the peritoneal cavity.

As Abbu pitched forward, the buibui figure behind him came into view, unprotected. The diving Roxana fired thrice in quick succession. Two bullets pierced the throat of the buibui figure, both travelling upwards and lodged into the brain. The third pierced the right eye, through the second assassin's veil. There was a muffled collective thump as all three bodies crashed to the floor.

Roxana got up and readjusted her stilettoes. One of them had almost come off in the dive. The other two figures were motionless; Abbu groaning on the floor. Roxana stepped up close and shot him again. Silence reigned supreme.

She reached forward and flicked off the veil; almost ripped off the buibui – the listless eyes and the face of a man threw her. The uncloaked figure was Shenzi. She shot him again. His psychotic behaviour was well documented by the cartel; the numerous contracts executed by the man dressed as a woman. As her understudy and a rival, she had made it her business to know all there was to know about Shenzi.

Roxana had not believed, not for a moment, the reports of Shenzi's capture and the alleged plea bargaining with the Kenyan police. The plan to execute Abbu and Shenzi had been a forgone conclusion. The deed done in one fell swoop meant that she was in charge: queen of her castle.

She smiled at the thought of all that booty and her final flight to Konya; she would retire there amongst the kindred spirits of Rumi and her father. It was a shame that Abbu would not be there with her to recapture the magic that they had once shared. His soulful renditions on the flute had added a poignancy and an emotional depth, that she never quite managed to share with any other man. Their chance meeting outside the ashram in Bangalore had been love at first sight.

She sighed as she muttered ruefully: 'C'est la vie! Not to be.'

As she readjusted the folds of her buibui, she saw the flute still gripped in Abbu's hand. She bent over and retrieved it, almost losing her balance and falling over as a spell of vertigo struck. It would be her memento – to remind her of what could have been.

She sat down briefly to steady herself – the Lamu incident flashed through her mind. She had ignored the spells as they rarely lasted long enough to cause any concern. She recalled the Harley Street physician's advice to keep an eye on her haemoglobin levels – she had forgotten all about her regular medical checks, missing the last few appointments.

She steadied herself and glanced at Shenzi again. He had been an accomplished killer; frequently using different disguises to evade detection. His frequent use of the buibui had rankled with her; making her job more difficult as the police had put out notices about a female assassin on the loose and even offered a reward.

'An accomplished assassin,' she repeated to herself as she walked out, striding towards her car parked well away from the villa. She clutched the flute even tighter as the twinge of pain hit her – the left side of her groin hurt with each step.

'Assassin? She had not contacted Shenzi, so...' she paused as she felt the pain again. It then came to her – she had been double crossed. She had not rejected the assignment and had not contacted the understudy to take over. Someone had engaged both assassins. It dawned on her, as she limped to her car, that Shenzi had been engaged to execute her.

'So, there was someone else who was orchestrating, pulling the strings? One more jigsaw piece. She was the puppet, not the head,' she mumbled to herself as she grabbed and yanked at the door handle of her car.

Just as she opened the door, another spell of vertigo hit her – more intense and prolonged. She half sat in the driver's seat, battling the dizziness. Her sense of betrayal heightened as her fingers traced the sticky trickle of blood along her left thigh.

'I've been hit,' she almost screamed. First time in all these years, she thought. She had to get to a hospital because the trickle was turning into a spurt. The flow of blood meant that Shenzi's second shot had punctured her left femoral artery.

She felt herself slipping down onto the road as flashes of the Harley Street consultant, Shenzi, and Abbu crowded into her mind. Her futile and belated attempts at staunching the blood flow hardly mattered as she slipped into an abyss.

The blood, now free flowing and unchecked, formed a pool of crimson around her ankles, the red stilettoes caked with congealed blood. The flute slipped out of her hand as she collapsed on the tarmac. It rolled out to the middle of the road.

They found her next to her brand-new Merc – one of the cars she had bought after settling with the Ray family; a model similar to her father's car back in Tehran. The flute had been smashed into pieces by a passing car.

The duty officer at Nazi Moja police station, the same one who had investigated Ava's disappearance, called Sam at his Naivasha farm.

On the flight to Mombasa, Sam could barely contain his
excitement. The details given to him about the crime scene where two
bodies were found and the presence of a buibui-attired woman close to
the crime scene, raised his hopes.

His intuition told him that the woman admitted to the ICU unit
at the Aga Khan Hospital must be the same as spotted on the ferry on
the day of the Lamu killing. His pulse raced as he contemplated the
final pathway to the cartel with victory finally within grasp.

When Sam walked into the Aga Khan Hospital, the attending
consultant gave him the bad news – the patient had bled to death.
Roxana's history of uterine fibroids, her anaemia and the profuse
bleeding following the rupture of the femoral artery had contributed to
her death. The post-mortem report also mentioned tranexamic acid in
the blood – the medic explaining to Sam that the TXA had been
prescribed to control excessive bleeding due to the fibroids. In her
case, the bleeding had aggravated the anaemia associated with her
genetic condition – thalassemia.

Sam's deduction that this was the female assassin who had left
behind the blood-soaked tissues in Lamu, after killing the Brit, turned
out to be correct – all the corroborative evidence dovetailed with that
presumption.

The dead woman's car identified the victim, leading the police
to her house, not far from the Nazi Moja police station; TXA tablets
and pairs of red stilettoes were found; as were several buibuis.

The ballistics report indicated that the bullets were fired from
two guns; one found at the crime scene and the other in Roxana's thigh
holster. Sam sat in his office in Nairobi, pondering. Roxana, his lucky
break, had died before he could question her.

Sam's look at her immigration file showed that Roxana Ray nee Shirazi had moved to Mombasa after her marriage to Sanjay Ray. The file had details of her lineage and her upbringing in Tehran and the stay in Bangalore where she met and married Sanjay. His pulse quickened as he came across details of her father, Dr Abbas Shirazi; the name rang a bell. He jotted a reminder to himself – to pursue the matter with the Tehran authorities; and yet he felt that the answer lay with him – here in Kenya.

Sam was due to interview Ray Senior in a few hours. He doubted the Ray clan had anything to do with his case; the family was well known with records going back four generations in Kenya.

He was quite hopeful of the new leads that had been thrown – the men had been identified as Abbu, the shaman, and Shenzi. Sam had provided the positive ID of Shenzi having infiltrated the poaching gang and his brief stints with Shenzi on several poaching expeditions.

Shenzi had disappeared with a trail heading towards Somalia. His presence in Mombasa did not surprise Sam – the poachers and the criminals drifted in and out of Somalia with impunity; the long porous border barely amenable to any immigration control.

Sam knew of the historical baggage of political animus in that part of remote Kenya – the decades of agitation in the Northern Frontier District, starting with the Shifta War, had left a bitter legacy of regional land disputes. The poachers took full advantage of the situation in the district. It would be virtually impossible to gather any background information about Shenzi or his associates.

The other dead man – identified as Abbu and associated with faith healing and grassroot political movements was an interesting lead. Sam was hopeful that Abbu was a break that he could pursue.

The ballistic report was his only substantive evidence of what had happened in the villa that day. Sam pieced together the findings – they knew for certain that Shenzi, Roxana or both had contributed to Abbu's killing; Roxana's and Shenzi's bullets had been retrieved from his body.

Shenzi had been killed by Roxana – the bullets found in the corpse fired from her gun. Shenzi had fired off a shot before he died - his bullet had ruptured Roxana's femoral artery. However, Roxana left the villa alive, albeit fatally wounded.

Ray Senior having read the reports of Roxana's death, following a shoot-out in Mombasa, knew that the police would come knocking on his door. Sam's call for a meeting did not surprise him; in fact, he was relieved. He'd rather get it over with.

As Ray Senior sat in his study in their mansion on Peponi Road, he knew that he would have to come clean about Sanjay's death and the history of Sanjay's drinking, drugs and his liaisons. It would soon be laid bare in due course anyway. He would urge the investigator to keep Sanjay's liaisons off the record – his son had suffered enough. Sanjay had died alone in London, away from the family. He blamed Roxana for his son's exile to London and his eventual death.

The interview with Sam lasted more than an hour and despite his initial reluctance, Ray Senior did come clean and mention the blackmail attempts by the local goons in Bombay. He recounted, without any qualms, the help he had to take from the local mafioso to get Sanjay out to Bangalore so that he could complete his degree. The thug had demanded a huge payoff to silence the smaller fry around him – Ray Senior had willingly parted with the money, secure in the knowledge that once Sanjay went to Bangalore and returned to

Nairobi, there would be no further interaction with the thug or his henchmen.

Sam listened patiently as the old man unburdened himself – the family dispute with Roxana, the separation, the financial arrangements and Sanjay's eventual self-imposed exile to London – to avoid a scandal in Kenya.

Sam perked up when Ray Senior mentioned his presence as a sponsor at the ivory-burning event in Nairobi. He had attended only briefly and had left straight after the burning – his interaction with the foreign sponsors had been very brief. His memories of the event were hazy and fragmented and not of much help to Sam.

The patriarch did not mention that among the group of sponsors in the tent, he had fleetingly thought that he recognised a face but had dismissed the thought as he got closer – the man did not match the physique nor the flamboyant style of dressing. He had hurriedly waved his goodbyes and exited the gathering.

Zubin's liaison with Sam and the information from MI6 had revealed details of the Mag Seven blackmail and the Lamu hoax, so Ray Senior's confession of blackmail and his presence in Lamu barely added anything new to the investigation.

It was much later, in a brain storming session with Alec and Ava, that it was decided that they have a look at Musa's film yet again – in the presence of Ray Senior.

The viewing did not trigger anything new. Even Ray Senior remained impassive, so the status quo prevailed. Alec had been closely watching the senior man as the film rolled.

'Anything, sir?' Alec asked Ray Senior who had seemed quite anxious at one point. The slight tremor in his voice as he answered in the negative was picked up by Alec but, before he could probe further, the clip ended, the lights came on and the man rushed off, citing an urgent meeting. Ray Senior had again dithered about recognising a face in the sponsors' tent at the event. He had kept silent and walked away.

The news from the authorities in Tehran lifted their spirits – Roxana had reported her parents missing and was later flagged because of her involvement with the militia groups. Her escape from Tehran, after the killing of her abuser, had incriminated her as a fugitive and she had been charged in absentia. The trauma of the sexual abuse and her subsequent actions had excluded her return to Iran.

Sam also recalled where he had come across Dr Shirazi's name – the scholar had represented Iran as an unofficial ambassador at Jomo Kenyatta's funeral in 1978. His attendance was coincidental as Dr Shirazi had been on a short visit to Masai Mara at the time of Kenya's national mourning. Sam had been assigned the task of escorting the Iranian politician to the funeral.

It was later that Alec realised that Drew, his father, had been at Oxford at the same time as Dr Shirazi's tenure in Oxford. They all felt that the Oxford link had raised more questions than answers.

Whilst the clique of Roxana, Abbu and Shenzi had unravelled, the spectre of the fourth member loomed like a Colossus. Or there could be other hidden cells and members.

The revelations by Zubin, as MI6 tip offs, about the Mag Seven club and the Lamu scam had convinced the investigating teams that ivory smuggling was just a small cog in a bigger wheel of fraud and scams. Based on the current findings and the stage of the investigation, they had no idea what the grand plan was or even if there was an impending finale.

TWENTY-SIX

Alec and Ava, Stone Town.

Alec and Ava were married on the beach in Stone Town,
Zanzibar. The first ceremony was a traditional wedding conducted by a
Hindu priest flown in from Nairobi - their marriage vows taken with
the priest reciting Sanskrit mantras as the sun rose from the eastern sky
over the island.

This was followed by the registrar legalising the union via a
special licence granted by the municipal authorities. The breakfast
reception was attended by a select band of friends and colleagues with
Sam proudly giving away the bride as Ava's parents were conspicuous
by their absence. Ian Ross, Alec's best man, had flown in from London
– they had been together at the private school in Harrow and at vet
school. Ian had been the only one who had managed to keep in touch
and occasionally standing in as a locum at Alec's surgery.

His comment on Ava's beauty was summed up with a tinge of
genuine wonder. 'Alec, your luck with the beauties is undiminished; all
of them used to swoon at the sight of you. You lucky dog. Does Ava
have a sister?'

'Ava, Ian fancies you rotten,' Alec said to Ava, loud enough for
Ian to catch the words. 'Shall we introduce him to Kay?'

It took an enormous effort on Ava's part to convince Ian that Alec was pulling his leg.

Her friends had frequently commented on Alec's strong resemblance to the American heartthrob, Sidney Poitier. One of them had gone to the extent of taping 'Guess Who's Coming to Dinner', one of Poitier's hits about inter-racial relationships in 1960s America. The gift-wrapped VHS cassette was presented as a wedding gift.

As they watched the movie in their honeymoon suite on a Panasonic VHS unit supplied by the hotel, Ava was enthralled by the unfolding drama of the 1967 Stanley Kramer film, which portrayed an inter-racial relationship between a black physician, Poitier's Dr Prentice, and his white fiancée. Ava had sobbed at the roller coaster emotional conflicts between both sets of parents – black and white – and had finally managed a smile as the movie ended on a happier note. The ending gave her hope.

Ava's angst at their own impending duel with her parents wasn't lost on Alec. He had maintained a dignified and diplomatic silence – worried that any attempt at humour would be ill judged; especially as Ava saw parallels between the celluloid drama and their own dilemma waiting back home in Mombasa.

'That was a different era of racial intolerance. I'm sure things will work out in the end. Your parents are medics, educated and urbane. I am sure we will have a similar happy ending – once I have them eating out of my hand with my Poitier charm,' Alec quipped, trying to pacify an overwrought and tearful Ava.

'I hope you are right. I don't want to fall out with them nor do I want to choose between you and them.'

'Really? They have your twin, Kay, to fall back on,' Alec

remarked, unable to resist the urge to lighten Ava's mood. He continued: 'Maybe, we could have had a cosy threesome if you had invited Kay to our wedding.'

'Aye, aye, dactari ya ng'ombe,' Ava retorted, calling him a cattle doctor. 'That's all you can think of? I am worried stiff and here you are conjuring up bedroom antics.'

'What else is there to think of?' Alec asked and then continued with sobriety. 'Don't be so hard on yourself and on your parents. I'm pretty sure if the roles were reversed, my Kikuyu relatives would probably have reacted similarly. I'll practise my new-found Poitier charm on them and win them over. It will be a cinch,' enthused Alec, trying to convince himself more than Ava.

Alec and Ava, on the last day of their honeymoon in Zanzibar, were winding down the day after spending the whole day at the beach. Alec, by now, was quite familiar with the local cuisine, having tried the Zanzibar Pizza, Date Nut bread and coconut bean soup and was leafing through the menu to try something different; his palate greedy for more exotica.

'What's mchuzi wa pweza?' he asked having spotted the item on the simple menu; all in Swahili but written in Latin/Roman alphabet.

'Octopus curry,' Ava remarked. 'For someone born in these parts, your Swahili is non-existent. You must get a lot of stick for that?'

'Not really, only from you and Sam. I get mistaken for an American and most understand when I explain that I have lived in the UK all my life, except for a few years here. The women specially are quite keen to teach me Swahili,' Alec remarked with a wee glint in his eyes.

'I bet they would be, the grandmas for sure. There's one over there, two tables across, who has been ogling you ever since we walked in.'

He had spotted the older woman sitting alone. Since Laikipia and the aftermath, Alec had practised memorising faces around him – especially in confined spaces. He had become quite adept at knowing what was happening around him. Laikipia and the cartel had taught him to be extra vigilant – constantly looking over the shoulder.

'Let's cut a deal – you teach me Swahili – the real lingo not the pidgin stuff most Brits get away with.' Alec proposed.

'What's the deal?' Ava knew what was coming. Alec's cheeky grin was a dead giveaway.

'The Kama Sutra in return for your Swahili one-to-one tutoring?'

'Single track mind, Sherlock. Order the mchuzi and satiate your taste buds; the Kama Sutra can wait. It's a treat, the octopus, I mean.' She said with a wry smile before Alec could comment.

As Ava got busy with their orders, her crisp Zanzibari Swahili impressing the waiter, Alec's gaze fell on a corpulent figure a few tables away. His animated exchange of semaphore of signals with the waiter at the other end caught his eye. As did the flannel suit which seemed a tight fit. Halfway through the meal, the man had unbuckled the belt with a sigh of pure relief.

Alec had noticed the lone diner wolf down the starters and the main course with great dexterity; using only the fingertips of his right hand. All seven pieces of the cutlery, lined up on the right of his plate, lay undisturbed.

The lip smacking and the gentle burp at the end signifying

genuine pleasure. Alec had witnessed similar displays of burping in the UAE and had been told that it was a cultural sign of appreciation of the host's hospitality; for the good food served. He saw the man unscrew a bottle and gulp down what looked like capsules. Even at that distance Alec recognised the distinctly marked bottle of cod liver oil capsules. The man burped again as the meds were washed down with water.

Alec had, subconsciously, forsaken the fork and knife – and used his right hand since Dubai, much to Ava's pleasure. Whilst the Arabs tended to employ both hands, the Indians were forbidden to use the left hand while eating. His short sojourn in Dubai had given him a great insight into the Asian subcontinent and Dr Reddy's input had been truly educational for Alec.

Alec had surmised correctly that the diner was Indian, having noticed the exclusive use of the right hand and the jewellery. The 'Om' symbol, a lavish pendant, was a dead giveaway – the gold chain dangling from a massive neck that even Mike Tyson would have envied. The chain glinted as it caught the sun.

The Indian shouted 'Saba, saba!' The waiter raised his right hand and cupped his ear to semaphore back; the restaurant chatter drowning all normal conversation.

In exasperation, the Indian raised both hands with seven fingers raised and shouted again. 'Saba, saba!' The waiter nodded in affirmation.

Having ordered item number seven on the menu, the Indian noticed a handsome couple watching him and smiled. He focussed on Ava and had that odd feeling that he had seen those elegantly sculptured features somewhere before. He noted the elaborate henna designs on her hands and the warm aura between the couple; guessing instantly that they were newlyweds.

He was dining alone and missed his mistress, one of seven that he had in his mini harem. A gal in each port as he was fond of saying. He had a fascination for the number seven. His Brahmin lineage could be traced back to the original seven sages from whom the Brahmins have evolved over centuries. The sages praised and venerated in the Vedic texts of ancient India.

Seven clove plantations in Zanzibar, each of his seven houses across his favourite seven capitals of the world had seven rooms with seven bathrooms; the list was endless. To top it all, the Lord had been kind to him – he was born on the 7th; his lucky number.

The Indian's appreciative glances at Ava were spotted by Alec, and he wasn't one bit embarrassed when Alec caught his eye. The Indian, in the creased suit, raised his shoulders, palms of his hands turned up, and shrugged as if to say 'what am I supposed to do – beauty prevails'. A prodigious smile lit up his visage briefly but the eyes held Alec's attention because the smile was not reflected in his eyes, the 'windows of the soul'. Inexplicably, Alec shivered.

Fortunately, the waiter arrived at the Indian's table bearing his dessert. Ava and Alec both simultaneously looked at the dessert menu. Saba (seven) was listed on the menu as 'faludo', an Indian dessert, a concoction of ice cream, vermicelli, milk and rose syrup. This one had a passion fruit topping as well.

The Indian could not shake off the feeling that he had seen the woman somewhere; he prided himself on his photographic memory. He never forgot a face, especially if eye contact had been made previously. As he mopped his high domed forehead with his own handkerchief, the restaurant napkin untouched, he gulped down the last of the ice cream.

As he pocketed the bottle of his capsules and got up to leave, their eyes made contact again. A flicker of recognition in her soft brown eyes or was he imagining things? By the time he got home, he had tried in vain to recall where he had seen her.

The following morning, he remembered – as he was finishing his daily routine of seven laps in the indoor swimming pool. The golden orb was just rising from the eastern azure sky, the seagulls screeching as they winged their way towards the sea. He would later make his way to his office – a house in central Stone Town converted into a sumptuous open plan office, not far from the house where Freddie Mercury had been born.

'Ava Patel.' He murmured with a note of smug acknowledgement. He had seen them together at the restaurant in Dubai.

Later that day, he made the decision to close down both premises and move to his Dar-es-Salam hub. It would take him a day or two to move all his private stuff and important documents; essentially 'cleanse' the office.

The presence of Alec and Ava in Stone Town so close to his operating hub worried the man. Alec had stumbled on to the ivory scam and he certainly did not wish to give him another gift by taking undue chances. He knew that the newlyweds had been watching him. He chided himself for not changing tables and moving away – the sheer beauty of the bride had tempted him to stay put. An error of judgement he reminded himself, sloppy and dangerous.

With his flagrant attention bestowed on the bride, he had made himself conspicuous. He had no reason to believe that their presence in Stone Town was in anyway sinister. Zanzibar was an extremely popular destination for honeymooning couples. Nonetheless, he could not take any chances.

Now that he was poised – at crossroads – on the final chapter of his grand plan, he could not ignore their presence so close to home. He fingered the Om pedant seven times for good luck.

Over at the other end of the town, Ava and Alec had just settled in the breakfast lounge of their hotel – their honeymoon almost over.

'Well, Mrs Dunlop. Habari ya asubuhi!' Alec mouthing the greeting as he forked bits of juicy pineapple and mango into his mouth. 'You recognised your admirer, the Indian, didn't you?'

The good morning greeting had a tinge of wonderment; he still could not believe his luck that this gorgeous Aphrodite was back in his world, making his life an absolute bliss. A second chance after the tumultuous events that had plunged him into a vortex of despair and depression.

'How did you guess?' Ava shot back, annoyed at herself for being so readable – she knew that Alec's powers of observation were razor sharp. Years of clinical practice, dealing with his 'silent' patients and pet owners had honed his skills and reading body language was very much part of his arsenal of diagnostic tricks. The eyes have it, was his oft-repeated refrain to his students.

'The flicker and the reflex averting of the gaze,' he shot back. 'Well, where from?' Alec continued munching the date nut bread, the unique, exotic Zanzibari staple with chopped dates and walnuts, truly manna from the heavens. Ava's hubby had taken to the local cuisine without any qualms though even she was squeamish about the octopus.

'Not sure, might have read something about him. He's very rich that much I know and those unforgettable eyes. Like being X-rayed.' She paused and then continued. 'The Russian, what's his name?'

'What Russian?' Alec shot back, puzzled. 'Russia? What's Russia got to do with all this? Too much sun, my dear.'

'Since I saw him last evening, I can't get this tune out of my head. You know how it is – the melody plays like a jingle but one can't put lyrics to the tune?' She looked away, trying to focus on the music in her head.

After a while, she hummed, a few lines and sang, 'There lived a certain man, in Russia long ago.....ra, ra ...something.' Her voice trailed off.

'Rasputin. The 1978 hit single by Boney M that the live band had played,' Alec said, referring to their tryst that night on the beach at the Orange Coral. Makeba's 'Malaika' song had become their song and both songs brought to mind their magical time together in Mombasa. 'We've come a long way from that beach encounter. So, what about your Rasputin...er...Indian?'

'I get the feeling that I've met him recently – Dubai?' she quizzed. 'That trip when Sam fetched me over to Dubai – so that we could meet; the matchmaking trip?'

'You mean the Indian couple – the Bollywood producer and his glamorous wife? Musa's bespoke safari clients. Really? I don't think I got a good look at him, the light was fading by that time.' Alec said.

'Of course, you didn't! You were too busy reading his wife's body language. The cleavage on display was something. She would have got into trouble here in Zanzibar, for sure. I am surprised she escaped censure over there. No, some other place – he was alone as he is over here.'

Fortunately, Alec was saved by the arrival of their breakfast. He knew that in the happily married future ahead of them, that cleavage and his reaction to it would rear its ugly head, time and time again. 'Punishment deferred, for sure,' he muttered under his breath as he attacked the masala scrambled eggs with great relish.

They were due to fly back to Nairobi later on – back to the high voltage tension that they had left behind. The pending confrontation with Ava's parents loomed and added a tinge of despair; the honeymoon truly over.

On the flight home, as Alec busied himself with preparing for a clinical presentation on tick borne diseases in dogs at ILRAD (The International Laboratory for Research on Animal Diseases), Ava's mind was still on the Poitier movie that they had shared. Her own contribution to Alec's presentation was minimal. In case her experience as a wildlife parasitologist was needed, she was going to be his back up at the Q and A session after the presentation.

The wedding present – the recording of the movie 'Guess Who's Coming to Dinner?' was the first thing that she unpacked when they got home. She retired to their bedroom with it as Alec finished off the presentation in his study.

The following morning, she despatched a small package by courier to Mombasa. And the unbearable wait for an answer lasted seven long days.

'Hi Mum, how are you and Dad?' Ava asked.

'We are both fine. How was Stone Town? Did you call any of

your Zanzibari relatives to your wedding?' her mum whispered, anxious to know if Ava had sought the presence of her biological family; most of them lived in Stone Town.

'No, Mum. I am so sorry…' Ava stumbled in mid-sentence and clammed up. Her parents obviously knew about the wedding; the gossip mills must have been on extra time.

'Bring Alec home. I'll expect you both by seven this Saturday. Spend the weekend with us – the Dobermans miss you as well.'

Ava knew all was fine, her mum's tone was neutral and she had referred to her hubby as 'Alec' rather than saying 'bring him home'. Ava was relieved even though no references were made to her brief letter of apology, her contrition and the enclosed Poitier movie. Her brainstorm of using the Poitier movie as a proxy for the prevailing trouble between them was a tad cowardly but she was hoping that her first salvo would pave the way to acceptance of Alec and his Kikuyu ancestry. Just like the movie, she was banking on a favourable outcome.

Ava's smile radiated across the room as Alec entered. 'What's the grin for?'

'You won't understand. Mum's invited us to Mombasa and she knows who's coming to dinner!' Ava beamed as she quickly explained what she had done.

'Well done. Are you sure I am not going to be ambushed by the Dobermans? Can't let them mar my Poitier looks.' Alec knew that Ava and her parents fawned on the two pet dogs – Romulus and Remus – and it was going to be a canine litmus test.

'If you pass the Doberman test, then my parents will be a pushover. Make sure you bring along your lucky red-tubed stethoscope

– the one that saved you in Laikipia. Give the dogs a once over – the best bedside manner you can conjure up. If they take to you, then mum and dad will be pushovers.'

The Patels lived in Nyali, not far from the Orange Coral where Alec had stayed on his first visit to Mombasa.

Dr Jay Patel, having married Dr Rani Patel, a Kenya-born GP, arrived from India as an intern and then set up a GP practice on Moi Avenue along with his wife. By the time they had adopted the three-month old Ava, Rani had known about her infertility for quite some time.

They had just finished dinner – vegetarian fare – much to Alec's initial disappointment but the evening had been redeemed by the free flow of Tusker beer. The beer, at Ava's behest, was grudgingly served to placate their son-in-law. For her parents the free-flowing alcohol, was the lesser of the two evils – even Rani had given up meat to keep matrimonial peace. Her father's chain of Tandoori restaurants, named after her – Tandoori Rani – had prospered and had provided the springboard for her private education. After her marriage to Jay, she had given up meat. She had turned veggie; lock, stock and barrel.

Alec had enjoyed the simple Gujarati cuisine and was at his best – his humour and talk about his work at Kabete had engaged the older couple. Alec's role in investigating the fungal contamination of maize flour and the resultant aflatoxicosis outbreak in Nairobi's canine population had endeared him to the two medics. The Dobermans had been saved from the toxic aflatoxin by their vet's quick action. The two pets, lavished with their wholehearted attention, had become even more special after Ava had left home for A levels and university.

The Doberman Pinchers, who had initially reacted ferociously to Alec's presence, soon calmed down as the vet, fearlessly, walked over and stroked both dogs, their docked tails wagging furiously as Ava joined in.

Ava's parents pretty much warmed to Alec – his expert physical exam of both dogs started the process of reconciliation and the awkward silences that Alec had anticipated never quite came to pass. Ava had played her cards cleverly by insisting that Alec play the starring role of the attending vet as the lead character, ably supported by Poitier as the new son-in-law. By the time the two guard dogs had been clinically assessed, the ice had melted.

At some stage the conversation moved to the destruction of Kenya's wildlife, poaching, ivory and Zanzibar.

'Did you know Zanzibar was, at one stage, the hub of ivory trading? And, the Indians, mainly Gujaratis, were at the forefront of the ivory trade?' Jay asked, more at ease now that Alec had gained the approval of the Dobermans. Both dogs had followed Alec around the house and had finally curled up next to the vet as the family settled down in the landscaped garden for the after-dinner dessert and coffee.

'Yes, the conference that I attended on my last visit here traced the history of poaching and the ivory trade. The Indian influence in Stone Town – the architecture and the cuisine – reminded me of the old town in Mombasa,' Alec remarked. He was given to understand that most towns in the coastal belt had similarities – the narrow lanes with the smells of Indian spices, the Indian and Arab facades, the minarets of small mosques ringing with the call to prayers and the salt in the air. Exotica par excellence for the London man accustomed to the uniformity of terraced houses, concrete office blocks, traffic jams and petrol fumes.

'You should read the English translation of the memoirs of Tippu Tip – his expeditions to Congo, the territorial power struggles and the history of his ivory dealings are all fascinatingly detailed. I haven't read it but am told that the geo-politics of the era are well documented in the book. Didn't you take Alec to Tippu's house in Stone Town?' Jay asked looking at Ava.

'Yes, I did. The various plaques at the museum were very informative, including his ownership of seven clove plantations and the somewhat unconventional trading practices. Notwithstanding his ivory and spice trades, his cruelty and notoriety stood out,' Ava remarked, shuddering at the recall of the gruesome black and white photographs at the museum depicting emaciated labourers toiling in the sun or living in shabby surroundings. Tippu Tip had, at one stage, become the Governor of Zanzibar – a remarkable transition from slave trader to political leader.

It was much later after they had returned to Nairobi that Ava realised that her parents had not discussed her marriage to Alec nor his Kikuyu lineage.

It was many months later that Ava's mum divulged that they had known about Alec's Kikuyu roots – friends in Nairobi had spotted the pair on several occasions and had alerted her. While they were hurt at not being taken into confidence, they were pleased that their daughter had the confidence and the strength of her convictions to marry the man of her choice. They would not have stood in her way. The regret of missing their daughter's marriage was allayed partly by watching the 8mm film record of the wedding in Stone Town and the stunning photographs – Ava had left behind both items in their safe custody. It was a minor sacrifice after the hurt that she had heaped on them by her impulsive decision to elope.

TWENTY-SEVEN

Sam, Naivasha

Alec and Ava had been felicitated by colleagues and friends after the wedding; Sam being the last to invite the newlyweds to his farm.

As usual, after dinner, they pondered on the latest news of the investigation. The discovery of the two dead men, Shenzi and Abbu, in the villa and the subsequent death of Roxana in hospital before Sam could interrogate her kicked off their deliberations.

They were having nightcaps in the lounge – the twinkling lights of Naivasha town could be seen clearly as the night chill and fog descended on the town. Alec and Ava were spending the night at the farm, so the descending fog and dangerous driving conditions hardly mattered.

'Ray Senior called me just after Roxana's death became public. He had not come clean to protect Sanjay but now with Roxana's death, he did not fear any comebacks. He admitted that he had been drawn into the blackmail scam and the Lamu hoax by Abbu.'

The shaman had treated Sanjay years ago when Ray Senior had turned to him for help. The resort to unconventional medicine and the shaman's shadier methods were prompted by Sanjay's promiscuous behaviour and increasing dependence on alcohol. Ray Senior was swayed by the shaman's unverified successes and marketing hype. He had personally flown to Mombasa and stayed with Sanjay until the shaman's treatment had been concluded. Soon after the treatment, Sanjay was recalled to Nairobi and packed off to Bombay.

The patriarch, after the Bombay debacle and Sanjay's marriage to Roxana, thought that Sanjay's problems were a thing of the past.

'Hardly the case as we now know. Sanjay's marriage was the start of the Ray clan's problems,' Sam continued, 'Abbu obviously blackmailed the patriarch and lured him into the Lamu scam.'

'We don't have details of the others? I thought Zubin, your contact as you put it, was planted into this Mag Seven club – he hasn't identified the others?' Alec asked.

'We know who the others are but the commission decided to offer immunity from prosecution on the grounds that the shaman and others had used coercion and blackmail – their exposure was not in the public interest. Even Ray Senior has been given special dispensation for his contribution to the investigation,' Sam explained.

'What is Zubin's role in all this, apart from offering himself as bait in the Lamu affair?' Ava asked.

'Without Zubin's entrapment of Abbu, the Lamu scam would not have been exposed. Zubin only became aware of Abbu's insidious role after his attempts to hijack the Y Foundation for his own divisive agenda.' Sam looked on as the other two digested the information.

'What does Zubin make of all this?' Alec asked.

'He is convinced that the Lamu scam was a dry run, a red herring, for something bigger. He has alerted the commission about fraudulent transactions; land purchases, shares and mergers. Not just here but across East Africa and possibly further afield – Zanzibar and Mozambique. Hallmarks of a cartel orchestrating everything,' Sam paused to let it all sink in.

The stunned silence broken by Alec. 'The deaths of Shenzi, Abbu and Roxana were pre-planned?'

'It would seem so, although Abbu and Roxana both probably thought they were at the helm of the cartel. What say you, Sherlock?' Sam smiled, kicking the can down to Alec.

'If your theory is correct, then either there is a fourth member out there or four more to bring the cartel number to seven,' Alec parried. 'This sequence of seven is a definite pattern; part and parcel of OCD rituals.'

'Seven innocent people have been killed or attempts have been made on their lives: Dr Pinto, the geologist, Musa, and the lab technician with all three of us escaping attempts on our lives. Seven in all. That is if we ignore the Arab's execution at the warehouse,' Alec said and then added: 'Maybe we three are still targets?'

'All circumstantial or do you have something else to justify your assumptions?' Sam asked with the worry lines etched clearly on his face. He knew Alec was methodical and must have been analysing all that had transpired so far.

'My first inkling of an emerging pattern was when Ava and I saw the Indian in Stone Town and Ava's conviction that she had met or seen the man in Dubai before. The 'seven' ritual with the food ordered and even the tip left behind – confirmed by the waiter – were definite pointers. The seven pieces of cutlery all lined up undisturbed on the right of his plate. Ava's déjà vu feeling about having met her 'Rasputin' and, that too in Dubai set the alarm bells ringing. Our conjecture about

Dubai being the cartel's base rounded off everything,' Alec elaborated.

'And then my dad mentioned a Zanzibari – a certain Tippu Tip. We had visited the usual tourist sites and ventured into Tippu Tip's house, which is a museum. The plaques mentioned all the gory details of his activities and curiously another seven reference. Tippu Tip was into gold, ivory and spices. And guess what? His main trade was spices – he owned seven clove plantations,' Ava reflected.

'I am lightly conversant with Zanzibar's history. Tippu Tip died in 1905 in Stone Town. So, what's the link with our times or to the cartel?' Sam was hoping that Alec was on to something.

'None as we stand. Maybe, as suggested by Ava's dad, we could read Tippu Tip's memoirs for further clues? Maybe, it's not Kenya but Zanzibar where the cartel is based? Could it be that Tippu Tip, considering his questionable ivory trading, is idolised by the cartel?' Alec ventured.

'Why do I get the feeling that there is more, the punchline?' Sam was now pacing with pent-up nervous energy. Ava was looking from one to the other, like a spectator at a singles tennis match – the back and forth of a long rally.

'Maybe we are dealing with someone who has been traumatised or depressed or both? Sometimes people with the obsessive compulsive disorder – OCD - get hooked on certain rituals and numbers. We may be dealing with such a compulsive personality,' Alec blurted out, hesitant and apprehensive that his seemingly wild conjectures could lead Sam and the investigation down a blind alley.

The OCD and the 'seven ritual' could just be coincidences. It was a long shot at best – at the moment without additional info to corroborate his assumptions. He recounted what he had seen the lone diner do at the Sheraton – the seven pieces of the cutlery arranged in a particular manner.

The arithmomania – the obsessive compulsion to count or arrange objects by numbers – that the lone diner had exhibited had convinced Alec that they were dealing with an obsessive-compulsive personality.

'This OCD – is it treatable?' Sam asked, hoping that it might open up another avenue of investigation.

'Yes. Most OCD patients, if the symptoms and rituals are so intrusive as to interfere with normal day to day activities, could be treated with antidepressants and cognitive behaviour therapy. CBT, in tandem with meds, helps to change behaviour patterns and compulsive actions,' Alec expounded.

'Meaning that evidence of therapy – medication and counselling – might be compelling clues?' Sam enquired.

'Yes, circumstantial evidence. There's another nugget of info I have forgotten to mention. That day at the ivory event, I found some capsules and tablets in the sponsors' tent that I had handed over to Dr Pinto. We now know that the capsules were cod-liver oil supplements and the tablet was identified as citalopram, an anti-depressant.'

'Mind you with so many visitors, the tablets could be anyone's, not necessarily a sponsor's?' Sam pondered.

'Agreed. Aren't we forgetting another important link – the original oil report? If that report is found then it would be incriminating. Assuming that it hasn't been destroyed,' Ava added.

'True. Oh, gosh I forgot the geologist – he was killed because of the oil report. The report in conjunction with this OCD link may strengthen our case,' Sam said, hoping that they were finally narrowing things down.

'The perfect scenario would be if we could tie up all those to an individual – the meds, the OCD including the number seven fascination and the oil report,' Ava said looking expectantly at both men.

'Just a thought, but do you know how many movies there are which have 'seven' in the title?' Alec posed a trivia question.

'Go on maestro, enlighten us. We are not movie buffs like you,' Sam retorted.

'A few but just to name two: 'The Seven Samurai and The Magnificent Seven,' Alec volunteered. Alec was a fan of Kurosawa and knew that 'The Magnificent Seven' was based on Kurosawa's earlier movie 'The Seven Samurai'.

'You forgot 'Snow White and the Seven Dwarves,' Ava added, thinking of poisoned apples, temptation and Eve.

'Indeed, Ava. And, you forgot the most important one – a wife's possible source of angst, especially after a few years of wedded bliss,' Alec said, baiting his new bride.

'You cad! Don't you dare! 'The Seven Year Itch'?' Ava answered, pretending to be hurt.

'We have pretty much zeroed in on the ivory-burning event – it seems central to our enquiries. Dr Reddy almost went to jail in Dubai but for your intervention.' Alec said, refocusing on the case. 'Your first interrogation revealed that him and his family went through a baptism by fire when they settled in Dharavi, after fleeing Zanzibar following the revolution. Musa with his Bollywood dreams also landed in Bombay; he was funded by the Bollywood producer. Do we see an Indian link?'

'This is the guy that you and Kay...er Ava met with his glamourous wife – the one that you were besotted with?' Sam enquired, adding fuel to the matrimonial fire.

'You forgot to add – the glamour gal with the deep cleavage,' Ava teased Alec as he shuffled and Sam grinned shamelessly, enjoying his friend's discomfort.

Alec hastened to add, before Ava had a chance to respond. 'I recall, from your notes, that the young Reddy worked, as did his mum, for this small enterprise in Dharavi when they moved from Zanzibar. The owner and Reddy both were loaned money by the Bollywood producer.'

'Yup. Dr Reddy did mention that he had to borrow heavily to fund his vet school fees and his flight expenses to Dubai. His stint in Dubai had enabled him to clear the family debt and secure their future.'

'Might it be worth pursuing that connection – the Bollywood producer?' Alec asked as Sam scribbled notes in his file.

'Looks like I might just get a chance to meet your glamorous gal, the one with the redoubtable cleavage, when I revisit Bombay. Anything you want to send to her, a small gift?' Sam asked, adding more salt to the wounds.

'Thanks, mate. With friends like you, who needs enemies?' Alec retorted.

Two weeks later, Sam rang Alec.

'Dr Reddy has confirmed that he had discharged the debt and bought adjoining flats for his mum and himself. He even took me to the cottage industry in Dharavi. It is still there in Dharavi. We spent a pleasant evening there reminiscing about Dubai and his time with you. He sends his regards.'

'And did you meet the owner and the Bollywood producer?'

'Alas, no. Both were unavailable. Met his wife at their fancy pad near Marine Drive. You were right, she is something!' Sam said. 'Apparently, the producer was out on location shooting in Korea; a Bollywood remake of the Japanese movie – the 'Seven Samurai'!' Sam exclaimed. 'Coincidence or do we have something to sink our teeth into?'

'You visited the cottage industry in Dharavi next to Reddy's old place?' Alec asked, ignoring the producer and his film.

'Yes. Apparently, the unit exports the entire production of gelatine overseas; mostly to Dubai. Reddy seemed to think that there are Kenyan importers as well who then supply other pharma manufacturers.'

'I'm sure with your ingenuity you can trace via the Chamber of Commerce who the importers are and match with the Dharavi address?' Alec ventured tentatively.

'Yes, Holmes. I've got the info. There's only one manufacturer in Nairobi who buys quite a bit from the Dharavi unit. Based in the Industrial Estate. I paid them a visit a few days ago – a small unit on Homa Bay Road. The unit manufactures pharma casings – the capsule shells. They import the raw material from Dharavi – gelatine, I am told,' Sam said.

Dr Reddy had elaborated, just before Sam flew back, that the bulk of the gelatine was probably derived from animal skins and bones – mostly sheep and goats; certainly not cattle bones because of the revered status of the cow in India. There were quite a few slaughter houses and leather and tanning units in and around Dharavi. Dr Reddy had suggested that the gelatine export unit probably was legitimate but could be a front for money laundering. He had added that the businessman who ran the unit had managed to secure loans for the Reddy household through a local loan shark; a financier who had also helped with the setting up of the gelatine unit.

TWENTY-EIGHT

The Mercenaries, Maputo, Mozambique.

Seven principal mercenaries with fourteen deputies formed the main first thrust of landings on the four main and three primary islands of the Zanzibar Archipelago. The mercenaries flew into Maputo and then split up into seven smaller groups; each group making the way northwards to mainland Tanzania and onwards to their designated island in the Zanzibar Archipelago. Each of the seven groups had an ancillary force of personnel – engineers and foot soldiers. Their numbers were proportional to the size of the island that they were taking over and there were several women in the group to justify the cover of being tourists.

The commanding officer of the principal task force and his deputies would take over the main Unguja Island – the seat of government in Stone Town. The other six officers and their deputies would fan out to the other islands. When the time came, these officers would see to it that the communication links were severed, thereby isolating each island – total radio silence except for the teams on the ground.

The arms payload per dhow consisting of 49 machine guns, 42 AK47s, 140 hand grenades, 70,000 rounds ammo, was being delivered by seven dhows from Mogadishu – to bypass all undue scrutiny and checks.

A force of 175 men, all mercenaries, recruited from the war-torn areas of Somalia, Mozambique, Zimbabwe, Angola and South Africa – a de facto mini UN force – was stationed in the Somali Sea awaiting further instructions. This marine force with the arms and the foot soldiers would sail out to Zanzibar in a staggered manner to avoid attracting undue attention. Each of the seven dhows would receive instructions from the advance parties via Hondo.

The six principal mercenaries and their deputies, forming the advance party, were hand-picked by Hondo and all were either South African or British. The Zanzibar Archipelago's seizure was given the operational code name - 'Old Spice' in keeping with the islands' local name – the Spice Islands. It also happened to be the Indian's favourite aftershave.

The flotilla of the dhows was based in the waters of the Somali Sea on the eastern tip near the Somali-Kenya border not far from Kismayo in Somalia and Lamu in Kenya. The presence of the dhows in the Somali waters was registered with the relevant authorities as a fishing expedition – to explore the Somali basin for its potential for fisheries and coastal development.

The warlords in Mogadishu had been paid retainers to protect the flotilla from rival ex-militia gangs and from foreign fishing vessels. Shenzi and the Indian had used these very same warlords in the past to afford safe passage to caravans carrying illegal ivory and other contraband goods through Somalia and beyond.

The South African mercenary heading the 'Old Spice' operation was nicknamed 'Hondo'; the other six had similar nicknames from favourite Western films. All their identities were hidden behind aliases and nicknames to avoid forensic audit trails.

These arrangements suited the Indian; his hawala network and transactions had survived on similar strategies. In the event that 'Old Spice' failed or had to be aborted, all the participants were promised their wages, irrespective of the end result. The onus would be on the authorities to prove that a coup had been mounted. The Indian was banking on Hondo and his professionals to ensure a smooth take-over and to forewarn him of any pitfalls. The final authority to proceed or to abort rested on the Indian.

The seizure of the Spice Islands, the Indian's brainchild, was inspired by the 'unilateral declaration of independence' invoked by Ian Smith, the Prime Minister of Southern Rhodesia, and his cabinet on 11th November 1965. The 'rogue' government survived for fourteen years despite British sanctions and international isolation. The Indian smiled indulgently as he noted that the figure fourteen was a multiple of seven – surely that was an auspicious omen for the success of 'Old Spice'.

The entire budget, which ran into two million pounds sterling, constituted a million pounds for operational costs, leaving a reserve of a million for contingencies. Only Hondo had been paid his full fees of £200,000; the rest were paid only half their fees with the balance payable on the successful completion of the operation. The contingency reserve included a slush fund of £500,000.

An advance task force of twenty-one officers had already entered Zanzibar, posing as tourists and had taken up positions on the islands, barring Hondo. He was holed up in Dar-es-Salam waiting for the final go-ahead from the Indian. Hondo had been promised a bonus – upon successful seizure and handover of power to a junta appointed by the Indian.

No one knew where the Indian was stationed. Honda had met him at the Ritz in London and after that all contact had been via secure messaging networks. Hondo was bemused when he was told that part of the network included a certain spice trader in Dubai, whom he had seen from afar only once – identified by his nutmeg-stained fingers. Hondo had deduced that the Indian probably spent a lot of time in Dubai.

The operation was scheduled for the 7th of July with alternate dates, at seven-day intervals, set for the 14th and the 21st. The 'proceed' signal for the three dates were the code words 'Apache', 'Comanche' and 'Sioux', respectively.

The abort signal was 'kukomesha', Swahili for 'stop'. A backup arrangement was also in place – seven green flares for the 'proceed signal' and seven red ones for the 'abort' one. A motorised dhow anchored off the coast of Stone Town was part of this backup to observe and monitor. All it had on board were packs of green and red flares. The captain and the two deck hands had been trained to use a VHF marine radio and instructed to use the flares only if the radio failed. The long antenna specially used was mounted as high as possible on the dhow – to enhance its transmission range from five to twenty miles.

The countdown had started, Honda and his deputies were anchored in their respective sites; Hondo in Dar-es-Salam and the others on the archipelago. The captain and his two-man fishing crew of the backup dhow were instructed to drop anchor offshore from Stone Town, effectively from 00.01 hours on 7th July.

TWENTY-NINE

The Indian, Dubai Airport

The Indian, originally scheduled to fly directly to Dar-es-Salam, was compelled to change his plan at the last minute to include a stopover in Dubai. The change gave him an opportunity to take stock in Dubai and keep an arm's distance from the theatre of action – if things went awry then he had the option to disappear, especially as one of his private jets was stationed at Dubai Airport. The scarcity of operational facilities in Dar-es-Salam could compromise a quick withdrawal in the event of trouble.

The last-minute change to his flight schedule was also because of a mix-up at his local pharmacy in Oadby, Leicester – his repeat prescription of antidepressants – citalopram tablets – was delayed. He was told that the three-month supply would be available for collection on the day of his flight.

He had picked up the boxes of citalopram and paracetamol from the pharmacy and had stuffed them in his hand-made and customised Boston Bag – the Aspinal of London bag had his simple customised monogram ''Seven'' embossed on both sides of the brown pebble textured finish. He never travelled anywhere without his lucky bag; it was his 'comfort blanket'.

Normally he would have flown by a private jet and avoided the hassle of security checks. His recent recurrence of headaches had made him edgy – even the fast tracking for first class passengers had him fuming. He regretted not taking a private flight but the sheer importance of his plans made it imperative that he did not draw any undue attention to himself. He liked the low-key approach by taking a scheduled commercial flight.

The young Emirati immigration officer at Dubai airport, eager and overzealous, ignored the plethora of visa stamps in the British passport that was presented by the tired looking and anxious passenger – the Indian had barely slept during the flight. The splitting headache, despite the seven tablets of paracetamol taken during the seven-hour flight, had made him edgy and anxious. The Emirati officer had picked on the state of anxiety and had signalled his colleagues for a random check. The edgy Indian with the Boston Bag was pulled up by customs.

The Indian, by now getting impatient to get to his waiting limo, testily remarked that he was a Dubai resident and had never been stopped in the years of travel through Dubai Airport. The officer, used to the lip that he suffered from the well-heeled, ignored the man and opened the Boston bag. The boxes of paracetamol and citalopram tablets were right on top as he unzipped the bag.

Before the Indian could remonstrate with the officer, he was led to a cordoned-off area. A minor verbal exchange ensued and a local reporter travelling on the same flight saw the commotion. He decided to wait and see if the detained passenger turned out to be a VVIP. He smelt a scoop and for want of anything better to do, parked himself in the arrivals lounge.

It took all the patience of Job for the Indian to curtail his natural instincts of demanding immediate attention and maintain a dignified silence when he was charged with bringing in controlled/ restricted medications. Unknown to him, both paracetamol and citalopram were on the list of restricted items. The look of consternation on the Indian's face barely masked his rising fury; the veins in his neck engorged. His protestations about having lived in Dubai and never having being stopped in all these years of travel in and out of Dubai fell on deaf ears.

This kind of stuff happened to others, drug peddlers, not to someone like him. He could, at a throw of dice, buy up substantial portions of the Dubai Gold Souk. The Emirati annoyed by the boasts of wealth and the arrogant posturing by the Indian ignored the man's outbursts. He was convinced that this was his chance to nab a drug dealer. In his eagerness to exercise his duties, the Emirati ignored the man's obvious aura of authority and worse still, his British passport. He ignored the inner voices of caution that forewarned him that the passenger wasn't some migrant from Karachi or Bombay. He sought the assistance of his supervisor as the passenger refused to admit any wrong doing – the pharmacy label confirming that the meds were dispensed legally.

After two hours of negotiation, trying to establish his bona fides as a resident, the tired Indian managed to track down Kostas.

The arrival of Kostas and his retinue of Emirati bodyguards dampened the ardour of the Emirati officers – Kostas was recognised instantly as the kingpin of the Emirati racing fraternity. Kostas, after the camel hospital takeover fights, had assumed a cult status and both officers promptly yielded to his menacing presence. The sugar-coated offer of VIP hospitality invitations to the next big racing event was enough for the officers to waive the Indian through without further ado.

By the time the harassed-looking Indian walked into the arrivals lounge, the local reporter had managed to find out that the passenger had been delayed because of the discovery of banned medications. He knew that there were restrictions on certain painkillers and anti-depressants.

His desk editor had agreed about the ruling on banned meds and had promptly despatched a photographer in anticipation of a front-page story. The local rag could do with a drugs storyline to boost circulation – the paper's emphasis on Bollywood gossip and cricket had lost its appeal for the Emirati readership.

The photographer went to work as soon as the Indian and Kostas emerged. Several close-ups were clicked – Kostas and the Indian in conversation. And shots of the limo being dismissed and the Indian getting into a taxi.

Neither the editor nor the reporter had a clue to the identity of the passenger. However, both recognised Kostas as the tycoon recently involved in the acrimonious takeover of a camel hospital complex. For Kostas to stick his neck out for an Indian and personally intervene, meant that the passenger must be someone important. The editor concurred with his reporter and decided to go to print. The story had the merits of a scoop.

Next morning's edition of the local paper had several photographs splashed on the front and inside pages with a brief write-up of the banned substances found – paracetamol and citalopram. The editor did not report that after producing a valid UK prescription, the passenger had been released without further ado. The emphasis was on the arrival and presence of Kostas and his intervention in the release of an Indian passenger. The report discussed the undue pressure applied on the Emirati officers to condone illegal behaviour and undue leniency shown to the passenger after the intervention of a prominent figure.

The Indian had been put off by the fracas at the airport. He had booked into a hotel rather than stay at his villa – the choice of a modest hotel was deliberate, as was the dismissal of his chauffeur and the limo. His actions afforded him anonymity – he was just another Indian face in an area well known to middle class Indians on shopping sprees to the gold bazaars of Dubai.

He was appalled when he saw the photographs in the morning paper, his unease and dread multiplied exponentially. He went back to his room and paced for two hours in a state of indecision – the presence of Kostas at the airport may well attract intense scrutiny, especially as the corporate takeover of the camel hospital had ruffled many feathers. His masterminding of the entire takeover was at the risk of exposure – the airport photographs with Kostas may well prove damaging; a domino effect that may even lead to 'Old Spice'. He paced for hours in his hotel room, indecisive for the first time and his confidence shaken.

Finally, arriving at a decision, he made two phone calls and checked out.

Full of angst, he reluctantly made the 'kukomesha' call to abort the mission. Thousands of miles away, the mercenaries saw the confirmatory seven red flares fired from the dhow. The seven teams melted away in the night, their outbound journey mirroring the inbound one. The marine force in the Somali Sea was put on hold.

THIRTY

Ray Senior and Sam, Nairobi.

The early morning call from Dubai had surprised Sam – Ray
Senior had been in Dubai when the story of the Kostas intervention at
the airport broke out. He had no clue who Kostas was nor knew about
the corporate dogfights but the close ups of the passenger triggered a
distant memory which was associated with Sanjay and the local thugs.

'It's the mafia boss who helped me when Sanjay was being
hassled by the local goons,' murmured Ray Senior. The man has put on
weight – maybe that's why I did not recognise him when I bumped into
him at the ivory event.' The patriarch was still breathless from the
shock of recognising a face from the past.

'Please bring along several copies of that newspaper for me.
Meanwhile, could you please let me have the editor's name and a
telephone number?'

Sam contacted the editor in Dubai and requested a set of all the
photographs by courier, explaining that the subject may well be an
important witness in a longstanding investigation.

The importance of the discovery of citalopram in the bag of
someone whom Ray Senior recognised as being present at the ivory
event and Alec finding the same drug in the sponsor's enclosure wasn't

lost on Sam and Alec. Both of them concluded that the man probably hadn't been identified earlier because of a simple and effective ruse – donning a buibui. The clip of the ivory event had captured a few buibui-clad figures. And Shenzi had used the same tactic to evade detection.

Sam's excitement at the turn of events dimmed considerably when he was told by Dubai police that the passenger had checked out of the hotel and disappeared. The police promised Sam that a name would be provided as soon the airline released the details.

That's what worried Sam – if this man was the head of the cartel, then chances were that he may well have been travelling on a false passport. 'This isn't over yet,' Sam reminded himself. The only saving grace was that the man had made calls from his room – to the private jet company and to a number in Dar-es-Salam. The third call to the mercenary force was not made from the hotel – a deliberate ploy to safeguard the secrecy of the operation.

Both Alec and Sam had one overriding concern – their adversary was just a mite too clever to commit such elementary errors. In fact, they concurred that the chances were that the so-called lapses – the calls from the hotel – were deliberate red herrings to throw them off course.

THIRTY-ONE

The Mercenaries, Stone Town.

The dhow with its three-member crew had over indulged on illicit liquor and the captain was the worse for the wear. When Hondo received the 'kukomesha' abort mission call, he set in motion several domino calls to all seven teams. The fall-back plan of the dhow was triggered and the young ambitious Zanzibari lad assumed, albeit briefly, full charge of operating the VHF marine radio.

It was when he could not tune into the right frequency and failed to relay the 'abort mission' message that he panicked. The non-compos mentis status of the captain and his deputy, brought on by the alcohol-induced intoxication, forced the second mistake of the lad's career.

If the first mistake was one of omission – not drinking – the second one was one of commission. He was forced to use the flares – he had no choice. He regretted not paying attention when the captain had showed him how to use the radio; even extolling the benefits of the longer antenna mounted at a height to substantially increase the range of the VHF radio.

He fired the seven red flares in quick succession, which were seen, not only by the Stone Town team but also by the port authorities.

A patrol was promptly dispatched to investigate. The patrol soon returned after having found nothing untoward – after chastening the young lad and his captain who was suddenly very compos mentis after having being roused by the five short blasts of the patrol's ship horn – the danger or distress signal. The officer noted the matter in the incident book and went back to chewing the miraa leaves; the Kenyan stimulant, also known as khat, that kept him alert through the night shifts.

The mercenaries hastily prepared to evacuate towards the dhow anchored in the harbour. It was then that the team lead realised that two of his men were missing. A frantic search revealed that, despite the curfew imposed, the two members had slipped out for a rendezvous with the 'ladies of the night' on the beach.

The team evacuated as scheduled towards the harbour with the leader and his deputy heading for the beach to rescue the two lotharios. As they approached the beach front, the bars and cafes across abuzz with tourists enjoying the party scene, they saw their two colleagues in a fracas with a couple of girls. Some of the Zanzibari males joined in the argument. The leader, even at the distance, could see that the pimp was making all the noise.

He signalled the two lotharios to move away to a quieter section of the beach, the two girls and the pimp following in hot pursuit. The trio, the girls and the pimp, now anxious that the two clients would melt away in the night without paying. Unknown to all, the waiter at the bar had called the police

The two lotharios, emboldened by the arrival of their rescue party, herded the pimp away from the two ladies and managed to silence him. The leader, well versed in the Krav Maga technique of disabling an opponent, deftly delivered a blow to the pimp's groin, who collapsed in pain. The girls, alarmed by the violent turn of events fled just as the police arrived with blaring sirens. They found him, incapacitated by the blow, doubled up and mouthing obscenities.

The quartet was halfway down towards their waiting dhow by the time the pimp had caught his breath and described the assault to the attending police. Within minutes they had boarded and sailed away in the dark. All along the other islands, similar evacuations were taking place – the mercenaries melted away in the night.

The incident of the seven red flares was briefly investigated by the marine authorities; the dhow's explanation of an accidental discharge was reluctantly accepted and, in the absence of any evidence of maritime impropriety, the incident was logged but not pursued any further.

The local paper carried the news of the fracas on the beach, the discharge of the flares and the boarding of the dhow by the marine authorities. The police were also informed about the disappearance of a team of foreign tourists without checking out. As the hotel bills had been paid in advance, the police saw no reason to investigate.

When similar hasty withdrawals from some of the other islands came to light, the bored editor of the local paper connected all three events; the discharge of the flares mildly less important than the arrest of the pimp.

One thing led to another and some of the local papers in Mombasa and eventually in Nairobi reported the mystery of the vanishing tourists and the discharge of the seven flares – matching the mystery of seven teams of tourists all leaving Zanzibar without checking out. All the hotels involved clarified that the bills for the tenure of stay had been paid in advance.

Sam's investigating team, primed and fully aware of the OCD rituals, the significance of the 'seven' pattern and the link to the ivory investigation, logged and indexed all the details. The Zanzibar incident, as it was dubbed, was reported to Sam.

THIRTY-TWO

The Indian, Nairobi.

The Indian never caught that private jet flight that was booked from the hotel in Dubai. He took a taxi and travelled by road to Doha, Qatar – a journey of roughly 700km, taking about 7 hours. The ploy of using credit cards intermittently was tried and tested. The credit cards issued to various business accounts of shell companies were used in a manner that almost defied an audit trail.

Using a card that he hadn't used for a while, he flew to Mogadishu and was then escorted to Kismayo via a warlord's network. He changed tack again and used a different network, one of Shenzi's favourite routes, to cross over into Kenya. The trek to Nanyuki and onward to Laikipia was much easier – all familiar territory.

He recalled the meeting with Shenzi and the Bollywood producer not so long ago. Musa's bespoke safari had given the Indian an opportunity to have an impromptu meeting with the producer. It was unfortunate that Musa had inadvertently walked in on them; his death sealed by the accidental intrusion. The thought that his identity had been breached preyed on his mind. It would be months before he would engage Shenzi to do the needful – Shenzi dressed in a buibui had carried out the execution of Musa in Eastleigh.

His logic for shacking up in Kenya was that he was taunting Sam and his team and, more importantly, with Dubai and Zanzibar in the news, they would not expect him to slip into Kenya. It was his double bluff strategy – they would not think him to be stupid enough to harbour in a place that was actively seeking the cartel. The master stroke was that he was holed up in a dingy flat in Eastleigh – not far from Musa's place of execution. And he had no reservations about using the buibui when required.

He was also sure, going by the precedents of previous such 'dogs of war' events, that bringing charges that could stand up in a court of law would not be easy – a failed idea, no matter how far flung, cannot be grounds for criminal charges. No law had been broken, apart from a breach of the peace; the fracas on the beach. The law would have to prove intent and as long silence was maintained, all of them were safe. And he was pretty sure that the mercenaries would not turn state witnesses – the 'wages of war' that he paid were, by far, the most attractive and tax-free by virtue of his hawala transactions.

The trauma of the enforced departure from Zanzibar, his birth place, had scarred him and many others who had to undergo similar forced ejections. The memories, still fresh, despite the passage of time had sown the seeds of his plan. All he had to do was borrow from the pages of history; his take on history repeating itself.

His timeshare club was a de-facto list of many who had shown an interest to return to East Africa. To most of his clients, the timeshare scheme was a genuine investment – holidays in the sun guaranteed.

However, for a select few – meticulously whetted and chosen – the timeshare investment was a planned return to the land of their birth; a back to the roots scheme; a secure homeland devoid of political upheavals.

For those committed and enlisted members two important criteria had to be fulfilled: birth in East Africa was paramount. And a minimum net asset value of £1 million with an annual disposable income of £100,000.

Initially, his intention was to recreate the lifestyle of a bygone era in Uganda; the richest of the three East African countries. Uganda's landlocked position forced him to look at other options; Lamu being high on the feasibility list. When he had stumbled upon the memoirs of the Zanzibari ivory and spice trader, Tippu Tip, Zanzibar Archipelago, the Spice Islands, became his automatic choice.

As he sat in the flat formulating plans for another onslaught on his dream island, he wondered how long he could stay off the radar before he could return to the UK or Dubai. He wondered how long he could stay holed up in Sam's backyard, under his nose.

He had been assured by Hondo that all the teams had successfully evacuated and gone underground. The mercenaries could be reassembled without any difficulties. They had decided to catch up after three months; the Ritz chosen again.

THIRTY-THREE

Sam and Alec, Nairobi.

The disappearance of the Indian had been as astonishing as the images of the man and Kostas that had landed on Sam's desk at the State House offices. Ray Senior's statement had opened up new avenues for the investigation. Kostas, the Bollywood producer and the owner of gelatine units and Dr Reddy all came back into focus.

While Kostas was still being investigated, Sam had been advised that it was very unlikely that anything incriminating would be forthcoming – at best Kostas's hostile takeover of the camel hospital may result in a slap on the wrist or a small fine. The Cypriot had cleverly manipulated the two vets – Dr Joshi and Dr Kingsley – to engineer the ketoprofen fiasco, the stock thefts and the expired medicines to discredit a competitor and then wrest control of the company. Getting rid of Dr Reddy was a doddle – his minions spread a rumour that the Indian's visa was being cancelled. Sam and Alec did the rest to arrange the vet's panicked exit from Dubai.

The link between Dr Reddy and the Bollywood producer was benign – loans given to the Reddy family all paid up and Dr Reddy's assets in Bombay being all legitimate – his tenure in the UAE had been very successful. His retirement plans had been sedate and safe.

The Bollywood producer was mired in complex systems of finance which defied clear demarcation between legal and illegal. It remained to be seen if the labyrinthine processes of the legal system enabled successful prosecution for violating foreign exchange and tax regulations.

The gelatine workshop owner had the only direct link to the ivory smuggling – the false invoices unearthed at the warehouses could prove troublesome for the units in Dharavi and Kenya. Sam wasn't holding his breath and thought at best a minor player would be apprehended. The cartel was still untouchable and free.

Sam's team, having established a money trail in Bombay, were working on the assumption that a shadowy underworld figure was the common link between the producer and the business man with the gelatine units in Bombay and Kenya.

Both the producer and the gelatine units were on Sam's radar and were being probed for any links to the cartel; if any. Sam's team had investigated extensively across borders – both manmade and political. 'Follow the money' became the mantra for Sam's handpicked team.

There was optimism within the various investigating teams but the cartel's maze of offshore tax havens, shell companies and private share-holdings was cleverly designed to confuse and derail enquiries. Offshore havens and tax shelters were part of the problem; getting past the political barriers even a bigger handicap.

If ever there was a time to invoke the 17th Law of the Universe - the Law of Serendipity – then this was it. A 'happy accident' was sorely needed to nail the cartel.

Ashwin Dave

THIRTY-FOUR

Zubin, Nairobi.

Zubin's help had been sought on the London company searches. His army of research analysts and accountants failed to find anything; even when the 'seven' ritual was factored in. It was during this phase that Zubin was notified about an East African link via an interview conducted by a local Asian network. The write up about a group of Asians – all from East Africa and their reunion bash had been reported and picked up by local radio stations.

The local paper had interviewed a tycoon who had prospered after opening a string of foreign exchange bureaux. His journey from Zanzibar to Leicester via Dubai and Bombay was briefly touched upon.

Zubin would not have paid any attention to the information passed to him by his team but for the tycoon's comment about his belief in numerology and how his fortunes had soared after the change in the spelling of the company name from 'Kubera Holdings' to 'Kuberaa Holdings'.

Whilst his UK team attached no significance to the numerology claims, Zubin was reminded of classified adverts in Kenyan papers, especially the ones in Mombasa and the coast, where astrologers professed expertise in numerology and the influence of numbers on one's destiny.

The tycoon in the article had gone on to glorify his rags to riches story – making his fortune running foreign exchange bureaux in the UK and the UAE. His UK journey to success had started with the setting up of forex bureaux in London – the first one in Seven Sisters and the second one in Seven Kings.

It was days later that Ava made the connection. The addition of the extra 'A' meant that the company title' Kuberaa' had seven letters. Also, her father had told her that Kubera, as per the ancient Vedic scriptures of India, meant the 'Lord of Wealth' in Sanskrit. It would seem the tycoon had got carried away and had inadvertently boasted about the 'Lord of Wealth' tag.

The Asian network, aware of the tycoon's taciturn persona, had deliberately chosen an attractive young journalist – a Joanna Lumley lookalike – to interview the businessman. It would seem the ploy had worked only partly – he had steadfastly refused to be photographed. Not even her flirtatious demeanour enticed him to pose for photographs.

The trio were having dinner at the Thorn Tree restaurant at the New Stanley in downtown Nairobi.

'The only common link, as far as I can fathom, is that the Asian group members are all from East Africa and most of them are Gujaratis,' Ava pointed out.

Life had come full circle – the migrants who had built the Mombasa-Kampala railway line – contracted by the British – were mainly from Gujarat. And many of their descendants, tens of decades later, had been ejected by political upheavals and landed back in India. Some stayed back permanently, while the vast majority, with the 'right of abode' and 'given leave to enter the UK for an indefinite period' stamps in their British passports hit the migration trail once again – to the UK. Many ventured further afield to Canada and the US. The ones who dared to go to the UK directly, suffered less compared to the ones who landed in India. The diaspora in the UK, despite the racial tensions that most encountered, prospered – hard work and ambition paid dividends.

It was much later that another link emerged – many of these East Africans belonged to several timeshare companies that only sold resorts located in East Africa. The groups that ran into several thousands of members belonged to mailing lists located in the West. Curiously, only a handful of British Passport holders, resident in India, were included.

It was later, as Alec and Ava were unwinding with a nightcap that Ava mentioned the press reports of the incidents in Zanzibar.

'Zubin may well be right about the Lamu coup being a hoax or a red herring. The Zanzibar Archipelago has three primary and four main islands -seven in total. The seven teams disappearing into thin air, the discharge of seven red flares and the police incident on the beach – all connected?'

Alec looked at Ava and nodded. He called Sam and mentioned Ava's theory that maybe, just maybe, Zanzibar was the potential theatre of activity. Sam promised to send a team to Stone Town to liaise with the police and the seven hotels.

Nothing of substance emerged from the liaison especially as details on the guest registration cards could not be verified. The Nairobi team assuming that forged passports had been used. Some of the hotel staff had guessed but weren't sure that British and South

African accents were detected. The captain of the dhow that had discharged the red flares eventually confessed that a white man with a military bearing had paid him to anchor offshore from Stone Town. The red and green flares and the VHF apparatus had been supplied by the man's deputy, who was also white.

'The Indian we observed in Stone Town on our honeymoon comes to mind. He might live there for all we know,' Ava continued in an excited tone, 'Do you remember he had that small bottle of cod liver oil capsules on his table?'

THIRTY-FIVE

The Indian, Nairobi.

The early morning phone call from Hondo woke the Indian – the flat echoing with the rings of the phone.

Hondo's information about the Zanzibari reports of the seven flares and seven teams disappearing did not alarm the Indian but he still decided to move out. It would be foolish to stay in one place for too long.

He was confident that after a spell of keeping a low profile and being 'off the radar' it would be safe to go back to the UK or Dubai or Zanzibar. The man pondered on his options as he made his plans.

As far as Hondo could tell, their foray into Zanzibar had not created any waves. He was sure that another attempt could be made at a later stage. The bonus promised by the Indian was quite substantial and he had every intention of earning it.

The Indian finally decided to retrace his way back to Somalia and with the help of his private militia make his way to the flotilla of dhows still anchored in the Somali Sea. He could easily sail to Lamu or even Zanzibar from there when the time was right. The seven dhows afforded the best protection from exposure. He could easily hop from one to the other to avoid staying in one place.

As he planned his trek to Mogadishu and onwards to the flotilla, he pencilled in a short return to Stone Town to retrieve the dossiers left behind after his hurried exit. He had decided upon the perfect temporary safehouse for all his documents – until Operation Old Spice could be resurrected.

He had been worried and anxious about the airport incident and the subsequent unwanted publicity. It had been months since that episode and Kostas had reassured him that there were no adverse repercussions or any ongoing investigation. The two Emirati officers had been lavishly entertained as promised and he had not heard from them. He considered the matter closed and advised the Indian to stop fretting.

By the time the Indian landed on the flotilla he had changed his mind. With the Somali militia shielding him, he stayed on the dhows for almost two months. It was his first vacation of doing absolutely nothing except read.

He re-read Tippu Tip's memoirs and T E Lawrence's 'The Seven Pillars of Wisdom'. He was biding his time before proceeding to Stone Town and resurrecting his plans. Hondo had been forewarned to expect his private jet for a meeting at the Ritz. It would be all systems go in a few months. The Indian smiled; things were looking up. Nothing had happened. The knock on the door and the arrest warrant were yet to materialise.

He was getting bored and thoughts of Operation Old Spice dominated his every waking hour. He would have to get a move on – his citalopram and cod liver oil capsules were also running low. He was finicky, obsessive, about getting his meds from anywhere except the UK. His constant worry was that he'd end up ingesting spurious meds. He knew the adulteration of medicines was a global phenomenon but his faith in the UK pharma supply chain was sacrosanct.

As he unscrewed the last bottle of the Seven Seas cod liver capsules, it occurred to him that he may be in the ideal place if he did run out. The shark infested Somali Sea had an abundant supply of shark livers. He wondered, as he spotted a few dorsal fins circling the dhow, if shark livers were good substitutes for cod livers.

THIRTY-SIX

Alec, Ava and Sam, Naivasha.

Kissinger had excelled himself – the simple fare of chicken curry and rice preceded by lamb kebabs – had the trio in raptures. They had gathered to discuss the events of the past few months. The Dubai Airport incident and the curious events in Zanzibar being instrumental in reinvigorating the team.

'That's him, my Rasputin,' Ava noted pointing to the several photographs that Sam had handed over; the Dubai airport ones. 'The eyes – unforgettable.'

'We have pretty much connected the citalopram, the 'seven rituals' at the beach restaurant in Stone Town and the links with Bombay and Dubai. Has he been identified?' Alec queried.

'Yes, from several sources. His name is A. Charya, a British Citizen born in Stone Town. During the Zanzibar Revolution, his father and other men in the extended family were butchered. His mother took him to Nairobi and an attempt was made to move to the UK. It would seem that their plans had to be changed and the family shipped out to Bombay. The struggle there, the criminal activity and the eventual journey to the UK via Dubai are all being confirmed and documented.'

'Great. So why can't you arrest the man?' Ava asked.

'We've got to find him first. He has vanished and we still have to get our hands on the evidence. The oil report, other incriminating documents and the cash,' Sam said.

'The stroke of good fortune was our honeymoon in Zanzibar – saw him at the restaurant and the tie up with his cod liver capsules – the Seven Seas ones was providential,' Alec said.

'He's Indian right? How would you spell his name?' Ava asked.

Sam complied and Ava rang her dad in Mombasa just as he was going to bed. She spelt out the name. After a lengthy question and answer session, she disconnected and beamed at her two male admirers.

'He must have changed his name by deed poll from 'ACHARYA' to A. Charya. Dad said it's an Indian surname - 'ACHARYA' - seven letters, one word!'

THIRTY-SEVEN

Sam and Zubin, Stone Town.

Sam's team in conjunction with Zanzibar Police staked out Acharya's offices – not far from the beach restaurant and Tippu Tip's museum. His mansion was also being monitored.

Two months later, Acharya was tracked from Dar-es-Salam to the offices and to his mansion on the other side of Stone Town. Despite finding six Chubb safes in the residence, very little of significance was found. It was quite evident that Acharya had either never stored documents there or transferred everything to another location.

Bottles of Seven Seas capsules and citalopram tablets were found in the walk-in wardrobe in the master bedroom. The three month's repeat prescription dispensed by a pharmacy in Oadby, Leicester, provided additional info – the pharmacy label on the meds confirmed the man's identity and, more importantly, opened other audit trails for the investigation. The medical history of OCD and its treatment proved decisive.

The cinema room's door had a brass plate with the legend 'The Den'. The room had, among other paraphernalia, books and VHS cassettes including 'The Seven Pillars of Wisdom', Tippu Tip's memoirs, 'The Seven Samurai', 'The Magnificent Seven' and several books on OCD and its treatment.

Having found six safes Sam's team was convinced that a seventh safe existed and had to be found. At Sam's insistence, the police returned to repeat the search. Eventually, the seventh safe was found in the pump room of the swimming pool. It was empty.

Without the incriminating evidence about the hawala transactions and offshore accounts, the case against Acharya weakened considerably. At best, he would be charged for the ivory smuggling out of Mombasa and for running the poaching teams.

The greater charges of fraud, illegal hawala transactions and tax evasion would have to be dropped. The strategy of 'follow the money' and charging Acharya had to be put on the back burner until the missing dossiers were found. There were rumours that his solicitors in London were assembling an array of barristers and QCs to defend him – the best that money could buy. Sam, Zubin and the team were disappointed and vowed to continue looking.

The Somali warlords on hearing of the Indian's arrest hijacked the fleet of dhows with the arsenal of arms. The mercenaries, on board the dhows, were issued an ultimatum to join the Somali rebels or walk away without getting paid. Most of the renegades took charge of the dhows and patrolled the Somali Sea and the Gulf of Aden – a mini franchise network that benefitted both factions; the rebels and the mercenaries. The ones who decided to walk away did so and were never seen again.

Acharya was in custody in Stone Town while the Kenyans, the Brits and the Tanzanians haggled about charges and legal jurisdiction. Eventually, the culprit himself realised that it was in his best interests to be tried in a British court. He had to fight to gain access to his medication – without which he would be reduced to a perpetual state of heightened anxiety and depression. He had instructed his London team of solicitors – via the consular staff – to facilitate his extradition to the UK.

He was extradited to the UK – despite the protestations of the Kenyans who blamed him for the poaching and smuggling of ivory on an industrial scale. The Tanzanians countered with their own protests as most of the illegal ivory was 'harvested' on Tanzanian soil and then shipped out to Zanzibar and onwards.

Acharya was relieved that the Kenyan investigation had not made any headway in locating the incriminatory documents – the dossiers that had every hawala transaction listed and details of the labyrinth of offshore accounts, details of Operation Old Spice and the private oil survey report of potential deposits in Zanzibar. It also held the notes on the history of oil exploration in Tanzania which he had managed to extract after years of cultivating sources in Stone Town and in Dar-es-Salam. The information provided reinforced his personal conviction that there was oil in this southern runt of the Rift Valley – he was born in the area where the oil seeps were first reported.

His childhood memories of oil seeps – shared by many of his school friends - had been the birth of Operation Old Spice. Commissioning the British geologist to conduct the private surveys was the first step and the first piece of the jigsaw.

He had, as an afterthought, added a generous bonus to the Brit to survey the Lamu Archipelago on his way back to the UK. The detour to Lamu was effectively a deferred death sentence when he read the Zanzibar report. The execution in Lamu was a diversion, a decoy strategy, to draw attention away from Zanzibar. He regretted his decision to appoint Roxana rather than Shenzi. Roxana, very astutely, figured out the ramifications and almost wrecked Operation Old Spice by demanding extra payments. Shenzi because of his Somali networks and his rapport with the warlords was a long-term asset whereas Roxana was eminently dispensable.

The missing dossiers also held details of the original 'Mag Seven' club – from which the cartel eventually evolved. Acharya had deliberately let Abbu borrow the Mag Seven title; using the Arab as a decoy. The arrangement gave him the leeway to sacrifice Abbu and others if it came to that. The cartel was also protected by its 'Chinese Wall' strategy.

The origin of the Mag Seven club could be traced to the protests and demonstrations held outside the British High Commission in Nairobi – Acharya was the only one who was denied the right to enter the UK; the others landed up in the 'refugee' camps in Leicester. A few had already arrived from Kenya and Tanzania or arrived soon after – all with their own horror stories of traumatic migrations.

Sam and Zubin were in a bind. They had Acharya, the head of the cartel, but not for the right reasons. Their worry was that he would get away lightly. The Kenyans were pleased that the Lamu affair was a hoax and that there was no substance to the separatist agenda for Mombasa or the coast.

Sam and Zubin were convinced that the timeshare enterprise with its membership in the thousands was a genuine investment initially, but had been deliberately hijacked by Acharya for its hidden purpose of creating a separate homeland for the Asian diaspora. The 'get back to the roots' scheme was his ultimate utopian dream.

For those, like Acharya, who were traumatised by the forced

expulsion from the land of their birth, it would be vengeance delivered. Their return to East Africa was poetic justice – justice delivered.

Part of the membership funds were earmarked for the purchase of several cruise liners and old used oil rigs and platforms; to be customised to accommodate, in great luxury, up to 5000 timeshare members. The offshore floating dwellings, anchored beyond the territorial waters of Kenya and Tanzania, would become 'homesteads on water' – self-sufficient and self-governed sea cities.

'The timeshare enterprise was kosher, albeit, breathtakingly grandiose. Very plausible, if not far- fetched but then Acharya obviously suffers from delusions of grandeur. And the quest for vengeance was passionately emotional; retribution lay in returning to Zanzibar in triumph,' Sam explained.

'The recent activity in Zanzibar – the seven teams, seven flares – suspicious to say the least. An attempted coup?' Zubin asked

'You mean like Ian Smith's unilateral declaration of independence for Southern Rhodesia? Smith's utopia never materialised – white Zimbabweans left as the country descended into economic chaos. Years later history repeated itself – the Asians were forced to quit and Uganda declined into economic chaos.' Sam recalled reading about the panic at both ends – departure and arrivals lounges.

'I guess we'll never know, unless Acharya breaks his silence and confesses,' Zubin retorted. 'He has confessed though to his plans of creating a homeland for the Asian diaspora. His sea cities.'

'It's a shame that we do not have a shred of evidence. We must persist – that cache of evidence has to be found,' Sam sighed as they terminated their conversation.

THIRTY-EIGHT

Alec, Ava and Sam, Naivasha.

Alec and Ava recognised, just as Zubin and Sam did, that the search for the missing dossiers, languishing in a safe somewhere, was crucial. Convicting the cartel would satisfy the three East African countries and appease all those who wanted a viable long-term solution. A lull in the poaching activities, after Acharya's arrest, was indirect proof that the cartel had been silenced; for the moment.

Ava was pregnant. She was struggling a little so she relished the chance to visit Naivasha whenever the opportunity arose – the peaceful and pleasant environs of Naivasha presented the best opportunities to unwind amidst the very many floriculture farms. Ava loved the feel of dew on her bare feet on her dawn ramblings in the rose farm next door, so when Sam invited them for the weekend, she accepted without hesitation.

She had grown fond of Kissinger's spicy offerings and arm-twisted Alec into picking up the second most valued produce of Naivasha, after its carnations and roses, tilapia, the freshwater fish, that Naivasha Lake was famed for. She had already discussed the menu with Kissinger.

The freshly grilled tilapia starter served on a bed of thinly sliced red onions was garnished with further dollops of butter by Kissinger. He was convinced that Ava was carrying a baby boy and, therefore, needed the extra energy. He had marinated the tilapia with freshly squeezed lemon juice and seasoned the starter with rock salt and freshly ground black pepper and cumin.

As Ava wolfed down the last of the main course of methi chicken and basmati rice, she complimented Kissinger on his Indian culinary skills. 'Mzee Kissinger, that was yummy. Where did you learn to cook like that?'

'Kampala – the Goan family that I worked for taught me two things – English and the use of Indian spices.'

As Kissinger cleared the last vestiges of their dinner, Sam recounted how Kissinger got caught up in Amin's expulsion of Asians. Mr and Mrs Vaz, their two young boys and the family Dachshund fled in their VW beetle to escape Amin's militias who were gunning for Asians and Christians. When they realised that Kissinger, their chef, would also be a target because of his Catholic faith, he was forced to join them in their dash to safety in neighbouring Kenya. The scale of Amin's carnage was discovered much later, when Mengo Palace which was used as a prison, opened up its dungeons to scrutiny. There were many such killing fields strewn all across Uganda.

When the Vaz family eventually migrated to Goa, Sam bought their Naivasha farm and inherited Kissinger. The family had pleaded with Sam to retain Kissinger, which he did without any qualms. Henry had made himself indispensable – as a chef, as a man Friday and, in time, as a revered elder - 'mzee'.

It was while they were having coffee that the trio went back to discussing Acharya and the elusive proof that was needed to indict him and the cartel.

'Where would you look, Kissinger – for the missing documents?' Ava remarked in jest. Kissinger's tilapia had resonated well with Ava's taste buds and a jovial mood had overtaken her. She felt a new person in Naivasha; away from the stresses of Nairobi. Kissinger's intermittent presence during all their discussions was accepted – the old wizened head preferred to listen and he sometimes came up with very observant insights. His grey hairs gave him an aura of an indulgent relative, looking over his wards.

Before Sam or Alec could intervene, Ava whispered in a conspiratorial tone: 'We are confronted with a missing safe and a villain who can't be tried without the crucial evidence that the safe guards.' The puzzle had flummoxed the best minds, so a fresh perspective and an unconventional approach might just do the trick.

'Where is this safe supposed to be – here in Nairobi?' Kissinger played along. He was sitting close to the fire that blazed away – the mug of coffee barely keeping the night chill at bay.

'We hope it is here somewhere. Fingers crossed that it's in East Africa. The villain has a fascination for the number seven. His six safes have not yielded anything, hence the inference that a seventh safe exists somewhere,' Ava said. 'He's a wananchi – born here in Africa,' she added.

Sam elaborated: 'The man has seven clove plantations, his houses have seven bedrooms, seven safes, always chooses item seven on a menu and so forth.'

'Your villain, he's from Zanzibar, right?' Kissinger queried.

'How did you guess?' Alec asked, impressed.

'Cloves, bwana. You mentioned cloves, the king of Indian

spices – my Indian recipes all use the spice. Zanzibar, the Spice Islands, is renowned for its cloves.'

'It's also his birth place,' Ava butted in.

'Did I hear Kampala mentioned earlier?' Kissinger asked.

'Yes, I was telling them of the Vaz family and how you were saved from Amin, the butcher of Uganda,' Sam explained.

'Have you checked out Kampala, bwana Holmes?' Kissinger asked looking at Alec. He knew that both men fought to assume the mantle of Holmes.

'Why, should we have?' Alec ventured. 'Don't think the Zanzibari is a fan of Amin, most East Africans aren't.'

'Seven hills. Kampala is built on seven hills. Our bungalow, the Vaz residence, was on Kololo Hill, one of the seven hills,' Kissinger replied

The trio stared at Kissinger. Of course, why hadn't they thought of it – Kampala, the Rome of Africa, may just be Acharya's bolthole; his safehouse.

Sam and his team went back to the drawing board – wondering where to start considering that the capital city, bursting at the seams, had expanded rapidly, well beyond the original seven hills.

Sam's team revisited their files to ferret out possible clues to the location of the safehouse and the missing dossiers. The team, acutely aware of the mounting pressure, pinned their hopes on Kampala.

It took a lot of hard work on the ground and a lucky break or two – but Sam's team found the dossiers and the evidence that they needed to put Acharya and the others behind bars.

A handwritten summary of oil exploration dates and a

'shopping list' of items needed for the Zanzibar timeshare portfolio
gave both men something to ponder on:

1950s: more than 40 wells drilled. No oil found.

1960s: oil seeps reported.

1980s: oil seeps investigated. No oil found.

The historical notes about the oil explorations led Sam and
Alec to believe that Acharya must have had access to someone in a
position of power to trigger the private survey for the oil exploration.
The handwritten information about the oil seeps became the impetus
for hatching the elaborate plan.

On piecing the three documents together – the oil exploration
notes , the private Zanzibar oil survey and the quotes for the oil rigs
and oil platforms – Sam and Alec deduced that oil was the spur for
Operation Old Spice. Everything else – the timeshare investments and
the 'back to the roots' Utopia – was just froth.

It was much later, as the investigation unfolded, that the real
'Mag Seven' club - the inner core of the cartel was exposed. Acharya,
as the head, had chosen the other six from the vast numbers protesting
outside the British High Commission in Nairobi – all those years ago;
all aggrieved by the trauma of expulsion from their land of birth. The
six were handpicked for their expertise – GPs, pharmacists, finance
and banking wizards, property czars and oil analysts. Acharya, the only
one without any formal qualifications, would never have dreamed that
one day the bottom of the class underachiever would end up heading a
cartel of six others – all qualified professionals at the top of their
respective games.

The investigating teams knew that they would never be able to
prove the existence of Operation Old Spice – unless Acharya or the

others confessed.

Acharya and his cohorts were charged for the scams and the hawala transactions. The creation of a homeland and unlocking the wealth of the 'black gold' remained just that – mirages.

The three friends were at the Naivasha farm with Kissinger in attendance, toiling over the charcoal fired 'jiko' (stove) in the kitchen. Despite having a fully fitted modern kitchen with its array of electric appliances, the chef preferred the traditional charcoal fired 'jiko'.

'What led you guys to the missing dossiers in Kampala?' Alec asked.

'Bit of thinking out of the box helped – your OCD and citalopram clues were hugely helpful. Reports from the Dar-es-Salam prison where Acharya was held tipped us off – apparently Acharya had refused his medication unless it is the same brand and flown in from the UK. Part of his OCD ritual,' Sam explained.

Just as Sam had suspected, the revelation of citalopram as Acharya's treatment for OCD, led them to Acharya's pharmacist in Oadby, Leicester. When the pharmacist confirmed that Cipramil, the branded version of citalopram, and Seven Seas cod liver capsules were dispensed at irregular intervals, it became apparent that Acharya only relied on the Oadby pharmacy when he was in town. Whenever he was away for long periods, which was quite often, the patient either made arrangements with a local wholesaler to export the meds or if he carried them with him, then he would get a private prescription from his GP. The pharmacist explained that stringent NHS guidelines on GP repeat prescriptions meant that only a fixed number of tablets could be dispensed.

The pharmacist, on being pushed, was unable to find any

records of a freight agent or wholesaler in his books who would have forwarded the meds overseas. There were a handful of private prescriptions on file, meaning that the patient had collected the meds before departing abroad. It was then that the pharmacist noticed a recent private prescription – for seven packs each of Cipramil and Seven Seas cod liver oil capsules.

An exhaustive survey of pharmaceutical export wholesalers and freight agents in the area for any despatches of Cipramil 40 mg tablets and Seven Seas capsules to Entebbe or Kampala did not bear any fruit, which is when Sam advised the team to shift the search to Kampala.

The seven-pack export order from the UK of branded products - Cipramil and Seven Seas – made the search fairly easy. The team quickly identified the pharma wholesaler in central Kampala.

The rest was history as they say – the wholesaler located on Seventh Street, Industrial Area, Kampala, provided a residential address on Impala Avenue, Kololo Hill. The safe and the dossiers were found in the seventh room of the huge mansion.

THIRTY-NINE

Premier Club, Nairobi.

Alec and Ava went through a second exchange of vows in the
presence of her parents, friends and well-wishers at the Premier Club
on Forest Road – in the huge marquee pitched on the edge of the
cricket ground.

The guests were mainly from Ava's side of the family. Alec's
party included Sam, Ian and Dr and Mrs Reddy and his very many
colleagues from the vet school at Kabete and the wildlife fraternity.
Zubin, who was in the country, had flown in from Mombasa,
accompanied by Simone.

Sam and Kissinger, bestowed with the status of honorary
Kikuyu elders for the day, conducted a short traditional 'ngurario', a
Kikuyu wedding, and, with a lot of fanfare presented Ava's dad with
the 'ruracio' – the traditional Kikuyu dowry.

The token dowry was wheeled in a covered golf buggy and
was duly 'unveiled' to reveal two goats. Amid the subdued laughter,
Alec explained that in keeping with his Kikuyu traditions, a bride is
worth '99 goats' and mindful of the logistics of bringing in all the
goats, he had settled on two goats representing the herd of 198 goats
that he owed Dr Raj Patel, Ava's dad.

When questioned by Ian and others as to why two goats were presented instead of one, he gleefully explained that he was paying a double dowry for the privilege of marrying the 'twins' – Ava and Kay.

At the wedding dinner that followed the brief ceremony, Zubin noticing a familiar face, walked over and greeted the octogenarian GP, Dr Arya whom he had met in Mombasa.

'Fancy meeting you here – didn't know you knew Ava and Alec?' Zubin said, concentrating on the elegant white goatee rather than the horse shaped fringe of jet-black hair.

'I have known the Patels for decades. Raj, Ava's dad, was my intern at Kenyatta Hospital when he first arrived from India. And when they set up a GP practice in Mombasa, Ava and her mum, Rani, became members of the same cultural groups that I was patron of.'

'You must have read the press coverage of the timeshare scam and the rumours of oil seeps and oil explorations in Tanzania?' Zubin asked the old timer.

'We East Africans, are all connected – by marriage and business relationships. You would be hard pressed to find a Kenya born Asian not have a connection with Tanzania, Zanzibar or Uganda or vice versa. Over the years, the bloodlines and the gene pool have mingled to an amazing degree. Not just the Asians but all the ethnic lines – Arab, Bantu, Portuguese, Anglo-Saxon, Persian, whatever,' Dr Arya remarked.

'You've dodged my question about the scams and the cartel?' Zubin persisted with his cheeky interrogation. He knew from past encounters that the old timer missed very little of the swirling political winds of the region.

The GP, long in the tooth and aware of the political 'tectonics' between the colonies and Whitehall, hesitated briefly and continued after touching the side of his nose and winking.

'I did. We are a melting pot. It is futile to point fingers at any particular group. The eternal 'them' and 'us' scenario. We are at the mercy of vested interests and invariably good intentions are hijacked by a tiny minority. We are all guilty.' Dr Arya paused to regain his breath. Although he had given up smoking years ago, the damage inflicted by chain smoking through med school and for decades later, had left his lung function severely compromised.

Before Zubin could probe further, the GP continued: 'Guilty by either making the wrong choices or, even worse, by keeping silent. Zanzibar has always had an uneasy relationship with the rest of us and indeed, with Britain. That troubled status quo probably still exists with the government in Dar-es-Salam on the mainland. In my opinion, the discovery of oil, especially in Africa, is a curse; a scourge that upsets the geo-politics of the area. The discovery of oil in a few countries – sited along the Rift Valley system – became the slippery slope of greed. Under the guise of development, investors arrived. So did the cartels and the carpetbaggers with their scams. Digging up the past is best left to historians, not to investors.'

A few weeks later....

Sam and his team were awarded a special Presidential award for their conservation efforts in protecting Kenya's elephants. Substantial cash awards were also approved for all the key personnel. Sam promptly donated his share to the bereaved families of the three who died under his watch – the two wardens and Joyce.

Zubin was felicitated in Whitehall and met up with his MI6 bosses at the Carlton Club in St James's Street. When asked to name his favourite poison, he said, deadpan: 'Martini, please. Shaken not stirred.' He was tempted to ask his bosses if they were aware of any British interests in the oil explorations of the past in the Zanzibar Archipelago or, indeed, in the other colonies. He did not ask – 'let sleeping dogs lie', the mantra of Sir Robert Walpole, the first PM of Britain, was good policy.

Ava's special present to Alec was an eight-pound baby boy, christened Sidney Dunlop.

The British government, after deliberating on what would be the ideal legacy for the confiscated assets of the cartel, promised to disburse the cash to various wildlife conservation programmes in East Africa and strive for a Royal Assent to ban ivory sales.

xxxxxxx

Acknowledgements:

Nilesh Trivedi, Dr Alkesh Dave and Dr Pinakin Dave.

Many thanks, once again, for the unflinching support. My frequent 'mayday calls' were promptly addressed. Nilesh's timely intervention, out of the blue, saved the incomplete first draft of 'When Elephants Fight' from being consigned to the bin.

Bhavika Patel – for the tech support in navigating the vagaries of my laptop and its programmes. I pine, in vain, for my HB pencils and manual typewriter.

Priyanka Patel – for allowing me to 'auction' the first print copy of 'The Ivory Towers & Other Stories' at her dinner and dance fundraiser. The event and her subsequent successful participation in the 2019 London Marathon collectively raised a substantial sum for CLIC Sargent - Priyanka's nominated cancer charity.

Kerry Barrett, author and editor.

A special thank you to Kerry for being the friendly 'googly' bowler, who helped me cope with the spin in a benevolent omniscient manner. Wicket intact, I live to bat/ write another day.

Tammy Barrett – for designing an impressive and exciting book cover which is replete with intrigue, mystery and veiled threats.

Aimee Horton – for formatting and other technical processes that go into transforming a manuscript into a viable entity.

Dr A K Dave and Mrs T A Dave.

Finally, without a doubt, my short story 'The Ivory Towers' would not have seen the light of day had it not been for Arvind kaka's persuasion for my return to Kenya. My licence to practice and the subsequent placement with the wildlife department had a lot to do with his tenacity of purpose.

Alas, both passed away several years ago and it has been my abiding regret that I never quite managed to acknowledge their immense contribution to my wellbeing during that difficult phase in my career. I am forever in their debt.

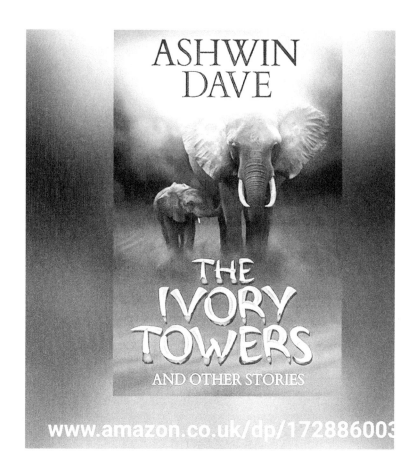

ASHWIN
DAVE

THE
IVORY
TOWERS
AND OTHER STORIES

www.amazon.co.uk/dp/172886003

Printed in Great Britain
by Amazon

65542698R00214